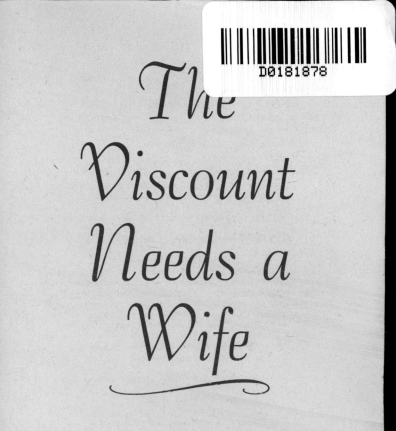

The Viscount Needs a Wife

Jo Beverley

A SIGNET SELECT BOOK

SIGNET SELECT
Published by New American Library,
an imprint of Penguin Random House LLC
375 Hudson Street, New York, New York 10014

This book is an original publication of New American Library.

First Printing, April 2016

Copyright © Jo Beverley, 2016

For more information about Penguin Random House, visit penguin.com.

ISBN 978-0-451-47190-1

Printed in the United States of America
10 9 8 7 6 5 4 3 2 1

Acknowledgments

With thanks to my editor, Claire Zion, and my agent, Meg Ruley, and to all my wonderful readers, who make creating books so much fun.

The Offspring of King George III in November 1817

Prince George, the Prince Regent, age 54

Prince Frederick, Duke of York, age 52

Prince William, Duke of Clarence, 51

Charlotte, Queen of Württemberg, 50

Prince Edward, Duke of Kent, 50

Princess Augusta, 49

Princess Elizabeth, 47

Prince Ernest, Duke of Cumberland, 46

Prince Augustus, Duke of Sussex, 44

Prince Adolphus, Duke of Cambridge, 43

Mary, Duchess of Gloucester, 41

Princess Sophia, 40

Chapter 1

November 7, 1817
Cateril Manor, Gloucestershire

"Kathryn, your dog is looking at me again."

Kitty Cateril looked up from her needlework to see that indeed her King Charles spaniel was sitting in front of her mother-in-law, eyes fixed on her face. She bit the inside of her cheek to hold back a smile as she patted her leg. "Sillikin, come."

The small black and tan dog cocked its head, then trotted over, as if expecting a reward for a job well done. Kitty wasn't sure why Sillikin sometimes stared at people, but it seemed to be in disapproval, and her mother-in-law sensed that.

What secret sins could lurk in the soul of straight-backed, gray-haired Lady Cateril? She was the sort of woman often described as beyond reproach. These days, dressed permanently in mourning black, she had been canonized by the heroism and death of her younger son—Kitty's husband, Marcus.

Had Sillikin caught Lady Cateril wishing that the heroism and death had come together? That Marcus hadn't lived, wounded and broken, for seven more years and married someone like Kitty? That devotion to Marcus's memory hadn't required her to offer Kitty a home? Kitty and her irritating dog.

"I will say again, Kathryn, that you should rename that creature."

And I will say again, Kitty supplied silently before saying, "She's too used to the name by now."

"She's a dumb creature. She cannot care."

"Then why do dogs respond to their names as people do, Mama?"

Names. So powerful and so often poorly considered. Six years ago, she'd named a wriggling ball of fluff Sillikin. Three years before that, when Kitty had married Marcus, she'd called his mother Mama, in the hope of pleasing the disapproving woman. It had never seemed possible to change to something more formal.

Her bid for approval had been a hopeless cause. Lady Cateril's favorite son, the wounded hero of Roleia, bound to a seventeen-year-old chit? Had she hoped that by using the name Kathryn, the chit would become a sober matron? "Kitty," she'd said at first meeting, "is a romping sort of name." There'd been a clear implication that Kitty was a romping sort of person.

Better that than being starchy as a frosted petticoat on a winter washing line!

The weather today wouldn't freeze cotton as stiff as a board, but it was raining. That trapped Kitty in the house, and effectively in this small parlor that smelled of wood smoke and the mustiness that came from long-closed windows. The larger, airier drawing room was rarely used in the colder months, so the fire there was unlit.

She would have liked to retreat to her bedroom even though that, too, lacked a fire, but in Lady Cateril's domain, bedrooms were not sitting rooms. They weren't dining rooms, either. The only time anyone was served food in her bedroom was if she was ill.

Kitty knew she should be grateful to be housed here. Her only other option was to live in cheap lodgings somewhere. At least there she had everything she needed and the estate to walk in.

She had everything except freedom.

In the beginning, she'd rubbed along well enough with her mother-in-law, united in grief. However, when six months had passed, Kitty had followed custom and prepared to put off her widow's weeds. When Lady Cateril realized Kitty had ordered new gowns in gray, fawn, and violet, she'd reacted as if she'd spat on Marcus's grave. When reproaches and then tears hadn't changed Kitty's intent, Lady Cateril had taken to her bed and sent for the doctor. Kitty had been badly shaken, but the rest of the family hadn't seemed alarmed, so she'd stuck to her guns. The first gown had arrived, a very plain gray wool round gown, and she'd worn it, quaking. The next day Lady Cateril had emerged. Nothing more had been said, but a frost had settled.

Kitty had realized then that in Lady Cateril's mind she had only one reason to exist: as Marcus's inconsolable widow. She was as much a monument to his magnificence as the marble plaque in the village church.

CAPTAIN MARCUS EDWARD CATERIL
OF THE 29TH
HERO OF ROLEIA
1782–1815

The words were inscribed on a large alabaster bas-relief that included a shrouded, mourning woman drooping over a plinth. The plaque was white, but the figure was black. Kitty had assumed at first that it was a symbolic representation of grief, but she'd since realized it was supposed to be her. Fixed in drooping black for all eternity.

She'd worn half mourning since then, but when her mourning year had ended, she'd lacked the fortitude to progress to bright colors. Her pretty clothes were stored away, becoming more out of style every day. She'd tried to think of ways to escape, but here she still was, eighteen months after Marcus's death. She had hardly any money and no possibility of desirable employment. She'd gone straight from school to marriage.

She picked up Sillikin. Through the most difficult times, the spaniel had been her confidant and consolation and had heard all that Kitty's pride had kept silent from people. *We'll find a way,* she said silently to the dog. *There has to be a way—*

The door burst open and Lord Cateril entered, eyes wild. "The most dreadful news!"

Lady Cateril started upright, a hand to her chest. "John?" she gasped, meaning her surviving son. "The children!"

"The princess. Princess Charlotte is dead!"

There was a moment of stillness as Kitty and Lady Cateril took in his words. Princess Charlotte, second in line to the throne, who'd been due to deliver her first child, the hope of the future, was *dead*?

"No!"

For once, Kitty and her mother-in-law were completely in harmony.

"The child?" Lady Cateril asked desperately.

"A son. Also dead." Lord Cateril sank into a chair by his wife's side and took her hand. "All hope is gone."

It was overly portentous, but Kitty knew what he meant. The king and queen had presented the nation with seventeen children, but now, nearly sixty years after George III had come to the throne, there had been only one legitimate grandchild, the Regent's daughter, Charlotte. With her dead, what would become of the nation?

The king was old and mad and expected to die at any moment. The Regent was nearing sixty, grossly fat, and led a dissipated life. No one would be surprised if he died soon as well.

His sisters were all middle-aged, and those who had married hadn't produced offspring. Few of his brothers had married, and none of those unions had produced a living child. With the perversity of fate, some had bastards, which were of no use at all.

Kitty's heart ached for the people involved. "Poor woman," she said. "And her poor family. Royal, but not beyond the hand of fate."

"Amen," Lord Cateril said. "The shops and theaters have closed in respect. The court has gone into mourning, of course. But I'm told people of all degrees are putting on black, or at least dark bands."

"We must do the same," Lady Cateril said. "The family must wear full black." In spite of her genuine shock and sorrow, she shot Kitty a triumphant look.

Kitty almost protested, but Lord Cateril agreed. "You're right, my dear. And black bands, aprons, and gloves for the servants. Please gather the household together in the hall. I must read out the news."

Kitty helped to pass the word, and soon the family and servants stood together in the oak-paneled hall as Lord Cateril read out the letter he'd received. All were affected and many wept. Afterward Kitty went to her room to put on one of her black gowns. If only she'd given them away . . . but it was provident to keep mourning by. No one knew when death would strike, as had just been proved.

As a red-eyed housemaid fastened the back, Kitty resolved two things. She'd return to half mourning after the funeral, along with everyone else except the court. And she would not live this half life any longer.

Somehow she'd find a way to escape. Here was evidence

that life was fleeting. She wouldn't waste what time she had left in the everlasting shadows of Lady Cateril's grief.

The princess's coffin, along with that of her stillborn child, was lowered into the royal vault at Windsor on November 15. Lord Cateril read a letter giving an account of the funeral to the assembled household, and they all prayed again for the princess and the bereaved family.

Kitty went upstairs to take off her black, tempted to move into brightly colored gowns now, but she truly was sorrowful over Princess Charlotte's fate, so half mourning felt correct. She chose gray and wore silver ornaments instead of jet. When she entered the parlor, Lady Cateril's look was flat, which seemed even worse than anger. Strenuous thinking over the past week had brought Kitty no closer to escape. The only prospect was to find employment. She'd discussed the situation with her sister-in-law and raised the possibility that Sarah give her a reference.

"Employment?" Sarah had asked, eyes wide. "Mama would never permit that."

"She can't stop me."

"But she can make my life miserable if I assist you." Sarah was plump, practical, and kind, but not courageous. She never tried to cross Lady Cateril over anything.

Kitty tried another approach. "Don't you think we should try to ease her out of her mourning? She has two fine children still, and six grandchildren—yours and Anabel's."

Anabel was Lady Cateril's youngest child, who'd married a man who lived three counties away, probably by design. Anabel had as much spine as her mother, so they easily clashed.

"She won't," Sarah said. "In some ways she likes the effect of it, but it reflects true grief. She always loved Marcus best."

"Doesn't John mind?"

"He's his father's favorite and he is the heir. Surely you're comfortable here overall, Kathryn. Why would you want to become someone's servant?"

On the surface it was idiotic. She was treated as one of the family, with everything provided for her. She hardly ever had to touch the small sum left her by Marcus, for any bills were paid by Lord Cateril without complaint.

Kitty had told Sarah the truth. "I want to wear rainbow colors and be joyful."

"I don't think governesses or companions are encouraged to dress gaudily, or romp around laughing."

Kitty had had to admit the truth of that, but it didn't change her mind. She was only twenty-seven years old and felt entombed.

Chapter 2

The next day, Kitty entered the parlor and found it empty. John and Sarah had driven out to visit friends who were celebrating the healthy birth of a child. Kitty could imagine how fearful the parents must have been with such a prominent example of the dangers. Lady Cateril must have been going over the household accounts with the housekeeper, for mourning had not led her to loose the reins of management. Lord Cateril would be in his office, where he spent most of his time when at home.

Kitty settled by the fire, Sillikin at her feet, to seek escape of another sort—in the delightful adventures of *Love in a Harem*. She'd enjoyed novels when young, but they'd become a precious escape during her marriage. The unlikely adventures had transported her far from the Moor Street rooms in London that she and Marcus had called home. Marcus hadn't liked her to leave him alone, but as long as she was in the room with him, he hadn't minded her reading. In good times she'd read to him, and they'd chuckled together over the most implausible parts.

He would have enjoyed *Love in a Harem*. The heroine had been plain Jane Brown when she'd set sail from Plymouth, but her ship had been captured by Barbary pirates and she'd been sold into the harem of the Sultan of Turkey and renamed Pearl of the North. She'd narrowly escaped being ravished by a number of men, including the captain of the ship, but now, trembling and dressed in the skimpiest silks, she awaited her lord and master. The harem door opened. . . .

"Silent reading, Kathryn?" Lady Cateril asked, coming in. "You know I don't approve."

Suppressing some salty words she'd learned from Marcus, Kitty did her best to be pleasant. "Would you like me to read to you, Mama? You might enjoy *Love in a Harem*."

She heard her own words only as she spoke them and had to fight the giggles. "Fulminating" was exactly the word for the look she received. Kitty was saved from another unwise remark by Becky, the housemaid, coming in with a letter.

"His lordship's sent this for Mrs. Marcus, milady."

She looked as if she might give it to Lady Cateril, so Kitty held out her hand. "Thank you, Becky. It will be from my friend Ruth Lulworth," she told her mother-in-law, for Ruth was her only correspondent.

"Ah." Lady Cateril's expression lightened a little. Ruth was a clergyman's wife and thus approved of. She sat. "You may read *that* to me."

It was revenge for that mischievous offer to read from the novel, and probably for Kitty's putting off mourning, but not worth fighting over. Kitty and Ruth were long past their school days, when they'd shared all the anxieties, dreams, and longings of their silly hearts. The letter would contain news about Ruth's home and family, and of her work in the parish around the Gloucestershire village of Beecham Dabittot. Kitty broke the seal and unfolded the letter, but was startled to see that Ruth had written a great deal. To save the cost for the recipient, she'd kept to one sheet of paper, turning it sideways and continuing the letter crossways. There were even a few lines on the diagonal. A sense of dramatic doings rose from the jumble, especially as one crosswise phrase stood out, because Ruth had underlined the "Yes!"

Yes! I'm sure your astonishment equals mine.

At least that didn't sound like tragedy.

Kitty needed to read the astonishing news in private, but Lady Cateril was waiting. The beginning of the letter seemed to be normal news and she didn't think Lady Cateril could see the crossways writing, so she'd make do.

My dear Kitty,

It's been a long time since I wrote, but we've been very busy here in Beecham Dab. Such terrible news about Princess Charlotte. All around put on some mark of mourning, and we tolled the bells at the time of her interment. The tragedy is a reminder to us all to be mindful of our brief lives and the judgment to come.

Sadly, we have been visited by death more frequently than usual here this year. In August a sickness carried off ten souls and weakened many others, even at harvesttime, so Andrew went out when he could to help in the fields.

"Andrew is Reverend Lulworth, Mama."

"So I remember. A charitable act, but not, perhaps, suitable for a man of the cloth."

Kitty was tempted to debate how any charity could be unsuitable for a clergyman, but she returned to the letter.

*By God's grace, we are all well. Little Arthur
is babbling very cleverly for three. Maria is still
quiet, but that makes her an easy babe.*

Kitty remembered that Ruth's second birth had been
difficult, but she and the child had survived, unlike poor
Princess Charlotte.

She continued to read more descriptions of the children, the work of the parish, and about a pair of clever
cats they'd acquired who were keeping the vicarage
completely clear of mice.

At that point she invented a farewell and folded the
letter. She longed to leave the room immediately to read
the rest, but that could stir suspicion, so she used Ruth's
comment about the cats to introduce a subject she needed
to discuss with her mother-in-law. The housekeeper had
asked her to try to persuade Lady Cateril to allow some
cats in the house.

"Mice are causing problems in the kitchen area,
Mama. A cat or two would control them."

"I could tolerate cats *there*, Kathryn, but cats do not
stay in their allotted space." Kitty had no answer to that.
"I'm pleased you see for once that I am right. It's a pity
that your dog doesn't kill mice. Dogs do generally obey
orders."

Sillikin half opened her eyes, as if commenting on
that.

"I've never known her to kill, Mama."

"If she weren't fed, perhaps she would."

Preferably kill you!

Seething, Kitty called Sillikin and left the room without
explanation. She retreated so she wouldn't say something unforgivable, but she needed to read Ruth's astonishing news.

Perhaps Andrew Lulworth had been offered a grander parish, or even a place in a bishop's establishment. Kitty had no idea how advancement in the church was achieved, but she was sure Ruth's husband deserved it, if only because Ruth had chosen him. Perhaps they'd received an unexpected inheritance, or found buried treasure in the garden. Perhaps the Regent had dropped by for tea!

Her flights of fancy were interrupted by the sight of the portrait of her husband hanging over the stairs in such a way that it always confronted her as she went up. It had been painted after Marcus's death, but based on a miniature done in 1807, before his heroic maiming. It showed a young, dark-haired officer in his gold-braided regimentals, bright with vigor and life. It showed the Marcus Cateril she'd never known, for she'd met him after he'd lost a leg and an eye, been scarred in the face, and broken in other ways that caused him pain till his dying day.

She fought tears, as she still often did, not of grief over his death, but of sadness for all he'd lived with. He'd often said he wished he'd died alongside others during that magnificent assault at Roleia, and she knew he'd meant it. The overdose of laudanum that had killed him had not been accidental, no matter what the inquest had said.

She hurried on into the refuge of her room and wrapped herself in two extra shawls. Fires in bedrooms were left to die down in the morning and not lit again until close to bedtime. Then she unfolded the letter, hoping for truly diverting news.

Now for the main impetus for writing, Kitty. The sickness carried off our local lion, Viscount Dauntry, and his only son, a lad of eleven. That was sad, to be sure, but it also produced an interregnum.

There's a daughter, but of course she can't inherit, so no one knew who the heir was or, indeed, if there was one at all.

Now the new Lord Dauntry has arrived. He's a very distant relation of the fifth viscount, who had no notion of being in line and has never been here before. By blessed good fortune, he and Andrew both attended Westminster School only a few years apart, though he was plain Braydon then.

Ah. A friendship with the new viscount might advance Reverend Lulworth's career.

Dauntry has joined us to dine quite frequently in the weeks he's been here, and thus we have become familiar with his situation.

At this point Ruth had run out of paper and begun the crosswise writing, so Kitty turned the page.

He did not rejoice to find himself a lord. He didn't need the wealth or want the running of estates. To make matters worse, the late Lord Dauntry's will makes his successor guardian of his daughter and imposes a duty to care for his mother, who lives on in the house. In short, Dauntry has decided he needs a sensible woman to assist him with these responsibilities. I immediately thought of you.

A laugh escaped. What was Ruth thinking of? Then she read the next line.

It would mean you living close, Kitty. Only think of that!

Oh. Yes. Only think of that.

She and Ruth had met when they were both parlor boarders at school in Leamington. They'd become inseparable, but when they'd left school their paths had gone in different directions. Ruth had found employment as a governess. Kitty had returned home and soon been wooed into marriage by Marcus. They'd rarely met since, and not at all since Ruth's marriage four years ago.

To be close again.

Wondrous, but surely impossible.

I know it would mean exchanging life as part of a noble family for one as a servant, but I have the feeling that you're not entirely comfortably situated.

It was so like Ruth to read between the lines. Kitty had tried to put a bright face on her situation here, just as she had during her marriage, for she didn't believe that a trouble shared is a trouble halved. It seemed to her that complaining of trials that couldn't be changed was merely sharing the misery.

Was this a possible escape? What would this position be? Surely the girl had a governess. Was she to be companion to the elderly lady? That might be no better than being trapped with Lady Cateril—except that she'd be free of mourning and have Ruth nearby. There could even be weekly visits.

Kitty focused eagerly on the page again.

I put forward your name and explained why you might be suitable, which I confess involved a little exaggeration of your sober nature, but then Lord Dauntry shocked me by saying he'd resolved that the lady he needs must be his wife. My hopes were exploded.

Kitty's were, too.

How could Ruth lead her on like that?

She crumpled the letter and threw it across the room. But Sillikin ran to retrieve it and bring it back to her, stub tail wagging.

"This isn't a game, you foolish creature."

But she took it, picking up the dog to hug. "I don't suppose I'd have liked the position anyway. I'd have been a servant, no matter how it was dressed up, and with no other company than my lady, who could be even worse than Lady Cateril." The dog licked her chin. "Yes, I know I have you. But would I be allowed to keep you?"

Sillikin turned to settle on Kitty's lap, but pushed the letter sideways with her paws so it slid toward the floor. Kitty caught it and realized she'd not yet reached Ruth's astonishing news. Perhaps that would raise her spirits. She smoothed the paper and found her place.

I was bold enough to ask why, and Dauntry pointed out that his ward is hard to handle and the dowager Lady Dauntry difficult in her grief. Then he asked if you would fulfill his requirements as wife.

Yes! I'm sure your astonishment equals mine.

It did indeed. Marriage? To a viscount? Was it a full moon?

I was cast into a tizzy. He, however, continued as if discussing whether to plant turnips or cabbages to say that he needs his household under sensible management without delay, and asked again if my friend might be suitable and willing.

I didn't know the truth about either, but the thought of you within miles, not to mention the opportunity for you to become my lady, was too much to resist, dear Kitty. I said you might be. Of course, that commits you to nothing, and I know you've said you will not marry again, but do please give it thought, for Lord Dauntry means what he said.

"He must be mad," Kitty muttered. "Would I marry a madman to escape?" She answered herself. "Perhaps. If he was safely mad."

Ruth was correct in saying that she didn't want a second husband, but that was largely because she couldn't imagine finding a comfortable one. After the storms with Marcus, she needed calm waters, but she was not in a position to pick and choose. She had no great beauty or elegance, and a pittance of money.

This offer tempted, but it was too good to be true. There must be something markedly wrong with a man who sought a wife in such a way. A difficult marriage would be far worse than life at Cateril Manor, and there would be no escape.

I respect your devotion to Marcus, but can you continue as you are for the rest of your life? Upon hearing of the death of Princess Charlotte, I found myself contemplating the uncertainties of life and our duty to use our time on earth well. I fear your current situation leaves you idle. However, my desires might cause me to overpersuade you, so let me tell you of the problems.

The writing was becoming even smaller. There must be a great many problems, and that was a relief. Kitty could feel the pull of this ridiculous plan, and she needed reasons to resist.

Lord Dauntry stated plainly that he sought a wife who would not seek to change his ways. Kitty, I fear those __ways__ include __carousing__ and wicked women. He behaves with complete propriety here, but he is a very __fashionable__ gentleman. I understand he is commonly called Beau Braydon, in the style of Beau Nash and Beau Brummell! His life since leaving the army has been mostly in London. You are more familiar than I as to what that might involve.

Kitty was, but she was fixed on the words "since leaving the army."

Kitty had lived in London all her married life, often surrounded by Marcus's army friends. He'd not been able to get out much, so his military friends and acquaintances had come to him when in Town on furlough or official business, sometimes in numbers that threatened to burst the walls. Some were good company, but she'd learned that soldiering often left scars, visible and invisible. Major Quincy had been silent, with such a dark look in his eyes. Captain Farrow had mostly been quiet, but occasionally he'd fall into a kind of fit in which he thought he was fighting the French; it had taken two or three others to restrain him. Lieutenant Wynne had a strong voice and had often led jolly songs, but she'd sensed something wrong. According to Marcus, his wounds had affected his manhood. Marcus had thanked heaven that his had not, but they'd affected so much else.

She wasn't attracted to the idea of any second marriage, and certainly not to another ex-soldier. She'd done her share in that regard.

He asked if I would put the proposal to you. I made no promise, but later Andrew and I discussed

*the matter. He is uncomfortable with the situation
for many reasons, but he sees how advantageous it
could be to you, and he confirmed my assessment
that Lord Dauntry would be a tolerable husband,
as long as you kept to his conditions.*

And if not? Rages and bruises, then weeping contrition and threats to kill himself?

If she'd been a meeker woman, perhaps Marcus's life would have been more tolerable, but his unpredictable anger had developed an echo in herself. To begin with, she'd agreed and soothed, and even apologized for imagined faults, but her patience had worn down until she'd answered sharp words with sharper, and rage with rage. She'd rebutted accusations with ones of her own. That had worked better, but she'd hated his dismal repentance for days afterward.

Men wanted meek wives, and she didn't think she could ever be one again. Ruth's plan was a fairy tale. But the next line leapt out at her.

*Remember, Andrew and I would be close by to
offer loving support.*

To be close to Ruth and have her loving support . . .

What was more, if she became Lady Dauntry—astonishing thought!—she'd be able to visit the parsonage whenever she wished. She could invite Ruth and her family to her own grand home. What was the name? Beauchamp Abbey. Was it pronounced in the French way—*BOW-shamp*—or did it match the village name, Beecham? That was irrelevant, but relevant thoughts, weakening thoughts, were trickling in.

Here, at last, was escape from Cateril Manor.

Might it be bearable?

The married life of Lady Dauntry would be vastly different from hers with Marcus, no matter how odd her husband was. She wouldn't be trapped in four rooms, and it seemed unlikely Lord Dauntry would demand her presence most of the time or insist on her sharing his restless bed.

She and he could have separate bedrooms, separate suites of rooms. Separate wings, perhaps! Given what Ruth had said, he might rarely be at the Abbey at all. In a normal marriage, she might object to his amusements elsewhere, but not in this one.

"Am I seriously considering this?"

Sillikin's cocked head seemed to send the question back at her.

"I am."

To escape Cateril Manor. To live close to Ruth. To have a home of her own again, with a frequently absent husband . . .

She read on, now fearful of something to make it impossible.

If you are willing to consider the matter, it must be soon. Dauntry is a man of brisk action. If you don't give him hope, he will proceed to other ways of obtaining the wife he wants. I can't imagine it will be difficult. He's a handsome man, though in a cool way.

Ruth had run out of space and turned the page to write diagonally.

If you agree to consider the match, he will arrange your journey here at his expense, and your journey

home if you decide he will not suit. You need only
reply to me for all to be put in hand, but remember,
it must be soon.

    I don't know this man well, Kitty, and I fear my
ardent desire to have you nearby influences me,
but Andrew believes you should at least consider
this, and his judgment is sound.

That was it.
Ardent desire.
Yes.
Kitty rose and paced her room, Sillikin in her arms.
Escape!
But through marriage.

She hadn't rushed into her first marriage, but she'd
been swept along on a torrent of ecstatic romance, with no
one attempting to slow her down. Her parents had been
dazzled by her being wooed by a member of the nobility.
If they'd suffered any doubts, Marcus's wounds and true
adoration had silenced them. Marcus had wooed her so
desperately, with gifts, flowers, and passionate entreaties,
that she would have had to have been made of stone to
refuse him.

Here was a very different situation. The offer was
cool, the promises minimal, and there were no tempting
gifts. The man was a stranger, but she must decide in a
moment, and this time she had no one no advise her.

"I must go to Ruth."

With that, everything became clear. She must go to
Ruth, for advice and for the joy of it. Once in Beecham
Dab, once she met Lord Dauntry, she'd know whether to
make this marriage or not. Mere travel there wouldn't commit her.

"How to escape?" she muttered. One thing was sure:

Lady Cateril would never tolerate Marcus's widow marrying again.

She thought she had enough money to cover the cost of a coach ticket to Gloucestershire, but how to escape the house? She was devising complicated ways, some inspired by novels, when she came to her senses. No one here knew about the offer of marriage. She could simply ask to visit her old friend.

She hugged Sillikin. "I don't know why I haven't done that before. I've allowed us to be glued here by Lady Cateril's grief, but even she can't object to a short visit to an old friend, can she?"

Chapter 3

Lady Cateril frowned but didn't argue against the journey. Lord Cateril, John, and Sarah all declared it an excellent idea, and Lord Cateril insisted on arranging her travel at his expense. Thus Kitty set out three days later in the Cateril coach, drawn by four post-horses. She was attended by a middle-aged housemaid for propriety, and the Cateril estate steward to see to all the arrangements on the way.

Such grand travel wasn't strange to her, but in the past she'd always been with Marcus. It did seem odd to have such arrangements only for herself, but she was grateful for them. The coach was well sprung, the squabs thick, and the carriage was warmed by hot bricks, with new ones brought at every change of horses. When they paused for refreshments or to dine, the innkeepers bowed low and the inn servants rushed to please in order to deserve generous vails when they left. Kitty couldn't help thinking that as Viscountess Dauntry, her life would continue in this way. As a governess or companion, it would not.

The maid, Tessa, never spoke unless spoken to, and occupied herself with knitting. Mr. Jones occasionally exchanged pleasantries but seemed content with his book. Kitty sometimes read, but for the most part she watched the world go by, enjoying liberation. She'd seen so little of England.

She'd been born and raised in Coventry, then attended school in Leamington, a short distance away. When she and Marcus married, he'd wanted to live in London, so, despite his mother's objections, they'd set up their household there. Kitty's entire married life had been spent in London, apart from the annual pilgrimage to Cateril Manor for Christmas. They wouldn't have made that journey except at Lady Cateril's insistence, because Marcus's wounds had made sitting in a coach for a long distance agony. He'd passed the journey in an opium haze and then suffered the results of taking so much.

Her last long journey had been in the cortege that had taken his body back to Cateril for burial, and she didn't remember much of that. She had grieved. Sometimes Lady Cateril seemed to doubt it, but she had. She always would. But she knew better than most how difficult life had been for Marcus. She couldn't regret his choice.

She shook off unhappy memories, but she wished she'd made this journey in summer. Now, in late November, the leaves had fallen from most of the trees and the sky hung gray and low. As they passed through towns and villages, she saw that the people were as somber as the weather. She'd read in the papers that people at all levels of society were keeping to sober dress as a sign of their sadness over the princess's death, but was surprised to find it still true weeks later. How long would it persist?

All the same, the changing scenery was interesting simply for being new to her. Over the day, the shackles of the past eighteen months fell away and she rediscovered a sense of lightness. She'd always been naturally lighthearted—yes, even romping. Her merry nature had probably been what drew Marcus to her. Perhaps he'd reached through her for the adventurous young man he had been. During her marriage she'd played the light part more and more to counterbalance Marcus's deepening gloom.

As the daylight faded and they approached their stop for the night, Kitty realized she wouldn't, couldn't, return to Cateril Manor, where Lady Cateril tried to impose gloom on everyone. *Let there be light!*

Life as a governess or companion could be as bad, however. Therefore, unless Lord Dauntry was a truly intolerable person, she *must* make this marriage.

But would he still propose it when he met her?

Ruth had admitted that she'd exaggerated Kitty's qualities. Perhaps she'd also falsified her appearance. Lord Dauntry, like Henry VIII with Anne of Cleves, could take one look at her and decide they would not suit. She'd heard that the Prince of Wales had had the same reaction to Caroline of Brunswick, but he'd not had the power to do anything about it.

Once they were settled in the Red Horse, Kitty surveyed herself in the mirror in her bedroom. Her nose and chin were definitely too assertive for a lady, and gray stole color from her complexion. In a reverse effect, gray made her reddish hair look brash, and her curls, as usual, were trying to riot.

"I'd look better in colors," she said to Sillikin. Perhaps the wag of a tail was encouragement.

She'd had to leave Cateril Manor in half mourning or raise suspicion, but what if Lord Dauntry was at the parsonage on her arrival and this was his first impression?

"I have brighter clothing in my trunk."

Sillikin went to the leather-bound trunk and put her paws up so she could look in, but then sneezed and turned away.

"The brighter stuff is underneath, you silly thing."

Kitty had never had a personal maid, so she'd been able to pack her trunk herself. She'd put three brightly colored gowns at the bottom, along with accessories, then placed two darker ones on top. She hadn't been able to squeeze in her blue fur-lined Russian mantle. It was wonderfully warm and suited her, and she could have worn it over the gray. She could wear the green gown beneath the gray pelisse and let the pelisse hang open on arrival. . . .

Her nerve failed her. Tessa and Mr. Jones would report the transformation to Lady Cateril. Reason said there was nothing her mother-in-law could do, but instinct argued for avoiding the remotest possibility.

"Oh, how I dislike squirming to please! If only I could be comfortably myself, independent of all. Short of winning a lottery, that can never be." She'd bought shares of lottery tickets in London. Hope had been better than nothing.

Hope.

She flung her gray pelisse over the depressing mirror and went into the private parlor for dinner.

The next morning, she hovered again over the idea of dressing in brighter clothing, but it would be reckless and she was determined to be full of reck. She smiled at the memory of how she and Marcus had sometimes played word games. He would describe her neat mending as ept, as opposed to inept. She'd encourage him to be gruntled rather than disgruntled.

Oh, Marcus, if you can see me from heaven, make this work. Please. And make him bearable.

She entered the carriage in gray for the final five hours, hoping she was the very image of sober, sensible reliability. That, after all, was what Viscount Dauntry sought. As if to encourage optimism, the sun broke through, catching the bronze and yellow of lingering leaves and touching bare bark with gold.

They dined just over the border into Gloucestershire, and an hour later turned off the main road, following a fingerpost that read BEECHAM DAB, 3 MILES. That shortening of "Dabittot" to "Dab" must be because of lack of space on the sign, but perhaps that was why the village was generally called that. It sounded so playful that she smiled as she waited for her first sight, pressed close to the window.

They passed one cottage on the right, then another, and then there were continuous buildings on either side, including the flaming mouth of a smithy and a substantial farmhouse. A barred gate protected the farmyard, where poultry pecked around and a man was leading two large horses toward an outbuilding. He paused to assess the passing carriage and four, and soon children began to run alongside in excitement. Adults came to their doors or paused in their work to see what was happening. Kitty was tempted to wave, but wasn't sure if that was appropriate for someone who might soon be the lady of this place. She sensed no hostility to strangers. That was a good sign.

Ruth had described Beecham Dab in her letters, but the village was larger than Kitty expected. It took some minutes to reach the green. She could see the square-towered church to her left, the Abbot's Arms to her right, and some larger houses among the cottages. They would belong to gentry.

She knew there was a squire, a doctor who served a number of local villages, and a pair of spinster sisters who were daughters of the previous parson. Puslow? She should have gone over Ruth's letters and made notes.

The carriage halted as the postilions asked the way. Kitty could have told them the parsonage lay behind the church at the end of the tree-lined lane to their left, but she let them find out for themselves.

In the center of the green stood a stone plinth. That

must be the memorial to three brothers killed in the Civil War. It had been erected by another grieving mother, the Lady Dauntry of the time, who'd lost all three sons to the cruelest kind of war. Two of the Braydon brothers had fought for the Royalists, but one had sided with Parliament. The recent wars had lasted longer than the Civil War, but had been abroad and less harrowing in that way.

The carriage turned down the lane, and soon the brick house came into view, looking exactly as it had in a sketch Ruth had sent. The chaise turned in front, and she saw Ruth coming out with her little boy by her side—a plumper Ruth but still as pretty, blond hair curling out from beneath her cap, waving and beaming a welcome. As soon as the steps were down, Kitty ran out and into her friend's arms.

"Oh, it's so good to see you!" she exclaimed.

"And I you."

But Kitty noticed an odd tone. "Is something the matter?"

"No, of course not." But then Ruth added, "You just seem a little wan."

"Perhaps that's because you have bouquets of roses in your cheeks."

"Country air." Perhaps Ruth remembered that Kitty had been living in the countryside, for she added, "Gray never suited you. What style you arrive in! Beecham Dab will be all agog."

"We certainly stirred excitement."

Ruth turned to her son. "Arthur, dear, be careful with the dog."

The four-year-old was giggling with delight but also waving his arms about, which Sillikin was taking as invitation to jump.

Kitty scooped up her dog. "She's very gentle, but I'll introduce her properly once we're inside. Good day to you, Arthur."

The boy bobbed a shy bow, but his eyes were bright. He was delightful.

"Come in, come in," Ruth said. "You'll be ready for some tea."

"I must thank my attendants first."

Kitty walked back to where a parsonage serving man was taking her trunk out of the boot, with Mr. Jones observing. Tessa was still in the coach. Kitty thanked them both and waved them on their return journey. The coach would come back for her when she wrote to ask, but she hoped that was never. Seeing Ruth again, even for just a moment, had only increased her desire that this plan work.

She joined Ruth in the entrance hall. It was much more modest than the one at Cateril, but Kitty instantly preferred it. It was wainscoted in dark wood, but the upper walls and ceiling were painted a pleasant eggshell blue and hung with watercolors that were probably Ruth's work. Potpourri and polish scented the air.

"You have a lovely home," Kitty said.

"We're blessed," Ruth agreed.

"I detect your clever hand as well as God's," Kitty teased, taking off her gloves. "Now, tell me more about Lord Dauntry."

"In a while," Ruth said, glancing down. "Little pitchers. . . ."

Little pitchers have big ears. Kitty knew from her niece and nephew that children could repeat things heard, sometimes at unfortunate moments.

She crouched down to introduce Sillikin to the boy. "I'll keep her with me for now, but I'm sure she'll like to play once she's become used to a new place."

"This isn't new," he protested.

"It is to her. Stroke her ears. She likes that." As the boy did, she added, "I understand you have cats?"

He nodded.

"We'll hope they'll be friends."

She rose, keeping the dog in her arms just to be safe. Ruth called for a maid to take care of Arthur, and they went upstairs.

"Here we are," Ruth said, opening the door into a bedroom.

The room wasn't as large as the one Kitty had in Cateril Manor and was much plainer, but as with the hall, she liked it better. Ruth had stenciled a rose design in places on the pale pink wall to simulate wallpaper. The bed had no posts or hangings, but a pink and white coverlet matched the curtains at the window, and a lively fire burned in the hearth.

"Perfect," she said, putting Sillikin down to explore. "Thank you."

"I hope you'll enjoy it. But not for long," Ruth added with meaning.

Kitty untied her bonnet and put it aside. "The prospect hardly seems believable."

"It is, Kitty. Completely. As long as you'll be practical."

"Practical?"

"You can act so impulsively. Kindly, but . . . Never mind. I'm sure you'll find Lord Dauntry unobjectionable."

Kitty considered her as she unfastened her pelisse. "That sounds grudging."

"I don't mean it that way. I don't know," Ruth said helplessly. "I can't know if you'll suit. It's a long time since we were schoolgirls together."

"I suppose so, but it doesn't feel like that now."

"It doesn't, does it? Oh, let me hug you again!"

Kitty happily complied, but then asked the important question. "When will I meet him?"

"We're to send a message when you arrive, and he'll call the next day."

Tomorrow. Thank heavens. She had time to work out how best to present herself.

She took off her pelisse, and Ruth pulled a face at the gray gown beneath. "I know we're all dressing soberly, but complete gray?"

Kitty didn't want to tell Ruth she'd been in half mourning forever. "It's practical for traveling."

"You, being practical?" Ruth teased. "But it's true. Let's see what else you have. Unlock your trunk."

"Bossy boots." Kitty said it with a smile, however, and found the key.

Ruth flung back the lid. "Violet," she said, putting that aside. "And fawn with black trim. Ah-ha!" She pulled out the blue and cream stripe. "This will suit you."

"Is it too bright? I hadn't realized until the journey how many people are still wearing somber colors."

"I know, and I hear it's worse in London. Very bright colors are looked at askance everywhere. Andrew and I think it's gone beyond reason, but what to do? The blue is quiet enough, and this russet brown, too." But then she sniffed. "Camphor?"

"I hoped that would fade. They've been stored away."

"Do you mean you've been wearing half mourning all this time?"

There'd never been hope of keeping secrets from Ruth. "It seemed easier. I'll spread them around the room to air."

"Better to hang them out—and most of the rest. The smell has spread."

"Foolish of me."

Ruth rolled her eyes, but Kitty hadn't been as foolish as Ruth thought. She couldn't have aired the colorful clothes before she packed them or Lady Cateril would have heard of it.

"There's an hour or two of daylight left and a breeze." Ruth lifted out an armful of clothing. "Come along."

Kitty grabbed the rest of the clothing, called Sillikin, and followed downstairs, feeling both happier and more anxious. It was wonderful to be with Ruth again, but the only way to hold on to that was to present the perfect appearance to Viscount Dauntry—definitely without the pungent odor of camphor!

Chapter 4

They passed through a cheerfully busy kitchen, and Ruth introduced her to the two women and the lad there. But then Sillikin saw a cat and trotted over to a new friend. The cat hissed, and Sillikin escaped under the table, tangling in the cook's feet. The woman yelled and waved a chopping knife.

Kitty dumped her burden on top of the one in Ruth's arms and went to her knees, coaxing the dog to come out to her. The kitchen lad scrambled under the table and brought Sillikin out, caught in the act of eating a dropped piece of meat.

"Bad dog!" Kitty scolded as she stood up with Sillikin firmly in her arms, knowing she was hot-faced and hair was escaping her cap. It was as well no one here would be asked to give her a reference as a suitable viscountess.

She apologized and hurried to catch up with Ruth. "You're going to spoil everything!" she scolded. The spaniel showed no sign of contrition.

"Round here!" Ruth called.

Kitty walked round the house and through a gate in a hedge to find a grassy area crossed by laundry lines. The area was edged on one side by a waist-high lavender hedge, over which sheets could be spread in the best weather to gather the fragrance as they dried.

"She's usually better behaved," Kitty said as she closed

the gate behind her. "But she's been cooped up in the coach for most of the past two days." And in Cateril Manor for so much longer. Perhaps Sillikin was feeling the same giddy relief as she was.

Ruth had draped the clothing over one line and was pegging the first garment in place on another. "You can let her run about in here. The hedge is dense and the gates are closed."

There was a second gate into the lane that ran beside the parsonage. As Ruth said, it was closed, so Kitty let Sillikin free. Once she was sure the dog was content with snuffling around the area, she helped with the pegging.

The sun was low in the sky and a breeze flapped the clothing on the line, but after her misadventure in the kitchen, the crisp air was welcome. The embarrassing moment hadn't been her fault, but she must avoid any more, especially where Lord Dauntry might hear about them. She paused to tuck hair back under her cap and then pegged her blue linsey-woolsey gown securely to the line. This was a good time to learn more.

"You wrote that Lord Dauntry is fashionable. My brighter gowns are years old."

"He's not expecting a peacock of fashion."

"What is he expecting? What did you tell him?"

Ruth pinned the green. "I can't remember exactly. That you're a widow aged twenty-seven. That you'd run your household in London for many years."

"Mere rooms," Kitty protested.

"But your own establishment. I tried to give the impression that you were sound in body and mind."

"An effort, was it?"

Ruth chuckled. "I sometimes wonder about the mind bit. I don't forget you persuading me to slip out of school to visit a fair."

"Nor do I," Kitty said as she pegged out a shift. "We fled back to the school in terror."

"You did it again the next year."

"And you refused. Very wisely, I'm sure."

"But that's when you met Marcus."

"Yes," Kitty said.

She'd repeated the adventure simply to prove to herself that she wasn't afraid, but she hadn't intended to stay long. When she'd seen the scarred and wounded man leaning against a low wall, however, crutch propped beside him, she'd felt his despondence. She'd asked if she could help him in some way. He'd smiled and she'd seen the vibrant man beneath, so she'd kept him company for a little while.

Older and wiser now, she could see all the ways that adventure could have been disastrous, but Marcus had never been that sort of wretch. They'd talked of trivialities, but the bond had been forged. He'd responded to her interest, and she'd fallen in love with the vision of herself as ministering angel to the wounded hero.

He'd been in Leamington to take the spa waters and consult with a doctor there. The school servants were easy to bribe, so they'd exchanged messages and even managed occasional meetings until he'd left. A month later, it had been time for Kitty to leave school. Marcus had turned up in Coventry to court her in traditional form. Not long afterward, they'd married in her parish church amid orange blossom, tossed wheat, and smiles.

"Sad memories?" Ruth asked.

"Just memories. What did you tell Lord Dauntry about my appearance?"

"I don't think he asked."

"That doesn't mean it won't matter."

"There's nothing wrong with your appearance."

"I've never been a beauty."

"If only beauties married, the world would be an odd place."

"Those without beauty or fortune often stay single. Don't look at me like that. You wanted me to be practical."

"And honest," Ruth said. "Whenever we schoolgirls encountered young gentlemen, they were attracted to your charm."

Charm? Kitty pondered that as she pegged out a pair of drawers. She'd forgotten those times, but perhaps Ruth was right. Swains had been drawn to Ruth's prettiness, but Kitty had never been neglected. Marcus had been attracted to her for more than her compassion for a wounded soldier, and his army friends had sometimes flirted with her.

Sometimes too much.

Marcus had liked her to be his hostess and been proud of her popularity, but sometimes and unpredictably, he'd take objection to one man's attentions. He'd even tried to duel with one of them. After that, she'd tried to deflect attention. When she thought back, it seemed it had become less necessary as she'd aged. Ruth was remembering a past nearly a decade old, not the way Kitty was today.

She moved to a new line to hang out her russet gown. Perhaps she'd wear that for her interview. It was the most sober color of her premourning gowns and it had long sleeves and a high neck. Unfortunately, it was trimmed with braid in a military style. That had been the fashion four years ago, but it wasn't popular in peacetime.

She told herself Lord Dauntry wasn't seeking high style. He wanted a sensible woman to manage his household. The brown could be just the thing. If not, it would have to be gray or fawn. The violet silk was an evening dress, and both the green and the blue too frivolous.

She picked up a pair of stockings, but then looked around. "Sillikin? Sillikin?"

She slung the stockings back on the line and hunted around the open area and along the hedge. Both gates were still closed. "Sillikin! Come, girl!"

She heard a bark, but it was at a distance. Over the lavender hedge she saw her dog, hindquarters wriggling in joy at her escape. "How did you get there, you bad dog? Come back."

Then Kitty saw that there were cows in the field. They were all at a distance at the moment, but that could change.

She ran to the gate that led into the lane and saw a small gap where the hedge met it. It hardly seemed big enough, but a bit of fur was caught on one twig. She opened the gate, calling back, "She escaped this way. She's not a country dog. She could get into trouble!" She ran into the lane, and Ruth joined her there.

"Call her. She should come."

"Sillikin! Come!" Beyond the wide barred gate into the field, the dog turned but stayed where she was, wagging her tail, inviting Kitty to the game. The cows were turning their heads to look.

"Devil take you," Kitty muttered, and then reminded herself to watch her tongue around Ruth. "I'll go and get her."

"I'll help."

But from the house came a call. "Mistress!"

"What now?" Ruth asked.

"Go. I can manage this."

Ruth helped Kitty to open the gate a little way. "Are you sure you'll be all right?"

"I'm not afraid of a few cows."

"She should be better trained, you know. She'll have to behave herself in the country."

"I know. She's never wandered during walks at Cateril, and in London I mostly kept her on a leash when we went out. Go. I'll manage."

Ruth hurried back to the house, and Kitty slipped through the gate, keeping an eye on the brown cows. She'd said she wasn't afraid of them, but that was true only if they kept their distance. She'd grown up in towns and then lived mostly in London. During her time at Cateril Manor she'd never ventured far from the gardens on her walks.

The ground was trampled to mud around the gate, so she picked her way along the drier edge, where some grass survived. Even so, she could feel dampness seeping through her jean half boots. She'd seen no need to wear her sturdier leather ones for travel.

"Pestilential creature," she muttered at the dog, who remained out of reach, in cheerful expectation of play.

Just in time, Kitty avoided some cow dung, but that had her continuing to employ some of Marcus's more colorful language as she navigated the field, holding up her skirts. Now three cows were watching her as they chewed. One took a few steps toward her. Sillikin danced farther away.

She had an idea. Despite what Ruth thought, Sillikin had been well trained and did usually obey a clear command.

"Sit!" she told her sharply.

Surprised but obedient, Sillikin sat. Kitty hurried over, but just as she reached for the dog, Sillikin looked past her and shot off toward the gate. Kitty turned and saw the attraction was a horse and rider.

They'd lived near the unfashionable side of Hyde Park, and Kitty had sometimes walked Sillikin there. That area was popular with men wanting a vigorous ride, so they'd often encountered Marcus's friends on horseback and always received a welcome. Now, ears flapping, the dog was lolloping over to greet new friends. But this was a stranger on a rangy gray horse that was sidling and staring with white-rimmed eyes at the little monster.

"Sillikin!" Kitty screamed, racing after. "Sit!"

The dog skidded to a halt and obeyed, but only feet from the horse, which was trying to rear, despite its rider's control.

Kitty dashed closer, grabbed her dog, and backed away. "My apologies, sir. She's overexcited."

"I'd say you were, woman. There was no need to screech."

Cold eyed, blond, and fashionable enough for a London park. Kitty *knew,* and here she was, in unbecoming gray, a complete mess head to toe, clutching an unruly dog who clearly hadn't avoided all the dung.

"Yes. No. I'm sorry, sir!"

With that, she fled down the lane instead of back into the parsonage gardens, as if she could somehow deceive him as to her identity. Perhaps Viscount Dauntry wouldn't connect a hoyden in a field with the sensible widowed friend of the parson's wife.

When she'd turned a corner, however, she collapsed against a low stone wall. It didn't matter. As soon as he saw her again, he'd know. He'd never believe she could control his household, and even less that she could be a suitable viscountess. Ruth had been right to worry. Within an hour of arrival she'd ruined everything.

She pushed despondently through the gate and followed a path through graves to the parsonage, too depressed even to castigate the pungent dog. It seemed that Sillikin's obedience had caused her to sit straight down in some dung, and she had more on her paws. Kitty couldn't take her into the house like this, so she paused in the garden to try to clean off as much muck as possible with handfuls of grass. The dog's coat was long, however, and grass didn't make much impression.

"Wretched beast. I might as well clean you off with my brown gown, for all the good it's going to do me now."

Ruth came out. "Is she all right?"

"Safe but filthy."

"The small washtub," Ruth said. She left and returned to fill it with water from the pump. "I'll get some soap and rags."

Kitty put Sillikin in the water and kept her there. "Yes, I know you don't like it, but perhaps this will teach you a lesson, milady. You know better than to run off like that."

Suddenly contrite as well as miserable, the dog licked her hand and whined.

"Very well, but you've ruined everything. We'll end up back in Cateril Manor, trapped under a dismal cloud forever."

Unheard, Ruth had returned. "Is it as bad as that?"

Oh, Lord. Kitty took the pot of coarse soap and began to wash Sillikin in the cold water. "Marcus's mother hasn't regained her spirits, so she doesn't want to think I have."

"That must be difficult."

"It is."

"What will she say when you remarry?"

"I don't know," Kitty said.

And now we'll never know.

Ruth went back into the house, and Kitty continued to clean the dog. She should have told Ruth the marriage would never happen, but she hated to shatter hope as much as she hated the prospect of returning to Cateril Manor.

Chapter 5

Viscount Dauntry, who'd been known most of his life simply as Braydon, trotted Ivor down the lane, trying not to let his annoyance travel to the unsettled horse. It would be pleasant to think the woman with the dog had been some servant, but her gown, though dismal, had been well made and her voice well-bred.

She had to have been the Honorable Mrs. Cateril, his prospective bride. He was astonished that Ruth Lulworth had been so duplicitous. That woman could never be a calming influence at Beauchamp Abbey or anywhere else. On top of riotous behavior, there had been riotous red hair escaping from her cap. He distrusted red hair.

He let Ivor canter to work out the fidgets, but that brought him back to Beauchamp Abbey all the sooner. He slowed to a walk as soon as it came into view. Was he the only new peer in Britain to so bitterly curse his fate?

Only weeks ago he'd been a happy man. He'd been plain Mr. Braydon, with ample funds, minimal responsibilities, and a comfortable suite of rooms in the most fashionable part of London. Now he was stuck here.

True, he'd become restless with an idle life, but he'd recently found occupation that suited him. A chance encounter with an army acquaintance had led him to an unofficial department of the Home Office that worked to prevent riot and revolution. It was headed by Sir George

Hawkinville, under whom he'd served at times during the war, and it provided interesting, challenging work.

The nation seethed with unrest because of the hardships brought about by the expense of the long war with France. That had been worsened last year by the bleak weather caused by the explosion of a volcano in the Far East. Some had dubbed it the year without a summer. That hadn't quite been true here in Britain, but crops had been damaged and prices of food had risen even higher.

The suffering was genuine, and Dauntry sympathized with the poor and with the honest reformers who were trying to bring about change. He had no sympathy with those who were exploiting distress to foment violence and revolution.

Hawkinville worked under the sponsorship, protection even, of one of the king's sons, Prince Augustus, Duke of Sussex. Sussex was sympathetic to reform and wanted to find and deal with the revolutionaries without oppressing the honest poor or the honest reformers. He was a useful counterweight to the Home Secretary, Lord Sidmouth, who would prefer to crush all dissent, but all in all, Hawkinville's task was as delicate as picking thorns out of a lion's paw.

Now the death of Princess Charlotte and the consequent succession crisis had added chaos to the brew. Britain needed a cool head in command. Instead, the Regent was hiding in Brighton, surrendering to grief over his daughter's death, and the government seemed paralyzed by his absence.

The situation could explode at any moment, and Braydon needed to be on hand in London, but damned duty tied him here. It was months since his predecessor died, and things had slid awry. Some of the paperwork was in disarray, possibly in order to obscure errors and even theft. Money was certainly unaccounted for. In addition, he had to handle the fifth viscount's mother, the dowager Lady Dauntry, and his difficult daughter, Isabella.

He was learning his new trade and beginning to put things straight, but accounts, documents, and land management were one thing; difficult females were another. It was only natural that the dowager Lady Dauntry was in deep grief over the loss of her son and grandson, and Isabella mourned the loss of her father and brother. He understood why they both resented the stranger who'd taken over their home and could throw them out on a whim. Facts were facts, however. They were all stuck in this mess and nothing could change it. He'd pinned his hopes of sanity on a quick marriage to a sensible widow—a woman like the excellent Ruth Lulworth. Clearly opposites attracted. Had he somehow offended the gods that they thwarted him at every turn?

Pale Beauchamp Abbey was his ball and chain, but it was a handsome house. It had been well designed and well built nearly two hundred years ago, in a simple style that had probably been based on the Queen's House in Greenwich, which was a notable work by Inigo Jones.

The gardens in front had a similar old-fashioned formality, and there, walking three small white dogs along a white gravel path, was Isabella, in deepest black. She was still in her mourning period, but she and her grandmother dripped with black and jet as a blatant reproach to cruel fate—that is, him.

He carried on to the stables and put Ivor in the hands of Baker, his groom. Nearly all the servants here were from the fifth viscount's time, so he appreciated the few of his own.

"Any problems?" he asked quietly. He'd been away for only six hours, but anything was possible.

"Nothing to speak of, milord. A Lord Nunseath paid a

call. Happened to be passing by, he said. From fifteen miles away."

A remarkable number of gentry and aristocracy did that, and Dauntry was glad to have missed one. They properly welcomed him to his new elevation, but they all bore invitations from their ladies, and most mentioned available daughters with handsome dowries, charming accomplishments, or both. He should have sought a bride from among those, but such a lady would not have welcomed a hasty wooing, nor her husband's intention to leave her in command here and live mostly in Town. In addition, she would have brought entanglements.

The visiting gentlemen all sounded out his politics, trying to discover what side he'd be on in national and especially local matters. Some had requested financial support for this good cause and that. Braydon would pour out guineas to be rid of them, but he'd detected local politics behind some causes, and a few seemed like outright fraud. It wasn't in his nature to ignore that. A wife without local connections had seemed to be a good idea.

He entered the house by the back door that lay close to his office, first entering the room used by his secretary. Worseley rose to hand him a message from the parsonage. As feared, it told him that Mrs. Cateril had arrived.

"Anything else of importance?"

"No, sir."

Braydon put the letter in his pocket as he progressed to the front hall, considering what to do about the widow. He could write to say she would not suit. She'd know why. But that brought problems of its own.

As he crossed the hall toward the staircase, Isabella entered by the front door. The little white dogs yapped the alarm as if he were a sneak thief, perhaps taking their cue down the leashes. This had to stop.

"Take the dogs to the dowager Lady Dauntry," Dauntry told an impassive footman. "Isabella, a word with you."

He indicated the library.

She gave him an icy glare, but she went into the room. He'd seen wariness beneath the glare, so he spoke gently.

"Isabella, I understand that you are upset by all that's happened, but perhaps it hasn't been made clear to you that I am not the worst result."

She stared at a bookcase, the perfect image of a rude child. She was nearly seventeen. She was a pretty girl with dark curls, a clear complexion, and vivid coloring, and would have no difficulty in finding a husband, especially with her large dowry. One of the complicating factors to his inheritance was that on his deathbed, the fifth viscount had put all the unentailed property and funds into Isabella's already generous portion. It was an understandable action from a father whose son had died, leaving only a daughter, but it made the viscountcy much poorer than it should be. Braydon wished Isabella well, however, and would do what he could to steer her into a happy life.

He kept his tone moderate. "If I didn't exist, the title and entailed property, including this house, would have already reverted to the Crown, and you would have had to leave."

She swiveled her head to look at him. "That's not true. The Regent would have promised to grant my husband the title."

"Highly unlikely."

"Grandmama is a friend of the queen."

That was putting it too strong, but the dowager had been a lady-in-waiting for many years, and Queen Charlotte had sent a personal letter of sympathy.

So this had been the hope lurking here between the fifth viscount's death and the confirmation of his own inheritance. He should have confronted Isabella sooner. The detail changed nothing, but now he could deal with the issue.

"Such a matter would be complex," he said, "and it's more likely that the title would have been restored, if at all, for your oldest son when he was of age. In the intervening decades, you and the dowager would have to live elsewhere."

He saw a flicker of uncertainty, but she shrugged.

"Now I'm in place," he said, "all such matters are moot."

"That's why you are going to marry me."

He'd suspected this plan and was glad to be able to scotch it. "No, I'm not."

"You'll have to," she said with a smug smile, "or you'll be dreadfully penny pinched. I have most of the money."

He could tell her that he had a fortune of his own, but he saw a better way. "Then I'll be obliged to sell off most of the extravagant bits and pieces the dowager has wasted money on over the decades."

The girl's chin dropped.

Report that back to your grandmother, and I hope it chokes her.

The dowager was the enemy here, however, and Isabella merely a foot soldier. If Isabella had been a French spy—and some had been as young and pretty—he'd know how to handle her, but nothing in his army experience or since had prepared him for Beauchamp Abbey and its female combatants. He'd put his faith in sensible Mrs. Cateril, damn her.

He attempted reason. "I can't imagine that you want to marry me, Isabella."

"This is my home," she declared, "and our family blood must continue here. It is *right* that it continue here."

"I have the Braydon blood," he pointed out. "You're talking of the Godyson blood, and that only came here with your grandmother. You will carry that to some other grand estate."

She had been well indoctrinated "You'll break Grandmama's heart!" she cried. "She made Beauchamp Abbey what it is." Here came the tears, which she seemed able to summon at will. "You're a monstrous usurper!"

"Then you certainly don't want to marry me."

She let out a wail that could probably be heard throughout the house, and ran away.

Dauntry sighed. Damn Mrs. Cateril for not being the woman he'd been promised. He'd have to find another bride, and speedily, for recently Isabella had been taking direct action. She'd sought his company a time or two and come too close to him for propriety. Once she'd tripped and fallen into his arms. It had been so clearly staged that he'd been tempted to drop her.

She was a child and his ward, but he was sure the dowager Lady Dauntry believed that all was fair in love and war, and she was waging war. He wasn't even sure the dowager loved Isabella. Whatever the truth of that, she was allowing her passion for Beauchamp Abbey and her precious Godyson bloodline to rule.

The Godyson family was one of the few aristocratic families that could trace its line back to before the Conquest, and the dowager was the sole remainder. When she'd married, she'd insisted on including the name, and the family had become Godyson-Braydon. She'd built the power and prestige of the family, and made the Abbey suitable for its glory. Braydon wouldn't be surprised if she'd had some plan to drop the Braydon name, and have her son become Alfred Godyson, Viscount Dauntry.

If so, any such plans were shattered, but she had not yet given up the fight. Thus he still needed a wife who was up to the task.

He'd go to Town and ask friends for recommendations.

There must be any number of worthy war widows who'd benefit from the arrangement, and some had followed the drum. They'd make short work of the dowager and Isabella. Before that, however, he'd have to deal with Mrs. Cateril. He could respond to the letter to say he'd changed his mind, but his friendship with Lulworth and his wife had helped preserve his sanity here, and Mrs. Cateril and Mrs. Lulworth were old and devoted friends.

Another delicate quandary, but with planning he should be able to manage it. He returned to his office to write that he would visit the parsonage at ten the next morning. He dispatched it, then sat back to plan how to get Mrs. Cateril to beat the retreat, saving him from any hint of having jilted her.

Chapter 6

Kitty tried to pluck up the courage to tell Ruth what a mess she'd made of everything. Instead, she clung to hope of a miracle. She thought she managed to appear normal through the evening, for Ruth and her husband must expect her to be anxious.

Andrew had arrived home accompanied by two large honey-gold dogs, which Kitty gathered served as gun dogs at times, retrieving rabbits and pigeons for the parsonage pot. Stocky, brown-haired, and cheerful, Andrew was made to be a country parson. Kitty could easily imagine him out in the fields, helping to bring in the harvest.

Why couldn't Viscount Dauntry be more like him?

His dogs were as amiable as he and tolerated Sillikin's excited greeting. The three soon ended up curled together in front of the fire, with the two cats nearby. Lady Cateril would have been appalled, but for Kitty that scene was a symbol of all she'd thrown away.

Over dinner Andrew spoke of the viscount, obviously assuming Kitty would be interested. How Dauntry was distantly connected to a duke, had been stylish even as a schoolboy, and had been mentioned in dispatches once in the war. Kitty assumed it was all intended to make him even more appealing to her, but it added to her blue devils. He most certainly wouldn't want a hoyden as his wife.

She went early to bed to avoid more talk of what she couldn't have and suffered a restless night of longings and fears. In the darkest hours of the night, she found a thread of hope. Lord Dauntry was clearly desperate enough to grab at any available bride, so perhaps his desperation would make him forgiving.

Dark-hour thoughts were never positive, however.

Why is he so desperate?

Has his cold harshness turned off all the women he's courted?

She tried to tell herself that he, too, had presented an unfortunate first impression. That he was easygoing beneath the ice. Or that she could cope with his coldness because he'd mostly be absent. She'd coped with a great deal worse from Marcus, after all.

None of it helped.

She awoke to a cold morning with the fire not yet lit, and huddled under the covers. What was she going to do when the ax dropped? She couldn't bear to return to Cateril Manor. She simply couldn't. But she couldn't stay here as a guest forever.

She'd have to find some kind of employment, but as what?

She realized that Sillikin was by the door, wanting to go out. At Cateril Manor Kitty would have simply opened the door, for the dog knew the way to the kitchen there and the servants would let her out. Here, she couldn't depend on that.

Ruth had only five servants—her cook, the manservant, the lad, a young nursery nurse, and the general maid. Clattering footsteps suggested that Sukey, the general maid, was dashing here and there. She shouldn't be asked to care for a dog.

Kitty wrapped up warmly and then, praying she wouldn't encounter Andrew, took Sillikin downstairs to the kitchen. The cook looked up, startled, and then frowned at the dog.

"She needs to go out," Kitty said. Yet again, she wasn't impressing the servants, and servants gossiped. "I didn't want to trouble Sukey."

The maid dashed in then. "That's kind of you, ma'am, but I wouldn't have minded."

"Bob," the cook said to the lad, who was topping up a copper of water, "take out the dog for Mrs. Cateril."

The boy leapt to the task with eagerness. Kitty thanked the cook, who had a twinkle in her eye. "He's my sister's son, ma'am, and a good worker. You must ask for him if your dog needs attention."

"You'll be wanting your washing water, ma'am," Sukey said. "I'll be right up with it!"

Kitty almost offered to carry it up herself, but she was conscious of the remote possibility that she might become Viscountess Dauntry, so she thanked the maid and returned to her room.

In her experience, servants didn't admire nobility who did for themselves. She'd heard such people referred to as not knowing what was due to their station, as if they were disturbing the order of the universe. The exception was men with their dogs, horses, and guns. They were allowed to muck around.

Good for the gander, good for the goose, Kitty thought. The makings of the fire were at hand, so she knelt down, cleaned out the ashes, and laid the kindling and wood. She was working the tinderbox when Sukey came in with the jug of steaming water.

"Don't you be doing that, ma'am!" she exclaimed, as if Kitty were a child likely to set the house on fire.

She put down the jug and claimed the tinderbox. Kitty retreated as Sukey fiddled with the arrangement, as if

Kitty had done it wrong. Only then did she strike a flame, ignite a wax taper, and light the fire.

"There," Sukey said, as if she'd snatched victory from disaster. "Now, ma'am, do you need me to help you dress?"

"I will," Kitty said. "But come back in a little while. I need to wash first."

And decide what to wear, she thought as the maid left. She doubted that Lord Dauntry would keep the appointment, but if he did, she'd do her best. That included a suitable appearance.

As she washed, she wished she could wear the gray so as not to be seen to be trying to hide the truth, but that wasn't even possible. The gown had been so smeared with dirt, some of it stinking, that it had been put to soak in the laundry tub overnight. It might never be wearable again, and she couldn't regret that.

So, the fawn with simple black braid, or the russet with military trimming? She longed to be out of mourning, even if unfashionably, so she chose the russet. Perhaps its being out-of-date would count in her favor. Sukey returned and helped her on with the stays and gown. Kitty released her then and sat to brush her hair.

She was still working at it when Ruth knocked and came in. "I'd forgotten how magnificent it is."

"I've often thought of cutting it," Kitty said, working the brush through the long, springy thickness, "but Marcus liked it. Unfortunately, he often said so. When I mentioned cutting off a foot or so, Lady Cateril protested that I no longer cared a jot for him."

"That woman has taken mourning to extremes," Ruth said, taking the brush. "You'll be better off away from her. Do you remember how we used to do this for each other? I always envied you the length and thickness of your hair."

"And I envied you your blond."

"Yours is a richer color."

"Red and restless. That's what Marcus said."

"He knew you well, but it's darker than most red hair, so perhaps not so wild. Marriage must have settled you."

"Of course, but . . ." The habit of keeping secrets was hard to break, but she wanted to tell Ruth a bit of it. "It was probably a complaint. Marcus's injuries meant there were many things he couldn't do. Travel far, walk far, sit in a theater for hours. Dance. Sometimes I was restless for new experiences."

Ruth rested a hand on her shoulder for a moment. "How shall I dress it?"

"Plait it tightly and pin it up. It doesn't show under the cap."

"You're not wearing a cap today."

"I'm a widow."

"You're almost a bride. I'll arrange something."

Kitty almost surrendered, but said, "No." She met her friend's eyes in the mirror. "There's no point, Ruth. When I chased Sillikin yesterday, I encountered a rider. I'm sure it was Lord Dauntry, so he saw me at my worst. He must have guessed who I was. He'll probably not even come."

Ruth did look dismayed, but she said, "He's written to say he'll be here at ten." Seeing the expression on Kitty's face, she asked, "Why don't you look relieved?"

"I'm wondering why."

"You know why. He needs a wife. You're a completely different picture now. And only think of the prize."

The hope in Ruth's eyes stifled further protests. Meanwhile, Ruth had been deftly forming smaller plaits. Soon a confection of them was pinned in place at the back of Kitty's head.

"You don't look a day older than when you left school," Ruth said.

Kitty laughed. "That would be an odd thing after six years a wife and nearly two a widow. I won't try to pretend to be anything other."

"It wouldn't be pretense. Oh, very well. I know that face."

"And I know that one. You think you know best."

"Because I probably do." Suddenly they were both smiling, carried back into the past. "We were so keen to leave school, but we had good times, didn't we?"

"We did," Kitty admitted, "and we didn't realize how leaving would separate us."

"But now we can be together again."

Kitty turned to face her. "Ruth, don't hope too much. Please. Oh, now we're both crying." She took out a handkerchief and blew her nose. "I won't have it. We'll enjoy the time we have."

"And you'll go without a cap?"

"It won't matter. I'm sure I ruined my chances yesterday. Oh, isn't it time? I want this done!"

At that moment, the clock in the hall began to strike ten. A moment later, Kitty heard the jangle of the bell that hung outside the front door. The precision of the timing struck her with sudden panic. It seemed unnatural.

He'd come, but had he come only to berate her for not being the lady he'd been told she was?

She didn't like anger, but if faced with it, she might fire back. It had probably been the best approach with Marcus, who could be shouted into reason. If she fell into an argument with Lord Dauntry, however, Ruth and her husband might have to take sides. She could cause discord that could last for years.

"Don't look so apprehensive," Ruth begged.

Kitty forced a smile. "I'm just a knot of nerves, but I need a cap for courage. I've not gone without one for so long, my head feels naked." She picked up the white one she'd worn yesterday and settled it on her head, tying the ribbons beneath her chin. "There, see? It doesn't make me a complete antidote."

"Nothing could," Ruth said, but adjusted it backward so it released more of the curls around Kitty's face. "Ready?"

Kitty stood. "Ready."

As she went with Ruth, Kitty prepared herself. No matter what she faced, she must not fight back. She would be meek, calm, and dignified, beginning to end.

Chapter 7

Alas for dignity—she'd forgotten Sillikin. Sensing her, the dog hurtled out of the kitchen area, a wriggling bundle of delighted greeting.

She crouched down. "Yes, I'm perfectly safe, but I have an important meeting." She could almost imagine a smile of anticipation. *Meeting? Yes! New friends!* "Well, why not? He's already encountered you at your worst. Do try to show at your best."

She rose and turned toward the parlor, to realize that the door stood ajar. Lord Dauntry would have heard that. In addition to being a wretched hoyden, she was now the sort of madwoman who conversed with her dog. She blew out a breath and walked in.

He should have seemed less formidable than he had on horseback, but she found him more so. He wasn't as broad a man as Marcus, but his elegant clothing didn't disguise the same sense of muscular power that her husband had retained even in his ruined state. Dauntry was perhaps taller.

Then she wondered why she'd thought his clothing elegant. He was wearing a brown jacket, buff riding breeches, and top boots, as most men did in the country But in some way his garments warranted the tag "beau." With his clean-cut features, fashionably dressed blond hair, and cool expression, the word that came to mind was "sleek."

Somewhere in the distance, Ruth was making introductions, but Sillikin disregarded formalities to trot forward and stare. That wasn't a good sign.

"Sillikin, heel," Kitty commanded, and, thank heaven, her dog obligingly trotted back to her side. Kitty dipped a curtsy. "Good morning, Lord Dauntry."

He bowed. "A pleasure to meet you, ma'am."

Kitty heard a silent *again*.

Pride afflicted her with an urge to break the arrangement first, but that would be foolish indeed. Innards churning with nerves, she sat and waved him to a nearby seat. Ruth mentioned last-minute arrangements and left, but Kitty saw her only from the corner of her eye. She couldn't stop looking at Lord Dauntry, rather as one might watch a predator that seemed likely to attack. His eyes were a light and rather icy blue.

He sat on a facing chair and crossed his legs. "Well, Mrs. Cateril?"

"Very well, sir."

"I wasn't asking how you are, ma'am. What questions do you have for me?"

Questions? Her mind went blank. "Mrs. Lulworth told me the essentials, sir."

"Are you not curious about the inessentials?"

The wretched man was toying with her! "I assume she didn't conceal that you are stark, staring mad?"

No reaction apart from a raised brow. "I might have concealed it from her, but indeed, I'm not. Are you?"

"No."

"Excellent. I also have all my teeth."

"So do I."

"Yet more harmony."

Oh, you wretch. Now she understood his abrasive manner. He'd come here to end the arrangement, but was going to avoid any hint of jilting her by making her do it. Well, he could work for his prize. She'd play his game, returning every shot, forcing him to produce the coup de grâce.

Now he was using silence. She saw the small piano in the corner of the room. "Is there a pianoforte in . . . the Abbey, my lord?" Thank heavens she'd spotted the hazard and not attempted the full name. Ruth and Andrew spoke of his house as the Abbey, so she'd not yet heard anyone say "Beauchamp." She still didn't know how it was pronounced.

"There is," he said, "though I've heard no one play it."

"Has the house in general been neglected, my lord?"

"Not as far as I can tell, but I know little of such matters. I was in the army, and since leaving, my home has been rooms in London."

For a moment she envisioned rooms similar to the ones in Moor Street she'd lived in with Marcus, but she dismissed the notion. No one had such deep polish and surety without luxury and privilege from the day they were born.

"I have no living family," she said. "Is that the case with you, too, my lord?"

"My parents and three of four grandparents are dead. I have two much older sisters, both married. We're not close. Some distant female cousins dangle on the family tree, but I don't know 'em."

Solitary, but careless of it. Like a cat. A fine-blooded cat, sure of its position in the world and that all should do it reverence. The cat was playing with a mouse, but this mouse wouldn't be trapped. She let silence settle.

"Of course, I have my new family," he said. "At the Abbey."

The reason for all this. "The previous viscount's mother

and daughter, I understand. The situation must be difficult for them."

"And for me. Your husband was the son of a baron?"

"My father was a shopkeeper." *There's your exit, sir. Take it.*

"A bookseller, I understand, and a scholar of some repute."

Dammit. Of course Ruth would have told him that.

He continued. "Your husband was an officer gallantly injured at Roleia."

"He was, my lord. You, too, were a soldier. You escaped without injury?"

She didn't mean it to be as insulting as it sounded. She would have apologized, but he seemed unmoved. "Superficial wounds only. I'm sound in wind and limb. Are you?"

She deserved that riposte. "Yes." She recognized an opening. "You will have noted that I have no children, my lord. That must be a concern to you." *Another escape. Take it.*

"Must it? If the viscountcy dies with me, I won't turn a hair."

"Of course not, being dead," she said tartly. "But when living you will want to provide for the continuance of the title. Any man would."

"Ma'am, until a few weeks ago, I'd never given a thought to the viscountcy of Dauntry, so its future is unlikely to disturb me now or in the hereafter."

"Are you *ever* disturbed?" *Oh, dear.* That shouldn't have escaped.

He stared, as well he might. "It rarely serves any purpose."

"Yet you don't seem idle."

"Activity is generally most effective when taken calmly. Do you have any other questions?"

She'd won. He was going to end it. But she did have one question plaguing her. "You truly don't consider yourself blessed to have so unexpectedly become a peer, my lord?"

"Rather more like one of the flies that the wanton gods amuse themselves with for sport. Perhaps we are done?"

With a silent apology to Ruth, Kitty met him halfway. "We are, my lord. We know this will not do."

"You don't consider yourself blessed by this unexpected opportunity, Mrs. Cateril?"

"I doubt anyone likes to be a fly, my lord. Or toyed with for sport."

He nodded in acknowledgment of that jab. "Why will our arrangement not do?"

Damn him. He was going to make her say it. "My origins are quite low, and though you didn't ask, I bring only a pittance to a marriage. On top of that, our encounter yesterday was unfortunate."

"Your appearance today might have reassured me, ma'am. As might your dog's obedience. Why is it staring at me?"

"She stares at people when they upset me in some way."

"How very perspicacious." He looked back at Kitty. "You lived your married life in London?"

Not a further inquisition. Kitty gave him the victory and stood. "My lord, have done with this. We cannot marry."

He rose smoothly. "Why not?"

Seeking any reason, Kitty found one. "My mother-in-law could not bear it."

At last that disturbed—or at least surprised—His Sleekness. "Why?" he asked.

Sillikin stepped closer to him. Kitty had no idea what the dog had in mind, but she picked her up to prevent mayhem. "My marrying again would offend against my husband's memory. I wouldn't want to hurt her."

"Yet you came."

"To see Ruth. I apologize for wasting your time, Lord Dauntry, and regret that I cannot oblige you." She dipped a curtsy. "I hope that won't affect your relationship with the Lulworths."

"I'm not so irrational." He made no move to leave. "Do I understand that you intend to return to your husband's family and live under a pall for the rest of your life?"

"It's a pleasant manor house," she protested.

"Where you'll be compelled to wear the sort of clothing you had on yesterday."

"You'd break a mother's heart without a blink?"

"I'd find a way around the problem."

"Oh, please do!" At her tone, Sillikin yipped, and it was like a call to order. "I apologize, my lord. I shouldn't sink to squabbling."

"If you have done so, so have I, and I never squabble. If the problem of your mother-in-law was swept away, would you consider my offer of marriage?"

"It can't be."

"Extend your imagination, ma'am."

He snapped it as a command, so she did. Could she marry this man? Moments ago she'd been sure she couldn't. That she couldn't bear him. Now she was reminded of the alternative. So could she marry him?

His title was almost as perfect a fit as his clothing. He was daunting. Like glass or marble, Lord Dauntry seemed smooth and impenetrable, and clearly that was his nature as well. However, "smooth" and "impenetrable" might also mean *calm* and *controlled*. She wasn't attracted by such coolness, but she could tolerate it, especially as he intended to spend much of his time in Town.

Sillikin licked her chin. "You have wisdom to offer?" she asked, then blushed for it. She glanced back at Lord Dauntry but saw no disapproval. She saw nothing she could make sense of. He was waiting as if he would wait forever, and, yes, as if it were a matter of turnips or cabbages.

"Why?" she asked.

He didn't pretend confusion. "I need to make a practical marriage as soon as possible. Apart from occasional lapses and an odd habit of conferring with your dog, you seem a direct, forthright woman who is not easily overwhelmed. Moreover, if you will excuse frankness, you are easily to hand and have the endorsement of Mrs. Lulworth, whom I admire. Why are you hesitant?"

"My mother-in-law . . ."

He waved that away with a gesture of a rather beautiful hand. "This marriage will be very advantageous to you. You will become Viscountess Dauntry and have all the wealth and privilege that entails. As husband, I will do my best not to distress you in any way, as long as you do the same for me."

There was a subtle threat in that, but one she understood. She wasn't to object to his absence or anything he did when away. That would be no challenge. She could imagine the kind of mistress this man would have, and the woman was welcome to him, as long as his peccadilloes took place far from her.

Peccadilloes.

Petty sins.

She didn't think Viscount Dauntry did anything in a petty way, but she'd be insane to refuse this opportunity, and the longer he waited patiently, the more she believed in his disinterested control.

She spoke before she lost courage. "I accept your offer, my lord."

"And your mother-in-law?"

She blushed for the deception. "As you implied, by coming here, I'd already decided not to be ruled by her concerns. If she's distressed, I truly regret that, but I can't live in mourning forever."

"Grief can be a consuming emotion, but the grieving are generally able to see sense. A love match might wound her, but I won't replace her son in that way. I suggest that you write to her and explain my predicament, presenting the marriage as a practical and charitable act."

"That's cunning."

"You see my attempt to ease her mind as a fault?"

In a way, Kitty did. It was as if he were moving pieces on a chessboard, but she could see how it might work. She'd prefer not to add to Lady Cateril's pain.

"You could also claim to need a purpose in life," he suggested.

How had he guessed that would weigh with her mother-in-law?

"I'll write the letter," she said.

"Good. Shall we marry tomorrow?"

"Tomorrow!"

"I've already acquired a license."

She took a step back. "You were so sure of me, sir?"

"My dear lady, for a few shillings I could be prepared. That is all. Mrs. Lulworth supplied all the necessary information."

It was completely logical, but what sort of person did such a thing?

"I would prefer to wait."

"For what?"

"For Lord and Lady Cateril's blessing! If I write as you suggest, to marry before they even receive the letter would make any hint of consulting them hollow."

His lids lowered slightly, just maybe because she'd

trumped his ace. She was hard put not to grin. She might be falling in with his plans, but she'd relish preventing him having it all his own sleek and dauntless way.

If there had been annoyance, it was masked. "Then will it suit you to marry in a week?"

Kitty would prefer a month, but she could find no reasonable objection. Over a week she'd get to know him better and be able to truly settle her mind. There would still be the possibility of retreat.

"It will, my lord."

He bowed, she curtsied, and then he left.

Ruth rushed in. "Well?"

"Perhaps." Kitty sat on the sofa before her legs failed her.

"Why only perhaps?"

"Anything could happen in a week."

"You're to marry in a week?" Ruth said, delighted. "What a tease you are!"

"Not so fast." Kitty explained about the letter to Lady Cateril. "I'm not sure what I'll do if she responds with anguish or fury."

It was a lie. Her doubts were internal. Until the vows were said, she could still back out and she might very well want to.

Ruth sat beside her. "You can't return to Cateril Manor, Kitty. You can't let Lady Cateril chain you in that way."

"That's what he said. Is he always so impenetrable?"

"Do you not like him?" Ruth asked, dismayed. "If so, you mustn't marry him."

"I don't know how I feel toward him. As you put it, he's unobjectionable. I can't express any reasonable objection, but . . ."

"You have doubts?"

A legion of them, but Ruth was clearly close to tears at the thought of the plan falling through.

"I'll write the letter," Kitty said.

"This is a very odd way to go about a marriage."

"This marriage has been odd from the start."

Ruth patted her hand. "A week will give you time to get to know him better."

"Exactly my thought."

Kitty went to her room, trying to assemble the right words. She didn't want to wound Marcus's mother any more than she already had, but she rebelled at any notion of asking permission. She sat and took out a sheet of paper, suddenly seeing the way. She needed her clothing and possessions sent here. The reason, the marriage, would be almost incidental information.

She uncapped the inkwell, dipped her pen, and began careful sentences. When it was finished, she read it over, then folded and sealed it. *There. Committed.*

She looked up and through the window saw Lord Dauntry talking to Andrew near the stables. His simple clothing did indeed look Town fine next to Andrew's cheerfully rumpled style.

Sleek.

Polished.

Marble.

Deep instincts wanted to throw the letter on the fire.

As if to prevent that, Sillikin came over to paw at her skirt.

"We have no other chance at a comfortable life, do we?" Kitty said. "And I'm not committed yet. Not until the vows are said. By then I'll be more settled in my mind. He is interesting, Sillikin. Cool and smooth as marble, but there's more beneath. I'm sure of that. The question is what lies beneath—good or bad?"

Braydon encountered Andrew Lulworth near the stables.

"Should I wish you happy?" Lulworth asked.

"The bird is not yet in hand," Braydon replied. "Mrs. Cateril is to write to her mother-in-law."

"Why?"

"To inform her. The woman seems unbalanced by grief."

"The loss of a child is never forgotten."

"Will her daughter-in-law's remarriage kill her?"

"I've never known such a case. Consider old Lady Dauntry. A devoted mother who was deeply distressed by her son's death, along with that of her grandson. She was almost mad with it for a time, I understand, but she resumed her life within a month."

"And the running of the estate. Has she always done that?"

"Probably. Certainly as long as we've been here. The fifth viscount was often away. Parliament, hunting, shooting, and such."

Ivor was grazing in the paddock, but came at a call. Dauntry set about saddling the horse himself.

Lulworth came to help. "How is the dowager taking your authority? You've never said."

"With outward sorrow and inner bile."

"Then how's she going to react to your wife?"

"I dread to think."

"I don't detect the shivers."

"I've faced worse."

"And won, I'm sure. Ruth's flying in alt at the thought of her dearest friend so close."

"Flying is a perilous business," Dauntry warned.

"Not for birds."

"None of us have wings."

"Taking refuge behind precision? My wife is anticipating high delight."

"Which might also lead to a tumble."

"It won't break her heart," Lulworth said. "Do you have one?"

Braydon took a breath. "If we squabble, you'll make a liar of me. I'm not heartless and I do have nerves. In arranging this marriage, I'm engaging in more of a blind chance than I'm accustomed to. But as always, I draw up a strategy to win."

Chapter 8

Kitty put her letter in the hall to go off with other correspondence, then returned to her room to consider what to wear for her next meeting with Dauntry. They'd come to an agreement, but he could still back out.

Might he come for dinner? She'd wear the violet silk this evening, just in case. Tomorrow the blue linsey-woolsey, but by then he'd have seen most of what she had with her. She should have brought more. If Lady Cateril sent her belongings it would probably be by cart, and that could take the week. She laughed, shaking her head. For nearly two years she'd thought little of clothes other than the desire to move out of mourning, and here she was, in such a fuss. Dauntry wasn't going to reject her now because her wardrobe wasn't sufficiently varied.

The engagement to marry had happened so quickly, however, and now it felt insubstantial and slippery, as if it could slither away with any wrong move.

It is settled, she told herself.

Nothing will change.

Which meant she must plan for her wedding.

What to wear for that?

The village would turn out to watch any wedding, but especially if they heard the local magnate was involved. She wasn't the right sort of bride for a viscount, but she must look right. *The green print, the russet, or the blue stripe?*

And what bonnet? She'd brought only two. One was the plain black and the other gray. That could be trimmed with something brighter to match the blue or the green. With the brown dress, it would have to be the black.

Oh, she hated to be in such a fiddle. She'd never been quite sure of style or what suited her, but in London she'd had an excellent dressmaker to advise her. Janet Saunders's premises had been in the next street and she mainly did simple work, but she'd been capable of anything. Together they'd contrived to stretch Kitty's money to provide a couple of stylish gowns a year, and Janet had firmly steered her away from disasters.

At school Ruth had been her advisor. Kitty smiled at the memory of once desperately wanting lace-trimmed pink. She went to consult with Ruth and found her checking her inventory of medicines in the aromatic stillroom.

"You make your own? I always bought what I needed."

"London ways," Ruth said. "Didn't you help at the manor?"

"What Lady Cateril has surrendered is done by Sarah. I suppose I could have pushed harder to take part, but I confess this sort of household management has never appealed to me."

"As well you're going to be a great lady, then, but I think even peeresses manage their stillrooms. You'd better learn. You can start by writing my notes."

Kitty hadn't thought ahead to the actual running of a country house and it dismayed her, but she could do anything if she put her mind to it. She sat at the table with the book and the pen and wrote as dictated.

When Ruth had completed her inventory of potions, Kitty said, "I must have Dauntry take me to the Abbey, so I'll have an idea of how the place is managed."

"That's a good idea."

"What's it like?"

"The Abbey?" Ruth said, moving on to shelves of glass jars holding leaves and powders. "I've been there only once. When I arrived here as a bride, I was taken to be presented."

"Heavens! As at court?"

"That seemed to be the idea. Lord Dauntry was pleasant enough—the previous one, of course. The dowager was gracious, but she sat as if enthroned. She is a Godyson, you know. The oldest barony in the country."

"Makes a point of that, does she?"

"Always. That visit was far too master-to-servant for my taste."

"Do they not invite you to entertainments?"

"They only ever entertain the aristocracy."

"Being a Godyson, you know."

Ruth chuckled, but then bit her lip. "We shouldn't be cruel."

"You started it. I've met people like that. Quite tiresome. Don't most country seats have traditional events when the lordly mingle with lesser people? Cateril Manor had some. Harvesttime, Christmas, Twelfth Night, May Day."

"Not while we've been here. Note that I'm low on woodruff. I'll see if anyone has an abundance. I gather the dowager used to go to London for long periods when younger. She was a lady-in-waiting to the queen."

"My goodness."

"Exactly. Far above our touch. Now she's troubled by an aging hip and doesn't travel."

"Don't highborn friends visit?"

"Rarely. That might be because of Lady Dauntry."

"She's haughty with them as well?" Kitty asked.

"Probably, but I meant the fifth viscount's wife. She ran off with an actor."

Kitty paused, pen in hand. "No!"

"Yes. Write what I said about fleabane before you forget. I shouldn't gossip, but you need to know. It was long before I came here—Isabella was young and her brother an infant—but off she went. From servants' stories, she was constantly squabbling with the dowager and raging at her husband for not taking her side."

"So she ran away. Good for her."

"Kitty! She ran off into adultery or bigamy and abandoned her children."

"She probably had no other choice."

"Nonsense. Bryony root."

Kitty wrote it down, considering the story. "Are you saying I'm going to face the same challenges?"

"Probably, but I can assure you of one thing—Dauntry will take your side. He'd like the dowager out of there."

"Then why hasn't he moved her?"

"Anyone would hesitate to evict a grieving mother and grandmother from the place where she's lived for forty years."

"She expects to stay there forever?" Kitty asked in dismay.

"So it would seem. You knew part of his reason for marrying is to have someone to manage his female relatives."

"I hadn't quite grasped the extent of it." Kitty put down the pen. "Yet that's not reason enough for this rush to the altar. I don't understand him, Ruth. Our encounter in the lane has to have exploded any idea he had of my being a pillar of stability. It wasn't my fault. . . ."

"It never is."

"Ruth!"

"I'm sorry, but you must confess you've never been the most conformable woman."

"So why is Lord Dauntry continuing with his plan, and why the urgency?"

Ruth leaned back against the shelves. "Perhaps he decided an unconformable woman would be a good match for the dowager."

"Is that possible?"

"If it came to skirmishes, I'd place my bet on you."

"Gambling? Horrors!"

"Oh, you. I can see Dauntry thinking that way."

"So can I. Choosing the piece to play. All life is a chessboard to him. I can see that already. And I can tolerate it, as long as I'm the queen."

"With him the powerless king?"

"Oh no. As I said, he's the chess player."

"He's simply a beleaguered man, Kitty."

They took up their work again, but it left time to think. Kitty had met beleaguered men, and Dauntry was beleaguered in much the same way as Wellington at Waterloo. He was planning for victory, no matter what the cost.

She'd know better what that might cost her after a week of encounters.

The next day she received a note from Dauntry and rushed off to find Ruth, who was scattering seed for the chickens. "He's gone to Town!"

"What?" Ruth turned to her. "Why?"

"He doesn't say. Of course. Merely that he's obliged to go up to Town for a few days, but will return by Wednesday." Kitty shook the letter. "He's avoiding me. What doesn't he want me to learn? And he's avoiding taking me to the Abbey. What is it? Bowshamp or Beecham?"

Ruth looked bewildered. "Bowshamp. He probably does have important matters in London. He's traveled there a time or two."

"Is his mistress so irresistible?"

"What mistress?"

"What else takes him to Town?"

"I don't know, but you always knew London was part of the bargain."

"Your reasonableness is unreasonable! He was to go to Town *after* the marriage. I was depending on this week to learn more about him." A hen pecked at Kitty's shoe, and she jumped backward. "Stop that!"

Ruth continued to feed the demanding poultry. Kitty kept watch on the beady-eyed birds. "I could visit the Abbey without him."

"I wouldn't."

"Why not? Are you too trying to hide something?"

"Of course not. But it would start your time there on the wrong foot. He must formally introduce you to his family and household."

Ruth was right, but Kitty didn't like it. "This is extremely frustrating."

Ruth shook out the last of the grain and turned back toward the house. "Would anything you learned there change your mind?"

"I assume he doesn't turn into a monster at night."

"And how would you discover that before the wedding?"

"Anticipate the wedding. After all, I'm not a virgin."

"Kitty!" But Ruth was laughing. "I wonder if Dauntry knows what he's getting."

"As well as I know what I'm getting in him. That makes me think. Marriage settlements."

"What?"

"We never spoke of them, but I'll have them, providing plenty of pin money, so I'll have some independence. Isn't there a solicitor in the village?"

"Mr. Whitehall, yes. But Dauntry might object to your dealing with such things in his absence."

"He obtained a marriage license without my say-so."

"Did he? Oh, dear. Talk to Andrew first."

Ruth was looking worried again, so Kitty said, "Of course, but I don't see why he'd object."

Andrew didn't. "I should have thought of it. We can have Whitehall draw them up, and Dauntry can review them when he returns."

Kitty relaxed a little. Settlements would give her some financial independence and provide for her in the case of her husband's death.

All the same, Dauntry's running off to London was a bad sign.

What did he seek to hide until after the knot was tied?

Lord Cateril considered the letter that had arrived that morning. Viscount Dauntry presented a good case for his need of Kathryn as his wife, laying out logical arguments like a lawyer. The postbag had also brought a letter for his wife from Kathryn. He'd thought nothing of it and sent it to her, but now he went to the parlor in trepidation.

She was sitting by the fire, the letter open in her hands, but staring at the flames.

"Is Kathryn enjoying her visit to her friend?" he asked.

She turned to him, seeming puzzled rather than distressed. "I believe so, but . . . She wants to marry again."

"Truly?" She seemed calm about it. He sat nearby, hoping for the best. Before he could find the right words, she burst out, "How *could* she?"

"She's a young woman, my dear. With her life ahead of her."

"But to replace Marcus!"

"Never in her heart, my dear. Never that. But perhaps she needs a purpose in life."

"That's what she says"—she rattled the paper—"but if so, I'll find her a position. As a companion. Not this . . . this *sacrilege*. I shall write to tell her so—"

He put out a hand to stop her rising. "Sarah, my dear, think about this. What sensible woman would seek employment when she could be a wife? Unless the man she has in mind is too low for her."

"Low! She claims to have an offer from a viscount! Perhaps she's deranged."

He sighed. Did all deranged people fail to see it in themselves?

"A viscount?" he said mildly. "Odd goings-on, to be sure, but I'm sure Marcus's wife is worthy of any peer of the realm."

He'd just used a sentence from Lord Dauntry's letter and suspected it had been planted there, but it had an effect.

"Of course she is. But how could it have come about? She's not been gone a week."

More arguments from the letter came to mind. "Its being so sudden argues against any unseemly passion, don't you think? Does Kathryn say how they met?"

"Viscount Dauntry's seat lies close to Beecham Dabittot, and he was acquainted with Reverend Lulworth in the past. She met him at the parsonage. But for him to make approaches to a woman in mourning!"

"It's well over a year since Marcus died, my dear. I believe Lord Dauntry has recently come into the title. There was something in the newspapers about it, because the search for the heir took some time."

"Then he has no business seeking a wife in a hurry."

"On the contrary. I have the impression that he is the last of the line. It is his duty to try to beget an heir."

"An heir!" His wife pressed her black-edged handkerchief to her face. "When she never bore poor Marcus a child."

Lord Cateril wasn't entirely sure Marcus had been able. It was not a matter he could have asked about. "Does Kathryn say why he's chosen her?" he asked.

"Only that he needs a helpmeet and finds that she fits his needs. He's mad, too."

"Perhaps not, dear. Kathryn was a good wife, and I'm sure Marcus's afflictions didn't always make him easy." He pulled out another argument from Lord Dauntry's letter. "Would Marcus have wanted his Kitty to live a half-life here when she could be useful elsewhere?"

He hoped his wife would see that the words applied to her as well, but she didn't seem to note it. "I can't bear her replacing him, Edward. I can't bear it. It would be as if he died again."

"Dead is dead, Sarah!" He instantly regretted the sharp words, for she looked so stricken, but he wanted his wife back. There'd been an argument in the letter that he hesitated to use, but he had to try. "Are you not perhaps expecting Kathryn to bury herself with Marcus, as the poor widows in India are expected to throw themselves onto the funeral pyre?" In better times they'd read about the practice of suttee, and Sarah had been horrified.

"This is not the same," she protested.

He let silence argue for him.

"It's not the same," she repeated. "But she shouldn't *want* to marry anyone else. She shouldn't be able to bear it."

He tried a different approach. "It's time for you to put off black, Sarah. For your own sake. Marcus wouldn't have wanted this. The grandchildren won't remember you any other way."

"They'll never know Marcus!"

"They'll know him from his picture and from the

stories we tell. Happy stories. He's gone, my dear, but so
are many admirable young men who defended us in battle so that we could live freely here. If we don't live our
lives to the full, do we not undermine their victory?"

"How have you become so eloquent?" she protested.
"You'll be making grand speeches in Parliament next."

Of course she'd detect borrowed words.

"I'm inspired by wanting my Sarah back. I'm only
half myself without you, my dear."

She cried again, but then blew her nose. "Have I been
so very selfish?"

"You needed time, my love. We all did. But it swallowed you, and you took Kathryn down with you. She'll
never forget Marcus or cease loving him, but she deserves
to live a full life. Can you follow her lead?"

She smoothed her black skirt as if she'd never seen it
before. "It will be hard."

Dauntry had mentioned addiction in his letter, but
Lord Cateril decided not to use that.

"I will help you," he said, and rose, holding out a hand.

She took it and let him help her to her feet. Her look
was questioning, but there was a bit of the old Sarah in it.

"I'm going to take you upstairs and help you choose a
gown that's not black. No, I'm not planning to undress
you, my love." He risked a tease. "Or not yet. But I'll help
you choose. Then when you're ready, I need your advice
about estate matters. There are many difficult decisions
these days."

"You've become very clever all of a sudden, Edward."
He delighted to see her sharp wit again. "But I admit
you're probably right. I have sunk too low for too long.
The sage green, perhaps."

"The very gown I had in mind."

He wouldn't mention the letter yet—the letter she must

write—or the matter of sending Kitty's belongings off to her new life. He hoped she'd come to that on her own.

He escorted his wife to the stairs, but left her to mount them alone, black skirts trailing the steps as if to drag her down. She'd never worn skirts of such an impractical length in the past. She paused at the best spot to study Marcus's portrait, but then nodded as if a decision was made and continued on.

Good lad, Lord Cateril said silently to his younger son, bright eyed and vital in his scarlet and gold. *You watch out for your wife, too. No dog with a bone about it. She's a grand lass. Let her have as much of a life as she can. I wouldn't have thought such a lawyerly type quite to her taste, but better than buried alive. Much better than that.*

Chapter 9

Kitty helped Ruth, trying to learn a bit more about rural household management. She also went with her around the village, alert for anything about Dauntry. She learned little of use. Everyone was interested in him, but it seemed he rarely visited Beecham Dab, and no one knew even as much as she did.

Some of the village women would smirk and say he was a fine, handsome man. Others judged him too fancy-dressed and haughty. A few were perceptive enough to say he was a London man who'd doubtless not be at the Abbey much, and declared that a shame.

She visited the Beecham Dab almshouses one day with Ruth and learned in conversation that some repairs were outstanding. A little more "idle" curiosity revealed that the problem was of long standing, but had become worse since the fifth viscount's death.

As they walked back to the parsonage, Ruth said, "Once you're Lady Dauntry, you'll be able to put that matter in order."

"Willingly. I'll take an active part in the management."

Kitty kept alert for other neglect but didn't find any, and she was constantly aware of needing to make a good impression as a sensible, decent sort of woman in case she did make the marriage.

"It's odd," she said to Ruth one day as they returned to

the parsonage from the village shop. "If I were a real viscountess, I could be as eccentric as I liked, but as a prospective one I must strive for perfection."

"You soon will be a real viscountess."

"But one from low origins. People will be alert for any vulgarity."

"You could never be vulgar."

"I pray that's true, but I don't intend to be haughty with the people here."

"True ladies and gentlemen aren't."

"I hear the queen is."

Ruth laughed. "I didn't mention royalty. Only think—you'll probably meet her and the Regent. You'll have velvet and ermine robes."

"I believe my post is in the country, and I'll be glad of that."

"If the king dies, there'll be a coronation. I think you'll be expected to attend that. In robes and coronet."

"Then I wish him a long life!"

"He's nearly eighty, Kitty, but he might outlive the queen. She's clearly unwell, which isn't surprising, given all she's had to bear. Being royal isn't proof against suffering."

"Stop it," Kitty protested. "You'll cast us both into the dismals. You, at least, are perfectly situated."

"Perhaps too perfectly," Ruth said, looking at the pretty parsonage.

"What's that supposed to mean?"

"Oh, nothing," Ruth said, and continued inside. But Kitty wondered. *How could anything be too perfect?*

She'd thought Ruth perfectly suited to being the wife of a country clergyman, but in the past few days she'd noticed something amiss. She'd caught Ruth in pensive moments and interrupted one serious discussion between Ruth and her husband.

Please let there be no problems there. If she was going to make this marriage, she needed Ruth to be her strong, reliable support.

By Saturday Kitty was desperate, and she decided to question Ruth more closely about Dauntry. She searched the house and finally found her friend in the scullery, surrounded by berried stems and a smell of vinegar. "What are you doing now?"

"Pickling barberries."

"Why?"

"They're a tasty addition to many dishes."

Kitty couldn't imagine the labor worth the result, but she said, "What can I do to help?"

"You could help pick the berries from the stems."

Kitty put on an apron and set to work. "I wish I knew why Dauntry is rushing into marriage. He's had months to consider his situation and decide he needs a wife. Months to find one."

Ruth paused in her work. "No, he hasn't. He learned he was the viscount only a few weeks ago. I must have said."

"Didn't the previous viscount die in August?"

"But no one knew who the heir was, least of all Dauntry. He came here as soon as the inheritance was confirmed, but he describes it as learning a new trade."

Kitty remembered his talking about being a plaything of the gods. "But all the same, why the rush? And why me? He could easily marry a grand lady."

"He made it clear he wanted to marry quickly and without fuss."

"And I was waiting to be plucked. Like a goose." Kitty removed some berries too forcefully, breaking a stem.

Ruth shook her head. "Isn't it more a case of your finding a goose that lays golden eggs?"

"Geese can be very unpleasant. We had some at Cateril

Manor that would chase away intruders and didn't always distinguish between us and thieves."

"Are you seeing Dauntry as an angry goose?"

Kitty chuckled. "Neck stretched out and hissing? Oh, what would you do in my situation, Ruth?"

Ruth had finished her basket of stems and she began to measure out vinegar into a pan. "I was a good governess in a kind family, but I was delighted to leave to marry."

"To marry a man you love."

"Yes." Ruth turned to her. "Oh, Kitty, I never thought! You'll be giving up all chance to love again."

"I'll be content with a tranquil marriage." It wasn't quite true, but it was more true than any other reaction.

"Perhaps Dauntry was wise to go away. To give you this time to think."

"I didn't want time to *think*. I wanted time to get to know him. He wanted to marry immediately, and when I refused, he ran away."

"Oh, dear. You're going to kick against the shafts, aren't you?"

"I'm not a horse, but if anyone tries to put me in harness, I'll most certainly kick."

"I don't know how you survived your marriage."

"Are you in harness?"

"Andrew and I are in harness together."

"A perfectly matched team." Kitty watched Ruth's reaction to that and didn't see any doubt, thank heavens. Perhaps there was a problem in the parish. "I don't imagine that will ever be the case with me and Lord Dauntry. We have very different paces. Oh, I'm out of sorts!"

"Why don't you take Sillikin for a long walk? I'm nearly finished here, and fresh air will do you good."

"I don't know what good means anymore," Kitty said, but she washed her hands in the bowl of water. "When I think back, I can't remember a time when I've not been in harness. My parents, school, and then I was swept into marriage to Marcus. Now here I am, approaching thirty years of age and still without free choice."

"Employment is a choice," Ruth pointed out. "You want comfortable choices."

Kitty was in danger of making a snappish retort, so she went to dress for the outdoors, called Sillikin, and headed out. She walked away from the village along worn pathways, keeping a close eye on the dog. Perhaps Sillikin had learned her lesson, for she didn't go far in her excited explorations.

Kitty paused on a rise to look around the countryside. It was a gently rolling and orderly patchwork of farmland, but no material for bucolic poetry in its gray, wintry shades.

She'd never enjoyed winter in the countryside. Life was so much better in Town then, with gas-lit streets, shops, theaters, and amusements in all directions. The coal fires could cloak everything in a pall of smog, but that hadn't killed the pleasure.

"Oh, Hades. Spring will come."

The dismal scene would burst from half mourning into vivid life. Daffodils, green leaves, frolicking lambs. She'd feel more in harmony with the area then. As for the present, she'd learn no more about Dauntry until he returned. Sunday should give her a glimpse, at least, of the Braydon family at church, and she might learn something from that. She looked forward to that, but on the day, the large box pew at the front stayed empty.

As she and Ruth walked back to the parsonage with the children and servants, Kitty asked, "Does the Braydon family often stay away on Sunday?"

"They never attend. Dauntry has, but no one else from the family."

"Are they Catholic?" Kitty asked in surprise.

"Heavens, no, but they have the chapel and a chaplain to offer services. A doddery old fellow."

"Isn't that unusual?"

"I'm not sure."

"I'll attend service here and I'll try to make sure my husband does, too. The dowager may worship in her chapel, but Miss Isabella can be compelled." She saw Ruth's expression. "No?"

"I know only what Dauntry has said, but 'stubbornly willful' seems to fit, with the dowager encouraging her."

"Why does the dowager still live there? Isn't there a dower house?"

"Used by the estate steward for at least thirty years."

Kitty frowned at an inoffensive gravestone ahead. "Do you think the dowager drove off the previous viscount's wife on purpose?"

"Kitty! Don't let your imagination run away with you. Why would she do that?"

"Mothers and sons. Is Andrew's mother protective of him?"

"Not particularly, but she has three other sons."

"Lady Cateril has one other son and two daughters, but that didn't help. I'd never thought before to be grateful that Marcus insisted on us living so far away. Life at Cateril Manor would have been unbearable."

On Monday Kitty was startled to receive two letters from Cateril Manor. Both were franked, so Andrew had nothing to pay.

When Kitty hesitated, fearing what Lady Cateril had to say, Ruth said, "Open them!"

"Both at the same time? Why are Lord and Lady Cateril writing to me separately? Heavens. Could my news have killed her?"

"Then she'd hardly be writing to you, would she?"

"No, but . . ."

"Why the hesitation? You're not going to let her disapproval prevent you from marrying, are you?"

"No, but . . ." Kitty broke the seal on Lady Cateril's letter. It was short, so she grasped the contents immediately. "She's sending me my possessions without objection." She stared up at Ruth. "She even says Marcus would have wanted me to live a full life. I can hardly believe it."

"Why doubt?" Ruth snatched the letter and read it. "It seems plain enough. You have her blessing, Kitty. All is well!"

Kitty opened the other letter. "Perhaps it's to tell me she's run mad. No. It's to thank me."

"For marrying?"

"Lord Cateril says my news has helped Lady Cateril return to life. She's put off her blacks and is taking her full part in life again."

Ruth was beaming. "A blessing all around!"

"But at the end, he wishes me well and hopes Lord Dauntry is worthy of me. That's odd."

"Good wishes?"

"That he say that. As if he has doubts. Do you think he knows Dauntry?"

Ruth took that letter. "He means worthy of Marcus's widow. Rejoice! You can marry without a cloud on the horizon. Andrew!" she called. "All's well! Lady Cateril makes no objection, and Lord Cateril thanks Kitty for bringing about a change in her."

"No celebration?" Andrew asked.

"Bridal nerves, perhaps."

"Everyone has them—grooms, too."

If Dauntry was quivering, she was the Man in the Moon.

"The best thing is to be busy," Ruth said. "We've still to retrim your bridal bonnet. Yes, you can go away again, Andrew. This is women's work."

Kitty surrendered to Ruth's excitement, but the removal of every obstacle along with Lord Cateril's possible doubts had made her newly aware that she'd spent less than a half hour in Lord Dauntry's company.

They'd never even touched.

However, it was too late to back out now. She could only pray she wasn't making another mistake, because this one could last a lifetime. She was unlikely to be granted an early release a second time.

Chapter 10

Kitty was rescued from bonnet trimming, at which she had little skill, by Sillikin's wanting a walk. She made it a long one, and they were both ready for a rest by the time she approached the front door of the parsonage. When she heard horses' hooves, she turned, alarmed that it would be Dauntry, catching her windblown and dusty again. Instead she saw a woman on a black horse, a mounted groom riding a yard or so behind. The woman was dressed entirely in black, and Kitty wondered if it might be the dowager Lady Dauntry, but then she saw that she was young. *Isabella?* She looked older than sixteen—erect, poised, and eying Kitty with haughty disdain.

The battle had come to her.

Kitty felt a flutter of panic, but despite the gloss, this was a girl and she was a woman of nearly twice her age and vastly more experience. She went forward, attempting bland amiability. "May I help you?"

"Are you Mrs. Cateril?"

"I am."

The young woman gestured, and the groom dismounted and hurried to lift her down. Once down, she arranged her skirts and walked forward. "I am Isabella Godyson-Braydon."

Kitty just managed not to express surprise at the extended surname. Why had no one told her about that? And how, exactly, did an Honorable widow greet an aristocratic girl?

She dipped a very slight curtsy. "Good morning."

Miss Godyson-Braydon merely inclined her head. Such petty battles didn't bother Kitty, but she was supposed to manage this girl?

Sillikin was staring, which wasn't at all surprising. If Dauntry was a marble box, his ward was a jet one. She was polished and perfect in every way, and Kitty was aware of being very much the opposite. However, she remembered that jet was a relatively soft stone.

"You've come to visit Mrs. Lulworth?" she asked.

"I've come to speak to you."

"Then shall we go into the house, Miss Godyson-Braydon?"

"No. We have heard an odd rumor, Mrs. Cateril. That you are to marry Lord Dauntry."

Kitty supposed word would have escaped. There was no way to deny it, despite an irrational wish to do so.

"I am, yes. On Wednesday."

"Impossible. He is betrothed to me."

Kitty couldn't help a laugh. "I doubt Lord Dauntry would have forgotten such a fact."

The girl flushed but said, "You wear no ring. I do." She pulled the black leather glove off her left hand to reveal a ring with a blue stone, presumably a sapphire.

Kitty was at a loss, stuck in this impossible situation, her heart fluttering with fledgling doubt. Could Dauntry be insane? But with deep certainty she knew that whatever else he was, he wasn't mad. Therefore, the girl must be lying.

"That is a lovely ring. But I have no reason to believe Lord Dauntry gave it to you. You're a child," Kitty said calmly. "Why would he marry you?"

The girl didn't so much as blink. "For my dowry. It's very large, and if I take it out of the family, the viscountcy's fortunes will be sadly depleted."

Kitty had to consider that. If the girl spoke the truth, Dauntry might be sensible to marry her. They weren't closely connected by blood. After the disastrous meeting in the lane, she'd been sure Dauntry would back out of the arrangement. Had he committed himself to her and then come to his senses? Then fled? That would be unbalanced, at the least, but then he was an ex-soldier. Who knew what chaos lay beneath?

"I fear," the chit said, a glint of triumph in her eyes, "he may have played a game on you."

Sillikin growled. It was so unusual, it snapped Kitty out of her paralysis. She quickly picked up her dog. "You speak nonsense."

"Do I? Ask instead why he would marry *you*, ma'am. You have no beauty or style, nor any fortune. I also gather that you are barren."

Kitty wished they were close enough for Sillikin to bite, because every word was horribly true. There was no reason for this marriage beyond some chilly convenience, and she'd been probing the puzzle for a week. The encounter in the lane had shown her to be not at all the bride he'd been promised. So he'd . . . what? Devised a cruel punishment? To build her hopes and then leave her at the altar, exposed to the sniggers of people surprised she'd ever thought to marry so unbelievably high? Had he assumed that she'd go around the village, boasting about it? Had he then returned to the Abbey and proposed marriage to Isabella?

She's his ward.

Is that even legal?

Her churning mind couldn't make sense of anything,

but her finger was bare, and that sapphire ring glinted as brightly as the girl's sharp blue eyes.

"I came to warn you," Isabella said. "If you go to the church on Wednesday, you'll be left standing at the altar."

Ah! So that is the plan. They think they can make me flee? Kitty almost smiled at the thought, but kept a sober face. "You have given me much to think about, Miss Godyson-Braydon. I bid you good day."

She turned and walked into the house, feeling the glare directed at her back. She walked faster, hoping it looked like panicked flight, then watched from the parlor window as the girl was helped by the groom to remount and rode away.

"What a paltry creature they must think me," she said to Sillikin. "They have much to learn." Brave words, but would anyone, even a sixteen-year-old girl, flaunt a false engagement ring? Logic was on Isabella's side, especially if she'd told the truth about having inherited most of the viscountcy's wealth.

What did Kitty have to offer? Nothing but convenience.

Dauntry had offered marriage, but then he'd run away.

With dismay, Kitty remembered Captain Jameston. He'd come home on furlough, visited a fellow officer's home in Kent, and met the man's sister. He'd made her promises but then hurriedly departed for the north. Later they'd heard he'd married a childhood friend there. It had almost led to a duel, but when the furor had been discussed in Moor Street, the other officers had seemed to understand. Plunged from battles and hardship into the sweet bosom of home, men's emotions weren't always stable or reliable. Men brave in war could be cowards in domestic complexities.

Kitty found it hard to see Dauntry as unstable or in

a cowardly panic, but she didn't know him at all. Even Ruth and Andrew didn't know him intimately, and Captain Jameston had seemed a rational man. She remembered Lord Cateril's implied warning. Did he know something about Dauntry that gave him doubts?

What on earth was she to do on Wednesday?

Chapter 11

Kitty went through Tuesday like a sleepwalker, which could be because she'd had little sleep. Ruth put it down to bridal nerves and left her alone. Kitty longed for Dauntry to turn up and make all clear, one way or another.

Would he make no contact until the wedding? They hadn't even set a time for it. Was she just to go to church and hope he'd be there?

Definitely not. She wouldn't even put on her wedding bonnet until she was sure.

But even if he was ready to marry her, should she go through with it?

She'd once brushed aside the idea of marrying a madman as a minor thing, but on the eve of her wedding, it wasn't minor at all. She prayed he'd visit her before the wedding so she'd have another opportunity to assess him. After so many days, she distrusted what flimsy impressions she remembered.

Cold, distant, calculating . . .

The arrival of her possessions from Cateril Manor provided distraction. It might turn out to be pointless to have them, but unpacking and hanging out clothing to air gave her something to do. She had her books as well, and the various ornaments and mementoes of her life.

She sat to reread Marcus's letters from when he'd courted her. They were faded now, but his vitality and adoration shone from the pages. They'd been different people then, still with hope. Then there were the gifts he'd given her over the years. He'd mostly given her small pieces of jewelry for her birthdays, but here was the china vase with a puppy on it that was very like Sillikin. Captain Edison had given her the puppy, and Marcus had been put out, but mostly because he hadn't thought of it. He must have asked a friend to seek out such a vase.

She smiled at the small model of the Parthenon made out of cork. There'd been a popular exhibition of much larger models of that sort, and Marcus had taken her to that. The promise of a working replica of a volcano had inspired him to a special effort. He'd hired a sedan chair for the journey, because it was a smoother ride than a coach over cobbles, and then a bath chair to go around the room. He'd claimed he was no more uncomfortable than sitting around at home, but even though the volcano had lived up to expectations, they'd rarely repeated the experiment. London was a treasure box of curiosities and amusements, but she'd experienced so very few of them.

She rewrapped the model and all the other bits and pieces. Whatever happened tomorrow, there was no point in putting them on display here.

She brought in the first load of freshened clothing and hung out some more. She had bright and becoming clothing again. None were up to the mark, but they raised her spirits, until she remembered that she'd not get to wear them as a governess or companion.

She'd start to wear them now, then. With the sun set and the candles lit, she changed into one of her favorites, a cherry red kerseymere gown with long sleeves and a high neck. It was quite plain except for a tapestry belt that had gold inset beads, but it hung beautifully. Marcus had said that with her hair, it made her look like a pagan warrior queen. That was how she wanted to feel.

Sukey was fastening the back when someone knocked at the front door. It could be a parishioner with a question or even an urgent summons, but it was just possible it was Lord Dauntry. Kitty sent Sukey away, checked herself in the mirror, and hurried to the top of the stairs to listen.

It was Dauntry!

Come to confirm their arrangement or cancel it in order to marry Isabella and her money?

Which did she want?

Ruth was saying, "Kitty received Lady Cateril's blessing, so all's well!"

"If you have the license," Andrew said, emerging from his study.

Kitty waited, breath held, and then Dauntry passed over a piece of paper. Relief made her clutch the stair rail for support. He intended to go through with the marriage, and he seemed sane enough. And she had no other reasonable option.

Andrew read it. "I was unaware of your given names."

"I assume it's essential that they be read in full at the service."

"Afraid so."

"What are they?" Ruth asked, trying to look. Andrew folded it.

Kitty realized she had to move. She descended the stairs. "Am I allowed to know?"

He looked up at her—and stared. Kitty couldn't help but smile. She'd not planned the effect, but it would seem he saw her much as Marcus had, and it would do no harm for him to know he was marrying a warrior. But did she see dismay at the prospect? Something had disturbed the cool sleekness.

As she reached the bottom of the stairs, he seemed to pull himself together. "I gather all is well?"

"Yes."

Ruth said, "Into the parlor!"

Her brightness was a little forced, so Kitty wasn't imagining the strain. Clearly Dauntry had come here intending to go through with the marriage, but he was troubled by something. Had he come to confess that he'd foolishly engaged himself to Isabella as well?

"We'll drink a glass of wine to your happiness," Ruth said, "and hear the latest London news."

They were soon all settled with a glass of blackberry wine, but Sillikin had taken up a staring stance.

"To the happy couple and a happy future!" Andrew said, raising his glass.

Dauntry drank. So did Kitty, but she had to ask, "Is something amiss, sir?"

He grimaced slightly. "Word has reached the Abbey that we're to wed, and the dowager is already on the attack. She can do you no harm, but she'll stir storms if she can."

Such as a false betrothal to Isabella? Or was he preparing a denial of a true one? "I can weather storms," she said.

"So I gather."

She stared at that. "So you gather?"

"In London I encountered some people who knew you there." Heaven help her, what had he learned to create this guarded expression? "They praised your care for your husband when his injuries distressed him."

"Ah. That's kind of them, but it's not hard to be patient when one loves." *So why do you disapprove?*

Ruth broke in again. "Town news! How are poor Prince Leopold and the Regent?"

"Both deeply distressed, as one can understand. It's expected that Prince Leopold will return to Germany soon."

"Far from everything that must remind him of Charlotte." Ruth sighed. "It's still hard to believe."

"But there are other problems, I gather," Andrew said.

Dauntry looked at Kitty as if expecting her to object to this discussion on their wedding eve, but what else were they to speak of? She was studying him for any hint of mental instability. At least Sillikin had relaxed and was lying by her feet.

"A general political and administrative disarray," Dauntry said. "It's as if London has gone into the grave with the princess. One good aspect is that mourning has tamped down unrest, and those most opposed to the monarchy keep their feelings to themselves. A ballad singer trilling against the Regent was pelted with rotten fruit, when a month ago she would have been applauded. Her song even had a legitimate complaint."

"What?" Andrew asked.

"Neglect of his duties. A ruler can't hide away, not even in grief. There are many matters hanging in abeyance. The only firm decision made so far is to put off the recall of Parliament until next year. That's largely for fear of someone raising the subject of the succession."

"Oh, dear," Ruth said, but then, relentlessly optimistic, she added, "I see one benefit—you won't have to go to London to take your seat in Parliament until then, Dauntry." She stood. "Come, dear. We must leave the betrothed couple alone for a little while."

In moments Kitty was enclosed with her husband-to-be, curtains drawn against the dark, with firelight and candlelight lending a deep intimacy. Now he seemed as cool and composed as before, and she became newly aware of how handsome he was and how elegant, not only in his clothing but in the way he sat, fingers lax on the stem of his glass.

Beau Braydon.

Beautiful . . .

"Lady Cateril approved without reservation?" he asked.

Kitty snapped out of distracting thoughts. Inappropriate thoughts, except that this beautiful, disturbing man was to share her bed tomorrow.

"She did," she said, surprised to be able to speak normally.

"Your letter must have been eloquent."

"I didn't think so." She needed to have things absolutely clear. "You do still want to marry me?"

A reaction at last. Surprise. "I thought I'd made that clear."

"Time changes things."

"You've changed your mind?" he asked.

"No. But you seem uneasy, my lord."

"You're an observant woman." She didn't think he approved. "Returning to Beauchamp Abbey always puts me out of temper, but this time I became aware that I'll be bringing you into a difficult situation."

With a jilted bride in residence? "I always knew that," Kitty said.

"In theory only. To give an example, I found the furniture in your dressing room still full of your predecessor's clothing."

That startled her. "The errant viscountess?"

"Yes. I'd ordered the rooms prepared, but only thought to check at the last moment."

"Someone should be held at fault for that."

"I made my displeasure clear to the housekeeper, but Mrs. Quiller's allegiance is to the dowager, so you can expect such petty annoyances."

Kitty welcomed a practical subject. "Is there a reason I can't dismiss her?"

"None, apart from the business of replacing her and her husband, who is butler. You must wonder why I haven't done so." He sipped at his wine and then put it aside.

Doubtless blackberry wine wasn't to his taste. "Firstly, this is the first blatant misdemeanor. Secondly, the Quillers are only one part of a web of annoyances. I have been waiting for a wife to see the way."

"I see. I know my duties, my lord, but if I dismiss all the servants, life could be uncomfortable for a while."

"No worse than other situations I've known. Do as you please."

"Do you truly mean that?"

"I always mean what I say. Finding replacements won't be difficult. Many seek employment these days. I had a particular reason for this visit. You must be in as strong a position as possible. Thus we need a story to account for the speed of our union."

"Your need of a helpmate won't do?"

"I suggest a little more than that. Would you object to us having met in the past?"

"A lie?" Instinctively, she did object, but perhaps it was necessary. "A white one, I suppose. But when? I went from school into marriage at seventeen, and from marriage into seclusion at Cateril Manor."

"I gather you kept open house for military officers."

"My husband and I did," she said, not liking his tone.

"My apologies. Of course that was what I meant. I had the impression that some of the men who visited your home see themselves as friends."

Kitty sat up straighter. "The impression from where? Have you been bandying my name around Town, sir?"

He raised a hand. "I mentioned your name in a military club, but in no way disrespectfully, I assure you. I learned of your husband's hospitality, and it provides a way in which we could have met."

Kitty still didn't like his behavior. "You're not suggesting a liaison, are you? That would dishonor Marcus and me."

"Of course not. Only that we could have met and liked one another. Your hospitality is fondly remembered."

She still detected criticism. "Marcus enjoyed the company. All I did was provide what refreshments we could."

"And an ear for those troubled and advice for the love-lorn."

"Who said that?" she demanded. "I merely smiled and nodded."

"Sometimes that's a generous gift. Will anyone question it if we say I visited your rooms a time or two and admired you?"

Another chess move. That's all it was. Kitty tamped down annoyance and gave his question careful thought. "I can't see how. The guests changed all the time."

"Then when I learned that you were a friend of Ruth Lulworth's, I arranged for you to visit here, and matters took their natural course."

"I can't ask Ruth and Andrew to lie."

"As long as they don't insist on the absolute truth, it should do. We won't volunteer our story, and if we have to use it, we'll keep it as vague as possible. The main point is that we are consistent."

"You seem practiced at deception, my lord."

"My work in the army wasn't always direct."

What was it, then? She didn't voice her question, for she might not like the answer. Had he been a spy? Most soldiers thought that dishonorable work, even though they benefitted from anything learned.

"Will you object to my calling you Kitty in private?"

The rather blunt change of subject confirmed that he'd been up to something shady, but it shouldn't affect their future. "Not at all," she said, "but what am I to call you? What are your Christian names?"

"Not to be used," he said, but then shook his head.

"They'll be read out tomorrow. My father believed that names could shape destinies. Plato Aristides."

Kitty couldn't help a smile. "Poor lad!"

"No wonder you touched young men's hearts. Fortunately, at school, boys are addressed by their surnames."

"And now?"

"I'm known as Dauntry."

"That seems somewhat formal for our private moments." Her words suddenly had extra layers of meaning. Marriage. Privacy. *Intimacy.* She bent down to scoop up Sillikin. "Thank you for not wanting to use Kathryn."

"You dislike it?"

"It was never used as I grew up." She was struggling to pull her mind away from an increasing awareness of him—of the body that would join with her in the marriage bed. Of those fine hands on her skin, on her breasts.

He was waiting for her to say more.

"Marcus's family are the only ones who've ever called me Kathryn," she said as briskly as she could. "Perhaps Lady Cateril was like your father and hoped that a more sober name would make me a more sober person. Don't think too badly of her. When she first met me, I was a silly seventeen-year-old."

"That's generous of you." Simple words, but something in his eyes and in his tone made her wonder if he shared her sensual thoughts and lurking doubts. He couldn't be unaware of tomorrow night.

"Were you silly at seventeen?" she asked. "It's hard to imagine."

"I expect I was. Are you wondering how old I am? Twenty-nine."

She'd thought him older because of his cool reserve. He couldn't maintain that in bed. Could he? "Perhaps you do have something of philosopher about you," she said, "but who was Aristides?"

"A statesman and general, sometimes called the Just."

"Not bad attributes to seek to give a child."

"No, but if we have a son, I'd favor a simpler name. So, we marry as planned tomorrow?"

This was the moment. The point of no return. But hot or cool, there was no reasonable alternative. "We do," she said.

"Good. The sooner the dowager realizes she can't prevent your arrival, the better."

"Especially as she still hopes you'll marry her granddaughter." She was pleased to surprise him. "Isabella came here to warn me of your cruel deception, armed with a sapphire betrothal ring."

Even better, he was speechless.

"I was encouraged to run from the shame of it," she added, "like the more foolish sort of heroine in a novel."

"They do both read those kinds of books."

"So do I, but I don't take them as a pattern card for behavior. I prefer the heroines who fight brigands with swords."

Perhaps he smiled. "I'm beginning to understand that you do. Tell me exactly what happened."

When she finished, he did smile. It was cool, but the first clear smile she'd seen on him. "Isabella is going to be very annoyed by your betrothal ring," he said.

"I don't have one."

"That's another reason for this visit. Rather last-minute, I know, but I thought you should have one before we wed." He came to her and took something out of his pocket.

After a moment, Kitty found words. "That's a rather large diamond."

"I confess to strategy. No one seeing it will think this a paltry affair."

"In particular the dowager? As you say, it knocks Isabella's little sapphire to flinders."

She realized he was waiting to put it on her finger, and that she was still wearing her wedding ring. She rose, trying to remove it, but she hadn't ever removed it. She had to lick her finger and even then she only just managed to wriggle it off.

He touched the groove as if it were a wound, but then slid on the diamond ring.

"A perfect fit," she said.

"I'm a good judge of such things."

She glanced up. "I suspect you're good at many things."

She meant it innocently, but awareness flared. They'd touched at last, and now they stood close together, looking into each other's eyes. He raised her left hand and kissed her knuckle near the ring. It brought him even closer, and she caught his scent. A male scent, but a different one.

Suddenly she wanted to kiss him. And more. She'd thought such fires well banked, but new fuel had been put on the embers. She was hungry for intimacy and ached to do more, much more, here, now, in the parsonage parlor.

He released her hand and moved away. Because he'd sensed her improper desires?

"Have you provided yourself with a lady's maid?" he asked.

"What?" It took Kitty a moment to make sense of his question and find coherence. "Should I have? I suppose I should. I've never had one."

"Not during your marriage?"

"I used the housemaid when I needed help. I'm sorry."

"No matter, for I thought of it. I asked my grandmother to send a suitable woman to Gloucester. I collected Miss Oldswick from there, and she's ready to move with you to the Abbey tomorrow. For now, she's resting in the Abbot's Arms."

"That sounds rather . . ."

His lips twitched. "We can hope she's enjoying it. You don't approve of my hiring her? You'd rather arrive at the Abbey without?"

"I'm sure it's ungracious of me, but I'm not accustomed to having my life so managed."

"And you resented your shackles at Cateril Manor. Miss Oldswick is my aunt's lady's maid, and so she's only on loan, but I can send her back to Lancashire if you wish. However, you could need allies in the Abbey, and she will be firmly on your side."

"Ah, I see. In that spirit, I thank you." She found it comforting that they could talk plainly of practical matters. "Why is the dowager so determined to be hostile, when it can do her no good?"

"It is not in her nature to give up on a goal. She plotted the union with Isabella because it would leave control of the Abbey in her hands, but mostly to preserve her bloodline there."

"One of the oldest baronies in England."

"I see you heard. But sunk quite low. When she married the fourth viscount, the Godyson family was in genteel, obscure poverty. She built her new grandeur by force of will and made Beauchamp Abbey a seat worthy of a great lord. She expected it to be the beginning of a long line of rich and titled Godyson-Braydons."

"Then her son and grandson died and you came, simply Braydon and without a drop of Godyson blood. But once we're married, she has to see the battle's lost."

"We can hope so, but I expect further sorties, and you'll be in the front line. Old women can be tougher and more vicious than many think, yet can't be opposed by men with brute force. I've seen men battered bloody by old harridans without feeling able to raise a hand. Are you deterred?"

"Not at all. I might relish a brisk encounter or two. I'm not suited to idleness."

"As husband, I approve."

"That might depend on where I direct my actions." Kitty hadn't intended a challenge, but she heard how it sounded. She let it lie.

A brow twitched, but he didn't make an issue of it. "The settlements were well thought of. I've increased the jointure and left the document with Whitehall. He'll bring it here tomorrow for us to sign and have witnessed before the ceremony. Is there anything else we should discuss?"

"I can't think of anything. Except what to call you. Dauntry is too daunting, and 'my lord' too formal for everyday moments."

"Why not Braydon? It's what I've been used to all my life, and how I still think of myself."

"Braydon. Perhaps if your surname had been Godyson, you'd never have been a beau at all."

"Beau Brummell is alliterative, yes, but there was Beau Nash. You don't think dandyism inborn?"

"I don't think of you as a dandy."

"Why not?"

"What a question to pose so late in the day! I suppose I think of a dandy as a man obsessed by clothes and appearance to the exclusion of all else. Perhaps Beau Brummell was such a man, but are you?"

"No."

"There you are, then."

"There we are," he agreed. "Is everything settled?"

Except my nerves. "The time," Kitty said. "Will ten o'clock suit?"

"Perfectly."

After this discussion she had no reason to fear his

not being at the church, but she still didn't relish arriving in doubt. "We could walk there together," she said.

He made no difficulty. "I'll present myself here at ten minutes to," he said, and took his leave.

To the very second, I'm sure.

After he was gone, she considered the ring. Had he known the dowager and Isabella would try such a ploy? That suggested almost supernatural powers, but then she remembered his surprise. It was good to know he could be ruffled.

How would that go in bed?

Had she imagined the passions weaving around them, or the way he'd looked at her in that hot moment? In the past when men had looked at her like that, it had been a warning—to be cool, to be careful. Never to respond or encourage. Tomorrow it would be her duty to respond. And her pleasure . . .

Ruth came in and then stared. "My goodness!"

"Armor against the dowager." Kitty held out her hand so Ruth could inspect the stone more closely.

"You're supposed to attack her with it?"

Kitty chuckled. "Only impress on her that our resolution is diamond hard."

"Are you more at ease now? I know you've had doubts."

"It's settled."

Kitty wanted to mention the marriage bed, get Ruth's opinion. On what, though? It was a simple enough matter. Only it didn't feel simple.

"He'll make you a good husband?" Ruth asked, looking worried again.

"I think so," Kitty said, because it was expected.

What would Ruth think if she'd said, *Something happened here, and it changes everything. But it shouldn't, because that's what marriage involves.* Yet in all her mental tussles over this decision, she'd neglected to consider the physical. Perhaps she'd assumed their coolly arranged marriage would be platonic, at least for a while. And she'd not even known that his name was Plato.

She'd put that part of herself away since Marcus's death. In fact, since a year or more before his death, when all desire had left him. But at Dauntry's touch—his first touch, and the light kiss on her hand—all parts of her had remembered.

Tomorrow she would be in a marriage bed again, with a man's hot body joined to hers in sweaty pleasure.

But a different man.

Would it be different altogether?

Would she satisfy him?

"Come!" Ruth said. "We must settle the final details for your wedding day."

Kitty went, telling herself that swiving was a straightforward business. Becoming a viscountess was likely to be much more challenging, and that was her destiny for the rest of her life.

Chapter 12

The next morning, Miss Henrietta Oldswick—short, sturdy, gray haired, and bright eyed—arrived at the parsonage.

"Quite a little adventure," she said in a comfortable Northern accent. "I'm happy to help out here for a while. Take me to your room, Mrs. Cateril, and we'll see what we have."

That sounded like an inspection!

Kitty had already laid out the blue stripe gown on the bed, with the bonnet and gloves alongside. The aired-out clothing was piled around the room, and the two trunks stood open and empty.

"I'll see to all this and to its delivery to the Abbey, ma'am," Miss Oldswick said. "Don't you worry about anything." She spoke as if Kitty were a helpless child.

Kitty said, "Thank you," but she'd hire a simpler servant in due course. She had no need of someone else to intimidate her. On the other hand, the confident Miss Oldswick could prove a big battalion in the war. "My gowns are mostly out-of-date," Kitty apologized. "I've been in mourning for most of the past three years. First my parents, then my husband."

"And then your husband's mother didn't like you to put off your blacks, ma'am. Yes, he said. Kind of you to comfort her."

Kitty hadn't thought of it like that. It was too generous, but she wouldn't argue.

"You'll have much to learn, ma'am, and I'll be able to assist you there. And, of course, I'm to report to Lady Sophonisbe."

"Who?"

"Didn't he say?" She tutted, but indulgently, as if Lord Dauntry, too, were a feeble child. "His grandmother, ma'am, Lady Sophonisbe Ecclestall. She'd have liked to attend his lordship's wedding, but she doesn't travel much these days and she's sensible of not intruding. Just thought I'd let you know I'll be a spy in the camp, but I'll be your ally in the wars."

"Thank you," Kitty said, not at all sure what to make of all this.

Lady Sophonisbe must be the daughter of a duke, marquess, or earl. Miss Oldswick was clearly on comfortable terms with the great lady, but that raised the maid rather than diminishing the lady. Thank heavens Lady Sophonisbe hadn't come. One tricky dowager at a time.

All the same, Kitty could see how Miss Oldswick's comfortable assurance would enhance her own situation at the Abbey. Dropping names such as Lady Sophonisbe's wouldn't hurt, either. *Excellent strategy, my lord.*

Then Kitty recalled that Andrew had mentioned Lord Dauntry was distantly connected to a duke. Distantly! Quite possibly he was the great-grandson of one.

"Is there anything else, ma'am?" Miss Oldswick asked.

"How do you wish to be addressed?"

"Henry'll do between us, ma'am. That's what Miss Ecclestall calls me. I don't care for this calling female servants by their surname. Mannish, that's what it is, and there's nothing amiss with being womanish. Your hair is well arranged, ma'am."

Kitty had surrendered to Ruth's insistence that she not wear a cap today.

"My friend Mrs. Lulworth is quite skilled."

"So I see." She looked at the bed. "This is your wedding gown?"

"Will it do?"

"As you say, ma'am, not in the latest style, but there's no shame in that, especially for a widow. In general, I'd say you're better suited by strong colors, but not for your wedding. Let's get you ready."

Henry Oldswick set to work, dressing Kitty like a child.

"Your jewels, ma'am?" Henry asked at last.

Embarrassed, Kitty unlocked her trinket box and let the maid choose from the limited selection. Henry took a simple silver cross and chain.

"Not the pearls?" Kitty asked.

"I hope I don't offend, ma'am, but they're small and contrast unfavorably with the ring. I believe you should move the ring to your right hand for the ceremony."

Kitty hadn't thought of that and did so, then rubbed at the mark beneath. Perhaps it would never entirely fade, but it did come from eight years of her life.

She turned to assess herself in the mirror. She didn't look her best, but her appearance was quiet and simple, which would be a good impression to start with. Would the Russian mantle spoil that? The deep blue, fur-lined cloak was hanging on a hook. Kitty took it down and draped it around her shoulders, then considered her appearance again. Her chin and nose were still too strong and her hair was red, but it was neatly arranged for now, and the blue cloak with the tawny fur did suit her.

"Is it too grand?" she asked. "In appearance, at least?" She was sure Henry knew the fur was cheap stuff.

"How could it be, ma'am?"

Of course, for a viscountess.

Ruth knocked and came in. "You look lovely. And that cloak is splendid."

"And practical. It's very warm. You could have one."

"A fur-lined cape for a parson's wife?" Ruth touched the fur that was turned out along the front edges. "Is this fox?"

Kitty chuckled. "Dyed rabbit fur. The lining's rabbit, too, so you could afford it. Here, try it on."

Ruth did, but then gave it back. "Not suitable, not even in a sober color and economical. It looks extravagant, but that's the right impression for you."

"There's a huge muff as well, also dyed rabbit."

Ruth admired that as well, but then said, "Dauntry's here, and Mr. Whitehall."

Silly to be startled and newly nervous. They needed to sign the settlements and be off to the ceremony. Kitty put on the freshly trimmed bonnet. "Time to go, Sillikin."

The dog stood, tail wagging with anticipation. She'd been lovingly combed to perfection and wore a blue ribbon over her collar, so she knew something exciting was about to happen.

Henry took Kitty's cloak, muff, and gloves and they all went down to the parlor. The solicitor was waiting with Braydon and Andrew, and the document was laid out on the table.

Today, Braydon undoubtedly suited the name Beau. Cream pantaloons, perfectly tailored brown coat, a waistcoat of cream and brown brocade just slightly woven through with gold thread, and perfect, pristine linen. Kitty had learned how to tie a neckcloth for Marcus and could manage some complex folds, but this design was new to her. Perhaps it was known in the ton as a Braydon. It was held in place with a glittering pale yellow stone that came close to the color of his hair.

This is the man his mistress knows. Kitty pushed that

thought aside. Time to deal with it later. No, not to deal with. That was their agreement. She was to leave his Town life alone. If she couldn't do that, she mustn't go through with this.

She eyed the document, tempted to read it before she signed, but she'd read the draft and she didn't think any of these men would try to trick her. In any case, it would have to be a heinous change to make her retreat now.

She signed, and then Braydon did the same in a strong, flowing script. Ruth and Andrew witnessed it. That part was done, but they still weren't wed.

Kitty thanked the lawyer and went into the hall, where Henry stood ready. But the viscount took the cloak to put it around her shoulders. Silly to feel cherished by such a simple act of courtesy, but it was as if no man had ever assisted her before. Few had, she realized. Marcus had never been capable of doing so and she'd not encouraged his friends to, but that was no reason to be flustered. *Bridal nerves,* she decided as she pulled on her gloves. She'd be sane again soon, and could only hope Sillikin would be, too. She was going from person to person as if she could learn all from sniffing boots and shoes. At least she wasn't staring at anyone. Kitty took her muff from Henry but pushed it up her arm so she could put Sillikin on the leash, and then they all left the parsonage.

There was quite a bite in the air today, and a wind to make it sharper. Kitty was grateful for her cloak and that they had no great distance to walk. They did so two by two. Kitty had decided to give a nod to the idea of the groom waiting at the church by letting the men go first and following behind with Ruth. She was glad to have Lord Dauntry in sight. She still worried that this event might evaporate.

The Whitehalls were to attend the wedding, along with the local squire and his wife, Sir Richard and Lady Green.

The doctor, Lowell, who was a widower, would also be in attendance. They were the local dignitaries and were to come back to the parsonage for cake and wine.

No one from the Abbey would be there—unless Isabella stormed in to denounce the match. Perhaps Kitty should mention such a possibility to Dauntry, but then she decided he would have thought of it himself.

As they approached the church, she saw villagers gathered to watch, with the Misses Purslow in pride of place. They were the spinster daughters of the previous parson and a power in Beecham Dab. Unwise to neglect potential allies.

"We should invite the Misses Purslow in," Kitty murmured to Ruth. Perhaps she was learning to be a chess player, too.

Ruth went over. Soon the two ladies, all aflutter, were coming to join their train.

"We had no idea," one said to Kitty, bright-eyed.

She'd have to remember which was Miss Martha and which Miss Mary. "I didn't wish to say anything too soon," Kitty said modestly.

Ruth said, "My dear friend's late husband was a military man, you know, as was Lord Dauntry."

Ruth had agreed to support the lie that far. The two ladies seemed to find it satisfying.

They progressed up the path and into the subdued light of the church porch. Sillikin was alert with anticipation of new experiences, but behaving perfectly. Dauntry and Andrew went inside, and the Misses Purslow followed. Kitty and Ruth waited, for Andrew would need to put on his surplice and prepare. Soon the verger came to nod that all was ready, and Kitty entered the church.

Ruth had been busy. Knots of ribbons decorated the altar, each set with a white silk flower. When Kitty arrived at the altar, she gave Sillikin's leash and her gloves and muff to Ruth. She heard an "ooh" and "aah" from the Misses Purslow at sight of the ring.

A good move, my lord.

The ceremony was soon done. The vows were said and the golden band slid onto her finger. Andrew declared, "May your union be blessed, Lord and Lady Dauntry."

Kitty's smile was spontaneous, summoned by surprise at actually being Lady anything. She thought she saw a trace of humor in Dauntry's eyes. For similar reasons, or laughter at her? They had so much to learn about each other. There would be surprises and disagreements, but they'd navigated the waters this far—to the point of no return.

Ruth was beaming. The Misses Purslow seemed in bliss over the romance of it all. Sillikin was looking between Kitty and Dauntry as if contemplating a stare. Kitty just managed not to tell her to stop. She remembered to put her diamond ring on top of the wedding band.

Marcus had given her a diamond ring, though with a much smaller stone. The stone had fallen out one day and never been found. Such tears she'd shed, but Marcus had been philosophical. She remembered him saying that they had each other and no need of a diamond to protect them. He'd wanted to replace the stone, but they'd had better uses for any money, so she'd sold the gold ring. He'd teased her, perhaps even complained, about her practicality.

How long ago had that been? Six years? What would happen if she lost this stone? Perhaps she'd not wear the ring every day.

When they emerged from the church, the villagers cheered.

Braydon murmured, "They must have heard that I've paid for a free cask of ale at the Abbot's Arms."

Kitty chuckled, but she thought most of the villagers' goodwill was from the excitement of a noble wedding on their doorstep, especially one connected to Beauchamp Abbey. They'd be hoping that in the future, the Braydon family would be more involved with matters here, providing charity, entertainment, and employment. If she had any say, they'd not be disappointed.

Braydon was prepared in another way. He pulled out a pouch and gave it to Mrs. Price, the shopkeeper. "Silver threepenny pieces, ma'am. If you'd be so kind, ensure that all the children under ten receive one in memory of this happy day. And then one for every household without such a child. Any remaining should go to Reverend Lulworth for benefit of the poor."

Another cheer, and a clustering of children and parents.

Kitty thought back to her first marriage. There'd been cheers then and flowers, for it had been a summer wedding. Marcus had tossed pennies, leading to a mad scramble. Braydon's way was more orderly and efficient, but the mad scramble had been fun. Back then, many people must have had doubts at seeing such a young lady marrying a damaged man, yet that had been a love match. This was not, but no one here showed doubts of their future bliss.

How odd weddings could be.

Enough. It was done.

Chapter 13

At the parsonage, they ate cake and drank wine. Real wine. Had Braydon provided it?

Toasts were made, and Braydon replied with a speech that contained all the appropriate sentiments but managed not to imply too many untruths.

As they all settled again, one of the Misses Purslow said, "So lovely to have a Braydon married here once more."

Ruth asked, "When was the last occasion?"

The sisters looked at each other. "That would have been the third viscount, wouldn't it, Mary?"

"Yes, dear," said Miss Mary, "for the fourth married in Hampshire somewhere. Before our time, of course."

"And the fifth in London."

Miss Mary smiled at them all. "It is quite customary to marry in the bride's parish, of course, but it's such a pleasure to see a Braydon wedding here. And perhaps . . ."

"Hush, dear," Miss Martha said with a touch of color in her cheeks.

Kitty fought a smile. Miss Mary had been about to mention christenings. That would never do. The implications!

But everyone knew what was supposed to happen tonight. Perhaps she was blushing herself. She wasn't nervous about the act, but the man beside her was still almost a stranger.

"I think it a great shame that the family hasn't worshipped here," Kitty said. "We will as often as possible, won't we, Dauntry?"

"Certainly. Of course, the dowager is something of an invalid these days. Does she consult you, Doctor?"

"No, my lord. Sir Percy Lansing comes from London twice a year, but I gather her limitations are not amenable to treatment."

What an odd, secluded life. Kitty wondered if it had always been this way. No wonder the fifth viscount's wife had run away. Kitty needed to know more, and this gathering was an opportunity. What bride wouldn't be curious?

"I understand my predecessor left," she said, trying for innocence with a touch of stupidity. Eyes slid left and right. Perhaps no one would answer.

Eventually Mr. Whitehall said, "That's true, Lady Dauntry."

"I suppose the fifth viscount divorced her."

"No, ma'am. For whatever reason, he did not."

Kitty sighed in a romantic way. "He must have loved her very much."

There was something significant in the way the long-time residents of Beecham Dab didn't answer.

"Father," said Miss Martha, "did not approve of divorce in any circumstance."

"But he was not against a separation, in the worst cases," said her sister.

"As with the Robertsons," Miss Martha agreed.

There followed a story of a local family a generation ago in which the wife had been very badly treated. Reverend Purslow had helped her to become separated from her husband in the eyes of the law.

"Not all approved," Mr. Whitehall pointed out, and perhaps he was one of them. "Apart from the morality of the situation, nothing could be done for the children, left in the father's care without motherly love."

Kitty saw that it might be a blessing to be barren. If she had children, she wouldn't be able to abandon them to cruelty. Yet the fifth Lady Dauntry had abandoned hers to her mother-in-law. Perhaps the woman hadn't been so odd then.

It was time to go. Again, her husband assisted her with her cloak. She trusted Sillikin to follow and took up her muff, pushing it up her left arm again. They left the parsonage on a wave of smiles and good wishes, which Kitty hoped had power.

She halted outside the door. "A curricle?"

The two-wheeled vehicle waited, with a groom at the highbred horses' heads. The groom was dressed in brown, red, and gold, to match the glossy paintwork. The vehicle looked so delicate, and she thought men mostly used them for racing.

"My luggage?" she asked. That thing looked as if it would be overloaded with three people.

"Has already gone ahead with Henry Oldswick. Do you mind an open carriage?"

"No, but I've never traveled in a curricle before."

"Then I hope you enjoy the experience." He handed her in, then passed Sillikin up to lie on the coach floor. He walked round and took his seat. "Are you warm enough? There's a rug if you'd like it."

"I have my cloak and muff," she said, pulling the muff down to cover her gloved hands. "I hope we won't go too fast."

"Between here and the Abbey and on a country road?"

What a stupid thing to say. He'd think her an idiot.

The groom took his seat at the back, and the horses started forward at a slow pace. Braydon's gloved hands looked light on the reins, but she had no doubt that he was in control.

"Don't your horses mind such a plebian pace?"

"I mind such a plebian pace, but we must all suffer in the cause."

I'm sorry you're finding this such a hardship. She just managed not to say it.

"Does Miss Oldswick suit?"

"I think so. And you're right. She promises to be an excellent ally."

"The servants at the Abbey nearly all date from the fifth viscount's time. Some of them have been there for decades. It would be unfair to dismiss them without cause, but having another agent in place will be useful."

"Another agent?"

"We already have my valet, my groom, and my new secretary, Worseley. All are my eyes and ears. Yes, Baker?"

"Yes, milord."

Was that a deliberate reminder that they were overheard? The man thought of everything. Unfair to cavil at that, but it set Kitty on edge. The groom had to be aware of the complex situation, so she asked, "What's the reaction at the Abbey to our marriage?"

"Guarded, for the most part," Braydon said. "Hostile from the dowager and Isabella."

"She could be sent to school."

"She thinks herself too old for that at sixteen, and it might be unkind. It's only a few months since the deaths of her father and brother."

"Of course. I forget. Perhaps she and the dowager will mellow in time."

"An optimist, I see."

"They will have to change. I won't live in a battle-field."

He glanced at her. "I'm not sure whether to antici-pate or dread the future."

"Always best to anticipate, don't you think?"

He gave a short laugh. "You're as changeable as the sea, Lady Dauntry."

Kitty's stomach clenched at the implied criticism, but she saw it could be justified. She'd not presented a con-sistent picture in their brief encounters. Hoyden, sober, firm, now brisk. She wasn't even sure herself which was the true Kitty. A change of circumstance could change a person as powerfully as wounds or illness, or a resto-ration to health.

They rolled between hedges with countryside beyond. Some fields were pasture holding sheep or cows. Some were empty. Did pasture need to rest? Many fields were stubble left after harvest earlier in the year. Others were plowed.

A bird burst out of a hedge to cross the road in front of them. The horses jibbed, but Dauntry controlled them with ease. Kitty realized that even at this leisurely pace, his whole body was involved, including his fine mind. Something about that was arousing, as was the thought of his hands, despite their being covered by leather gloves. The seat held them close enough to brush against each other if the vehicle swayed. Kitty's thoughts slid again toward the coming night. Perhaps a stranger would be exciting. True or not, it would happen. . . .

She launched into a mundane subject. "How much of the land hereabouts belongs to the viscountcy?"

"Most of it. I can show you maps. There are freehold properties, such as Duncott Manor, the squire's place, but most people are tenants. It's good land, well tended. My predecessor did a good job there."

"But a less good one with his family."

"Unfair, perhaps, to criticize a man for being indulgent to his widowed mother and then to his motherless daughter."

"If the result is unhappiness, someone is at fault."

"How very trenchant you are. We could lay all the blame on the errant Lady Dauntry."

"We could, but I'd like to meet her."

"Why?"

"To hear her side of the story."

He looked at her. "If I prove intolerable, will you run?"

Kitty gave that a moment's serious thought. "No."

"Good."

They went through a crossroads and began to follow a high stone wall that must surround the estate. Kitty could see nothing beyond it until they turned left toward great wrought-iron gates. Beyond, the drive ran arrow straight toward a pale rectangle of a house.

The gatekeeper and his family came out to bow and curtsy.

"Franklin and his family," Braydon said to Kitty.

The man, helped by an older child, hurried to open the gates. Braydon paused the carriage as they went through. He dug in his pocket and brought out some silver coins. "I saved a few for your children, Mrs. Franklin."

Four bright-eyed children, one in her mother's arms, came to receive their silver threepenny bits and say their thank-yous.

Kitty was impressed by her husband's thoughtfulness, but was any part of him not calculated with a cool head? How did that work in the marriage bed? She supposed some women discussed such matters among themselves, but she'd never had that sort of female friend. Except Ruth, of course, but there'd been few opportunities since Ruth had married, and none taken up.

They continued on through the gates toward the house. "Abbey" had made Kitty think the place would be ancient and rambling, but the house before her was the complete opposite. Two regular rows of tall windows ran along the middle of the house. Those would be the principal rooms. A lower rank of smaller windows close to the ground must serve the kitchens and such. Tiny windows in the roof would be for servants' bedrooms. There were no grand embellishments or crenellations.

She'd prepared to become mistress of ancient, slightly crumbling Beauchamp Abbey, but how was she to rule this austere place?

As they continued forward, she looked to one side and the other. Beyond straight, leafless trees, deer of some kind cropped smooth grass that was set with the occasional pale statue of a Greek or Roman. A smooth lake held an island crowned with a small, white temple. The various trees, both solitary and clumped, seemed neatly arranged.

"Your thoughts?" he asked.

"It's lovely," she said, "but perhaps too perfect?"

"Everything should have a flaw?"

"I think so, or it would be intolerable."

"I'm not sure I agree, but comfort yourself that there are any number of flaws in Beauchamp Abbey."

Her unease was probably irrational or just wedding-day nerves, but his words stirred questions. "Has the history of the family here always been difficult?"

He glanced at her. "The house might be malign? An interesting speculation."

"Not a ridiculous one?"

"I don't believe in ghosts or evil spirits, but it's not a happy place, and the recent family history hasn't been blessed."

"Digging further back will give me something to do in my idle hours."

An elusive smile told her he'd caught the irony, but it didn't unseal any mysteries, about the house or about him.

"If your father were alive he would have inherited this," she said. "Would he have welcomed it more than you?"

"He'd have reveled in the title, but I can't imagine him spending much time here. His life was London and government."

"As is yours?"

"Not government any more than my title obliges. Did you not enjoy living in London?"

Kitty had to think about that. "I preferred it to Cateril Manor, but I'm not sure how much was place, how much circumstances." They were close to the house now and she refused to be any more nervous than the situation called for. "I, too, don't believe in ghosts and evil spirits."

He drew up the curricle in front of straight white steps that led up to large double doors, again white. The doors opened to let out a parade of servants. The maids wore dark gray dresses and black aprons, and the footmen a livery of paler gray and silver braid along with black stockings and armbands. *Is gray the regular livery or a special mourning one?*

When Braydon's brightly liveried groom hurried to the horses' heads, he shone like a cheerful fire in a wintry scene.

Kitty was glad to see Henry Oldswick there in her apronless dark blue. The sour-faced, black-clad man beside her was probably Braydon's valet. Did he not approve of his master's bride? Henry smiled, but every other face was blank or hostile. Kitty wondered if the same expressions showed when a conquering army entered a defeated city.

She would conquer, but she would be a kindly conqueror, if allowed.

Braydon came to hand her down. Once on the ground Kitty lifted Sillikin down, quietly commanding her to heel. The dog obeyed, but how would that go in hostile territory? Sillikin was venturesome, and in the parsonage she'd soon made friends with all. Kitty couldn't let her wander here until she was sure it was safe.

Braydon led her toward the dozen or so servants, but she noticed one dripping nose and that none of the women wore gloves. Here was a chance to make a point. She spoke loudly enough to be heard by all. "We can't have our people out in this cold, Dauntry. Go in," she said to the servants. "Go in!"

After a startled moment, they hurried inside. Kitty and Braydon followed, and the door closed behind.

First step complete.

Kitty surveyed a large, pale hall that reached the full height of the house to a glass cupola that let in the cool November light. The floor was white marble, as was the wide central staircase in front of her. White marble pillars to left and right supported galleries above, and there were more pale pillars up there supporting the floor above. Doors and woodwork were also white. There was some color in the walls, but that was a pale and particularly cool shade of blue.

Kitty saw what Ruth had meant by "chilly." Sillikin was keeping close to her side, which was an interesting sign.

There were touches of color—a cream and gold vase on a plinth and some paintings—but they served to emphasize the pallor of the rest. It was an elegant space—Kitty could see that—but oddly unwelcoming. In one corner a long-case clock, also white, ticked ponderous seconds.

She smelled . . . nothing. The parsonage held hints of polish and potpourri, and probably of dog, cat, and children, and whatever was cooking in the kitchen. She'd not noticed, because homes always harbored smells. Did marble absorb them?

A fire would definitely have warmed the space in all means of the word, but there wasn't one. However, the air wasn't cold because an extraordinary Dutch stove gave out heat. She'd seen such a thing only once before, and that had been smaller than this ornate tower of white ceramic. It must have been six feet high and nearly as wide. Kitty could feel the warmth from where she stood.

"What an excellent device," she said, grasping something she could honestly praise.

"My predecessor made a number of improvements. Come and meet the Quillers."

The gray-haired butler and housekeeper were both in black and, as she'd been warned, hostile. Both acted and spoke appropriately, but she had no doubt they saw an interloper. Kitty was surprised they were able to show their feelings to the new mistress of the house. Foolish of them—unless they thought she'd run off like the last one.

Mrs. Quiller introduced the senior servants, and then all were dismissed to their duties. There was no sign of the dowager or Isabella, and that was just as well. This hall had galleries on the right and left of the upper floor, which made the entrance hall like a theater stage; anything said here could be heard by many. If there were to be explosions, Kitty preferred they happen in private.

"Thank you, Mrs. Quiller," Braydon said. "I'll take my wife upstairs."

Kitty shot him a look. Did that mean "to bed"? She'd assumed they'd wait until night, but what did she know of such things? Her wedding day with Marcus had taken such a toll on him that it had been days before they'd been able to consummate their marriage. Then it had happened in the evening, with the sun still up and birdsong and conversation heard through an open window. Summer versus winter.

Not a good thought.

Chapter 14

Braydon led her toward the stairs. Kitty picked up Sillikin and began the climb, saying quietly, "So much marble."

"Unwise in Britain, yes. The first viscount saw too much of Italy. Be thankful for the stove and that the upper floors are wood and sometimes carpeted."

They turned right at the top of the stairs and right again along one gallery. Kitty glanced across the open space and thought she saw a flicker of dark movement on the other side of the house. When she looked more closely, no one was visible, but that had probably been Isabella.

Would the girl continue the claim of a betrothal? Perhaps even that she'd been jilted? It would come to nothing in the end, but could be unpleasant.

There were white-painted doors to her left. Braydon opened the first. "Your boudoir, Lady Dauntry."

She entered, relieved to be offstage, but then shocked by a strident burst of color. The walls were papered in a pink flower print, and a green and brown carpet covered most of the floor. The curtains and hangings were an odd shade of green that didn't go well with either, and the upholstered chairs and a chaise were yellow.

"No one's used these rooms for some time," Braydon said.

That didn't explain the colors, unless some had changed over time. But she said, "It's a pleasant size. Not too large to be cozy, especially with that fire." She put down Sillikin, then discarded her muff and walked toward the hearth, even though she wasn't cold. "After the snow palace, it's a relief."

"Snow that never thaws," he said. "Your rooms have been cleaned but otherwise unchanged. You must alter or arrange them as you wish. The same applies to the whole house, of course."

She wandered over to inspect a lovely table with a marquetry chessboard on the top. "Do you think the errant lady played?"

"I've no idea. I've hardly thought of her at all." He came and opened a drawer. "Two packs of well-worn cards imply she enjoyed them, at least." Another drawer contained fish-shaped counters, and a third, chess pieces.

"Surely they must have played games here in happier times," Kitty said. "There must have been happy times." But what if they'd married as strangers and never come to enjoy each other's company? Was the unpleasant decor a violent protest against cruel fate? Would her fate be similar? "How would you feel if I had the walls in the hall painted a warmer color?"

"Relief," he said, "but I advise you to pick your battles, especially on the first day."

"He thinks I'm impetuous," Kitty murmured to Sillikin, then winced. She must break herself of that habit.

He politely ignored her eccentricity. "Your dressing room is next door."

Kitty went through the adjoining door into a smaller room, but that was by excellent design, as this was also a bathroom. The bath sat in the center, crowned with a rail from which hung curtains to keep off the draft. With a fire burning, as now, there'd be no shivering through a hasty bath.

"Delightful!" she said, and meant it.

"There's a boiler in the basement, so hot water is always available. A stirrup pump brings water to my bath, but there was no Lady Dauntry when the system was installed, so buckets will be needed from there to here."

"The dowager and Isabella have the piped water?"

"Of course, though they share a bathroom. Isabella's room is on the other side of the house, alongside the dowager's."

"What of guests?"

"There are three additional bedrooms on this floor but no extra bathrooms. It seems there have been few guests in recent years."

Shame over the errant viscountess, or a lack of interest in company? Kitty didn't ask. Though they were alone, she felt as if they were being overheard. *Lurking servants who were merely curious, or a lurking dowager?*

The dressing room was lined with wooden cupboards and drawers, but her trunks were only half unpacked. Henry must have slipped out when she heard them approaching. Perhaps that was why she'd sensed someone.

They progressed on into the viscountess's bedroom. She'd expected it to be grand, but again it was of a practical size. The bed made up for it, being tall with heavy, mustard-colored hangings trimmed with a long gold fringe, which again managed to clash. The coverlet and window curtains were in the same bilious color, and the flowered carpet was a dazzle of white and blue. The blue was picked up in the painted walls.

"That yellow could have changed with time," Kitty said faintly.

"Or Diane Dauntry didn't have a good eye."

"Perhaps that's why she and the dowager were at odds. If so, I have some sympathy for the dowager."

"There is ground between snowy perfection and garish havoc."

"Some people never choose the middle way."

Sillikin began an exploration, and Kitty did the same, wandering idly from bedside stand to upright chair, absorbing the fact that this was the viscountess's bedroom. Hers alone? She and Marcus had shared the one room and the one bed.

"You're troubled?" he asked. It was as if he could read her mind.

"Merely warm." She took off her cloak. He moved to help her, but it was already done. Was she going to have to learn to be less self-reliant? She shed her bonnet and gloves as well, laying all on the bed. She hadn't worn a cap for her wedding and now felt underdressed.

"If the previous Lady Dauntry returned, how would people distinguish between her and me? She can't be the dowager, can she?"

"No. There can only be one. She'd be Diane, Lady Dauntry. It's unlikely to be an issue."

"Does anyone know where she is?"

"Not that I'm aware."

"If she's heard that her husband and son are dead, she might return. She might be concerned for her daughter."

"Somewhat late in the day."

He was unsympathetic, but Kitty was increasingly curious about the previous occupant of these rooms. The decor suggested turmoil, and it couldn't have been easy to abandon children.

"I wonder if she even knows she's a widow."

"A point," he said. "I'll ask my secretary to look for any correspondence. I have the impression there's been none since she left, but the paperwork is not in good order."

"Your predecessor was disorganized?" She was sure Braydon was the complete opposite.

"He didn't employ a secretary and was often absent."

"Perhaps not surprising," she said. "This is not a comfortable house."

"And yet he is presented as a devoted son and father."

"Why didn't he seek a divorce? He must have wanted to remarry."

"Perhaps he didn't. He had his son."

"Or didn't want to expose another wife to his mother."

"Melodrama? He could have sought someone of sufficient steel."

"As you have done?"

"Your steeliness is my good fortune, but the dowager isn't my mother. I have no special duty of respect or care. I suspect that like most men, he simply didn't want unpleasantness."

"That's not entirely my experience," she said, but her mind was mostly on the bed. Perhaps he didn't have his own. Perhaps this one was shared. There was one way to find out. "May I see your rooms?" she asked.

"Of course."

He opened the door, and there was her answer—a bedroom similar to hers, but with a more comfortable atmosphere. Of course, it had been lived in until the fifth viscount's death, and then by Braydon for the recent while. It was also more pleasantly decorated, despite a darkening use of brown. It seemed the fifth viscount hadn't had a taste for winter, but not for summer, either.

"Did he spend most of his time away because of the house," she asked, "or did it become as it was because of his neglect?"

"Perhaps he simply avoided the war between his women."

"Then he shouldn't have complained of the result."

"I have no evidence that he did."

The conversation was wandering because of her awareness of the bed.

A book lay open on a table by the chair. What did a man like this read on the night before his wedding? A riding crop lay on the chest at the foot of the bed. A sheathed cavalry saber hung from the raised escutcheon in the back of the bed. Marcus, too, had kept his sword on display. Did that indicate that Braydon felt some nostalgia for the war?

She'd given Marcus's sword to his mother. Lady Cateril had been touched to tears, but it had been no sacrifice for Kitty. The sword and other war remnants reminded his mother of his glory days, but to Kitty they were symbols of his suffering.

The silence felt oppressive. "How long is it since you came here?" she asked.

"Five long weeks."

She turned a look on him. "It can't be so dreadful as that."

"I've never had a taste for country living."

"Poets have poured out praise of it."

"Then they are welcome to it."

She had to fight a smile at his hint of surliness. He must have seen it.

"I'm London born and bred," he said. "I find fields and coppices pleasing enough to observe in passing, but severely lacking as a habitation for anything but cows and sheep."

"This is hardly living in a field," she pointed out.

"But if I walk outside, how far is it to civilization? You're a town person, too. Do you not feel the same?"

"Perhaps living in Beecham Dab reduced the suffering. May I suggest that you suffer from lack of congenial company, sir, not from an excess of fields?"

"You may, but it would be discourteous of me to agree."

She felt heat rise in her cheeks.

"I apologize," he said. "That wasn't meant as it sounded."

"It takes time to discover congeniality," she agreed, but they were walking on eggs here. Was he, too, unsure of marital-bed protocol? He'd never been married at all.

She strolled idly about the room, past a glossy wooden washstand that held shaving equipment. She'd shaved Marcus when his hands had been unsteady. Braydon would need no such service. Marcus had favored clove-scented soap, but the scent here was different. Rosemary, perhaps, but with other ingredients.

This was the bedroom of a different man. A different husband. Would he expect different behaviors? Was he waiting for her to initiate something?

"I have a dressing and bathing room next door," he said, "but my office is downstairs, easily accessible from outside when people need to see me on estate matters. Would you like to see more of the house?"

If she'd failed to do the right thing, he should simply tell her! She wouldn't mind consummating the marriage now. Her body had been simmering for hours, and she wished the first time over and done.

But all she said was, "Of course. Come, Sillikin. Sillikin? Where on earth has she gone to now?"

The dog wriggled out from under the bed, a woolen stocking in her mouth, and presented the prize with pride.

"Well done," Kitty said as she took it and brushed a tuft of dust off one of the dog's ears. "When did you lose this?" she asked, dangling the sturdy stocking in front of Braydon.

"It's not one of mine."

His disdain made her laugh. "I suppose your stockings are tailor-made by fairies."

"Finely knitted by elves," he responded.

Had he actually made a joke?

But then he said, "Shall we progress?"

Kitty dropped the stocking on the chest, making a mental note to check the quality of the cleaning everywhere in this house. Once in the corridor she realized she might have been wise to keep the cloak. The Dutch stove could do only so much. She was hardy, however. She'd survive.

He indicated the matching doors on the other side of the central open space. "The dowager's suite and Isabella's bedroom. There are guest bedrooms at the end of each gallery and another tucked in a rear corner. We'll go that way."

Kitty kept silent, aware that anything said up here could be heard by many. She hoped it wasn't like St. Paul's Cathedral, where a whisper on one side of the dome could be heard on the other.

The guest bedrooms seemed adequate, and Sillikin's exploration revealed no more neglect. The style of decoration was along the middle line that Braydon had mentioned between snowy and garish, making the viscountess's rooms even more peculiar.

Chapter 15

He took her next to a short gallery with windows looking over the rear of the estate. It would be a pleasant place to sit in summer, and was large enough for exercise in bad weather. One large fireplace provided warmth, but again Kitty regretted not having her cloak.

Paintings hung on the walls, and Braydon took her to one.

"My predecessor."

The smoothly plump man sat by a desk on which documents were spread. That was common when the sitter was a landowner, but it seemed to Kitty that the papers were mere ornaments. He had thinning dark hair and a slightly anxious expression, as if he was thinking, *Will she approve of this?*

"Odd that a loving mother can make life particularly difficult."

"You're thinking of Lady Cateril as well?"

"She tried to force Marcus to live at Cateril Manor, where she'd have fussed over him all the time. As it was, she fretted over him in letters and sometimes dispatched doctors to torment him with pointless treatments."

"It must be hard to accept that there's no hope."

"I see that, but she sought a miracle that would make him what he'd once been. I don't think she truly loved him as he'd become. Oh, that's unfair!"

He startled her by taking her hand. "You loved him as he was, and you did what you could to protect him."

She looked into his cool blue eyes. "It was little enough."

"Sometimes that's all we can do."

His touch and understanding were so unexpected that tears threatened. She twitched away to look at the portrait again.

"There's an open locket on the table," she said, looking closer, "with a picture of a woman. Mother or wife?"

"You're observant." He came close beside her. "Youngish, I'd say."

"Wife, then. He must have loved her when this was painted."

"Or done the conventional thing."

Kitty was tilting her head to try to make out the features of the brown-haired woman in the miniature. "It might be of his mother when young. Is there a painting of the dowager here?"

"A family group over here."

The large painting showed a seated young woman with a boy at her knee and an older man standing behind. Though they were dressed finely, they were presented outdoors, with the park and house behind them. Lady Dauntry was plump and pretty, with dark curls, but not at all like the woman in the miniature. Lord Dauntry had rather heavy features and wore an old-style gray wig.

"They look content," she said.

"I see them as smug. Prosperous, satisfactorily married, and with a healthy young heir. Within three years," he added, "the fourth viscount will be dead and she will raise the fifth alone."

"In the midst of life we are in death," Kitty murmured, quoting from the funeral service. She turned away from the disturbing painting. "Are there any later pictures of her?"

"One. She keeps it in her boudoir."

"I assume she's gray haired by now?"

"Somewhat. She wears ostentatious mourning caps, so it's hard to tell."

Kitty looked around at generations of Braydons. "I suppose you'll have to have your portrait done."

"And you. We could wait until we have a son and reproduce that one."

"No."

"No," he agreed. "Portraits are odd things, aren't they? They show sitters like flies in amber, oblivious of the fate stalking them."

Kitty thought of the painting of Marcus. "Some people lead tranquil lives," she argued. "Consider Ruth and Andrew. They could be captured in contentment now, and there's every chance it could happen again in twenty years and then forty."

"We'll pray for that."

"You doubt it?" *Has he, too, detected trouble there?*

"The future is a mystery to everyone. My father died when a wall fell on him."

Surprised by a personal revelation, Kitty sat on a cushioned window seat, ready to hear more. "How?"

"Pure ill luck," he said, strolling to sit beside her. "He was walking along a London street toward his Whitehall office. Some building work was being done, and an old wall crumbled down on top of him. A young lad nearby was killed at the same time."

"In life we are in death, indeed. A lesson to enjoy the moment we have."

"I agree. How did your parents die?"

"In a fire. A stove kept the chill off the bookshop in winter, and it somehow set fire to the books. They lived above. The smoke killed them. I was scarcely out of mourning when Marcus died. And now Princess Charlotte. Women do die in childbirth, but it was such a shock. Perhaps because she was a princess?" she asked.

"We believe that royalty are immune to cruel fate?" he asked. "History hardly bears that out."

"We might at least believe that they receive the best medical attention. Many are blaming her doctors."

"Perhaps with cause. But I suspect the universal grief is for a belief that innocents are safe. Whereas fate is a malign old crone."

"Not for us." She said it in instinctive reaction to his bitter tone. "Many people are fortunate, and we will be of that party."

"By force of will?"

"If necessary. Consider this—how often have royal women died in childbirth?"

"I have no idea." But he was thinking. "Not the queen, certainly, despite nearly twenty births. George the second's queen died long after the birth of her last child. Queen Anne suffered endless unsuccessful pregnancies, which might have harmed her health, but none directly killed her. Queen Mary died of smallpox, and James the Second's queen of cancer."

"You've studied such matters?" she asked, astonished.

"I have a retentive memory. Elizabeth, of course, had no children, nor did Mary Tudor. Ah . . ."

"Jane Seymour!" Kitty said. "Henry the Eighth's third wife. But that's nearly three hundred years ago. So, we may all have taken as fact that queens and princesses don't die in childbirth. Hence the shock at the affront to natural order."

"You're smiling."

Kitty realized she was. "Such speculations are fun. Is there a natural order?"

"I'd like to think so, and to preserve it."

"How?"

"In any way I can."

"I'll help you if I can." Kitty looked around. "Speaking of which, is there a portrait of Diane Dauntry here?"

"There must have been, but it was probably destroyed."

"Thrown on a bonfire, with the dowager dancing around it, cackling?"

"Hush."

She looked round quickly, but there was no one there. He was correct, however. She must guard her tongue.

He walked to the fireplace and rang the bell beside it. When a maid came, he sent her for Mrs. Quiller. The woman entered with a guarded expression and seemed relieved by the simple question.

"There were two portraits, milord, a miniature and a large one. They were returned to her family."

"What was she like?" Kitty asked.

Mrs. Quiller bridled, as if insulted. "It is not my place to say, milady."

"I simply meant in appearance."

"Ah. Thin and blond, milady. Will that be all?"

"Yes, thank you."

When the woman had left, Kitty slid a look at Braydon. "Perhaps she thinks I, too, will be soon gone."

"I expect you to prove her wrong. Onward."

"A moment." Kitty returned to the portrait of the fifth viscount to study the miniature again. It didn't help. The woman was definitely brown-haired and youngish, but didn't really resemble the young dowager. It wasn't important, but the fifth viscount's marriage and the flight of his wife tweaked her curiosity. The answers must be here somewhere.

She left the gallery feeling more comfortable by the moment. She still didn't know her husband in all the many ways possible, but she could enjoy his company, which was something. It was a great deal.

He showed her the drawing room, which was in the wintry-perfection style but warmed slightly by a carpet in shades of peach and a number of paintings on the walls. It was not warmed by a fire, so must have seen little use recently. It was typically a lady's room, and the dowager had her own.

A pianoforte and a harp sat in one corner. Kitty had been taught to play a keyboard but not kept up the skill. She'd never played a harp. Was an aristocratic hostess expected to entertain her guests in that way? In that case, she'd have to apply herself to practice, which had never been her forte. She found it hard to imagine herself staging grand entertainments here. Who did she know other than the village gentry?

A house like this should host events, however, even if only local ones on high days and holidays. What was she to do about that? What was she to do about anything?

Her comfort curdled.

Beauchamp Abbey was a large and complex house, and she knew nothing of the running of such a place. It was elegant, and she was not. Everything here was luxurious and spoke of wealth, and she didn't know how to be rich. She'd known people who had come into money and wasted it or hoarded it or made ridiculous show with it. It took familiarity to deal with wealth graciously. Braydon had that. She didn't. How was she to learn?

"I require coffee after my exertions," Braydon said, "and relief from rooms like this. We'll enjoy it in my quarters."

They returned to the staircase, and Kitty let Sillikin make her own way down, claws clicking on slippery marble. She'd have a carpet laid there, but that wouldn't remove the sensation of entering a snow-palace stage or the presence of an invisible and hostile audience.

It was a relief to leave the hall toward the back and enter a part of the house with wooden floors and brown wainscoted walls. Not summer, but perhaps a dull autumn.

They passed the door Braydon had mentioned—the back door through which people could enter on business. People like his estate steward, she supposed, and perhaps his head groom and gardener. How many servants did he—did they—employ in total? An alarming number, she was sure.

A short corridor held three doors, and the first was open to show a young man at a desk covered with books and papers.

"My secretary, my dear. Worseley." The man standing was surprisingly young for such a post and even blushed a little as he bowed. "Any discoveries today?" Braydon asked, then turned to Kitty. "As I said, I found the viscountcy's minor papers in disorder. Worseley attempts order—in his idle moments."

The young man smiled at the wry comment. "I've assembled and annotated the records to do with the Lincolnshire estate, sir. The one the dowager Lady Dauntry brought into the marriage. All seems in order now, and there's reason for the lack of income."

"That being?"

"It's a mere remnant, sir. A house and garden."

"Ah. Perhaps those details were obscured on purpose. What an excellent fellow you are."

Worseley blushed with pleasure. Here was a different Braydon. He was almost playful, but there could be no doubt who was lord and master.

Of course, he'd been an officer in the army, and good officers knew how to bring out the best in their men. She tended to forget Braydon's past because the soldiering didn't show through the gloss. She found it impossible to imagine him muddy and tattered, even in the heat of battle.

He showed her the next room, which had glass-doored shelves packed with ledgers, folders, and document boxes. "The muniment room. Most of the important and current estate papers were properly kept. It's only the more personal papers that are out of order. On to my inner sanctum."

They entered, and Sillikin explored while Kitty assessed it by eye. It was a room much like his bedroom, and designed more for comfort than work. The pedestal desk, even holding neat piles of documents, seemed subordinate to a thick carpet, a large fire, and two very comfortably upholstered chairs by the fireside.

Kitty smiled. "I sense the fifth viscount overlaid by the sixth."

"Sounds deuced odd."

She was startled into a laugh. "I mean that your predecessor used this as his haven, not for work, and probably spent most of his time in one of the chairs. Who used the other?"

Sillikin abandoned hope of treasure and flopped down in front of the fire.

"I don't know," Braydon said, "but the one on the left is significantly less worn. The overlay?"

Kitty considered. "The desk gives off an aura of hard work—that's you—and that cabinet is out of place." She indicated the glossy black cabinet whose doors were decorated with inlaid wood and mother-of-pearl. It was about five feet high. "You had it moved in here to hold more business papers than he ever bothered with."

"You're very shrewd."

She didn't like his tone. "At least you added the D."

"I've seen no sign of shrewishness."

"That's because you haven't crossed me yet."

"Perhaps I should practice taming."

"I recommend not!"

"You, my lady, are a shrew after all."

"A word applied to any woman who speaks her mind."

"Only when the mind is fierce."

"And is there anything *wrong* with fierceness?"

He began to speak, then clearly thought better of it. "Not always, I grant you, but may I point out that I am not the enemy?"

That was a just reprimand. She'd almost lost her temper there, over nothing.

"I apologize."

"But you enjoyed that."

She almost protested, but he was right. "Your turn to be shrewd? True, it's been some time since I've felt able to let rip."

"You didn't fight with Lady Cateril?"

"How could I? She was deep in genuine grief."

"So, perhaps, is the dowager Viscountess Dauntry."

"Is she?"

"In one sense, yes. But it's a grief that leads to war."

Kitty moved toward the desk, curious about the papers there and what they would tell her about her husband, but realized in time that it would be nosy. She turned back. "Should I not meet her soon?"

"A delicate question. Would you wish to be presented to her for approval?"

"No."

"Thus, not yet."

"And Isabella?"

"Will be taking her cue from her grandmother. I could summon her."

"To be presented to me for approval? Not the best approach."

"No. The dowager uses Isabella as a foot soldier. A reluctance to harm foot soldiers can lose a war."

She considered him. "Yet you are reluctant. I find that admirable."

"Despite her attack on you?"

"It was a feeble sortie. Is she a resolute foot soldier?"

"A shot over her head usually sends her in retreat."

"Poor girl. Can her allegiance be changed?"

"I hope you can find a way."

She supposed that was part of her duties.

"As for warfare," he said, "if you need a sturdy sparring partner, I'm unlikely to bleed."

"But you could be bruised. Will you take offense?"

"No."

They were on an edge again, in danger of losing balance. "Didn't you mention coffee?" she asked.

"I did. I take it dark and sweet, in the Turkish style. How would you like yours?"

She could try for harmony in this. "May I try your Turkish coffee? I, too, like it strong and sweet."

A look in his eyes suddenly gave added meaning to her words, sending a hot tingle over her. Perhaps they wouldn't wait until the night. . . .

But he turned away to call the order to his secretary and then returned, closing the door, indicating that she should sit. Simply sit. She did so, but with an inner wail. It had been so long, and now she felt sure their consummation would be satisfactory. Highly satisfactory.

He sat in the other chair. "What was your first wedding day like?"

She hoped he didn't mean her first wedding night. She didn't think she could talk about that without completely losing control.

Chapter 16

"Summer," she said, "and more of an event. A number of my friends attended, and his. We spent the night at an inn, then traveled on by easy stages to our London home."

"And you'd known each other for some time."

"Three months, though we hadn't met frequently until the last weeks. I was at school at first." She told him about sneaking out to the fair and then exchanging letters and arranging the occasional meeting. "All irresistibly exciting at seventeen."

She realized that begged the question of whether she'd regretted it later, but thank heavens he didn't ask.

"Who were your witnesses?"

"Half the parish, but principally Ruth and Marcus's brother. His family was there, of course, his mother still trying to persuade us to return to live at Cateril Manor."

"Mothers," he said. "The queen is a difficult one, too."

She raised her eyebrows at him. "Is that, perhaps, treason?"

"Probably. But everyone acknowledges that she's cold to most of her children, and a tyrant as well. She refuses to acknowledge the Duke of Cumberland's wife because of some old grudge."

"It must be hard to have her husband in such a terrible state and for so long."

"True, but that doesn't excuse her."

"Perhaps it's worn her down," Kitty said, thinking a little of herself, but there was no comparison. "She's old and in ill health. Perhaps to be pitied."

"You have a kind heart," he said, but without notable approval.

"I'm not ashamed of it. What was your mother like?"

The question seemed to take him aback.

"It's hard to say." He rose to put more wood on the fire. "She died when I was eleven, and I doubt any child that age judges a parent clearly. I didn't see a great deal of her, but she was beautiful and charming. She sang when there were guests. I'd slip out of my room onto the landing to listen." He stood, dusting off his hands. Those beautiful hands, which sent her mind in improper directions. "Until I went to school, my time was mostly spent with my nurse and tutor."

An aristocratic upbringing. Why be surprised?

Because he was beginning to feel like an equal and that could be dangerous to her sanity. She was a glorified housekeeper and governess, and his life was in London.

"Lady Sophonisbe," she said. "She must be the daughter of an earl, marquess, or duke."

"Duke."

Kitty had hoped for the lowest level of aristocracy, not the highest.

"But she ran off with a commoner," he said, with a smile that might even be fond. "Plain Sir Barnaby Ecclestall. An excellent fellow, though my mother didn't think so."

"She disliked her father?"

"She died when I was young, so I don't know. But my father said once that she resented being born a commoner when her mother should by rights have married high. You asked about my father and the title, and I said he'd have liked it. My mother would have been in alt to become Lady Dauntry."

Kitty wanted to ask more. Here was another difficult mother lingering in her husband's memories in ways that might affect their future, but this wasn't the moment.

She looked around the room for a safer line of talk. "What do you keep in the cabinet of curiosities?"

That term was usually applied to a place to keep an eccentric collection, but when he rose and opened the doors, she saw shelves holding orderly ranks of open-topped boxes.

"My predecessor didn't believe in filing his personal papers, and, as I said, he had no secretary. He tossed them into the nearest receptacle—a box, a drawer, even sometimes a vase. We've been gathering them. The top shelves are unsorted boxes and the lower ones sorted."

She saw neatly written labels—*Plas Blaidd, Parliament, Town House*. There were a number of boxes for correspondence, each with a subtitle, including *Personal, Commercial, Petitions* . . .

"Poor Worseley," she said.

"I do my share when I have time."

"Why bother?"

"The alternative would be to burn them all unread."

Kitty rose and went to dip into an unsorted box and found a recipe of some sort in faded ink.

"Perfume?" she asked.

He looked over her shoulder. "Snuff, I'd think. Those are types of tobacco, with the addition of herbs for scent."

She looked at him in surprise. "You use snuff?"

"No."

Of course—that memory. And now he was so close, they were almost touching. Whatever this snuff had smelled of, Braydon had his own subtle smell, and it stirred her. She was tempted to turn to him, to put her hand on his chest, and invite a kiss.

But where might that lead?

Here? In his study.

With coffee ordered.

She moved away. "Why bother with such petty details?"

"Knowledge is power. Ignorance is vulnerability. I intend to know and understand all about my new responsibilities."

She looked at him, alert. "You think there have been irregularities? Under the dowager's rule?"

"Money is unaccounted for and aspects are murky. I suspect the oddities rise from sheer bloody-mindedness . . . if you don't mind such language."

"After so long a soldier's wife? But you wonder if there's been some wrongdoing." She considered the boxes in a new light. It would almost be like a treasure hunt. "I might enjoy going through the papers."

"Then do so, but record each item in this ledger." He took out a large book and opened it on the desk. She saw on each line a note about a paper and where it had been put. She recognized his handwriting in some entries, but another hand in others. That must be the secretary's.

Letter, March 15, 1813, from Lady Pierrepoint to 5th V. NOI

"NOI?" she asked.

"No obvious importance. All those go in that box." She saw one with simply those initials. "If there might be some importance, they are stored in boxes according to subject." He pointed to one line, which said, *Letter, September 12, 1814, from W. Hughes to 5th V PB.* "That deals with a small estate in Wales, so is in the box for Plas Blaidd. In time that box will be incorporated with the one in the record room."

This meticulous organization stole some of the appeal of a hunt through the papers, but Kitty supposed she should have expected it. This was a man who turned up at ten o'clock to the very strike.

Looking down the lines of writing, she saw many NOIs. "Why not burn the unimportant ones?"

"There's a gap between unimportant and no obvious importance, and it could be disastrous."

She looked at him in surprise. "You think there's criminality here? Or even danger?"

"No, but until I'm sure, I'm on guard. If you turn up crimes and scandals, come to me before you shout them to the world."

"Well, really! I don't think I deserve that."

"Of course not." But then he added, "I don't know you, Kitty, any more than you know me. Our encounters have been few, and form more of a patchwork than a picture. I don't know what you might do or how you might react."

"Nor I you," she pointed out.

"I am as I am."

"So am I." What did he want—that she be only one version of herself? Presumably the composed, calm one. That had been as close to deception as she'd come. "I might have presented a motley impression," she said, "but nothing was put on for show."

He didn't like that. He lifted a box out of the cabinet and put it on the desk. "Explore, if you wish."

A test? If so, she'd pass.

She sat at the desk and took out a paper. Then she wrote in the ledger, trying to be as neat as he: *Receipt for repair of ormolu clock, Stelby & March. February 3, 1810.* "I assume I can put NOI?"

"Miscellaneous household receipts have their own box. Add H, and give it to me." She passed it over and he put it into a box in the cabinet. "The inventories might indicate which house, though I suspect there are a number of ormolu clocks."

And how can it matter? Kitty thought, but she returned to the box.

The next paper was a letter dated September 25, 1810, from a Charles Day to the fifth viscount about a house in Edgware. The Edgware Road ran north from London close to Moor Street, where she'd lived, but she didn't know how far away it was. She wrote the essentials, then asked, "Is there a box for a house in Edgware?"

"No." He came toward her to take the paper, but the coffee arrived then, the aroma very welcome. Kitty was pleased to see a plate of tiny cakes came with it. She'd only nibbled at the wedding breakfast. She put the letter on the desk and rose.

The footman placed the slender coffeepot and tiny cups on a small table beside one of the armchairs and set the cakes alongside, together with a jug, plates, and serviettes. He left, and Kitty sat in the other chair, curious.

Sillikin, always aware of food, came to her knee. "No," she said. With a reproachful look, the dog lay down again, head on paws, half over Kitty's feet. "You wouldn't like it," Kitty said, then bit her lip. She was going to stop doing that.

"She wouldn't," Braydon said as he sat, "unless she's a very unusual dog." He poured coffee for them both and passed her a cup. "I requested cream in case you'd like it."

"I assume it's not normally used?"

"No."

She sipped, and felt her eyes open wide. It was very strong and very sweet. And very delicious. "I don't think I want cream."

A smile in his eyes might even be true approval. "Try one of the cakes."

They were tiny squares, and when she picked one up she could tell it was dense. She nibbled. "Marzipan? But not quite."

"It's halva, made of ground sesame seeds and sugar."

"The kitchen here makes these?"

"Hardly. I recently purchased a new supply from a Turkish bakery in London. Do you like it?"

"The taste is a little odd, but I think . . . Yes. I do enjoy new things." She sipped more of the coffee, which went well with the little cake. "You've visited Turkey?"

"In 1809, and occasionally at other times."

"You were a diplomat?"

"It was on army business."

That intriguing army business again. "Did you visit a harem?" she asked.

"And lived to tell the tale?"

"Perhaps you wore a disguise to slip in and rescue an English slave."

"Perhaps you read too many novels."

She smiled. "Perhaps I do. But I don't take them as a textbook for my life." She twitched her toe under Sillikin. "In a novel," she said to the dog, "he'd have a mad wife locked away, or a chamber of bloody mementoes."

Without opening her eyes, Sillikin snuffled.

"Not a great conversationalist, is she?" Braydon remarked. "I can merely offer a deranged dowager and an ice palace. How long have you had her?"

"Eight years. She was a gift. Marcus didn't mind."

"A gift from a gentleman?"

"Why ask that?"

"Why else would your husband mind?"

"Having a dog in a small place. The mess when she was a puppy."

"I see."

"As it happens, it was a gentleman. Captain Edison.

His mother breeds them." She smiled at the memory. "She was such an adorable bundle of fluff."

"And made you happy." He was watching her from beneath lowered lids in a way that unsettled her.

"Yes. Yes, she did. And does."

"I must set myself to make you even happier."

He meant it. *Lord above, please let him not be plagued by jealousy.*

To cover the moment, she sipped a little more coffee, but he said, "Don't drink too deep. There'll be a thick layer at the bottom. Would you like more?"

She put down the cup. "Not at the moment, thank you. It seems a little like ratafia or some other sweet alcoholic drink—deceptively treacherous."

"You won't become drunk on it."

"It feels potent enough. I think I heard that the dowager has dogs. Will they be friendly?"

"It shouldn't matter. They're rarely outside her rooms."

"That can't be healthy."

"For either of them. A footman walks the creatures twice a day around the gardens. Sometimes Isabella does that."

"It can't be good for her to be cooped up here."

"No, but she resists change."

She picked up another piece of cake. "What was Isabella's life like before her father and brother died?"

"She receives some letters from friends, but none have visited since the deaths. She had a governess, but Mrs. Riverton was dismissed when Isabella turned sixteen and decided she no longer needed lessons."

"Indulged, then."

"Assuredly."

"Which must mean she had the life she wanted."

"I've known people who had all the choices in the world and yet managed to make themselves miserable."

"That could include Napoleon."

"Cursed with an appetite for conquest that could never be satisfied," he agreed. "If he'd taken Russia, where next? That's the worst curse the gods can place upon us—insatiable ambition."

"Like Tantalus, chained, thirsty, in water that never quite reached his lips."

"Indeed. The old gods knew their tortures."

"You are free of ambition?"

"Yes, thank God."

The pleasure of sweet coffee, halva, and the fire's warmth led Kitty to ask, "There's nothing you want?" She watched for his reaction.

He sipped coffee, taking his time. "To not die with regrets. What of you?"

"Nothing significant at the moment. I wanted to escape Cateril Manor, and you provided the key. I wanted to escape tedium, and you've provided purpose. When I discover a new want, I'll seek a way to satisfy it."

"Do you want children?"

The question startled her. Because it felt too personal, she realized, and that was ridiculous.

"In truth, I don't know. I've become accustomed to not having them, and to it being unlikely. What of you? You said you're not concerned about an heir, but do you want to be a father?"

If he was taken aback, it served him right.

"I've had little to do with children," he said. "I doubt I'd be good at it. I'm not like Andrew Lulworth."

Impossible to imagine him romping with a child as Andrew romped with Arthur, but he was relaxing here with her. In this modest room, in comfortable chairs by the fireside, with a plain mantel clock slowly ticking time, Kitty could forget the grand house above and around them and all the problems it contained. Perhaps the fifth viscount had done just that. If so, she didn't blame him.

"I'm enjoying this," she said. "The coffee and the cake, but mostly the conversation. It's so long since I've enjoyed a long and sensible one."

"Your dog doesn't oblige?"

As if aware she'd been mentioned, Sillikin raised her head.

Kitty chuckled. "She employs the supportive silence."

"Which can be extremely effective."

Sillikin got up, stretched, and went to the door in a meaningful way.

"And sometimes she's direct." Regretfully, Kitty rose. "I need to take her out, and she should have a walk. You'd be welcome to accompany us, but I suspect you have tasks awaiting you, having been away."

He rose, too. "What an understanding bride you are. Are you truly so composed, or is this a brave front?"

The question surprised her. "I am as I am, Braydon. If you want something other, I'll try to oblige, but I fear I'm no hand at acting a part."

"No. Be yourself," he said. But he didn't sound easy about it.

She prayed she soon understood him better. Attempting to interpret every little thing would be exhausting, and she must make this work.

Chapter 17

He opened the door for her, inclining his head slightly as she passed. That seemed too formal between husband and wife. But as she walked down the short corridor, she acknowledged that she knew nothing of how it should be between a viscount and viscountess. Perhaps the nobility were different in all ways.

Kitty opened the door to the outside so Sillikin could relieve herself. The air was still cold, so she'd need cloak and gloves to go far.

"Come, Sillikin."

The dog drooped like a disappointed child.

Kitty scooped her up. "Unlike you, milady, I don't have a fur coat on. Once I'm warmly dressed we'll have some fun."

She'd entered the front hall speaking, and only just suppressed a curse at the thought that people could hear. Their hearing a curse echoing through the house would be even worse. She'd said she couldn't act a part, but could she ever be herself here?

Henry dressed her in cloak and gloves and would have handed her a bonnet, but Kitty declined.

"I can walk in the garden without," she said, "even if the garden is acres large." She found Sillikin's leather ball and they headed out, using that convenient back door.

Braydon's door, straight ahead, was closed.

They crossed a small courtyard to emerge into formal gardens. Beyond lay the grass cropped by deer. The animals were in the distance, and she hoped they stayed there. They looked delicate and gentle, but they were wild animals and the males had large antlers.

Sillikin was looking at her expectantly.

"Yes, I remembered," Kitty said, taking the leather ball out of her pocket. She threw it over the garden onto the grass, and Sillikin raced to follow. A movement made Kitty aware of someone watching. Over to her right she saw a gardener peering over a bush. She wanted to wave, but what should Lady Dauntry do in such a situation? What would the servant think of Lady Dauntry romping with her dog? *Never mind.* That was exactly what Kitty intended to do.

She followed Sillikin, meeting her halfway and engaging in the obligatory tussle for possession of the ball. When Sillikin surrendered it, Kitty threw again, but parallel with the house. She'd like to venture farther, but not with those untrustworthy animals around, some of them watching her.

The estate was probably called a park, but it was unlike any park she'd known before. Hyde Park was large and untamed in places, but it pushed up against a million people, and they could be heard, even if only as a kind of hum. Here, in winter, her surroundings were almost silent, and in the distance she saw only trees. The rolling grass was dotted with specimen trees, statues, and deer. It seemed a great waste of space. Cateril Manor had only modest gardens because most of the land was put usefully to agriculture. She remembered that here beyond the dense woodland, the estate was walled. She couldn't see the high wall, but it was there, keeping the world out, and perhaps keeping things in. *The deer,* she reminded herself. *The people are free to come and go.*

Who knew what lived in those woods? She didn't think there were wolves in England anymore, but were there still wild boar? What of wildcats? Even a fox could attack Sillikin, who'd never had to fight anything. Kitty resolved to stay close to the house until she knew it was safe to wander—for her dog and herself. She was sure it was ridiculous to worry about actual danger, but she felt a creeping worry. She looked back at the house and caught movement at a window in the upper floor.

A face. The dowager or Isabella, looking down with a sneer at the romping, hatless interloper who dared claim to be Viscountess Dauntry.

Then she'd romp! She wouldn't be intimidated by shadows. Kitty ran with the ball, Sillikin running alongside delighting in the chase.

Braydon watched his wife playing with her dog. He'd never owned a dog and never regretted it. Some officers in the army had kept one or two, or even a small pack of hounds to indulge in the occasional hunt. He had no objection to dogs, but he'd never felt the need for one. Would he benefit from a canine companion? Not if he came to talk to it.

"My lord?"

Braydon turned to Worseley. "Yes?"

"I have those documents prepared, if you have a moment."

Dauntry read and signed the papers, then asked, "What do we know about the fifth viscount's wife since she left?"

"Nothing so far, sir."

"Her family home must be in the records, for I'm told two portraits of her were returned there. Find out. If she's in distant parts, she might not know she's a widow."

Worseley left, but Dauntry realized the secretary's

window faced the same way as his. What did Worseley think of the Viscountess Dauntry romping hatless with her pet? What would anyone else think?

Of Kit Kat.

He now knew that's how his wife was known to a host of enthusiastic officers. After his offer of marriage had been accepted, he'd traveled to Town, mostly to avoid Isabella. Her efforts to tempt him had been merely annoying, but word of his intent to marry might have pushed her and the dowager into drastic action. Her visit to Kitty had been a weak ploy, but it showed he'd been right.

The prospect of Town had delighted his valet, Johns, who would probably abandon him if obliged to spend much more time in the country. That would be an inconvenience. He was a fashionable valet of the highest sort, and tempting him from his previous employer had almost led to a duel.

He'd traveled post chaise rather than in the curricle, which had pleased his groom, Baker. Baker liked the countryside and had set up a flirtation with a farmer's daughter, who seemed very willing to flirt back, so he'd been happy to be left behind.

Such a natural business, billing and cooing, but one that came no more naturally to him than a jovial night of drinking at a local tavern. He could flirt, but as sophisticated play with a certain sort of woman. He could even protest devotion as long as he knew the woman in question was playing the same game.

He would never have married any of the women he played with, and they'd had no more desire for commitment than he. Thank heavens Kitty Cateril showed no sign of wanting spurious emotions and declarations. That was probably what had decided him a week ago—that and her fighting spirit. By God, she had a fighting spirit.

In London he'd visited his military club and out of

curiosity mentioned meeting Marcus Cateril's widow. There'd been universal approval, which should have pleased him, but he'd seen interest as well when they'd realized that Kit Kat was free to wed. Most men had lamented that they were in no position to marry anyone and probably hadn't been serious in the first place, but there'd been a few others. He'd lied to one, a Captain Edison, about where she was. He hadn't wanted an old admirer racing in to snatch his bride. His instinct had been right. Edison had given her the dog and might have been a serious admirer all along.

He'd left the club unsettled by the men's reactions, but it hadn't dented his determination to marry the woman. She met his requirements, and once she was established at the Abbey he'd be free to leave. Now, however, he was discovering a new Kitty every minute. He shouldn't be surprised. Women could be as changeable as the English weather. He'd seen hard-bitten whores become sighing fools over a man no better than any other. Usually one much worse, which only proved the female brain was chaotic. He'd seen coolheaded ladies gibber and coo over a baby—but, then, he'd seen men do the same if it was their own.

Children.

Odd to think he might have a bunch of them.

Unlikely, she'd said. That answered one question. She wasn't a virgin, so he needn't consider that in the coming night.

The coming night. His body stirred at the thought of it. When she'd relaxed in the upholstered chair, firelight playing on her russet hair and bold features, he'd felt her sensual power. A sliding, quizzical glance had caught his breath, and he'd been suddenly aware that though her strong nose and chin could be somewhat mannish, her full lips were anything but, especially when parted. . . .

He'd have to guard against that or he'd end up ensnared like all the rest. *Kit Kat.* Apparently her husband's London rooms had been known as the Kit Kat Club.

He dragged his mind back to the practical.

Eight years married and no child, so in all probability she was barren. That was probably a blessing. He had no idea how he might react to a child of his own, but he was sure having a wife die in childbirth would be the deepest sort of hell.

Kitty played her way around the house, encountering the occasional groundsman. If she passed close by she said, "Good afternoon" which seemed to startle them. Was it extraordinary that any of the family acknowledge their existence?

When she'd completed the circuit of the house she was feeling better for fresh air and exercise, but reluctant to return. That wouldn't do. She couldn't retreat, so she must advance. And if she were advancing, it would be with a strategy and as great a force as she could muster.

Perhaps worrying about how to conquer the dowager and Isabella was the wrong approach. The servants might be a better target. *Rather than attack the fortress, undermine it.*

A first step would be a celebration of the viscount's marriage. She was sure that was normal. The villagers had received coins and free ale. The servants here should do as well or better.

She'd consult Braydon.

No, Henry. Henry will know.

The outdoor servants must be included. What of the tenants, laborers, and local tradesmen outside of Beecham Dab? There was the hamlet called Stuckle, and there might be other places.

Lord Pately's heir had married during her time living at

Cateril Manor. The Caterils hadn't attended because of mourning, but they'd heard all about the celebrations. There'd been the usual coins and free ale, but there'd also been a servants' ball a few days after the event and invitations to the most prosperous local farmers and tradesmen.

Perhaps there was something in the records about how the fifth viscount's wedding had been celebrated. If not, people could be asked. It might have been no more than twenty years ago.

She strolled about as she thought, but then a speck of rain drove her inside. She closed the door just ahead of steady rain and went to Braydon's office. The door was open, but he wasn't there.

She stopped by the secretary's office. "Do you know where Lord Dauntry is?"

He rose. "No, my lady."

"Do you know if there's any record of the events around the fifth viscount's wedding?"

"I believe there are some accounts. A moment, my lady."

He went into the muniment room and returned with a ledger, flipping through the pages. "Here are some costs to do with the ring and various gifts. All in London, of course."

Of course. He'd married there. "Were there any celebrations here?"

"That would be in a separate account, ma'am. A moment, please." He found another ledger and ran through the pages. "Ah, here. On the same day, a special dinner for the indoor servants, with wine to toast the couple. The next night, a dance in the long barn, which included the outdoor servants, with ale and cider. Ale and cider provided for the villagers of Beecham Dab and Stuckle. Special provisions for the residents of the almshouses. More of such benevolence."

"Thank you." She turned and came face-to-face with Braydon. "May I have a moment of your time, my lord?"

"As many as you wish," he said, but once they were in his study he asked, "A problem?" as if he expected one.

"Not at all. I was thinking there should be a celebration for the servants and others."

"Of course. How remiss of me. I've never been involved in such an affair before. What do you suggest?"

"I don't suppose we can arrange a special dinner for the servants tonight, but they could have wine to toast us. Perhaps we should attend the toast. Then a ball in a barn as soon as it can be arranged, and the special dinner. But what of the local dignitaries?"

"Apart from the Fields, there are none nearby and I've not gone farther in search of them."

"Then that will do for now. What of the dowager and Isabella? It feels unnatural to ignore them."

"And perhaps petty. I'll invite them to dine with us tonight."

Kitty didn't relish that, but she agreed. "Shall I put the rest in hand?"

"I will be very grateful."

That seemed sincere, and Kitty left in a pleasant halo of purpose. This was the sort of thing he'd married her for, and this she could do.

Chapter 18

Consulting with Henry about appropriate wedding celebrations and then making plans with the Quillers took up most of the rest of the day, but Kitty didn't have to prepare for a grand dinner. The dowager declined the invitation for herself and Isabella, in brief and without explanation.

Kitty wondered what Isabella thought of that and was tempted to invade the other side of the house to speak to her directly, but she remembered the hostile young woman she'd faced before. She doubted Isabella would appreciate any concern.

If the meal would be only for herself and Braydon, they would eat in the small dining room, and though she was hungry, she wanted nothing grand. She summoned the cook to her boudoir and discussed matters.

The woman was guarded, but perhaps not hostile. When Kitty explained that she wanted the servants to enjoy some treats tonight, the cook suggested that beefsteaks could be cut from a sirloin joint.

Kitty suspected that she was supposed to balk at that, but she agreed. "And for dessert?" she asked.

"There's a suet pudding cooking, ma'am."

"Then we won't waste it, but are there any little treats that would finish up the meal?"

"There's some nice cheeses in the larder, ma'am, but

to speak plainly, most of the servants wouldn't appreciate them. They prefer sweet to savory. Er . . . there are the candied fruits, ma'am."

"Yes?"

"The dowager Lady Dauntry is particularly fond of those, ma'am."

Kitty sensed another test. "I presume we can obtain more. Very well. A small piece to go with the wine. Would the servants prefer a sweeter wine?"

"Yes, ma'am, most of them."

"I'll consult Lord Dauntry about that."

Kitty sent the cook on her way, then hurried to talk to Braydon.

"You want to serve my finest port to the servants?"

"Do you count the cost of ammunition, sir?"

"Always, but you're right. However, may I suggest a punch? Rum, brandy, and such, as sweet as you like."

She smiled. "Brilliant! We'll overrun them entirely."

He took her hand, a smile in his eyes. "Tell me you're enjoying this as much as it seems."

"I am. I enjoy a challenge."

"Then I expect to give you great pleasure."

She took his words at face value, but then he raised her hand and kissed it, his lips pressing warmly against her skin. The look in his eyes told her he was as aware of the coming night as she was, and perhaps with the same anticipation. But first they had the evening to navigate. All must go perfectly.

Kitty had Henry choose her gown.

"The red, ma'am. It's elegant but not ostentatious. A pity you don't have grander jewels to wear with it. There should be some belonging to the viscountcy." A gentle hint.

"I'll look into it."

"Sit you down, ma'am, and I'll brush out your hair and redress it."

"It will do."

"It will not. It's coming out all over."

"Cap?" Kitty saw the maid's expression and sat down with a sigh. "It's completely appropriate for a married lady to wear a cap."

"Not on her wedding day, ma'am," Henry said, pulling out pins. Kitty had forgotten that Henry had never seen it down. "That's quite a sight," the maid said as she started to brush it.

"And quite a lot of work. My first husband liked it."

"I'm sure your second will, too."

Kitty sincerely hoped that was true. She still feared disappointing him. "I've often wished it was smoother," she said. "I've tried rinses and oils, but it has a mind of its own."

"Like the head beneath it, I suspect."

Kitty chuckled. "You suspect hair grows out of the mind? What of the men with none at all?"

"Certainly they're not all stupid, so there's an end to that theory."

Kitty was thinking about jewelry. To demand the viscountcy's jewels on her wedding day seemed grasping, but the toast in the servants' hall would be a formal appearance, and she wanted to impress.

She remembered that Henry was an old familiar servant to Braydon's family. When her hair was cleverly pinned up in rolls of curls, Kitty said, "You could mention jewelry to Lord Dauntry."

In the mirror she saw Henry give her a look, but she said, "I could, ma'am. I'll dress you first." She went to pick up the red dress.

Kitty stood. "Could you call me Kitty? In private."

Henry smiled. "I could, yes. As I won't be here for long."

Kitty was suddenly saddened by that.

"I won't abandon you," Henry said, "but my place is with Miss Ecclestall, and in time you'll find a maid to suit you." She dropped the gown over Kitty's head and then fastened it. "There. Now you're ready, I'll go and speak to his lordship."

She soon returned with Braydon, who had remained in the town finery he'd worn for the wedding. Kitty thought his look was admiring, and perhaps more than that. She hoped so.

"No one admits to knowing where the Braydon jewels are," he said. "The dowager has some that she claims to be gifts to her, and as best I can tell, that's true. I will uncover the truth, but I've made minor amends." He had a box in his hands. "If I'd known of that gown, I would have chosen red stones."

He gave her the box and she opened it to see a necklace. Smooth, translucent yellow stones were surrounded by what must be tiny diamonds that sparkled in the candlelight. The size of the stones and a clustering design made it a fit companion for the ring. It was probably too splendid for the occasion, but it would impress.

"It's lovely," she said. "Thank you."

He took it out of the case. "May I?"

She turned so he could put it around her neck and fasten it, his fingers brushing at the nape. That had always been a particularly sensitive area for her, and she inhaled. Hands on her shoulders, he turned her toward the long mirror.

"Perhaps it isn't so poor a choice," he said.

The cider-toned stones were a bridge between the cherry-red dress and her red hair, and they picked up details of the beaded tapestry belt. The diamonds sparkled. She put in the matching earrings herself.

"I have another gift," he said. "Which will also suit, I believe."

Kitty hadn't noticed that Henry had brought something wrapped in white muslin. Unwrapped, it proved to be a gorgeous shawl in shades of brown, red, and gold. As soon as Kitty touched it, she knew it was genuine cashmere, made of wool but smooth as silk, with the design all hand embroidered. Imitation shawls were woven in Britain, but this must have cost a small fortune. He'd purchased these things in London between proposal and wedding.

She didn't know whether to gush thanks or be careless about it, so she simply said, "Thank you."

Henry arranged it, draping it over Kitty's elbows so that the fringes on both sides fell just short of the ground and the lush end embroidery was displayed. Undoubtedly, she looked magnificent. Magnificent enough to be a duchess rather than a mere viscountess.

He'd provided the weaponry she needed.

She turned to him. "I feel I should have a wedding gift for you, but I've not so much as embroidered you a handkerchief. If I had, it wouldn't have been a treasure. I'm not an elegant seamstress."

"You've made a gift of yourself, my dear. I could want nothing more."

A suitable thing for any bridegroom to say. Weak of her to wish it meant more.

Kitty told Sillikin that she'd have to stay in the room, where she had food and water. She'd swear the dog sighed. Probably she was missing the lively atmosphere of the parsonage.

They went downstairs, and Kitty again felt as if she were going onstage. Was Isabella watching from the gallery? She hoped the girl was, and would see she was outmatched.

Even so, it was a relief to enter the small dining room, but even there she couldn't be entirely comfortable. Quiller supervised, and two footmen served them. Kitty was strongly tempted to order them away so she could relax, but for today at least, she would attempt nobility.

"Have you traveled to Kashmir, my lord?" she asked as she ate some excellent clear soup.

"Never farther east than Turkey. The court there is known as the Sublime Porte, after a gate that leads into the state apartments."

"Rather like British administration being referred to as Whitehall, after a street?"

"Very like."

He went on to speak of foreign places of interest, and she supplied the occasional question. As the next course was laid, they moved on to the war, where she could contribute some of Marcus's stories. Braydon dwelt on Marcus's glory at Roleia, and she realized that was for the servants. She was the widow of a hero. She dropped Cateril Manor and Lord and Lady Cateril into the stream of words. Her husband had been of the aristocracy. Neither of them spoke of her more humble origins.

At last she could rise to leave him with his port and brandy, but he rose to go with her. "As the drawing room is unheated, my dear, perhaps we can take coffee in your boudoir."

"Of course, my lord." Kitty turned to Quiller. "Please let us know when it's time for the toast."

They went upstairs and into her sitting room and closed the door. They looked at each other and Kitty asked, "Do actors feel like this as they come offstage?"

"I have no idea, but you played the part extremely well."

"I did my best with the reality," she countered. "This is who I am now."

"You say it with the voice of doom."

"Do I? Like flies to wanton gods? But no. Unlike you, I had a choice."

"Regretting it?"

Kitty was saved by a noise. "There's Sillikin scratching at the door." She opened it, and the dog rushed in as if deprived of her company for weeks. Kitty picked her up for a cuddle, but Braydon was waiting for an answer.

"No regrets. I've had a more purposeful day than in a long time and I've found it satisfying."

"And tiring?"

She almost said yes, but realized he could be delicately asking if she would be too tired for her duties.

"Not at all," she said with a bright smile.

She'd strip naked now if not for the servants' toast.

Braydon knew he should be keeping a cool mind, but how, when alone with Kit Kat in her red and gold pagan magnificence? He was no more immune than any other man.

She'd played her part splendidly before the servants, never taking a wrong step. When he remembered their first encounter in the lane, that could have been a different woman, and yet he knew that she'd been honest when she'd said all aspects were true. How was a man to deal with such a wife? Coolly, but that could prove impossible with the thought of the marriage bed woven through every moment. Were her thoughts of anticipation or trepidation? Were his?

He desired her now, but the lack of prologue made this too much like an encounter at a high-class brothel. At the same time, the delicate steps of a courtship would be mere playacting with the denouement already decided. They could get the first engagement over now, but there was the performance in the servants' hall to get through. So they drank coffee, this time with brandy, and spoke of foreign parts and lighter army matters.

When she mentioned the premature peace celebrations of 1814 he said, "You must have enjoyed them, all the same."

"When I could. By then, Marcus couldn't get out much."

Angry on her behalf, he asked, "Didn't he have a manservant to keep him company?"

"He did, but Tranton served as footman as well and much more. We had only three servants—Tranton, Lindy as general maid, and Mrs. Ipple, who came in once a week to do the hard scrubbing."

"No cook?"

"Lindy and I could do simple cookery, but we often bought in."

He should have realized how different her life had been to his, but Cateril Manor had come between, like a veil.

"Yet you kept open house for military men."

"Marcus couldn't get out, so they came to him. He was well liked, you know."

"Yes."

She looked at him over her cup. "I remember. You asked about me in London."

He could understand her disliking that, but he thought she seemed wary. *Zeus. Had her intimate experiences been not with her crippled husband, but with one or more of the young men who remembered Kit Kat with such enthusiasm? Would some of them have sought her out now for reasons other than marriage?* If Cateril hadn't liked her jaunting out with his friends, perhaps he'd had reason.

She suddenly rose and excused herself. It was probably to use the chamber pot, but she might have read his thoughts. She was damnably perceptive. The dog lifted her head to observe, gave him a stare, but then clearly decided there was no need to intervene. Would that the animal were right.

He remembered returning to the Abbey doubting the wisdom of marrying Kit Kat, but he'd ended up going through with it. But that was because of Isabella, not a sorceress's spell. Or was it? He couldn't lie to himself. When he'd gone to the parsonage and seen her in that gown, he lost all remnants of the ability to let her go.

Perhaps it went back further. He wasn't a liar, but he'd lied to Captain Edison about her whereabouts.

He was stuck now. As the marriage service said, for better or for worse.

She returned just as Quiller came to announce that all was ready. He gave her his arm, and they went down to find most of the servants around the long table. A few of the lowest stood ready to serve their betters. There were layers at every level of society.

Everyone rose. Quiller made a congratulatory speech and proposed a toast with the punch. Everyone had a glass, even the servants' servants, and even the youngest. Everyone drank. Undoubtedly they were enjoying the treats, but the mood was still guarded. They were still unsure who was in command at Beauchamp Abbey, and to whom they should give allegiance.

Braydon thanked them and announced that there would soon be a ball for the servants and tenants to celebrate the event. Then he added that all the Abbey servants would receive a bonus of ten percent of their wages on the Christmas quarter day. That brightened a few faces.

He and Kitty returned upstairs in silence, for while the servants were all belowstairs, the dowager and Isabella could be lurking and listening. How would it be if he took her into his arms and kissed her in the way he was burning to?

Marble stairs.

Most uncomfortable.

Once they were in the boudoir again, they would be free. Some sweet words, some kisses, and on to bed.

Sweet words would be false.
Straight to kisses?
Would that be to fall straight into Kit Kat's enchantments and become another adoring fool?

Again they were in an awkwardness. Kitty was tingling with expectation but also fretful about the hows and whens. She wanted to suggest they get it over with, but there was something odd in his manner. She didn't want him to think her a shameless hussy.

When they entered her boudoir she saw the pretty gaming table with the marquetry chessboard on the top. She had no intention of playing chess with a man like Braydon. She fiddled with the top and found how to flip it to reveal a baize-covered surface with indentations at the corners to hold the players' coins or counters. "Do you play cards?"

"Doesn't everyone?"

"Some have moral objections. We could play piquet."

"I have an excellent memory for cards," he warned.

"Then I'll hope for luck, but as my husband is responsible for my gaming debts, it hardly matters. In any case, I've only ever played for penny points."

She took out the cards and counters, but he said, "Counters aren't much use in piquet. There's paper in your desk."

She hadn't yet explored the walnut writing desk, but indeed there was paper, and he brought a sheet to the table, along with a silver inkpot and a pen. The paper was monogrammed. She picked it up, surprised that it looked so fresh. The imprint read KD. Kathryn Dauntry, her new name.

"Mine?" she asked.

"I purchased it in Town."

"Thank you," she said, absorbing his thoughtfulness.

Or was it simple efficiency? She could ask, *What if I'd jilted you?* He would have responded, *It was only a small amount.* How did she know him so well and yet not understand him at all?

As he shuffled the cards, she wondered if many wedding nights were as awkward as this. She supposed most couples had courted for some months and were ready when the time came. She'd heard of one couple who'd scandalized their servants by rushing upstairs as soon as they entered their house, shedding clothing as they went. Such impetuous passion sounded like fun, but there'd be nothing like that tonight.

She remembered hearing about the Regent's wedding night. He hadn't been the Regent then, only the Prince of Wales, obliged to marry before Parliament would pay his debts. The marriage had taken place in Germany by proxy, but when he'd met Caroline of Brunswick, he'd taken an instant dislike of her.

Braydon suddenly asked, "Do you like cognac?"

"I've only ever drunk it for medicinal purposes."

"Then I hope it wasn't the finest. Cateril didn't drink it?"

"He was a claret and ale man, but he didn't overindulge."

Opium. That was another matter.

"I'll get some."

It was as if he wanted to escape.

It was said that the Regent's bride had been unclean and uncouth, which was possibly true, for she'd behaved oddly ever since, creating scandals all around Europe and supposedly taking lovers. They must have consummated the marriage, for Princess Charlotte had been the result, but they'd soon separated.

Kitty fiddled with the quill pen. How had Caroline been so intolerable that they'd never conceived other children? It was a simple enough business, and if they'd done their duty, there wouldn't be such fears about the succession.

She put the pen down. She couldn't imagine why she would be intolerable, and she'd thought she'd felt the earthy desires between them at times, but clearly there was a reason for wooing and courtship. This situation was odd.

He returned with a decanter and two glasses and poured some brandy for each of them. Then they began the game.

It had been some time since Kitty had played, and he was good. Very good. She didn't think it was entirely his memory. He knew what to do with what he remembered. She began to enjoy the challenge, even though she was losing. She was having to stretch her mind.

"Ten shillings down," she said later, placing her cards on the table. "My luck was insufficient to overcome your skill. You could make your living as a card sharp."

"'Sharp' implies cheating," he objected, but mildly.

"Perhaps any extreme talent is." She sipped more brandy. The fine cognac was far more pleasant than the brandy she'd drunk before, and this was her second glass. "Is it fair if a strong man fights a weak?"

He seemed relaxed, one hand at ease on the table, fingers light on the stem of his glass. "You'd have wars fought between scrupulously balanced armies?"

"I'd not have wars fought at all."

He raised his glass and toasted her. "I crown you queen of the world. But are talents not of God's providing?"

She shook her head. "No, please. Not a philosophical discussion this late in the day." She glanced at the clock. Ten o'clock. Not so very late, but she couldn't bear to draw this out any further.

"Time for bed," she said. Damnation, the brandy had made her blunt.

But he responded, "It is."

He rose, picked up the decanter and his glass, bowed slightly, and left.

Kitty rang for Henry, then drained the last of her brandy. She'd never expected to be so nervous about this.

Chapter 19

In his bedroom Braydon rang for Johns, still plagued by ridiculous uncertainties.

Nightshirt or no nightshirt?

He should probably have asked which she'd prefer, given that she was a plain-talking, experienced woman. Nightshirt would be the safe choice, but when had that ever been his way? Wise if possible, wary sometimes, but cowardly safety? No.

Even though they'd rarely touched, he was aware that she was a sensual woman. She showed it in the way she enjoyed sweet coffee, cake, and brandy. He saw it in her movements and her glances. She didn't ogle him, but at times her gaze had heated his blood.

She'd been a widow for over two years, and he doubted that she'd sought consolation. No matter what her previous behavior, impropriety would have been close to impossible at Cateril Manor.

He didn't even know what he wanted. If she was as hungry and passionate as he sensed, this night could be memorable. Too passionate, and it would support his fears that she'd not kept her marriage vows. Could a badly injured man have satisfied an adventurous wanton? He recognized a base instinct beneath these concerns. Whatever and whoever Kit Kat had experienced before, he needed to outdo every man jack of them.

Johns arrived with the washing water and the usual sour face.

"I'm not willingly lingering in the rural wasteland, Johns. Sometimes fate dictates."

"Yes, milord." Johns used "milord" rather than "sir" as a rebuke.

"In a while we'll be able to spend more time in Town."

"It is to be hoped for, milord."

Braydon reined in his temper. To be picking a fight now was proof he was all on edge. Why? Kit Kat was a box of surprises, but she'd have no shocks for him in bed.

Then he remembered how often she'd surprised him. *To hell with it.*

He dismissed his valet. His wife should have had enough time to prepare.

Kitty told herself there was nothing to be nervous about, but she couldn't block awareness that she'd be coupling with a different man. After a day spent mostly in Braydon's company, she felt she should know him, but the marble box remained closed. She liked him better, but she couldn't guess what he was thinking. Or expecting.

Henry had undressed her and brushed out her hair in a way Kitty could only think of as motherly. How peculiar. The lady's maid was unmarried, so Kitty could read her a lecture on the subject of marital duties.

Before her marriage to Marcus, her mother had not been particularly informative. She'd given a mechanical description of what would happen and then added, "If he's able. If not, don't mention it."

It had all sounded so odd, Kitty hadn't been sure which to hope for, but above all she'd been curious. She'd arrived at her delayed wedding night eager to learn more, but also eager to do her wifely duty. If he were able. She had loved

Marcus—adored him, in fact—and after a couple of days in his company, she'd been even more deeply devoted. He'd been so kind, so tender, and so *grateful*.

He'd also begun to touch her and kiss her in more intimate ways, which she'd enjoyed very much, so when the time came, she hadn't been confused or fearful. She'd been carried along by love, desire, and Marcus's kindness. She remembered that he'd apologized at least three times for the awkwardness. Despite the pain of losing her maidenhead, it had been lovely, and she'd learned how to do it better so that it brought both of them pleasure, despite his injuries.

This husband was uninjured, so it should present no difficulties at all.

After Kitty had washed behind the screen, Henry passed through the nightgown. That showed how little she knew.

"Just the robe," Kitty said.

Once wrapped in the blue woolen robe, she emerged and sent Henry away. She needed a moment to steady herself against returning doubts.

Marcus had always seemed pleased with her, but he'd been so damaged. Perhaps that had led him to overlook her flaws. She didn't have the body of a Greek goddess or the face of a Botticelli Madonna. What's more, Braydon hadn't chosen her from a host of others. She'd been conveniently to hand.

She was sure he could have—had!—attracted the finest, most beautiful women to his bed, in England, France, Spain, and even Turkey. Now he had her.

She studied herself in the mirror. Her nose seemed even longer than usual and her chin squarer. At least her hair was unchanged. Henry had thought Braydon would like it, but what did Henry know? He probably preferred hair as sleek and polished as he was.

Enough. The choice had been his. It would be unreasonable for him to find fault now, but he could complain of tardiness. She extinguished the candles and hurried to the adjoining door.

Sillikin came with her.

Kitty crouched down. "No. I'm married again, so you can't sleep in my bed. Oh, I wish you could truly understand me. Stay!" Then she slipped through the door into her husband's bedroom, closing it quickly in case the dog disobeyed, and turning.

He wasn't in bed. He was standing facing her, in a fawn banyan robe. He, too, had extinguished the candles, so only firelight lit him, casting a ruddy tone on his blond hair.

One difference from before: this husband preferred less light.

"I'm sorry," she said, slightly breathless. "I took too much time."

"You must always take as much time as you wish." His tone seemed strange, but that was probably her nerves. Her heart was thumping.

And he wasn't in the bed.

Another difference.

All she could do was carry on. She undid her robe and took it off. His intent look could be appreciative. Or not. He was so damnably unreadable.

After a moment he said, "Your hair is magnificent."

A small, relieved breath escaped. "It will never be smooth and shiny."

"Nor should it be."

She placed her robe neatly over a chair, wondering how to proceed. She was sure he was experienced, but perhaps not of marriage. Whores and concubines could well do things differently. In fact, she'd seen some interesting pictures. In chairs. On swings. Almost upside down. She could only continue as normal, but he was still standing there.

"If you would get into bed, husband?"

He smiled. Perhaps it was only the softening effect of firelight, but it seemed untarnished by other emotions. He took off his robe and laid it neatly over a chair, just as she had. With Marcus, his valet had already settled him in bed and he'd worn a nightshirt.

She was glad Braydon had turned away to disrobe, or he might have seen her reaction to a naked male. And such a one! She'd known he lacked significant wounds and was well formed, but not that he would be perfection. His long, sleek muscles reminded her of a statue she'd seen of a classical athlete. She'd read that such athletes oiled their bodies. A vision of oiling her husband turned anxiety into a flush of pure desire. Instantly she clenched inside.

He glanced at her only briefly before climbing into the bed and lying there, on his back, just as he should. And ready. There'd be no need to help that along. Thank heavens, for she was ready, too. It had been so long, so very long, and he was stretched out in manly perfection, waiting for her pleasure.

She climbed onto the bed and straddled his thighs, smiling at him. It was only polite to smile, but it was genuine. He was so beautiful, and his thick, thrusting cock promised her such pleasure.

She slid a finger inside herself, then stroked the cream up his penis to the tip. It jerked. He inhaled. Smiling even more, she slid down over him, slowly, slowly, appreciating every inch, but watching him for signs of discomfort. But this man didn't have poorly healed bones and knotted sinews, and the way he was filling her was pure ecstasy.

She forced her eyes open to be sure he was all right.

He was watching her. His lips were parted, but in the dim light she couldn't read much. It was for him to object if he needed to, or to guide her if he wanted something more.

She was aching with need and could race toward her pleasure, but she made herself move slowly, trying to serve his needs, as a good wife should. But her eyes kept closing on their own as she sank deeper into the sliding heat.

His hands gripped her knees. She looked, but he wasn't objecting. The grip was from his passion. *Thank heaven.* She leaned forward to brace her hands on the bed on either side of him, and raced to the relief she so desperately needed.

Suddenly he pumped up into her, meeting her movements and thrusting her up again and again and again. Marcus had never been capable of such strength and she gasped at the power of it, driven by him into a blinding white heat.

After the release, she almost collapsed onto him, but corrected in time and settled beside him, heart pounding, hot and sweaty, still rippling with pleasure, but so very, very satisfied. She kissed his shoulder, stroked his chest. She could very easily purr.

His hand covered hers, but the silence became uncomfortable. Marcus had always thanked her. It had become a rote courtesy, but she'd come to expect it. He'd meant it, but she'd sometimes thought it would be pleasant to break the pattern. Not into complete silence, however. Had she done something wrong? She leaned up to look at him. He was looking at her, but his lids were lowered, his face in shadow and completely unreadable.

Then he took a handful of her hair, raised it, and let it drift down. She almost said, *Marcus used to do that,* but stopped herself in time. Then he cradled her face and kissed her gently. Perhaps that was his way of saying thank you.

It seemed she was acceptable.

Braydon considered his sleeping wife. In general he preferred to sleep alone, and if they'd been in her bed he would have left, but it would be churlish to send her on her way now, especially after such generosity. Especially after a silence he hadn't seemed able to break. What should a gentleman husband say after such a performance?

He hadn't expected that, though he might have if he'd accepted that she'd known only one man, Marcus Cateril, crippled by serious wounds. Cateril would have been put to bed by his manservant, and Kitty would have joined him. When summoned? That wasn't Cateril's fault, but it seemed too much like a sultan summoning a woman from his harem. Had Kitty been allowed to decline?

Irrational to be vexed on her behalf. In truth, he was vexed with himself for his doubts about her. She'd known only one man, and Cateril had not been a thoughtless husband. She'd expected to find her own pleasure. Now she lay sound asleep, tangled in her magnificent hair, her generous lips relaxed. There would be more kissing next time. Abundant kissing, and other pleasures that might be new to her. He didn't think she'd object.

Here was one blessing from the mess his life was in. He had a frankly sexual lover in his marriage bed.

He sank into sleep himself, thinking that every man should marry a widow. And then smiling at the impossibility of it.

Kitty woke in a strange bed to strange smells and strange everything.

Of course, she was in Braydon's bed. She was turned

away from him on the very edge, where she'd used to sleep with Marcus to try not to bump into him in the night and possibly hurt him. And to avoid the way his arms sometimes flailed around, as if he were fighting.

She rolled toward the center but she couldn't see much in the dark. The fire had gone out and the air was nippy on her nose. It must still be the middle of the night.

She considered the event.

She thought it had gone well. There'd been something about that kiss that denied any anger or disappointment. She certainly felt none.

It was going to be lovely not to have to worry about putting weight on a painful place. She could probably bounce up and down on his hips if she wanted, which had her fighting a chuckle at the thought.

But the way he'd surged up into her. *Oh, my!*

He might be easy to rouse again, but she stopped herself from reaching out to try. She had the impression from Marcus that there was no such thing as a too-demanding wife, and that only his physical state had constrained him, but that might not be true of all men, and Braydon seemed to prefer control.

She began to fall back into sleep, but then remembered that she had a bed of her own. Heavens, she'd made a mistake! A viscountess was supposed to return to her own bed.

She slipped carefully out of bed, shivering in the cold air as she fumbled around for her robe. She wrapped it closely around herself and picked her way out of one dark room into another. She heard Sillikin, so didn't yelp when warm fur brushed against her in eager welcome.

"Yes, yes," Kitty said quietly, "but I'm going to trip over you."

She finally made it to the bed and climbed into it. Sillikin scrambled up the bed steps, claws scratching.

"Oh, very well. Come on in."

It was a long time since the warming pans had been worked through the bed, and the sheets were cold. The small dog did little to warm them. Huddling and rubbing herself, Kitty thought that the aristocratic way of doing things was stupid. But, then, Marcus had been an aristocrat. Perhaps it was the wealthy way of doing things. Whichever, it was most unfair to the woman. She was still grumbling in her mind when she fell back asleep.

Chapter 20

Kitty woke to a noise. Sillikin was already out of bed, snuffling around the gray-clad maid who was making up the fire.

"Beg pardon for waking you, milady." It sounded like a sincere beg, as if she expected to be scolded or worse.

Kitty realized she was naked and stayed under the covers. "No matter. Carry on."

Sillikin went to the door. This was definitely a problem. At Cateril and the parsonage, Kitty had let the dog out to find her own way to the kitchen and the outside, but she might not know the way here as yet. More important, Kitty wasn't entirely sure it was safe. She found it hard to imagine anyone hurting a friendly little dog, but there were problems in this house.

When the fire was going, Kitty said, "Thank you. Please take my dog down and let her outside. Then return her here. And send Miss Oldswick to me."

The maid curtsied. "Yes, milady."

Sillikin went with her trustingly, already seeing a new friend. Soon Henry arrived with chocolate and fresh-baked bread, followed by the maid with a large jug of steaming water and Sillikin, tail wagging with enthusiasm for a new day.

Kitty was already in her nightgown and robe, sitting at the small table by the window.

Once the maid had left, Henry said, "I didn't ask what breakfast you like."

"That's excellent, thank you. When there's good fresh fruit, I'll have some of that as well."

Kitty could sense Henry wanting to ask about the night, but of course she didn't. Kitty tried to give an impression of contentment, because Henry was a spy for Lady Sophonisbe. It wasn't difficult, but she couldn't relax until Henry left.

Kitty was spreading butter on her second piece of bread when the adjoining door opened and Braydon came in, only partly dressed. It was startling to see him less than perfectly turned out. He wore boots and breeches, but only a shirt above the waist, and it was open-necked. That glimpse of chest was enough to light a spark in her, but he said, "I'm going for a ride. Do you ride?"

"No."

"Would you like to?"

"I don't know."

"So many things to explore."

Kitty sensed underlying meanings to that.

She glanced at Sillikin. The dog was lying in front of the fire. She'd raised her head to look, but she wasn't staring. A step in the right direction.

"You don't object to my being out for perhaps an hour?" he asked.

Kitty did, but only because of lust. She'd wondered how they'd be together this morning, but the answer seemed to be *the same as before*.

"Of course not. I have plenty to do." She finished buttering her bread. "But I'm not going near you-know-who until you're by my side."

"Ah, I did hope to avoid that."

She glanced at him and saw that hint of a smile in his eyes. It had become precious to her. "Shirking the battle, sir?"

"There are times when it would be a very wise thing to do."

"Dishonorable to be wise?"

"In this crazed world, frequently."

She thought he might kiss her again, but he inclined his head and returned to his rooms. She regretted the lack of a kiss.

Kitty spread black currant jam on her bread and enjoyed a bite, thinking. She had not displeased him, even by lingering in his bed, but it would be pleasant to have a more positive response. Open approval, or even admiration. Was the hint of a smile as much as she would ever get? In the biblical sense, she knew her husband today, but in other senses, he was still a mystery.

Oh, by their agreement, they would be mostly apart. Why bother about these things?

Kitty washed and began to dress, by which time Henry had returned to put her into her outer clothes. She chose a sage green woolen gown because it was her warmest, and an extra flannel petticoat underneath. Today she planned to go through the whole house with Mrs. Quiller and put her stamp on it.

She added a cap with relief. She'd worn one for a decade and felt undressed without. A check in the mirror confirmed that she looked like the lady of the house. Perhaps not grand enough to be a viscountess, but there was the ring to compensate.

"My cloak, please, Henry. First, I'll take Sillikin for a walk."

Henry brought it and asked, "What bonnet, dear?"

She probably should wear one, but she was walking in

her own garden. If she was mistress here, she could set the rules.

Once outside, Kitty found the air even colder for being damp and the sky overcast, but she felt immediate relief from escaping the house. That wasn't a good sign, but in time, with changes, it would become a comfortable home.

She decided to explore the outbuildings, heading first for extensive ones that were probably the stables, despite being built as a miniature of the house and painted as perfectly white. When close, she realized the first high wall was roofless. It was a walled garden, so probably the kitchen garden.

Kitty put Sillikin on the leash and explored. When she went through the door she encountered an affronted stare from a wiry man who was directing two others in some digging project.

But then he doffed his hat and said, "My lady."

Kitty gave him good morning and asked his name.

"Garrison, m'lady."

"Everything looks in good order, Garrison," she said, trying to look as if she understood what she saw. She gave him leave to return to his work and strolled a path in spurious inspection.

Much of the ground was empty, but there were some tall green plants and other smaller ones beneath glass bottles or inside low glass frames. From Cateril Manor she knew vegetables could be kept beyond their season by such means, but no more than that. She was skilled at choosing good fruits and vegetables at market, but knew nothing about growing them. A closer look at the tall plants showed little cabbages growing along the stem, larger at the bottom and smaller toward the top. Heavens, they were brussels sprouts. She'd never known they grew that way.

Branches wired to walls would be fruits, she supposed.

A glass house ran along one wall, full of plants. She'd like to explore in there, but not under the wary observation of the gardeners, who seemed worried that she'd run amok in their domain.

She left and continued on to the stables. They were unmistakable because of the smell. Remembering the alarmed and alarming white horse, Kitty picked up Sillikin before going into the stable yard. A black dog slunk out of a building, growling.

A bowlegged, sinewy man followed. "Down, Roller." He touched his forelock and said, "Milady," but with a wariness that was becoming tiresome.

Then Baker came out of a stall, smiling. "Good morning, milady. Can I do something for you?"

No sign of the white horse. *Ah. Braydon is probably riding it.*

"Does someone have time to show me round?" Kitty asked. "I know little of horses and stables, having spent most of my life in London."

She saw Baker silently defer to the older man and be given the job. *Excellent.*

Baker took her through rooms where food, straw, tack, and other necessities were kept. Sillikin wriggled, keen to explore, but Kitty said, "No."

"Most of the horses are in the paddock, ma'am," Baker said, "but Corsair's here. We're keeping an eye on him 'cos of a bit of a limp. He's Miss Godyson-Braydon's mount."

Kitty remembered the black. "Has she had Corsair a long time?" Kitty asked.

"Not as I understand, ma'am. She had a gray before."

So upon the deaths, even the stables had been adjusted to mourning. "Are all the horses black?" she asked.

"No, ma'am." Baker took her to the paddock rail, and she saw five horses there. Two brown ones stood out as prime specimens, and she recognized Braydon's curricle team. The other three were various shades of brown and didn't look highbred.

"What are they used for?" Kitty asked.

"Not much," Baker said. "Toby and Trump were the late viscount's riding hacks, and Teapot is used with the dog cart."

"Teapot? Who named her that?"

"Miss Isabella, as I understand, ma'am."

So Isabella had been playful when younger, and a romantic more recently. She'd named her black horse after Byron's *The Corsair*. That could be something to build on.

"Do they all just loll around doing nothing?" she asked.

"They're exercised, ma'am, and Teapot sometimes takes Mrs. Quiller on errands."

"She drives herself?"

"Yes, ma'am."

"Is it difficult?"

"Not with Teapot, ma'am."

"Could I try?"

There were probably a host of duties she should attend to, but being able to drive would offer freedom. Kitty acknowledged that the real reason was that she didn't want to return to the house until Braydon was back. Cowardly, but there it was.

"I don't see why not, ma'am," Baker said. "Unless Mr. Varley has any objection."

He, Kitty assumed, was the head groom. There was probably an interesting balance of power between Varley and Baker, his lordship's personal groom, but it seemed Baker could handle it. Kitty suspected all Braydon's servants were carefully chosen.

Kitty let Sillikin explore on the leash as the gig was brought out and checked, and Teapot was brought in from the paddock, placidly ready to oblige. Kitty was glad she'd never have to harness the animal, for it all seemed very complicated, but the two-wheeled vehicle itself was much sturdier than the curricle.

All the same, when it was time to climb into the seat, she had to hide nervousness. Baker was already in position and clearly had the animal under control, but the thought that she might soon be in charge could almost make her back out. She put Sillikin down by her feet and told her to stay still, hoping that made sense.

"Shall we go anywhere in particular, ma'am?" Baker asked.

"No," Kitty said, but then changed her mind. "Let's visit the parsonage."

It would be eccentric to go there the day after her wedding, but Kitty smiled at the thought of driving up to the door and of seeing Ruth.

Baker drove round to the drive and out through the gates, turning onto the road. Then he paused to pass the reins to Kitty. "It's a simple route from here, ma'am— flat and almost straight, and Teapot is as calm as could be. But you should learn to hold the reins right."

He showed her how to wind them through the gloved fingers on her left hand so that she could tighten the left or right by turning her hand. Then he put the whip in her right.

"I can't whip the poor beast."

"And you'll not need to, ma'am, but you should start right. The whip's mainly in case the horse misbehaves. A touch brings it back in line. Now just say, 'Go on.'"

Kitty did, and Teapot set off at a walk.

"Say, 'faster.'"

"Faster." Teapot sped to a trot. "Does it understand?"

"Only the sound, ma'am."

They were rolling along a little too fast for Kitty's comfort, and the gig's springs didn't provide a smooth ride, but she could truly say, "This is splendid! I'll soon be able to go where I want, when I want."

"Early days, ma'am," Baker said, sounding worried.

She flashed him a smile. "Don't worry. I won't attempt the curricle."

He might have blanched. "Nor anywhere alone for a while, ma'am. Think about stray dogs, birds, even cows in the road."

Kitty remembered when a bird had flown out in front of the curricle. "Teapot might go wild?"

"I doubt that, ma'am, but his lordship'd have my hide if you harmed yourself."

"Don't worry. I have no idea how to harness her, and I'm not even sure I'm strong enough. I won't attempt anything without a suitable companion."

In reality, Teapot was following the road for herself, giving Kitty nothing to do, but she still enjoyed the sense of control and the confidence that she could soon be able to come and go around the area with ease. The only hazard they encountered was a two-horse cart lumbering along and taking up a good part of the road. Baker took the reins to steer past that.

They approached the parsonage down the lane toward the village, so Kitty didn't have to deal with the busy green. She managed to turn the vehicle into the space before the door, only ending up at a slightly odd angle.

"Victory!" she declared.

Teapot jibbed at the sharp voice, but Baker was already at the horse's head.

Ruth came out and stared. "Kitty! What on earth are you up to now?"

Kitty managed to climb down without assistance and lifted Sillikin down. "Driving lessons."

"But it's the day after your wedding."

"Braydon's out riding, and I want to be independent."

"Without a bonnet?"

Kitty put a hand to her head. She'd completely forgotten that. "Don't fuss. No one saw me."

Ruth shook her head and asked, "Have you come for any particular reason?" Then, "Is something the matter?"

"No, not at all. I merely needed a destination. Oh, there goes Sillikin, in search of friends." The dog had shot into the parsonage. Kitty turned back to the groom. "Can Teapot stand for a short while?"

"Yes, milady. And if you're longer, I'll walk her around a bit."

Kitty went into the house with Ruth. "No need for alarm. I simply took the impulse to learn to drive. It's quite easy."

"Not necessarily."

"Oh, very well. It's easy on a quiet road with a groom at my side. But it will be delightful once I'm more experienced. It's also delightful to speak without wondering who's listening."

"What do you mean? Come into the parlor. This might not be the Abbey, but do you want everyone here hearing everything?"

Kitty went in, but she was feeling scolded and wondered if it was justified. She certainly shouldn't have gone driving without a bonnet. "I'm not intending to share scandals," she said when the door was shut. "But when you visited the Abbey, did you notice how the entrance hall is like a theater stage, with the upstairs galleries seeing and hearing everything?"

"No, but I can see what you mean. Oh, Kitty. Are you unhappy?"

"No! Not at all. The place is a challenge, but I expected that. Dauntry and I are coming to understand each other quite well. I came here simply to practice driving, and because I wanted to see you. But I do have a few questions."

"About what? Sit down."

Kitty did so. "About the fifth viscount and his wife."

"Oh. Why?"

"Because I sense a mystery. Diane Dauntry left before you came here, but does anyone ever mention the event? She can't have simply disappeared."

Ruth shrugged. "It's one of those subjects that people don't talk about, and as you know, the Abbey keeps its distance."

"But some of the servants come from local families, and I'm sure the Misses Purslow will know what's to be known. People gossip."

"And shouldn't. Why are you poking into it?"

"Don't make a prune face at me. Dauntry pointed out that ignorance is weakness. He's trying to understand everything about the Abbey and the family there, and I want to help him." Kitty thought of a nobler motive. "In addition, Isabella might want to know about her mother."

"Ah. I'm sorry if I was sharp. What of the lady's family? They must know where she went. Probably abroad, you know."

"Yes. It just seems odd that the fifth viscount didn't divorce her. It's as if he and everyone simply said 'good riddance' and went on with life."

"They must have said something to Isabella. Have you asked her?"

"I haven't met her there yet. Or the dowager."

"Why ever not?"

"It's not my fault. They've stayed out of sight, and Dauntry dissuaded me from approaching them. He seemed to think it would be a weak move. Yes, yet more chess. I'll meet them today, one way or another." She stood. "I'd better go back, but if you get the chance, please raise the subject of Diane. It's not just idle curiosity. I have a feeling there's something lurking there."

"Whatever can you mean?"

"If I knew, I'd be further forward. There are all kinds of oddities at the Abbey, Ruth. According to Dauntry, there's money unaccounted for, though that could be because the fifth viscount had a very haphazard way of dealing with paperwork. It's early days, but I sense something peculiar about him. He's spoken of as a devoted son, but it seems he spent little time at the Abbey."

"That's certainly true in recent times."

"You see? I intend to get to the bottom of it, as well as turning the servants to my side, taking over control of the Abbey, and wooing Isabella from allegiance to the dowager."

"All in a day?" Ruth teased.

Kitty chuckled, but wasn't feeling humorous when she said, "I've a lifetime." She hugged Ruth. "As I said, nothing is amiss is my marriage, and I'm relishing all these challenges. Thank you, thank you, for putting me in the way of it. I'll visit frequently as I take my driving lessons, and in a few days, you and the family must visit me."

Ruth's hug was fierce, but did she, like Kitty, feel a divide? They weren't schoolgirls anymore, and their situations and stations were now very different. And they might not even be in accord on all matters. How was Kitty to cope without Ruth's support?

Chapter 21

Kitty reentered Beauchamp Abbey by the comfortable back door, hoping to find Braydon in his office. However, Worseley told he her he'd not yet returned.

He was taking a very long ride.

Was he escaping both the Abbey and his wife?

Kitty was tempted to go back outside and stay out until he returned, but that would be childish. She went upstairs, determined to take up her duties to the house and the family. *Which one first?*

At the top she was confronted by a black-clad woman. For a moment she wondered if it was the dowager, but, if so, she'd been mistaken in all her impressions.

"The dowager Lady Dauntry wishes you to visit her, my lady,"

Ah, the Irish maid, as was confirmed by a slight accent, and sent with a summons. Not at all surprising that Sillikin was staring.

"Of course," Kitty said pleasantly. "In a little while."

She went on to her rooms. Perhaps she was seeing skirmishes where none existed, but she'd go odds the dowager knew Braydon was out and hoped to get Kitty alone.

Henry was waiting to take the gloves and cloak.

"I've been commanded to the presence," Kitty said. "I'll go, but after a meaningful delay."

"You don't want to wait until his lordship returns?"

That sentence was open to various interpretations.

"I don't know when that will be, and it might be best to meet woman to woman. Am I suitably dressed?" The sage green gown was rather plain.

"Perfectly adequate," Henry said, "but you could wear the shawl."

"The cashmere?"

"The house is chilly between rooms. Let's see." Henry took the shawl and placed it around Kitty's shoulders, as if it had been an everyday one. Then she crossed it at the front, as a simple woman might do, and tied the ends at the back.

"I can't wear such a shawl like this," Kitty protested.

"A viscountess may do as she pleases. A wealthy viscountess may be careless of expensive items."

A wealthy viscountess. The pin money arranged in the settlements was generous, and this house was very fine, but if Isabella had spoken the truth about her inheritance, there might not be funds for extravagance.

She wouldn't ask anyone else, but Henry was his aunt's maid and confidant. "Is Dauntry wealthy in his own right?"

"There's many richer, dear, but his uncle had a way with money and left him well provided for. With all my worldly goods . . ." she reminded.

Which meant, in theory, Kitty was also now well provided for.

She studied herself in the mirror. The dull green was an excellent background for the shawl, but as the deeply embroidered ends were now behind, it didn't look completely outrageous. The embroidery running along the edges was simply pleasing.

"Very well. Which door across the way enters the dowager's boudoir?"

"The second. Cullinan will be with her." It was a warning.

"You don't have a high opinion of her?"

"I can't decide if she's haughty or uncouth, but I've no time for her."

Kitty was surprised to hear such disdain. "Perhaps you could test her out by asking advice."

"From *her*?"

"Not about your work," Kitty said quickly. "About where something is, perhaps."

Henry's ruffles smoothed down. "I could do that, I suppose, though she's the last I'd ask in the normal way of doing things. I see her only at meals. She's the sort who spends all her time with her mistress."

"Is that common?"

"With some. Like a lady-in-waiting at court, always to hand. But that went out of fashion when bells became common. Most people don't want servants at their elbow all the time, seeing and hearing everything."

"I certainly wouldn't. Not even you, Henry. I would like a deeper opinion of Cullinan, however."

"Quite the little general, aren't you, dear?"

It was said with a smile, so Kitty didn't object. "I lived with soldiers for so long that I'm used to looking at the world that way. Here it seems appropriate. I'm going to leave Sillikin with you. I don't think she'll need anything whilst I'm on the far side of the world."

"Where there be dragons?"

"Precisely. Into the fray."

Kitty crossed the hall and knocked briskly on the second door. When it didn't quickly open, she opened it herself and went in. "You wished to see me, ma'am," she said cheerfully to the woman in black, equal to equal. "I'm sorry it didn't seem convenient for us to meet yesterday. I completely understand that you were unable to travel to the wedding."

The overheated room was crammed with expensive furniture and ornaments, its walls thick with paintings. The air hung heavy with rose perfume, wood smoke, and dog. Three tiny white dogs were appropriately all in the dowager's ample black lap. The three of them would just about equal Sillikin.

The dowager stroked them with plump, beringed fingers. "See who we have here, my darlings. The new Viscountess Dauntry."

She was fat, but could be described as comely, as some well-fleshed women could, with smooth, plump cheeks delicately aided by rouge. Her eyes were largely hidden by puffy lids. Black suited her, giving dignity to the mass, and her black cap with lappets and gauze veiling concealed most of her graying dark hair.

Kitty wondered for the first time how old she was. In her sixties, at least.

She was seated on a large chair that decidedly resembled a throne, her feet on an embroidered footstool. Kitty doubted even Queen Charlotte sat in a chair like that on a daily basis.

The maid was standing sentry just behind.

There was no sign of Isabella.

Kitty looked around, saw a straight chair with an upholstered seat, and moved it to a convenient spot, not too close to the fire, but facing the dowager. She sat and said, "Please accept my condolences on your losses, ma'am."

"A hollow sentiment when it has provided you with such an opportunity."

"I, too, grieve, ma'am—in my case, for my first husband."

"That is not the same as the loss of a son!"

"Truly anyone can appreciate that, ma'am."

"Not until they have suffered it." Was the dowager truly wishing Kitty would one day?

"I lived with my mother-in-law for quite a while," Kitty said, "and saw her grief daily. It is a bitter loss."

"Cateril. A very *recent* elevation." The sneer revealed long, darkened teeth.

"Nothing at all by comparison to the Godysons, ma'am. I understand they can be traced back to before the Conquest."

"And the barony to 1176. A proud line brought down in the end to a mere woman—myself."

"And to your granddaughter, ma'am."

"The new viscount jilted Isabella to marry you."

Kitty had expected that. "That can't be true," she said calmly. "And a marriage of sixteen to nearly thirty is undesirable."

"Not in dynastic situations. He raised her hopes and broke her heart."

"I doubt that, ma'am. I remember that age. It's so easy to fall into infatuation with no encouragement at all. Whatever the case, he's married to me now, and that's an end of it."

The dowager Lady Dauntry stared, definitely not accustomed to such blunt speech.

"As to Isabella," Kitty continued, "I look forward to helping her to a good marriage in time. Thus your bloodline will continue."

"Not in this house," the dowager shouted, thumping the arm of her throne. "My life's work! And my name will die. Isabella is a Godyson-Braydon, but that will not continue."

"It would become cumbersome," Kitty agreed. "Godyson-Braydon-Cavendish or some such."

"I see I provide you with amusement."

"I was merely agreeing with you, ma'am."

A dog yelped. Perhaps it had been squeezed. The dowager soothed it, but her eyes fixed on Kitty. "If any of my *other* sons had survived, I would have demanded that the Godyson barony be re-created for the eldest of them. God did not choose that it be so."

And that put God on the list of enemies, Kitty suspected. Here was a woman obsessed with one thing, but Kitty was shocked to realize that she'd lost a number of children. However, she'd aimed that tragic information as a weapon. Cullinan's comforting hand on the dowager's shoulder was a supporting volley.

Kitty was tempted to point out that if the dowager had made Diane Dauntry happy here, there might have been many more vessels of the Godyson blood, but she wouldn't sink to petty cruelty. She took up a different line of attack. "I see that you won't want to continue to live here, ma'am, in a place that must remind you of all your losses."

"I would never abandon my duties."

"You may do so with honor, now I am here to shoulder them. I'm sure Dauntry will arrange for whatever home you prefer. He and I have only your best interests at heart."

The woman's face was so set it could have been one of Madame Tussaud's wax models of victims of the guillotine, and the rouge looked garish. "I have lived here for more than forty years," she said.

"And have made it beautiful."

"You have the ability to recognize that?"

Kitty ignored the sneer. "I'm sure anyone would, ma'am. The viscountess's rooms were something of a shock."

That brought the dowager back to life. "That woman had deplorable taste and she thwarted every attempt by me to improve matters. I was glad to see the back of her. Glad. She probably squandered her fertility on her low-born lover."

That sounded authoritative. "Do you know what happened to her, ma'am?"

"I have no interest in the strumpet."

"Did she ever write to your son?"

"If she did, he didn't tell me of it."

"Why didn't he divorce her so that he could marry again?"

"I have no idea, and he can no longer satisfy your impertinent curiosity. You may go."

Kitty considered defying the command, but it would be a meaningless skirmish and she'd be glad to escape the heat and smell. But she had one point to make first. "I'm about to speak to the cook, ma'am. I will be ordering some dishes to my and Dauntry's taste, but I'll make sure ones that please you are always included. Please let me know if you perceive any lack. In that, or in any other aspect of the running of the house."

A lapdog yelped again.

Having asserted her command, Kitty rose and left. The coolness outside was a relief, but she was careful not to show any reaction as she crossed to the other side of the house. She could have grinned. She'd met the dragon and there was nothing to her but bile and bluster.

She hoped Isabella would be as easy. Surely the girl would welcome escape from the dowager, and the prospect of a normal life.

Chapter 22

Close to her door she saw Braydon coming up the stairs and turned to meet him at the top. They should have a pleasant exchange for attentive ears, so there'd be no sign of strain over the recent encounter.

"Did you enjoy your ride, husband?" she asked.

His brows twitched, but he responded, "Very much."

They turned to walk together. "I took Sillikin out. The kitchen gardens are well kept. Yesterday I admired the flower gardens, but I saw no roses."

"Perhaps they're not sufficiently amenable to drill and discipline."

"Flogging them does no good?"

"Not sure if it's been tried. Perhaps a pagan whipping dance at the winter solstice."

She laughed as they entered her boudoir. The laugh was spontaneous, but it would convey the right impression. A happy couple. A strong team.

He closed the door. "That is an unusual way to treat a cashmere shawl."

"I visited the dowager."

"Ah, armor. I see no blood."

"We had a frank discussion."

"I see no blood," he said again.

"I believe we came to an understanding. Did you know she had other children that died?"

"No. That softened your heart?"

"To an extent, but she wielded the information like a battle-ax."

"She would."

"She also tried to claim you'd jilted Isabella. I take that as a sign of weakness—that she has no better weapon— but is it possible that Isabella truly fancies herself in love with you?"

"No."

"Think, please. As I said to the dowager, sixteen tumbles into infatuations very easily."

"I've seen no sign of that. Only of calculated acts."

Kitty supposed he would know. He was the sort of man girls would have been tumbling over since he was in his teens.

"Very well. I suggested to the dowager that she wouldn't want to live on in a place that had such unhappy memories for her."

"*Still* no blood?"

"If eyes could pierce . . . What places are available?"

"She won't go, but in addition to the Dower House here, there's a house in Bath that has been rented out for a decade or more, her old house in Lincolnshire, and the place in Wales. Though that's more of a farm."

"No London house?"

"Yes, but we'll need that at times."

A London house. It would be a grand one in Grosvenor Square or some such fashionable quarter. Another place to manage, and being there would mean tackling the haut ton.

"Do you live there now?" she asked.

"I keep my rooms."

She'd like to see them. She suspected they'd tell her a great deal about her husband. "Is the house rented?"

"No. The fifth viscount used it fairly often."

"But it's stood vacant for at least a six-month. That's a waste."

"The viscountcy is not so desperate for income." He might as well have looked down his fine nose, and she wanted to snap something about pampered privilege, but she must try to think and speak like a grand lady.

"I plan to speak to the cook," she said. "Are you content with the meals provided?"

"They've mostly been edible. I offended you?"

"Not at all. Mostly?"

"Inedible was tried once. I put a stop to it."

"Flogging?"

"Beating servants was outlawed long ago."

"But not beating wives," she pointed out.

"Wives are chattel. Servants aren't."

He might be teasing, but in her present mood, Kitty couldn't tell. "Why was the food inedible?"

"The dowager instructed the cook to it. Oversalted soup, rubbery meat, scorched potatoes."

"And she obeyed?" It felt good to turn her anger on a worthy object.

"It was early days," he said. "I put an end to it by making it clear that another meal of that sort would lead to the instant dismissal of all the kitchen servants."

"Somewhat drastic, and very unjust."

"It never serves to slap at arrant insubordination. At least in civilian life, we don't have to hang people to bring the rest to heel." He halted and inhaled. "I apologize. That's not the sort of thing—"

"To say to a lady. Think where I spent most of my adult life, Braydon."

He'd been growing angry, however, as angry as she, perhaps responding to her emotions, and because of his cool restraint, she hadn't been aware of it. At least with Marcus there'd been no concealment.

"You went driving," he said.

"You object to *that*?"

"Not object . . ."

"Was I supposed to seek your permission? I beg your pardon, my lord. I am not yet accustomed to this form of marriage."

"Devil take it! Am I at fault for being concerned for my wife's safety?"

"I was perfectly safe! Baker took good care of me. If you've dismissed him—"

"Of course I haven't, you termagant." He inhaled. "This is a storm over nothing."

"Then why . . ." But Kitty pulled in her anger. "Perhaps the dowager . . ."

"Put you on edge."

"I don't know how she can bear that overstuffed, overheated room."

"Nor do I."

Thus, carefully, they arrived at a point of fragile agreement.

But then he said, "They called you Kit Kat."

She eyed him warily. "Yes."

"You didn't mind?"

"Should I have? It isn't some lewdness, is it? No, no, Marcus would never have allowed that."

"Of course not. It just seemed . . . I apologize. I was taken aback by so many men having a fond name for my wife."

Please, not jealousy as well! She'd suffered from that for years. She couldn't bear it again.

"I accuse you of no wrong," he said.

"Good," she said, striving for a moderate tone, "for I did none."

"And you couldn't help being so engaging."

"I was merely *there,* Braydon. The only woman among many young men."

"I've been in situations where women were scarce. Not all of them were adored."

"No one adored me!"

"No one?"

She wished she'd instantly said no, but she'd faltered on the lie and probably her expression gave her away. "A few," she admitted. "And briefly. They forgot me as soon as they were back with their regiments. Believe me or not as you please, but if you play Othello with me, you'll find no meek Desdemona."

He raised a hand. "I apologize again. What a treacherous business marriage is." But there was more in his eyes—a keen awareness that made her feel as if he could read her mind and even her memories. As proof, he asked, "What did Cateril do?"

To deny everything would be pointless. "Sometimes he fretted about the embarrassing adorers. Once he tried to challenge a captain for giving me roses. Of course, Bullock refused to fight a cripple, which reminded Marcus of what he'd become. Sometimes he could forget that."

How he'd raged—at Bullock, at the French, the Portuguese, and at fate. And then at her. A flailing fist had struck her in the ribs. She'd swung the pottery jug she'd had in her hand, opening a gash on his head. He'd collapsed into miserable self-pity and weeping contrition, and she'd retreated into wary silence, nursing her bruises. They'd been estranged for days. She'd given out that they both had head colds and couldn't receive guests. They'd recovered, but it had never been the same, and it hadn't been the only time. . . .

She started when Braydon took her hand. Was surprised to have him ease open a fist.

"I'm sorry," he said.

"So am I." But she meant for the way things had been, and perhaps he understood.

He kissed her hand and then her lips, gently, probably offering comfort, but it became warmer, inviting more. But this time resentment and disquiet simmered in her and she couldn't respond.

He stepped back. "I leave you to your domestic labors, my dear."

Kitty was left feeling guilty about having rejected him, but she couldn't change the way she felt.

Why had he questioned her right to drive?

Why had he asked about her around Town?

Why did he seem determined to probe matters she'd rather forget?

Braydon took refuge in his bedroom, needing time for his anger to simmer down. He wanted to thrash Marcus Cateril, but he couldn't do it, even if the man were alive. How many of Kit Kat's admirers had felt the same, guessing that Cateril's surly rage at his condition was sometimes vented on his wife? Had they seen bruises, or even witnessed attacks? Had the puppy been offered in consolation?

How had she responded? When she'd said she'd be no Desdemona, she'd meant it, but had she felt able to hit back? She would have given as good as she got with words—that was sure. He'd married her for her fighting spirit, but he wished she'd not had to learn to fight.

He wanted to return to her and find a way to make it right, but her simmering anger had been like a wall.

Breaking it down would do no good. He sought refuge in his office and paperwork. The sooner the administration of the viscountcy was in solid order, the sooner he could leave for London. He could be gone by Christmas and only obliged to return on occasions.

After mere minutes he tossed down his pen, realizing how little he wanted that now.

He'd be leaving Kitty alone in this hostile house, as she had perhaps been alone in a hostile marriage, despite her flock of admirers. More than that, he'd miss her company already, in and out of bed. There was so much to learn and explore in bed. And out of it . . .

Perhaps he could remain over Christmas. Town would be thin of company, and the troublemakers had gone quiet. There were probably rural rites he was supposed to take part in. Wassailers. Mummers. Gathering holly and mistletoe.

Quite likely the dowager was of the modern mind that saw such things as pagan.

He smiled at that. He'd encourage a riot of them.

Kitty paced her boudoir, tense with the residue of anger and with anxious unhappiness. She'd let out another side of herself—her ability to rage.

But then he'd guessed.

She hated that. *Hated* it! The violence in her marriage was her secret, hers and Marcus's, and he'd taken it to the grave. It shamed her that she hadn't been able to avoid it, to be kinder and gentler. In that, she'd failed as a wife.

Sillikin whined, nudging at her leg.

Kitty picked her up and hugged her. "At least he never hurt you, little one. Even when you told him off."

Kitty sat to comb Sillikin's long coat, easing tangles and removing leaves and twigs. Sometimes it was a tedious task, but often it was soothing.

"You cared for him, too, didn't you? And he for you on his better days. You knew when he was most in pain."

Marcus had tried to hide his pain, largely, she thought, because it was proof of his damaged state. In some ways he'd been like his mother in trying to pretend that the damage was less serious than it was, and that some of it might heal. Sometimes Kitty had thought he'd married her in expectation of a miracle cure, and that his bursts of anger grew out of disappointment.

"Braydon isn't Marcus," she said, working on a little tangle. "I must remember that."

The task did ease her mind, but that allowed in other concerns.

"I'm woefully unprepared for this. I knew that, but I didn't expect to trip over little things. Like the Town house. It *is* foolish to leave it empty for such a long time. If the viscountcy doesn't need the money, it could have been given to the poor." She paused, and examined her dog's solemn expression. "The supportive silence, I see."

Sillikin's silence was bliss, not philosophical.

"He's going to be jealous. Already is, because of Kit Kat. Why does that upset him? I never did anything wrong. A good thing that he'll be away most of the time. Though I might be tempted to go up to London and catch him with his mistress. Sauce for the goose . . . You don't approve?" she asked the dog with a smile. "You're right, of course. It would achieve nothing but to make me a figure of fun. Women, especially ladies, are supposed to never talk of their husband's unkindnesses, and to pretend ignorance of his infidelities. At least Marcus never strained my discretion in that department."

She cleaned the comb of hair for the last time and put it aside. "Perhaps I'll take a lover," she said, but Sillikin was asleep.

Kitty didn't need a reaction from her dog to know she'd

never do that. It would be dishonorable, and a husband being equally dishonorable wouldn't absolve her. But that meant that when Braydon left for London, she'd be returned to celibacy. For the past few years, she'd felt the lack of a man, but dully amid the darkening days of her marriage and then the enclosing atmosphere of Cateril Manor. Now she was alive again, but he would soon leave.

Perhaps not till after Christmas.

Whatever happened, what she must do was keep her side of the bargain—and her temper—and become a perfect Viscountess Dauntry in all regards.

As a first step, Kitty put the sleeping Sillikin down near the fire, summoned the cook, and discussed menus for the coming week. At the end, she asked, "Is there anything you need in order to do your work to the best, Mrs. Northbrook?"

"Not unless there's stuff needed for new dishes, milady. Turkish-like."

"Turkish? Ah, you mean like Lord Dauntry's coffee and cakes."

"Nasty, thick stuff." The woman went red. "Begging your pardon, milady!"

"That's quite all right, Mrs. Northbrook. The coffee is very strong, but delicious if one has a taste for it. You don't make it?"

"I do not, milady. His lordship's gentleman does that, though I understand that in London his lordship's cook prepares it."

So he had a cook in his Town rooms. That implied considerable space. "I'm sure he's not concerned that you have no experience of it."

"I certainly hope so, milady. I'd be willing to learn, of course, but . . ."

But he won't be here much? Kitty was surprised the

servants knew that. No wonder they seemed uncertain about which side to support.

"But it would be difficult," Kitty supplied. "As long as Johns is here to prepare it, that will do, but have one of the kitchen servants learn from him in case. As you know, Lord Dauntry has many duties in Town, and in the New Year there'll be Parliament, but he will be here as much as he can be, and I will be here most of the time."

"You won't be going to London with him, milady?"

Kitty wondered if people hearing that war is to be fought on their doorstep had the same frightened look. She was sorry for it, but the servants were going to have to choose their sides.

"Only occasionally," she said. "There's so much to do here. What will we need to provide for the tenants' and servants' ball?"

Mrs. Northbrook still looked anxious, but she had some good ideas. In the end, Kitty could thank her warmly and hope they parted on reasonably good terms.

So far, so good. What next?

It was approaching noon and she was hungry, but it was time to deal with Isabella. *Two birds with one stone?* She braced herself and then went down to Braydon's study, annoyed to feel nervous about being with him again.

Her tone was probably too brisk as she asked, "Do you see any reason not to invite Isabella to eat lunch with us?"

"No, but what if she refuses?"

"It won't be a command. If she chooses to stay cloistered, so be it."

"Forever?"

"I feel sure I can outwait her."

"So do I."

That sounded approving, and Kitty relaxed a little. "I wonder . . ." she said.

"What?"

"Perhaps she's caught in a trap similar to mine at Cateril Manor, tangled in the dowager's mourning like a fly in a spider's web. I'm sure she feels her losses as I felt mine, but is she mostly acting out of fear of upsetting her grandmother?"

"More likely out of fear of angering her."

"You can't be sure of that. The dowager has been mother to her for ten years."

"And a dominant figure in this house all her life. You might be right, but how to break such chains?"

"We can offer escapes."

"By all means, but open doors don't always tempt a caged bird."

"Because it's afraid. We'll have to overcome her fears." *As I'll have to overcome mine.*

Kitty left, considering whether her experiences with Marcus had caged her in some way. Was she afraid of breaking free of watchfulness and readiness for war?

She was who she was, however, and she couldn't bear to start bending and pretending in an attempt to placate an angry man.

She stuck to the matter in hand and sent Henry with a verbal invitation to Isabella. She was surprised, but pleased, when the girl accepted. Isabella would doubtless come with cannons at the ready, but Kitty hoped she'd soon have a better idea of how to sweeten the girl's mood.

Chapter 23

Kitty made sure she was tidy and went down to the small dining room. She found Isabella already there, no longer wearing the ring. The girl was in the deepest mourning but also in the latest style. *So she is interested in fashion. That is a beginning.*

Sillikin hurried to make friends.

Isabella stepped back, snapping, "Go away!"

Kitty picked up the dog. "She's not at all dangerous, I assure you."

"But not suitable for a dining room."

There was some justice in that. "If her presence upsets you . . ." Kitty summoned the footman from the hall and told him to take Sillikin to Henry.

When she turned back, Isabella said, "I understand you were raised in a shop, my lady. That must have been interesting." Clearly "interesting" was not desirable. The girl had been sent here with prepared lines.

"It was," Kitty said cheerfully. "There's always something to read in a bookshop, and when I was older, I acted as shop assistant at times, which was fun."

"Fun?"

"I enjoyed helping people find the books they wanted, and writing the bill and taking the money. Of course, I didn't have to work long hours, as a real shop clerk might. And then I went to school. Have you attended school?"

"*I* had a governess."

"I sometimes thought I would like that," Kitty said, "and not have to go away, but I enjoyed being with other girls and the variety of subjects and activities. I assume you've learned music and dance?"

"I have been well educated in all regards, ma'am. I would have attended a ball this year if not for our tragic changes."

Tragic changes; not losses. Before Kitty could react to that, Braydon arrived, followed closely by servants bearing food.

"Do let's sit," Kitty said. "I confess to being hungry." Once they were settled and the servants had left, Kitty said, "We've been speaking of dances and balls, Dauntry. When Isabella's mourning is over we must arrange some—here or perhaps in London." She dangled that as bait, but Isabella didn't twitch.

"Of course," Braydon said. "And presentation at court."

Isabella stayed silent, eating tiny morsels perhaps as a reproach to hearty appetites. Kitty reminded herself that the girl's father and brother had died. Her mourning wasn't false.

"We can do nothing as long as you're in your blacks," she said to the girl. "But when you're in half mourning, we could host a small social gathering here. Don't you think, Dauntry? Perhaps a musical evening."

"I don't see why not."

"And if there were to be a little spontaneous country dancing, nothing more than a hop, Isabella could join in. I never had the advantage of such social events, but I believe that young ladies often do host parties to practice before going to London."

Isabella spoke at last. "Grandmama would not approve."

"She may not be here to be disturbed. She and I spoke of her moving to Bath."

Isabella's jaw dropped. "She'll *never* leave the Abbey!"

"She might find she'd like a change," Kitty said cheerfully, and ate more of the excellent pork pie. "Would you want to move with her?"

"No!" The girl's cheeks flushed. "I mean, this is my home." She looked at Braydon. "You can't send me away. You can't!"

"Of course not," he said. "Kitty meant that you are free to leave with your grandmother, if you wish."

Kitty hid a smile as she poured more tea. He'd caught the idea.

"I don't," Isabella said. But then she added, "And nor does Grandmama."

"Wherever you choose to live," Kitty said, "you'll be able to visit Town in due course, and perhaps Brighton as well."

"Brighton?" Isabella did a good job of delivering it flatly, but the flicker of excitement in her eyes was a breach in the citadel.

"And eventually Almack's," Kitty added carelessly. Young men spoke of the Almack's Assemblies as an arduous duty, but for a young lady, attendance was heaven. She asked Braydon, "Will Isabella have the entrée there?"

"Of course, though whether she'll wish to go, I don't know. Your large portion could attract fortune hunters, Isabella."

"But true admirers as well," Kitty said, playing along. "She'll have her pick—earls, marquesses, and even dukes."

"I may not like such attention," Isabella said, but her eyes were fixed on her plate.

"It will be as you wish," Braydon said, "but at the least you must be presented at a drawing room." He looked at Kitty. "So, of course, must you."

"Me!" She looked at Isabella. "I'll have to take lessons with you."

Isabella looked up then. "I have already been well instructed," she said, and rose. "Please excuse me."

She went to the door, but at the last minute turned and sank into the sort of deep curtsy required at court, then rose again with impeccable smoothness and a triumphant glint in her eye. Then she left.

The saucy minx. But Kitty liked her better for it, and she saw Braydon did, too. That hadn't been rehearsed.

Isabella had left the door ajar. Was she hovering in hopes of hearing Kitty complain of her? How would she like being forgotten?

"I never thought of having to be presented at court," Kitty said. "How will it be arranged?"

"Easily enough once the court recovers from mourning. A suitable lady will present you."

"What suitable lady?"

"An excellent question. Not one of my sisters."

"Are you so very at odds?"

"No, because we rarely meet, but they wouldn't add to your consequences, neither having a title. I could, I believe, summon a duchess or two."

"A *duchess*?"

"They're not quite as rare as unicorns."

But near enough. Being presented by a duchess would definitely add to her consequence, but it would also make her a center of attention and curiosity. Kitty had never expected to want anonymity, but the thought of being an object of attention before the critical eyes of the fashionable world turned her off her food.

She moved the talk to household matters, including food and the servants' ball, and only slowly realized they'd rediscovered their ease. He still knew things about her she'd rather he not know, and she'd revealed her warrior side, but they had both put all that aside. They'd worked together smoothly in dealing with Isabella. This marriage could work, as long as she was careful.

As they finished the meal, Braydon asked if she'd object to his riding out on estate business. *Is he not as comfortable with our situation as I thought?* She pushed that worry down and gave him permission. They both rose. Then, instead of leaving, he tilted her chin and kissed her in that soft, warm, promising way.

This time she responded, as she should, but also as she wanted to. Whatever their problems, the desire was honest. She put her arms around him and kissed him back, unabashedly suggesting that he escape his burdens in another way. She thought she'd won, but then he gently put her away.

"I truly do have business to attend to, my dear. Until later."

It was an excuse, but also a promise, one that left Kitty unable to settle to household duties. She collected Sillikin and went to Braydon's office, simply because it was so very much his, with his essence all around. She opened a book on the desk. It was all to do with yields of different crops. Riffling through the neat piles of papers seemed intrusive, so she decided to work on the loose papers in the cabinet as an excuse to stay there. She took down a box.

She found the simple task soothing. Take a paper from the box, read it, write the brief description and decide where to put it. She could easily denote some as ONI—of no interest—but as that wasn't an option, they went under NOI.

Scribbled names of horses, perhaps from a race meeting.

Bills for all kinds of small items—a cravat pin; garters; soap, in this case almond and rose. Rose soap wasn't usually a gentleman's choice. *For the dowager or Isabella?*

Trite letters from acquaintances acknowledging a favor or offering one, or informing him of a meeting in Town. He seemed to be a member of a number of worthy organizations, but that was probably a requirement of the peerage. She came across nothing to suggest active involvement.

There was a bill for the repair of the leading on a window. It should go in the box for the appropriate property, but there was nothing to indicate which house. The tradesman's address was in Edgware, so it must be connected to the document she'd found before. Where had that letter been filed?

She made the note in the ledger, then put the bill on top of one of Braydon's piles of paper to catch his attention. It seemed the viscountcy owned some property in Edgware. It might be a similar case to the Beecham Dab almshouses, in danger of neglect.

Then she came across a letter from the dowager to her son, dated three years earlier. Kitty smoothed it, surprised that it had been carelessly stuffed somewhere.

The handwriting was ornate. The dowager wrote of estate matters and urged her son to return to the Abbey soon to deal with a rental issue. It was hard to detect any emotion. She mentioned the good health and educational progress of his two children, but without any sense of doting. She probably would think doting for her dotage.

Kitty went into the secretary's room. "Is there a special place for family correspondence, Worseley?"

"Yes, my lady. In the cabinet." He went with her and took out a box from the bottom shelf. "This is for recent correspondence. Older letters are stored in the muniment room."

"How long a period does this box cover?"

"Three years, ma'am."

He returned to his office. Kitty considered the scant

contents of the box, sorely tempted to read the letters. That would be rudely intrusive, however, so she put the letter with the rest and noted the location in the ledger.

She put some more wood on the fire and returned to the muddle of paper, enjoying the simple room and the placid routine of the task. The bits and pieces built up a picture. The fifth viscount had been fussy about his boots and shoes but haphazard about his clothing. He'd certainly been no dandy. In fact, his concern over his footwear was all for comfort. Had he had bad feet?

Chapter 24

"There's no need for you to be doing that."

Sillikin leapt up and went over to Braydon, tail wagging. That was a great improvement, and Braydon hunkered down to stroke her, but he had a small wooden chest under one arm. More papers?

He had that glow that comes from fresh air and exercise, and she wanted to eat him.

"I needed a routine task," she said as he rose, smoothly and easily. "Just as you, I suspect, needed exercise and open air."

"Astute as always. Have you found hidden treasure?"

"Not unless you count the fifth viscount being very concerned about his feet and his thinning hair. I've come across bills for three different hair tonics."

"I seem to remember others. I, on the other hand, have found treasure for you." He put the chest on the desk. "I decided the dowager must still have the family jewels, so I faced the dragon and wrested them from her."

"And lived to tell the tale!"

"She has an impressive safe and suggested she was the best custodian. There's a safe here as well, however. Remind me to show it to you." He unlocked the chest and opened it. "I can't be sure this is all of it."

Kitty didn't try to hide her excitement. She took out boxes and pouches and began to open them, finding jewelry of all sorts in all stones, and a beautiful necklace of large pearls. She cradled it in her hands, but when she looked up she saw amusement.

"Who wouldn't be excited to explore a treasure chest?" she protested. "If I have to face the world as a viscountess, I'll have the chance of glittering as I ought."

He picked up an emerald necklace and studied it. "Good stones, but ugly setting. We'll have it reset." He picked up a diamond pin. "This needs cleaning. Probably most of it does. All the same . . ." He came round the desk and slid it into her hair. "Ice and fire."

His look was admiring and his touch flowed heat down her spine, making her sway. She put a hand on his chest, hoping he felt as she did. That they could—

"Coffee," he said.

"Coffee?"

But it was a warning. He must have already ordered it, for it arrived then, again with little cakes, but these were golden and glossy. Kitty sat, reminding herself that the night was not so very far away.

He poured and passed a cup to her. "Have you questions for me?"

He meant about the house, but she chose to take it another way.

"Tell me about your life before you became Lord Dauntry."

He was surprised. "Including the army?"

She'd be interested, for it didn't seem his career had been commonplace, but it might be a difficult subject. "No, after you sold out. Was that soon after Waterloo?"

He relaxed back and sipped. "Late in 1815. I didn't intend to. I liked the life, all in all, and considered it my career, but as it became clear Napoleon was truly done for, the work became less appealing."

"You enjoyed the fighting?"

"Does that offend?"

"No. I can't quite understand it, but I know it's common enough."

"If I'd wanted armed combat, there are postings around the world where it's available, but I didn't fancy a life in Canada or India, and there are even worse places. The West Indies, for example, and the penal colonies of Australia. I'd no mind to be a jailor."

"I've listened to men discuss the same options," she said, enjoying her own coffee, feeling as relaxed as Sillikin, who was dozing by the fire. "In the same manner. After Waterloo, something seeped away—and left a swamp."

"A good way of putting it. Most military officers need their profession, but I didn't. I had a modest inheritance from my father, and then an uncle left me a larger one. When another regiment was sent to keep the peace in Yorkshire, enforcing the Riot Act against desperate Englishmen, I sold out before I was entangled in a similar mess." He poured himself more coffee. "I couldn't mend that situation by staying."

"Of course not. And your concerns were justified. The dragoons were ordered to charge the gathering at Spa Fields last year. People could have been killed. It was outrageous."

She expected him to share her disapproval, but he said, "You didn't read the handbills distributed before the meeting. I quote: 'The whole country awaits the signal from London to fly to arms! Haste, haste to break open gunsmiths and other likely places to find arms! Run through all constables who touch a man of us. No rise of bread! No Regent! No Castlereagh! Off with their heads!'"

"Heavens! You know it by heart?"

"My very retentive memory."

"It's horrible that people preached such violence. But the hardships are great."

"It would be pleasant if life was black or white, but it rarely is. Try some baklava. It's sticky, but you're allowed to lick your fingers."

She took a tiny square and nibbled. Crisp layers of thin pastry with honey, spices, and some sort of nut. "Have you introduced the dowager to this?"

"No."

Clearly he saw it as sweetmeats before swine.

Kitty took another nibble and drank some coffee. They went together perfectly. "I'll end up fat."

"Not if you eat only small pieces." He'd finished his and sucked honey off his fingers and thumb.

Kitty realized that she'd licked her lips only when she saw the way he was watching her. She ate another nibble of cake; then she put down the remainder and moved her hand up to lick off the honey.

He leaned forward and captured her wrist. Watching her, he brought her hand to his mouth and sucked at one finger, his tongue swirling to clean off every trace of honey.

It wasn't night, but her body didn't seem to care. He moved on to the next finger, watching her, a smile deepening in his eyes. He knew what he was doing to her, and he, too, didn't care that it was still light outside. He drew her to her feet, still sucking at her finger, then drew it deeper and out. Kitty felt as if she were melting, deep, deep inside.

Here?

Why not? The floor was carpeted.

At the sound of voices he moved apart.

After the briefest knock, Worseley came in. "A message, sir. Courier."

Outwardly cool again, Braydon took the letter, broke the heavy seal, and read. "How very inconvenient," he said. "I apologize, my dear, but I have to leave for London immediately."

Kitty could have wailed a protest, but she could see

the issue was serious. "Of course. Is something terribly the matter?"

"Nothing that need concern you." She thought he'd leave on that curt sentence, but he came over and kissed her hand. "It's a comfort that I can leave Beauchamp Abbey in your excellent care."

With that, he was gone.

Kitty took out the diamond pin, feeling tragically noble. This was why he'd married her, but they'd been married for only a day, and she ached with desire. She put away the jewels and locked the box, but she didn't know where the safe was. She put it in Worseley's charge.

Should she supervise her husband's packing? She'd packed for Marcus before their annual visit to Cateril Manor, but Braydon and his valet could manage such things. She was fighting tears, which was ridiculous, but then suddenly it wasn't.

She hurried upstairs and found him in his bedroom, instructing his valet about what to pack in one small trunk.

"A word with you, my lord."

His look was impatient, but he came with her into her bedroom and closed the door.

"I need to come with you."

His lips tightened. "I dislike being blunt, Kitty, but your being here to take care of the Abbey was a key point of our negotiations, was it not?"

Kitty almost apologized and left, but she couldn't. "Yes, and I'll keep my part of the bargain, but not now. Consider—we've spent one night together. One! If you leave now, what will people think?"

"That I have urgent business?" But he grimaced in exasperation. "You're right, of course. Some will see disappointment or rejection. I'll be traveling without consideration for comfort."

"I'll survive. I'll have to ask Henry whether she wants to come."

He nodded and returned to his room. Kitty tugged the bell. By the time Henry arrived, Kitty had already laid shifts, drawers, and stockings on the bed, despite Sillikin running around, trying to understand what was happening. Perhaps the dog hoped they were returning to the parsonage.

She quickly explained to Henry. "What should I take for a few days in Town?"

"Something for all eventualities," Henry said. "I'll make the selection."

"Will you come?"

Kitty had meant to phrase it more generally, giving the older woman more option to refuse, but she wanted Henry with her. London she knew. Town was foreign territory and probably hostile.

"Of course, dear. I'm no delicate flower, and you'll need me."

While Henry packed, Kitty invaded the dowager's parlor again. She found Isabella there, seated at a distance from the roaring fire, looking resentful. When Kitty informed the dowager that she and Braydon were going up to Town for a few days, the girl's sulky lips tightened. Kitty truly meant to do something for Isabella, and for a moment thought of taking her with them, but heaven knew what the summons involved. It would be folly.

"How will Beauchamp survive without you both?" the dowager asked with a smirk.

Kitty kept her composure. "The servants seem well trained, and I'm sure you will advise them as necessary, ma'am. I don't expect to be gone long." That pinched her face. Kitty added, "We will certainly return by Christmas. There will be festive traditions to follow."

"Yokels," said the dowager.

"I don't know that one, ma'am. We must have the wassailers up to the house, however, and mummers if there are any hereabouts. A yule log and greenery about the place."

Kitty saw a glint in Isabella's eyes, and though it pleased her, she knew she was taunting for the joy of it.

"Now I must make haste, ma'am. If there are any items you would like from Town, please send me a note before we leave."

No note came from the dowager, but Kitty did receive one from Isabella, asking for some new novels. *Perhaps a slight breach in the citadel.*

Chapter 25

They left before sunset, but traveled mostly in the dark, grateful for moonlight and hardly slackening speed along the good toll roads. Abbey horses had taken the traveling carriage to Chipping Norton, but from there they used four post-horses with frequent changes. One of the postilions sounded his horn as they approached every toll, so the gate was already opening for them when they reached it. Only rarely did they leave the coach at a change, for necessary relief.

Kitty had never before traveled at such unremitting speed and could only attempt not to show her exhaustion.

There was little conversation. Whatever the cause of this race to Town, it was not to be spoken of in front of Henry and Johns, and there was no need to speak of anything else. Sillikin seemed to pick up the mood and mostly slept on the floor, though she opened an eye now and then, as if to check that her humans were still all right.

The coach drew to a stop, and they could finally climb out into the biting night air. Kitty was bone-weary and her breath was misting, but the fashionable street was warm with gaslight, and the sounds of London were all around. She couldn't help a smile as she recognized its fast, familiar pulse.

They hadn't stopped in front of a typical Town house

that had been divided into two or three sets of rooms. This building stretched on either side of her with only one central door. Johns used the brass door knocker, and the door was opened by a sturdy, broad-shouldered manservant in greatcoat and gloves.

"Welcome 'ome, m'lord," he growled.

A retired prizefighter to guard the door?

Dauntry gave his arm to Kitty and they went forward. "Thank you, Clark. Lady Dauntry will be with me for a while."

The entrance hall was narrow but the staircase wide and gracious, and the whole was of fine, polished wood. Braydon escorted her up the stairs for one flight, and then they turned left, where he used a key to enter his rooms.

Kitty remembered once thinking, for the merest moment, that his rooms might be similar to the four rooms she'd lived in with Marcus. She'd known they'd be grander, but she'd had no idea.

His private entrance hall was small, but again the wood was fine and polished, and two paintings hung on the walls. They were small and probably Dutch, judging from the interior scene and the costumes. A mahogany wall clock ticked the seconds above a small table that held a Grecian vase, a silver tray, and a candle lamp. The candle wasn't lit, but a fire in a room ahead spilled warmth, and a manservant was already lighting branches of candles there.

He turned to bow. "My lord! We weren't expecting you."

Yet he'd been preparing before we entered. A bell from the porter below to alert the household?

"I wasn't expecting myself," Braydon said. "My dear, this is Edward. You'll find he's a useful, knowledgeable young man." Again he said, "Lady Dauntry will be here for a little while."

Was he making sure the servants knew she wasn't his light-o'-love? Or was the emphasis on the temporary nature of her stay? She knew some gentlemen's rooms were bachelor only.

The candles illuminated a sitting room of modest size, but elegant enough to be called a drawing room. She almost felt she should apologize for putting her travel-worn half boots onto the thick carpet, and there were more objets d'art and pictures on the cream-colored walls. She saw two glossy mahogany doors to the left and right. Five rooms? Only one more than she'd had in Moor Street—but no. There must be a servants' area somewhere, and as he had a cook, a kitchen. Her small kitchen had been one of the four.

"My apologies, my dear," Braydon said to Kitty. "I must go out immediately. The servants will take good care of you."

And then he was gone.

Kitty, Henry, Johns, and the footman stood in silent uncertainty. It was Sillikin trotting to the footman with friendship in mind that alerted Kitty to the fact that she was in charge here.

"Tea," she said. "And something decent to eat, please, Edward. Johns, kindly show me what accommodation we have."

Braydon's rooms contained all one might find in the smaller sort of fashionable town house, but with the usual three or four floors laid out on one level. In addition to the parlor, she was shown a dining room where at least ten could dine and a small library with walls entirely of books. There were two good bedrooms, and off one, a dressing room with bath. That was clearly Braydon's room.

She didn't inspect the servants' quarters, but she suspected that all the servants here were male. For tonight,

at least, Henry must sleep with her in the second bedroom.

What struck Kitty was the quality. In its way, Braydon's
home was as fine as Beauchamp Abbey, but infinitely
more welcoming. All the principal rooms were decorated
with gleaming wood, papered walls, and beautiful objects
that seemed chosen one by one rather than acquired for
show.

She paused to admire a small bronze of a horse and
rider.

She'd thought once that his rooms would tell her
much about him. They did, but again it was daunting.

The unwelcoming atmosphere at Beauchamp Abbey
had given them common ground, like people of very different backgrounds and natures thrown together in a
wintry storm. These rooms made their differences plain.
As she'd once acknowledged, Braydon had been accustomed to graciousness and wealth since the day he'd been
born, and she had not.

Fires were being hastily lit in all the rooms, but the air
wasn't frigid, so Kitty shed her cloak, bonnet, and gloves
and washed her hands before going to the dining room.
As Braydon wouldn't command that food be ready for
him at any time, it must have been rushed from a nearby
inn or tavern, but everything was served on fine china
and silver chafing dishes.

Kitty would have liked to have Henry's company at
the meal, but she couldn't see how to invite her maid
without inviting Johns. She assumed they would eat in
the kitchen. Perhaps they'd be more comfortable there.
As she finished, the clock in the hall tinkled ten, and
distantly she heard other clocks sounding the hour.

> *Oranges and lemons*
> *Say the bells of Saint Clement's.*

You owe me five farthings,
Say the bells of St. Martin's.
When will you pay me?
Say the bells of Old Bailey.
When I grow rich,
Say the bells of Shoreditch.
When will that be?
Say the bells of Stepney.
I do not know,
Says the great bell of Bow.

Most of those old bells were in the City of London, but she'd heard some of them at times in Moor Street, marking the passing of the day or night.

She shook herself. She was falling asleep where she sat. Foolish to even think of staying up for Braydon. She drank the last of her tea, realizing she was clinging to hope of more marital adventures.

In her weariness, doubts crept in. Perhaps he was pleased to be free of such duties. Perhaps that was why he'd seized on whatever summons had brought him here. Perhaps he had some other woman's bed to go to when his business was done.

Braydon had gone to the Home Secretary's home.

"Avoided by the merest chance," Lord Sidmouth said, pacing his office. He was a spare, bony man with thinning hair and deep-set eyes, plagued more by an anxious nature than ill health. "If a servant hadn't moved a barrel out of his way . . . three princes gone!"

Sidmouth lived in fear of insurrection. There was true danger—it had happened in America and France, after all—but that meant a steady head was even more important. Braydon believed he had a steady head, and he was willing to serve. He hoped to steer a good course, but also to turn aside the more draconian acts of suppression.

"May I have the full story, sir?" In violation of etiquette he sat, which led, as he'd hoped, to Sidmouth also sitting down.

Perhaps it hadn't been outrageous. He realized that he now outranked the Home Secretary in the peerage. They were both viscounts, but Sidmouth's was a new creation, whereas Braydon was the sixth of his title. The thought amused.

"Kent, Clarence, and Sussex gathered together last night to discuss the current problems," Sidmouth said, "and find a way to get the Regent to take control."

There were seven surviving sons of the king. One was the Regent and the rest were royal dukes—York, Clarence, Kent, Cumberland, Sussex, and Cambridge.

"I thought Kent resided in Brussels for the health of his purse," Braydon said. Being royal didn't mean being wealthy.

"He does, but he sometimes returns, supposedly incognito. Clarence is in regular attendance on the queen in Bath, but he came to Town for the meeting. Sussex, of course, resides in Kensington Palace."

"But they gathered in a private house?"

"In Holles Street. Someone learned of the gathering and put gunpowder in the basement in the guise of barrels of beer. The plot was prevented only by chance! A servant moved a barrel out of his way and thought it didn't contain liquid. Suspecting a fraud on the part of the beer merchant, he summoned the butler, who tapped it."

"And black powder dribbled out. How was it to be set off?"

"Someone would have had to slip into the basement, but that wouldn't have been difficult. There's a hatch through which the beer barrels and other heavy goods are put in. We set a watch, but no one turned up. The servants have been kept quiet as much as possible, but word is bound to escape. There could be panic!"

"The story can be denied," Braydon said soothingly. "The world is awash with rumors. Whose house was it?"

"The Honorable Mrs. Courtenay. In the past she was part of the queen's household and was trusted by the princes."

"Is she under suspicion?"

"She seems an honest enough old lady, but who knows where evil lurks these days?"

It's your job to know, Braydon thought with asperity. For Sidmouth, every protestor was a potential revolutionary, every orator a potential Robespierre, and every servant a potential traitorous spy. Braydon sometimes wondered if Sidmouth truly trusted anyone.

"You said in the letter that Hawkinville is unavailable?" he asked. Sir George Hawkinville ran an unofficial antirevolutionary department for which Braydon worked from time to time.

"In Paris. Ostensibly a pleasure jaunt with his family, but there are some issues there. You will handle this?"

It should have been a command, but came out with an anxious question mark at the end.

Braydon considered claiming his very new marriage as reason to decline, but that would be vile. This was a dangerous incident and could be smoke from deeper fires.

"Of course."

"Good, good. Find the spy in that house. He or she will be the one intended to set off the bomb."

"You said that access was possible from outside," Braydon reminded him. "Moreover, if we find such a person, we'll have a mere minion. We need to know who is behind the plot."

"Find the minion and we'll get the truth."

By any means? Braydon hoped he was correct in believing torture chambers a horror of the past. "Even the rack wouldn't overcome ignorance," he said, "and such means are, of course, unthinkable. If I were devising such a plot, the lowest wouldn't know me, and the links from layer to layer would be very hard to follow."

"Damnation. *Damnation!* We could still hang the vermin. Hang, draw, and quarter 'em for an attempt on three royal lives. That should deter any future attempts."

Braydon prayed no jury would condemn anyone to death for such a nonevent, but in these times who could be sure? Most juries looked kindly on protestors, but in the current mania over Princess Charlotte's death, a jury might turn vicious with anyone threatening the royal family.

"People fired up by a purpose are rarely rational," he said. "What measures have been taken to prevent future attacks?"

"Their royal highnesses have instructions not to cluster. Kent is en route back to Brussels, and Clarence should be in Bath by now. Both are under extra guard. Sussex is a damned irregular, but he should be sensible in this situation."

Braydon thought the Duke of Sussex admirably free-thinking, but it was a shame that his rebellious streak had led him to marry in contravention to the Royal Marriages Act. He had children, but the Act made any royal marriage null if it didn't have the approval of Parliament, so his were technically bastards. If matters were otherwise, there'd be no succession crisis. Prince Augustus and Princess Ellen would stand ready to ascend to the throne if needed.

"But who was behind it?" Sidmouth demanded, thumping the arm of his chair with a clenched fist. *"Who?"*

"Rather, ask why," Braydon said. *"Qui bono?"*

"Someone who wishes to disrupt the kingdom!" Sidmouth declared. "The death by explosion of three princes. Alarm. Shock. Fear."

Certainly in you.

"There could be a more practical purpose," Braydon said. He left a polite pause, but when Sidmouth didn't take up the subject, he did. "The explosion would have removed three of the four princes who are free to marry and provide an heir."

"By Lucifer! *Jacobites?*" Perhaps Sidmouth's hair really did rise on end.

"Any Jacobite claim would be feeble, but there are plenty of German Protestants with a line of descent."

The Jacobite fragments were Papist, which was why Parliament had made a law to say all future monarchs must be Protestant. That was how George of Hanover, a rather distant branch on the royal family tree, had become King George the first in 1714. If the Hanoverian line failed, a number of other Protestant German principalities had people with claims.

Sidmouth shot to his feet to pace. "I can't believe it of any of them. It's the French. It has to be the French. Create mayhem. Weaken us. Open the way . . ." A knock at the door ended the tirade. "Come!"

A footman entered with a letter on a silver tray. Braydon heard him murmur, "From Carlton House, my lord."

The Regent's London residence.

An explosion there, too? Thank God the Regent wasn't in residence.

Sidmouth waved the man out and broke the seal. "Good God."

Braydon waited, aware of his heartbeats.

"He's here," Sidmouth said. "The Regent. Demanding my immediate presence."

Not a new disaster.

"You'd better come, too."

"I'm still rough from travel," Braydon pointed out.

"So must he be if he's hurtled here from Brighton. Come."

Sidmouth hurried out, and with a moment's wistful thought of his wife and his marriage bed, Braydon followed.

Chapter 26

Braydon was pleased to see that Carlton House was adequately guarded, though it was possible the number of soldiers had been increased today. They were challenged at the railings that barred the forecourt, and scrutinized as they left the coach beneath the massive portico and climbed the steps to go inside. In the hall Braydon saw only liveried footmen, but there could be other guards concealed by the elaborate architecture.

He'd attended levees here and one banquet, but never been admitted beyond the public rooms. Now he accompanied the Home Secretary through the famous octagon room into the back of the house and the more private areas. The decoration did not become simpler. The anteroom was hung with remarkable paintings. The furnishings were sparse but opulent, most probably obtained from the spoils of the French Revolution. Perhaps their former owners would be pleased to see them in a royal setting.

Bourbon visitors might also like the fleur-de-lis carpet, which continued into a salon, and at last, into the Regent's presence. He was seated in a large chair with upholstered arms and seat, but it bore no resemblance to a throne. This room was smaller than the previous one, but just as fine—if one favored blue panels and hangings amid gilded walls, doors, and cornices. Thankfully, the grand chandelier was unlit, and the room was illuminated only by candelabra, but a great many of them. They and the large fire made the air unpleasantly hot.

No wonder the Regent was half-undressed and swathed in a silk banyan of blue embroidered with gold. *Someone so very large should avoid strong colors.*

"Sidmouth! At last. Who's this?"

The Home Secretary introduced Braydon, with explanation.

"Hawkinville's away?" the Regent said. "I like Hawkinville, even though he can be damned impudent. Wellington trusts him."

Braydon was tempted to point out that Wellington trusted him, too, but silence seemed wiser. In private, people sometimes poked fun at the Regent for his extravagance, size, and folly over women, but he was the ruler, with a ruler's powers.

As he and Sidmouth made their bows, Braydon assessed the man. There'd been optimistic reports in the papers that the Regent was recovering his spirits in Brighton and was seen out riding, but if they'd been true, he'd suffered a setback. His complexion was blotchy and his eyes almost haunted. A foot raised on a stool suggested gout, but even so, he had a decanter of port at his elbow and was drinking from a glass.

"Very well, very well. Tell me this tale."

Sidmouth related the attempted assassination.

"Courtenay," the Regent said. "Remember her. Always giving me sorrowful looks. Was she in on it?"

"I very much doubt it, sir."

"Then who?"

Sidmouth went through their arguments. Braydon's mind drifted. He could be much more pleasantly engaged. But, then, the journey had been taxing, and Kitty was probably fast asleep by now. Would she sleep in his bed and be there when he finally managed to get home? A delightful prospect, but she'd probably prefer a bed of her own. She'd returned to her own bed last night.

"Balderdash!" The Regent's exclamation snapped him back to the moment. "The succession?" the Regent continued. "Even if the plot had succeeded, there'd be no benefit from it for decades!"

He was right. Despite the Regent's bulk and ill health, he was showing a sharp mind.

"M'father's living a long life," he continued, and Braydon thought he heard resentment. "And there's no reason we shouldn't all do so. Go odds some of my sisters'll live to ninety. Could end up with a succession of doddery old virgin queens! Queen Augusta, Queen Elizabeth the Second, Queen Mary the Second, Queen Sophia . . ."

He laughed and swigged more port, but the laugh was bitter. None of his brothers and sisters could reign until he died. Perhaps he spent sleepless nights fretting that his father might outlive him, stealing his chance of coronation and kingship. From all reports, the mad king was in better physical health than his heir.

"It's one of those damned revolutionaries," the Regent said. "Arrest 'em all!" Braydon must have moved, for the Regent's eyes turned on him. "You think that unwise?"

Now, there is a tricky question. "Not in principle, sir," Braydon said carefully, "but the recent tragic event has reminded everyone of their devotion to the royal family and particularly to yourself, and strengthened their desire for peace and good order. Anyone speaking treason now is chastised by those around. To arrest people without explanation would disturb that situation, but would it be wise to explain? Might it not be best to keep the event from public knowledge?"

"Don't want to create new fear and uncertainty, eh?" The Regent pouted, but didn't repeat his command. "Leave it in your hands, gentlemen. Find the culprit and ensure there's no repetition. I hold court tomorrow. Excuse for coming, don't you know, in order to keep this quiet." It was the Regent's way to make good decisions his own. He'd even been known to claim a part in the victory at Waterloo.

They were dismissed, and Braydon was glad to escape. He and Sidmouth left in silence, aware of listening ears, but Braydon was rearranging the pieces.

They'd ignored the princesses. They were probably all past childbearing age, and only two were married, but if their brothers all died, they would ascend the throne, one after the other. The royal dukes might not make old bones, but some of the princesses might. Even if there were no new legitimate grandchildren for the king, it could be forty years or more before the Hanoverian line was exhausted.

So what would have been the point of killing Kent, Clarence, and Sussex?

Once in the coach and on their way, Sidmouth said, "Insurrectionists after all. I thought so. Hawkinville's staff is still in place in his house. Use them."

Does Sidmouth not trust his own Home Office or the military in this matter? Paranoia or reason? "If you'll let me down at Mrs. Courtenay's house I'll begin my enquiries."

"This late?"

"Carelessness with gunpowder deserves some inconvenience."

Sidmouth shrugged, and soon Braydon was ruthlessly knocking until a sleepy servant opened to him. He learned that the lady had fled to the country. *Or fled the country?* That could be discovered.

Her absence gave Braydon free rein to tour the house and ask questions, though she seemed an unlikely conspirator. The Regent had confirmed her royal service, and her servants described an elderly widow of a sober, religious disposition.

There was nothing informative about the three-story house. Its elegance was rather faded, but it spoke of conventional tastes and deep propriety. The hatch into the basement was as described, accessed from a small backyard that had a gate into a delivery lane. The hatch was near the kitchen, and two servants slept nearby. Could anyone trundle a beer barrel into the basement unheard?

"Oh no, milord," the butler said. "It was delivered, regular, in a manner of speaking. That is, the usual people, but we weren't expecting it."

"Yet you took delivery."

"Danny, the footman did. We were in such a flurry of preparation for the royal dinner, so Danny said no one had time to stow it properly. When the delivery men offered to do that instead of carrying it back to their cart, he agreed."

"The usual delivery men, you said?"

"I didn't see them, milord, but different men come every time. Waller Brothers supply half the town."

Braydon nodded, but he'd be astonished if Waller Brothers had anything to do with it. "When did you learn that the royal dukes were coming to dine?"

"That morning, my lord. Which is why we were at sixes and sevens."

"Have members of the royal family gathered here before?"

"No, my lord. That is, the princesses Mary and Sophia have visited a time or two, without ceremony, for Mrs. Courtenay was in the royal household when they were younger. But not recently."

"Have you hired new servants within the last year, or even sooner?"

"The footman, milord. Danny."

"Send him to me. And prepare a list of all your servants and when they were hired."

It was possible that in a few hours, one of the servants had passed on word of the opportunity, but Braydon found it hard to believe. That would imply that a potential spy had been conveniently in place in an old lady's house. He'd known luck to settle more momentous events than this, but it ranked unlikely.

He spoke to the nervous young footman and crossed him off the list. Danny Onslow was nineteen and had worked in the house for only three months. He'd been new in London then, up from Essex, where he'd worked for a Sir Dillerby Vernon from the age of fourteen.

Braydon would check all the details, but it seemed more likely that the informant was in one of the princes' households. One or more treasonous factions might have infiltrated servants there, but that would be hard to investigate. One household was in Brussels, and at the moment Clarence lived as part of the queen's household in Bath. Sussex had apartments in Kensington Palace, but even his liberal principles wouldn't make him happy about being questioned.

Braydon left the house, thinking that even if he found the source of the information, the culprit could merely be a gossip, as had been the case with a government leak earlier in the year. It might provide a salutary lesson to hang, draw, and quarter a few gossips!

Clocks struck eleven disjointedly. Unreasonable to wish that the London clocks were adjusted to strike in synchrony. He could return to his rooms, where bed beckoned, even without a wife in it. However, he dutifully detoured to visit a place where he might encounter unruly gossip.

The smoke-filled Castle Inn was raucous, and many

there were well on their way to being under the table, but that tended to loosen lips. Braydon mingled, hearing the latest scurrilous jokes and incendiary remarks, which might prove useful later, but mostly picking up the atmosphere.

Men of all ranks gathered there, but it wasn't a fashionable venue, so he got some looks and even comments. But on the whole he was known and accepted there. Not everyone was a revolutionary, but it was a haunt of radicals. Among the drunken jocularity were groups deep in fierce political and philosophical debates. Some were frankly for a republic, but not the sort that guillotined the royal family. A few would cheer each falling head, but had more sense than to say so at the moment.

Could the French Revolution have been turned aside by the tragic death of Queen Marie Antoinette in childbirth? Unlikely.

He joined a group of men who were looking to the Regent to lead the cry for better justice and fair wages. Braydon had little faith that the Regent would go so far, but he put in a word. "He might. He led the campaign to bar French silk, demanding that everyone wear English silk products."

"Aye," said a few. But "Silk!" said another, and spat on the floor.

"Even silk weavers deserve jobs and fair wages," Braydon pointed out.

No one argued with that, but the spitting man said, "What wage is fair with bread the price it is because of the bloody Corn Laws?"

That set them off in another direction.

Braydon moved on, listening in particular for any mention of the royal dukes. All he heard was a joke about the middle-aged princes probably scrambling for wives of childbearing age in order to provide an heir.

"You know what brothers are like," an old man said, showing long teeth and few of them. "All out to show up the others."

"My money's on Clarence," another said. "A hearty sailor, and look at the family he had with Mrs. Jordan!"

The Duke of Clarence had lived openly with the actress Mrs. Jordan for decades and sired ten children with her, all known as FitzClarence. There was another bunch of potential monarchs if only they were legitimate.

The Royal Marriages Act had created problems, but a prince's marriage to an actress was exactly the sort of thing it had been designed to block. Clarence and Mrs. Jordan had parted six years ago, and she'd died last year. Even if Clarence had considered himself committed to her, he was free to marry now. In moments, a betting book was out and wagers were being made on which of the princes would sire the first son.

Braydon had learned what he could for now, so he found a hackney and traveled home. He let himself into his rooms, but Johns was waiting up for him.

"Lady Dauntry?" he asked quietly.

"Is sleeping in the second bedroom with Miss Oldswick, sir."

Braydon nodded, disappointed. Strange, when he'd always preferred to sleep alone.

"Any problems?" he asked as he undressed.

"No, sir. Do you require food or drink, sir?"

"Only hot water, and then get to bed."

Once Braydon was washed and ready for bed, he sat to make brief notes. His memory was such that he didn't need them, but he sometimes found it useful to lay out key points in search for connections. Something dangerous was afoot, and he must put a stop to it.

Chapter 27

Kitty woke, and for a moment thought the body in the bed beside her was her husband's, but, alas, it was Henry's. Some daylight came in around the curtains, but she sensed it was early. She realized that she must have been woken by Sillikin's mind power, for the dog was standing by the bed, staring the message that she needed to go out.

"At least I should be able to trust the servants here," Kitty muttered.

She climbed out of bed, shivering in the chilly air, and put on her robe. As soon as she opened the door, Sillikin went straight through and toward the back.

Kitty heard a man say, "You need to go out, little one? Very well."

Clearly, Sillikin had the matter in hand. Kitty left the door open a crack so the dog could return, and rubbed her hands to get some warmth into them.

Was Braydon home? The thought of him being out all night stirred her worries about a mistress, but by day and rested, she couldn't believe that. He'd come here on important business. In addition, she might not know him perfectly, but she felt sure he wouldn't go to a mistress the day after his wedding night. It would simply be ... unsmooth.

Henry stirred. "What time is it?"

"I'm not sure. We need the fire started and washing water."

"I'll get it."

Kitty almost protested, but Henry was the servant here. "It's odd being in a bachelor household, isn't it?" she said.

"It is, dear. There's a house, I understand."

Kitty heard the hint. "So there is, and left empty for quite some time. I should at least inspect it. And if we're to stay in London for any length of time, it could be opened. But would Dauntry want to leave here?"

"That's something you'll have to discuss with him, milady. But marriage brings changes."

Secure in robe and cap, Henry left. Kitty considered getting back in the warm bed, but instead she put on her fur mantle over her dressing gown and went to the window.

She drew back the curtains a little and saw that it was raining. It was only a soft, almost misty rain, but servants were hurrying about their duties with their hoods up, and a gentleman strode along beneath an umbrella. The fashionable world still slept.

The street wasn't much wider than Moor Street, where she'd lived, but it was grander. She'd been too weary to follow their direction yesterday, but she suspected they were in the heart of Mayfair. All the houses were in fine condition, and each had a railed entry at the front with steps down to the basement area. The front of her house had met the pavement, the house had only had two stories, and there'd always been wear and tear. Of course, this building was not a terrace but a solid block. Were there servants' quarters in the basement, or did each set of rooms have its own servants' quarters?

A coal cart clattered by, and here came a cow and goat, each with a bell around its neck, led along to provide milk. A maid hurried out of a house with a jug to be filled. Seeing the milk drawn from the animal was proof against adulteration, but it would be thinner stuff than Kitty had enjoyed recently. Animals needed good pasture to provide rich milk. Some London cows were kept in sheds.

Henry returned with hot water, and she was accompanied by the footman in shirtsleeves and apron with a bucket of coal. He soon had a fire burning in the small gate.

Carefully looking at the wall he asked, "May I know what you'd like for your breakfast, milady?"

Kitty was tempted to ask for the Turkish coffee, but that felt presumptuous. "Chocolate, bread, and butter, please. Henry?"

"Tea and bread and butter. Thank you, Edward."

There wasn't anywhere to eat in the bedroom, so Kitty added, "We'll eat in the dining room, Edward. And my dog will need water and meat."

As if summoned, Sillikin bustled in, ready for the next adventure.

Kitty realized only when the footman had left that she'd implied she'd be eating with her maid. So be it. She enjoyed Henry's company and her advice.

Kitty went behind the screen to wash. Once she was in her shift, she came out to be corseted. She had to help Henry with her corset and gown, and then Henry helped her into the brown.

Henry said, "While we're in London, you could order some new gowns." Another hint, and one Kitty was happy to take. Her seamstress here was a friend and it would be an excuse to visit Moor Street and meet many friends and acquaintances there.

They went to the dining room. Their breakfast came promptly, beautifully served, with jewel-like jams as well as rich butter that must have come up from the country. On the floor, Sillikin had a china bowl of water and a dish of what looked like chopped steak. Her stubby tail was vigorously approving.

"Still-warm bread," Henry said, cutting open a roll. "An excellent kitchen."

"It will be from a local bakery," Kitty said. "I'm surprised Dauntry keeps a cook here. It can't be only for his coffee." Then she had to explain about the coffee.

"I don't like coffee in any form," Henry said, "so I'll decline that treat. But I think you'll find he enjoys a range of foods not readily available from the local chophouse or tavern." Henry could be a deep well of information about Braydon, but the door was open, so Kitty wouldn't indulge in curiosity yet.

She was enjoying her second cup of chocolate when Braydon entered the room, already perfectly shaved and in faultless Town elegance similar to his clothing for their wedding. If he'd come home late and slept little, it didn't show.

"Good morning," he said to Kitty as he sat. "I hope you've found everything to your satisfaction."

Henry rose, curtsied, and left. Kitty almost protested, for Henry felt like a friend, but she did want to speak privately with Braydon.

Edward brought an ordinary coffeepot, bread, and cold meats.

"Close the door as you leave, Edward." Once they were alone, Braydon said, "I'm sure you have questions."

He was perfectly polite, but that was the problem. They'd come to do better than this in Gloucestershire. Was he cool because she'd insisted on coming here with him?

"Not if you don't want to provide answers," Kitty said, in as no-nonsense a way as she could. "I understand that matters might be confidential."

He took his first sip of coffee. "Thank you." He buttered some bread, put ham between two slices, and took a bite. He saw her watching him. "You disapprove?"

"No, but I'm surprised."

"That I like a sandwich for breakfast? I found in the army that they're an efficient form of food. If I was interrupted, I could put what was left in a pocket and have rations later."

"That can't have been good for your clothes."

"I couldn't always afford to be particular."

Again, she was curious about his army career, but the current mood made personal questions impossible.

Two days, she reminded herself. It had been merely two days since their wedding, and they'd had only one night together. Alas . . . She watched as he poured himself more coffee and then added milk, admiring his long, strong fingers.

He put down the milk jug. "I'm in the same dilemma as before, Kitty."

She pulled her wits together. "About what?"

"I don't know you. I don't know if you can be trusted. Not," he said with a raised hand, "in the deepest sense, but might you let information slip? To a friend, for example."

"My only close friend is Ruth."

"You may meet old friends here. Male as well as female."

"Ah." She sipped more chocolate. She'd looked forward to meeting Moor Street friends, but he was thinking of military men. "I don't think I'd carelessly let anything slip, but if it would create problems or danger, then it's better not to tell me."

"What an excellent woman you are."

It was more statement of fact than high praise, but Kitty couldn't help but smile. "Thank you."

He ate another bite of his sandwich, then said, "What I'm doing isn't life-and-death, but you have no need to know, except that I'm going to be very much engaged."

"I'd enjoy your company, but you needn't be concerned. London is very familiar to me."

"But not, perhaps, fashionable London? Remember your changed station. I had a momentary awareness of that myself last night when I remembered that I'm not Mr. Braydon anymore but the sixth Viscount Dauntry, and thus took precedence over the Home Secretary."

Kitty noted that tidbit of information. Nothing would slip out accidentally, so he was letting her know that he'd come to Town at the request of the Home Secretary. Lord Sidmouth was the man principally responsible for the safety of the nation. That told her little, but it was more than nothing.

"When you go out," he continued, "take Henry and Edward."

"Go about with an entourage?"

"It's appropriate, but Edward might prove useful."

"As protection?" she asked, startled.

She'd surprised him in turn. "I don't expect any unusual danger to you, Kitty, but London has dangers enough. In addition, Edward is familiar with this part of London, skilled at finding hackneys in the trickier locations, and can advise you—on the best shoemakers, for example, and furnishing warehouses."

Kitty took a moment to appreciate his clever mind. Most men would have said something like "shoemakers and milliners," assuming a woman would have no interest beyond clothes. He'd remembered that she had rooms to redecorate.

"That touches on a subject," she said. "I have very little money to hand."

A blink revealed surprise. "My apologies! Your pin

money is theoretical at the moment, isn't it? I'll provide some money immediately and make proper arrangements. If you purchase anything for the house or estate, have the bill sent to me."

Kitty buttered another piece of bread. "Which touches on a second subject. Have you any objection to my visiting the town house?"

"I'm sure it's your duty to do so. There's only a small staff, however, and everything's under Holland covers."

"We will want to use it at some time, and it must be ready. Which brings us to a third subject. How long are we likely to be here?"

"That I don't know. At least a week. Are you uncomfortable? We could remove to a hotel."

"I doubt that would be any more comfortable."

"Clearly you haven't visited the finest hotels."

"If some are more luxurious than here, you tempt me!" Kitty sipped her chocolate, considering whether to speak her thoughts. She saw no reason not to. "I don't suppose there's any way I can assist you with your duties, Braydon, but I hope you know I will if I can."

"I do, and I thank you." He'd eaten and drunk efficiently and was finished. "A moment." He left and returned with some banknotes, coins, and a key. "To the house. You shouldn't have any difficulty in gaining entry, but take a key in case. I suggest sending a note to alert the servants there. Mrs. Grant is the housekeeper, and she has two housemaids and a manservant to help care for the place. As best I can tell, she's excellent, but it's better not to surprise."

"Some would say it's better to surprise."

"Only if expecting problems. You remind me that the viscountcy has theater boxes, which are rented out by the night when not needed. I'll see if any are vacant while we're here."

"That would be delightful! I've never been to a London theater."

"Never?" Again, she'd surprised him. He had no conception of her London life.

She wouldn't be ashamed of it. "We couldn't afford a box," she said, "and Marcus couldn't have sat for hours in the pit."

"Then we will certainly go to the theater." He came around the table, raised her hand, and kissed it. He didn't press his lips, but they touched and perhaps lingered. "Please forgive a neglectful husband, Kitty. I hope to do better."

Did she imagine a silent "tonight"?

He left before she could properly respond, so she stroked the place he'd kissed and imagined. What a lustful jade she was....

Enough of that. There were at least twelve hours between then and now, and she had things to do. She did need to order new clothes more suited to her station, and she should visit the viscountcy's town house. She hoped it wasn't another ice palace.

Chapter 28

Braydon was surprised to realize that he would rather have spent the day with Kitty, even if it involved inspecting the town house and visiting upholsterers and wallpaper manufacturers.

Unexpected, and peculiar.

As it was, he had a dangerous situation to investigate, and he needed allies. Hawkinville had a coterie of gentlemen with a variety of skills, but who would be in Town in December?

One he could count on. Major Hal Beaumont was married to a Drury Lane actress, and the theater was open. Braydon had known Beaumont in the army years ago, but met him again earlier in the year, during another dramatic episode. Despite losing an arm in Canada, he'd been cool and effective. He'd already sent a note asking Beaumont to meet him at Hawkinville's house in Peel Street.

It was a fine gentleman's residence, but three rooms were set apart for Hawkinville's secret administration, disrespectfully dubbed by some as the Hawk's Nest. Braydon found four ex-military men engaged in routine work, collecting and dealing with information from London and around the country, and sending out messages as necessary. There was a pigeon loft in the attics.

Braydon asked what news had leaked about the attempted assassination.

"Only rumors, my lord," Bob Adams said. He was a stolid, middle-aged man who'd been an undistinguished corporal in the army, but Hawkinville had somehow spotted his cleverness. In fact, Hawkinville had said a clever man was wise to be undistinguished in war. Adams now ran these offices.

"One version," Adams said with a wry smile, "has it happening in Carlton House."

"Rather difficult to roll a barrel of gunpowder in there undetected."

"Easier to roll it to the moon, sir."

"What villains are active at the moment?"

"If you mean *active* active, sir, no one. There are people writing handbills, and some suspect private meetings, but it's as if rabble-rousing's gone into hibernation."

"We'll hope it doesn't emerge till spring. Keep alert for anything that might have bearing on the princes' affair, and set a watch on the house where it happened. See if you can discreetly discover the whereabouts of Mrs. Courtenay, and find out if Waller Brothers delivered ale there on Wednesday. The answer is almost certainly no, so what we really need to know is if any of their carts could have been used, and, if so, how. As it happened, the footman never saw the cart, but the villains might have been thorough."

"Right, sir."

Beaumont arrived, and he and Braydon went into Hawkinville's office. Braydon told the story.

"Dashed odd," Beaumont said. He was a handsome, dark-haired man with an easygoing manner that Braydon knew could be deceptive. His empty sleeve was pinned to his chest.

"I've been going over it," Braydon said. "If not a Protestant German hoping to inherit in decades, what about the Jacobites?"

"After all these years? Are there any claimants left?"

"I believe the next in line is the King of Sardinia."

"If I were him, I'd stick with a simpler situation and a much better climate."

"Resist a bigger realm and greater wealth and power?"

"I'm not ambitious. Don't understand the disease."

"Blessed soul. Very well. What about the French? They're always ready to set Britain at sixes and sevens, and another spurt of Jacobite action here would suit them."

"There'd be nothing to it. Scotland's not going to rise again, and who else?"

"The Irish?" Braydon offered. "Supporting a Catholic claimant?"

"Any attempt to put a Catholic on the British throne would lead to civil war."

"Which would suit France nicely."

Beaumont grimaced. "Ah. It would indeed. It's a long plan, though."

"It is. The Regent pointed out that working through the existing royal family could take us into the second half of the century."

"You've discussed this with him?"

"For my sins. Sidmouth was summoned, and I had the misfortune to be with him at the time."

"A large part of military survival is not being in the wrong place at the wrong time," Beaumont remarked. "The royal dukes aren't the healthiest lot, are they? I don't see old bones in any of them, but, as you say, the princesses, especially the spinster ones, are tougher."

"Queen Charlotte, Queen Augusta, Queen Elizabeth—"

"Hold on," Beaumont said. "Charlotte is the Queen of Württemberg! The King of Württemberg might well wish to add Britain to his domain, and he'd only have to knock off the males to get there."

Braydon hadn't thought of that. "Damn you. How the devil do we investigate a foreign monarch?"

"More to the point, why have you dragged me into this?"

"Desperation."

Beaumont smiled. "Fair enough. At least the solution's simple. All the princes who are free to marry must do so with all speed, and provide an abundance of legitimate British heirs."

"But will they do it? They've been altar-shy all their lives."

"Fault of the damned Marriage Act, but a brush with gunpowder might have toughened their nerves."

"Death or marriage?" Braydon asked. "The would-be assassin might have done Britain a good turn."

"As long as he or she doesn't succeed on another occasion."

"I was wondering who else of Hawkinville's gentlemen are in at the moment. Lord Arden? Lord Amleigh? Mr. Delaney?"

"None of those, though Amleigh's in Sussex, thus close enough to summon. Sir Stephen Ball's in Town. M.P. and lawyer."

"Isn't he a radical?"

"Say, rather, a reformer. Hawkinville often consults him."

"Then I'll do so if needed," Braydon said, but he had reservations. "He's not a military man."

"Can't see that makes a difference, but I know some military men who are kicking their heels and could be useful."

"No outsiders as yet. We're to avoid alarm, and I'm not yet clear about what useful action to take. Hawkinville's people here can undertake the routine investigations."

Beaumont rose. "Then if I'm of no further use, I have another appointment."

"I'm sure I'll find more uses for you," Braydon said with a smile. "Thank you. At the least, I need someone to talk this mess over with. Your insights have been helpful."

"Always willing. Are you free to dine tonight? Blanche isn't performing, and the Balls might be free."

A cleverly presented opportunity to assess Sir Stephen.

"I'll have to consult my wife. You may not have heard that I'm married."

"We'd be delighted to meet her."

"Then unless she's managed to commit us elsewhere in the past few hours, it will be a pleasure." Curious about the reaction, he said, "She was Mrs. Cateril."

Beaumont's smile was warm. "Kit Kat! Lucky man. I've wondered what became of her since Cateril died. I'll be delighted to meet her again."

He left, and Braydon wasted a few minutes probing that response like a tender tooth. Why the hell did it bother him that men lit up like beacons at mention of her? Would he rather have an unappealing wife?

No, but a treasure who'd been tucked away in the country, undiscovered, would be preferable.

He turned his mind to work. Neither he nor Sidmouth had considered that one of the royal family might be trying to do away with others. Even if Charlotte, Queen of Württemberg, wasn't coldhearted enough to try to kill three of her brothers, her husband might be. He was known to be a very unpleasant man.

If the explosion had killed Kent, Clarence, and Sussex, that would have left only the Regent, York, Cumberland, and Cambridge.

The Regent was still married to Caroline of Brunswick.

York had been married for twenty years without issue.

Cumberland had been married for only two years, but there were no children yet and his wife was in her late thirties. Why the devil couldn't he have married a younger woman?

Cambridge would be the only other good possibility for an heir. He lived mostly in Hanover and was effectively ruling it, but that might make him more vulnerable to attack from Württemberg.

He asked Adams if Hawkinville had people in place in the royal residences. Of course he had, so the one working in Kensington Palace was summoned. By good fortune—or perhaps good planning—he worked in Sussex's household.

In the meantime, Braydon paid a quick visit to Sidmouth, who scoffed at the suspicion of Württemberg. "It's radicals, I tell you."

"We can't ignore the possibility," Braydon said. "I recommend that Cambridge be urged to take care. Once the princes are gone, there's a string of sisters, yes, but Charlotte is the first. The stability of Britain will not be increased by a German taking the throne."

"He'd be consort only," Sidmouth objected. "We did away with joint rule after William and Mary."

"He's known to be a bullying tyrant. He'd rule, and everyone would know it."

"He and Princess Charlotte have no children. It'd be a dry twig."

So many details slipped people's minds.

"He has four by his first wife," Braydon pointed out, "and his first wife was the king's niece. Care to lay odds as to whether Württemberg would try to establish his eldest son's claim to rule after him?"

Sidmouth sat as if his knees had failed him." I'll write

to Hanover," he said. "For God's sake, Dauntry, find out the truth and deal with it."

Braydon left wondering exactly how he was supposed to deal with Württemberg. He'd met the man once. It was rather like meeting a mountain. He was seven feet tall and was said to weigh more than thirty stone. In addition, he had a sharp, cunning mind and a very unpleasant nature. His first wife had fled for protection to Tsarina Catherine of Russia.

He focused on one question: *If Württemberg had been behind it, who had been his tool?* He needed to know more about that meeting.

When he arrived back at Peel Street, the Kensington Palace footman, John Goring, was waiting for him. Goring knew of no suspicious servants or unusual goings-on. Goring himself hadn't known of Sussex's plans for the night.

"His highness's man might have known, sir, but his highness doesn't stand much on ceremony."

"Do you know where the Duke of Kent and the Duke of Clarence might have lodged in Town?" Braydon asked.

"No, sir."

"There must have been messages and replies. Find out about them."

That was a reminder to himself, so when Goring had left, he returned to Mrs. Courtenay's house.

"Messages, sir?" the butler said. "Only one that I know of, from the Duke of Sussex to my mistress, upon which she commanded the dinner."

So Sussex had coordinated the event. Therefore he must be interviewed, and not by one of Hawkinville's staff. *Sidmouth? Hell, no.* It would have to be the highest-ranking man available, and that was himself.

As Braydon put on his greatcoat, he went over what he'd learned. But as he left the house, his mind turned toward home. Or, to be precise, toward his wife. Would she be in his rooms or gallivanting around Town, shopping, as women seemed to like to do? She'd have to return home eventually.

Damn Beaumont's dinner. But he couldn't drag his wife to bed as soon as it was dark.

What did dark have to do with it? He could drag her to bed as soon as he returned home—except that he wasn't that sort of man.

The dinner would end at a reasonable hour. Tonight his wife would sleep in his bed and learn ways of enjoyment that Kit Kat had never known.

Chapter 29

Kitty inspected the town house, accompanied by Henry and Edward. She'd decided to leave Sillikin behind in the care of the cook, who had become the dog's devoted slave. The spaniel would need plenty of exercise or she'd become fat on the tidbits he fed her.

The Dauntry town house was a typical Mayfair one similar to the row opposite Braydon's building. The door was promptly opened by a short, plump woman in black bombazine, who seemed rather anxious as she bobbed a curtsy.

"We're all shrouded up, milady. I hope you don't mind. I didn't think you'd want everything uncovered, but we will if you prefer, milady."

"Of course not," Kitty reassured her. "I simply wish to get a sense of the house. Edward, you may wait below."

She'd already asked the footman to assess the servants' area and the servants, such as they were. He might welcome that task, for it was probably warm down there. Up here Kitty was very glad of cloak and muff.

"Are you warm enough?" she asked Henry, and the maid confessed that she'd be happy to go belowstairs.

It was possible that Mrs. Grant was cold, but perhaps some of her roundness came from extra layers, and she wore a thick shawl and woolen fingerless gloves.

The ground floor held a small reception room, a reasonably large dining room, and a larger parlor that had enough book-filled shelves to perhaps be called a library. There were paintings on all the walls, but all were shrouded in dust cloths.

Narrow carpeted stairs led up to a drawing room that took up the front width of the house. Three windows gave good light, and Kitty thought it could be a pleasant room in a warmer season. In fact, she thought this could be a pleasant home.

She'd expected a viscount's house to be grand, but there was nothing overwhelming here. The rooms were a decent size, and what details she could see, such as papered walls were . . . unobjectionable. She smiled at that word. If the unobjectionable house turned out as well as the unobjectionable husband, she'd have no cause to complain.

At the back of the house she found two bedchambers and a smaller room, which the housekeeper described as "His lordship's dressing room, ma'am."

It contained a narrow bed. Kitty had heard of this, that some fashionable people kept the fiction of a shared marriage bed, but that the gentleman had a separate room disguised as a dressing room. Perhaps it was simply that these town houses were quite small, so an additional bedroom would take up too much space. Perhaps it was so that the husband could come home late or not at all without disturbing his wife. All the same, the arrangement confirmed that it wasn't the usual thing for aristocratic couples to share a bed. She thought it a shame.

A higher floor contained another small bedroom and two even smaller rooms that were unfurnished.

The housekeeper said, "This could be a nursery area, milady."

"Did the former viscount's children ever visit here?"

"Not as I know, ma'am, but I've worked here for only eight years."

They had to use the servants' staircase, plainer and even narrower, to reach the attic rooms. The servants' accommodation seemed adequate.

As they returned downstairs, the housekeeper invited Kitty to take tea in her parlor. Perhaps she hoped to be refused, but Kitty accepted and asked Henry to join them.

The housekeeper had quarters just off the kitchen—a small parlor and an even smaller bedroom, but very cozy. Kitty shed her layers. The tea was good, as were the sweet buns.

As she poured, Mrs. Grant said, "Are you likely to be using the house soon, my lady? I hope it's not impertinent to ask, but it will be grand if so."

"Not soon, Mrs. Grant—there is much to do at Beauchamp Abbey—but probably next year for the season."

"Oh, that will be grand, my lady."

Henry spoke then. "There's some as think that being in a closed house with no work to do is a treat, my lady, but most don't find it so. There's still plenty to do to keep up the place, and the servants reduced to almost nothing."

"You have it exactly, Miss Oldswick," Mrs. Grant said. "I find it hard to keep good servants, even on full pay, for there's no excitement, you see, and no vails."

Ah. The gratuities guests would pay.

"Were you lively here earlier in the year?" Kitty asked.

"Lively, ma'am?"

"When the fifth viscount was in Town for Parliament."

"We didn't see much of him, my lady. The house was kept in readiness, but he mostly stayed at his club."

More ridiculous waste.

"I suppose it is large for a single man." That wasn't quite the right term for an abandoned husband, but Kitty couldn't think of a better. She was trying to frame a question about the house in the time of Diane Dauntry when she realized Mrs. Grant wouldn't have been here then. "Who was housekeeper before you, Mrs. Grant?"

"Mrs. Hopgood, ma'am. She died."

"Were any of the servants here then?"

"No, ma'am."

It was as if Diane Dauntry had vanished beyond an impenetrable veil. *Because someone wanted it that way?* Kitty tried not to let Gothic novels influence her, but there was something odd in the Braydon family story.

She accepted another cup of tea. "Is there any matter that needs attention, Mrs. Grant, or any improvements you'd suggest?"

"There's no problems with the upkeep, ma'am. Mr. Southern, his lordship's man of business in London, pays all bills for such and inspects the house at times. If the family were to be in residence, ma'am, one of the new water boilers would be useful, so as to have hot water readily available. And, perhaps, a Rumford stove in the kitchen?"

"I'll discuss it with Lord Dauntry," Kitty promised.

She would have liked to wander the rooms again and perhaps unshroud some furniture and paintings in search of clues about Diane. That would be a waste of everyone's time, so they took their leave.

Once they were in a hackney, Edward made his report. "The two maids are her nieces, milady, but both seem sensible girls and good workers. Comfortable in a situation like that to have family around. I caught a suggestion that Mrs. Grant might not be as robust as she seems."

Henry said, "I noticed that her ankles were badly swollen."

"So she might be glad of an easy position," Kitty said.

She had a number of thoughts about the fifth viscount and his wife, but didn't want to share them with Edward. Once they were back at Braydon's rooms, she intended to go over them with Henry, but Sillikin expressed rapture at her return and an insistence on a walk. A long walk. *Now.*

"If Cook's been feeding you tidbits, you'll need it," Kitty said. "Come along, then. Henry, you can stay here."

The park was quiet at this time of year, so Kitty let Sillikin off the leash and had Edward throw the leather ball, for he could send it farther. After retrieving the third throw, Sillikin was racing back when she paused, turned, and ran in another direction, toward a pair of strapping young men in long cloaks over scarlet regimentals.

One bent to take the ball and ruffle Sillikin's fur, then threw it again. The men came over to Kitty, grinning.

"Kit Kat, as I live and breathe!" declared Captain Claudius Debenham. "Town's alive again."

"Less of your nonsense, Cully," Kitty said, laughing. Debenham was blond, connected to a dukedom, and far too handsome for his own good. "And, in truth, my blue cloak seems too lively."

Cully pulled a face. "Good to be in uniform and spared that dilemma. Present Captain Barlow. Barlow, Mrs. Cateril."

Kitty acknowledged the other young man, but said, "It's Lady Dauntry now. A recent event."

"Congratulations! Wasn't Dauntry Beau Braydon? He'll keep you up to style."

"Are you saying I'm wanting in that department?" Kitty teased, turning to stroll with the men, enjoying the lighthearted exchange.

"Never," Cully said.

She let the officers take turns throwing for Sillikin. The dog would be ready for a long nap after all this.

"It is good to see you back in Town, Kitty," Cully said. "The Kit Kat Club is missed."

"Someone else will have to offer a gathering space."

"No easy matter. It's a rum old world these days. We soldiers had a purpose once. Defeat Napoleon. Save the world. But now it's all riots and mayhem. We're more likely to be ordered out to fight Englishmen."

Another officer joined them. Kitty greeted lanky Captain Edison, who'd given her Sillikin.

"I see she's in good form," he said, hunkering down to make a fuss of the dog. "Thought of breeding her?"

"I'd be too softhearted to take her babies away."

He shook his head as he rose. "Typical Kit Kat." The look in his eyes was too warm.

"Did you hear my good news?" she said brightly. "I've been elevated to the peerage!"

"What?"

"By marriage. I'm Viscountess Dauntry."

He congratulated her, but his smile didn't reach his eyes. "You married from Cateril Manor, I suppose."

"No, I met Dauntry when visiting a friend near his seat in Gloucestershire." She remembered the story they'd concocted. "Re-met, for we had known each other in the past. We married in a nearby village. Now tell me all your news."

But Edison demanded, "When was this?"

Damn his eyes. What business was it of his? But the only way was lightly. "A mere few days ago. We're honeymooning in Town."

"Then he's neglecting you shamefully."

Cully Debenham intervened and talk became general again, but Kitty was aware of Edison fuming at her side. She knew he'd been overly fond of her, but she was surprised his feelings had lasted. Even if they had, there was no reason for outrage. He'd had nearly two years to pursue her if he'd cared.

What would have happened then? If he'd visited Cateril Manor once her mourning year was over, she might have grasped the chance to escape. As matters had turned out, that would have been unfortunate.

Other officers joined them, again greeting Kit Kat and seeming truly delighted to see her. She hadn't known how much she'd missed being called by that cheery name. They came to a halt, sharing news, one man or another throwing the ball for Sillikin as required. Kitty teased one on his promotion and another on the news that he was a married man. She commiserated with a third on his difficult wooing.

Then Cully said, "Here's your husband."

Kitty turned to see Braydon approaching, escorted by Sillikin, ball in mouth, who seemed to be saying, *Look what I found!* Braydon's expression was less readable. Kitty suddenly became aware of being the hub of a group of seven officers.

Chapter 30

Two of her coterie knew him, and they all congratulated him on his title and his marriage. He was amiable, but Kitty wasn't surprised when the others took their leave. Perhaps she shouldn't have encouraged such a cluster in public, but she hoped he wasn't going to be tiresome.

"Are you here for a walk?" she said. "I think Sillikin and I are ready for home."

Indeed, the dog was lying down, panting.

"I was headed there myself when I spotted her." He offered his arm, and she took it.

Very well. As long as he wasn't going to express jealousy, she'd ignore his coolness. She was probably imagining it anyway, fearing that he'd be like Marcus. She mustn't do that. "I went to the house," she told him as they walked toward the edge of the park. "It seems well maintained, but apparently the fifth viscount rarely used it. He preferred a club."

"Some do."

"It seems wasteful. I'm not being penny-pinching, but why?"

"If he used the house, people would call and then he'd be expected to entertain, and thus he'd need a full staff. So it could be seen as economical."

"In a very odd way. Better to have rented it out for the season. If I had a house, I'd not choose a hotel or club." Or rooms, for that matter. His rooms were spacious and excellent, but as she'd gone through the house, she'd realized that she liked the feeling of it all being hers, with no strangers above or below. "I wonder if he had something against the place," she said.

"Memories of his wife? He married in London, so they might have lived there together for a while, in happier times."

"A grand love and tragedy," Kitty said, but then she pulled a face. "That doesn't match his portrait, does it?"

"No. Why are you fascinated by him?"

"It's not so much him as the situation. It's odd." She looked at him. "You're going to think I'm being Gothic, but is it possible that the dowager did away with Diane?"

His brows went up. "And buried her in the shrubbery?"

"I know it sounds ridiculous, but it seems she simply disappeared. How is that possible?"

"If she had any sense, she'd have wanted to disappear. If she'd set up house in England, her husband would have had the legal right to seize her. He might have challenged her lover to a duel."

"The man in the portrait?"

"Placid men can be pushed into drama if sufficiently embarrassed. At the least he could have sued her paramour for damages, which can be set at ruinous amounts."

"So she went abroad."

"Possibly her lover was from abroad. It might have been his foreignness that gave her the courage. And once in Greece, Italy, or some more remote spot, they could pretend to be married and live in peace."

"Then I hope she's happy."

"You're very forgiving of unfaithfulness."

Kitty chose to ignore the edge to that. "Would she really not let anyone know? Not even her own family?"

"Perhaps they were estranged."

"I wish I knew how to contact them."

"The name is Hartley," he said, "and they reside near Chipping Ongar in Essex."

"I didn't know that!"

"I didn't know you were curious. Worseley gave me that information shortly before we left."

"I could write to them. Or visit. Essex is close by."

"Do you not have enough to do?"

Without gathering gentlemen in the park. Kitty was tempted to pull the simmering issue to the front and let it boil, but she made herself be sensible. "I'll not neglect my duties," she said, "but the puzzle intrigues me, and Isabella might like to know."

"How much does a six-year-old remember? She's probably been raised to hate her."

"You have a bleak view of the world, sir."

"Long experience, but am I unreasonable to have a bleak view of the dowager?"

"Thus she might be capable of murder to rid her son of a troublesome wife."

They turned into his street. "If that were true, you'd want her to hang?" he asked.

"No, but the threat will make her do as we wish."

"Gads, you terrify me."

She gave him a look. "I very much doubt that." When he didn't respond, she lost patience. "Do you object to my being with some officers in the park?"

"It was disconcerting," he admitted, his tone unreadable.

"I won't turn away old friends."

"And they will gather. How could they not? What if

you find Diane is alive and happy in Herzegovina or China?"

How could they not?

Had that been praise or accusation?

Kitty sensed it would be unwise to pursue the issue. She hated her own reluctance, but she had no wish to test her husband's limits as yet.

"I'll rejoice and inform her she's a widow," she said. "She might be conventional enough to want to marry her lover. She might have children."

"I'd not considered that."

"Who knows what drove her to flight?" Kitty demanded. "It might have been the dowager's cruelty or her husband's. But it could have been the irresistible pull of love. That is a wild force."

"Only in novels and plays."

"Your view of the world is excessively mundane, sir!"

"If only it were."

She remembered why they were in Town and welcomed a new subject. "Your business doesn't go well?"

"It hardly goes at all, but we have a diversion. We're invited to dinner tonight, if you've made no other arrangements."

"An assignation with my host of admirers? We hadn't had time to come around to that." *Damnation.* She'd been determined to let that issue rest.

"If it was a host," he said, "I might not object."

"I assure you, Braydon, there will never be assignations with an individual."

"Very well."

It could be acceptance, but she felt his simmering suspicion, and that triggered her next words. "If we move to the town house, I might like to hold an open house for officers once a week. There is a need. I know they have their clubs, but sometimes they want something else."

"Someone."

"It's *not* about me."

"I think it is, but if it came to that, I wouldn't object. I assume I would not be excluded."

"Of course not. And I'd welcome other ladies, especially wives. And widows. There must be too many military widows."

"You'll set up a matchmaking agency?"

She couldn't read his tone, so chose to take his words at face value. "Why not? Alas that so many military men can't afford to marry, especially on half pay."

"And any number might prefer the single life."

Like you? With your comfortable, female-free rooms. "All the more need for a gathering place," she said, "without gaming and hard drinking."

"A benevolent cause," he agreed. "But the Abbey can't be ignored."

Kitty managed not to curse. For a moment she'd enjoyed that vision of the future, with the Kit Kat Club revived, but in the spacious town house with the funds to be generous. However, at best she'd spend a couple of months in Town, and that would be during the season when there'd be less need for a gathering place.

As they entered his building he said, "Our box is available for tomorrow at Covent Garden. I gather the theaters are never full these days."

"Mourning has gone beyond reason. I've even had narrow looks because of my blue cloak. Perhaps some think I should dye Sillikin black!"

"Do you have half mourning to wear to the theater?"

"It's necessary? Then it's good that I brought some. What about tonight?"

"I doubt anyone there will care. The invitation was from Major Hal Beaumont. You might know him."

Did she detect an edge to that? "There were a great many men, and I don't have your memory."

"He's without an arm now."

"Ah! Such wounds are more memorable, though too common by far." They climbed the stairs. "He served in Canada, yes? A very pleasant gentleman. Didn't he marry an actress?"

"He did. Will you object to dining at their house?"

"Of course not."

"Of course not," he echoed, but he didn't seem displeased.

They entered his rooms in a sort of harmony, but Kitty was aware of discord beneath. He would simply have to learn to trust her. They took lunch together, talking about a safe subject: the house.

"Mrs. Grant would like a water boiler and a Rumford stove in the kitchen," she told him.

"By all means. We can see if it's possible to install the hot-water piping to the bathroom."

"There isn't one. Only tubs to be set up in bedrooms and no space to create one, either. But it needs a general refurbishment. I need not count the expense, need I?"

"Short of silver-plating the walls, no."

"Would anyone?"

"Nothing is beyond the foibles of the insane rich."

Which touched on the question of how rich they were. As she poured more tea, Kitty said, "I gather that much of the viscountcy's money went to Isabella."

"The investments and such, but the viscountcy produces a decent income, and I have money of my own. You needn't count the pennies."

"That will be pleasant." The discussion itself was pleasant, but would he turn moody whenever he encountered her with her military friends?

As they finished their meal, Braydon said, "I've been considering what you said about the fifth viscount. He mostly stayed at his club?"

"That's what Mrs. Grant said."

"I don't recall any expenses from a club. Some memberships, yes, but if he was living in one for months on end, there should be more."

"Somewhere in the boxes of curiosity?"

"We've gone through most of the papers."

"Does it matter?"

"If he wasn't living at the house or at a club, where was he?"

Kitty considered it, then exclaimed, "A mistress! Why didn't I think of that? One he'd set up in a house. He wouldn't want his servants to know, so he'd claim to be at a club."

"Then there should be expenses relating to that."

"Oh, I suppose so. You think he was up to something shady? From his portrait, it seems unlikely."

"It does. When we unravel this, we'll discover something completely banal."

"Should we pity him for that assessment?"

He gave a wry smile. "Probably envy him, but I don't think either of us is suited to a dull and tranquil life."

"No." She liked the way he linked them. She remembered thinking that Braydon's longing for London was because of a mistress, but now she doubted it. He was simply enjoying being in Town and whatever work he was involved in. They were both suited to London and its challenges, but the Abbey and estates hung around their necks like . . . like slave collars.

She remembered another scrap of Shakespeare. Something about things gone wrong, and someone cursed to have been born to set it right. Flies to wanton gods indeed.

"Is something the matter?" he asked.

She put on a cheerful face. "Only the thought of a dull and tranquil life." She raised her teacup. "Lord save us from that!"

Braydon left to return to Peel Street. He could have remained at home, for there was nothing pressing to do, but he didn't trust himself. He couldn't rid himself of the image of Kitty in a circle of admiring military men, glowing with enjoyment.

Had she ever glowed like that for him?

Reason shouted that they'd known each other for only a couple of days, but that underlined that she'd known some of those men for far longer. *Known . . .*

Their wedding night had wiped away any notion of her having many lovers. She'd seemed to come to bed with an assumption of one, clear way of going about it. That didn't mean she hadn't loved. Had she wished one of her established admirers had made her an offer so she'd not had to accept one from a stranger out of desperation?

One of the military cluster had been Edison. He was the one who'd given her Sillikin, but also the one Braydon had lied to about her whereabouts. No wonder Edison had sent him a coldly furious look, but that proved a depth of attachment.

He'd returned the look with interest. *She's mine now. Abandon hope.*

The last thing he should do was to show his jealousy, which was why he'd left, but perhaps if he returned, he could do better. . . .

"Lord Dauntry!"

He snapped to attention to see a florid Mrs. Motely approaching, her eldest daughter in tow. She was his sister Justina's sister-in-law and keen to increase the family connection.

Despite the nip in the air, the two Motelys were willing

to linger. At the earliest opportunity he mentioned his wife. That led to exclamations of surprise and smiling good wishes, but also to their abrupt lack of interest. His marriage was serving that purpose, at least.

It wouldn't have been hard to find a wife, but as he'd always known, a conventional wooing would have required more time and promises he hadn't felt able to make.

And it would have been a shame, because then he'd not be married to Kit Kat.

Damn her.

Chapter 31

Kitty lingered at the lunch table, fretting over Braydon's attitude and depressed by thoughts of the Abbey; but dwelling on either could only make matters worse. The Abbey was her destiny, and Braydon wasn't like Marcus. His jealousy wouldn't turn violent.

She abandoned her cold tea to investigate Diane Dauntry in Braydon's library. The information could be useful. The dowager might be a forlorn hope, but Isabella might come around. Having news of her mother could help.

Sillikin accompanied her, but after a brief investigation flopped down in front of the fire.

"A pity you can't read. You could make yourself useful."

The Hartley family of Chipping Ongar. If the family had a peerage, they'd be in Mr. Debrett's useful book. As soon as she opened it, however, she realized that unless the peerage title was also Hartley, she had no means of finding them there.

She found nothing under Hartley.

Next she checked a gazetteer, and there, under Chipping Ongar, she found Sir Allenby Hartley, baronet, of Keys Court. The mention was brief, however, and mostly about the house, which seemed ordinary enough. Probably not a wealthy family, and pleased for their daughter to become "my lady." Had the fifth viscount married for love, against his mother's wishes? That could have been the seed for endless discord.

The library was well organized, which was hardly surprising, and all the reference works were in one section. She hunted for something else and found that Mr. Debrett also had a book about baronets. There she found the detail she needed. Sir Allenby was married to Catherine Forbes, daughter of Sir Charles Forbes of Cheshunt. He had issue, a son, Allenby Forbes Hartley, a daughter Susanna Maria, who was married to Henry Filstowe, Esquire, of Tonbridge, Kent, and a daughter Diane Alice, married to Viscount Dauntry of Beauchamp Abbey, Gloucestershire.

Kitty checked the date of publication. Only five years ago, but the entry had been technically correct. Diane had still been married to the fifth viscount at that time. It was no business of Mr. Debrett's if a couple chose to live apart.

She made a note of all the details.

Sillikin stood, stretched, and came over with a look that strongly suggested a walk.

"In a moment. Should I write or should I visit?"

The dog whined.

"If you're in a hurry, it will have to be without me." Kitty opened the door and called for Edward. Sillikin greeted the footman like a relieving army and went with him without hesitation.

Putting aside grievance over that, Kitty returned to her problem. She was tempted to order a coach and rush out to Chipping Ongar. But on a short winter day it could be dark by the time she arrived, and the Hartleys might be elsewhere.

She'd do the sensible thing and write. It was a delicate letter to compose, but she tried for a sympathetic tone and asked if they knew about Diane's whereabouts, as she wanted to give the information to her daughter, who had lost so many of her family.

Her signature presented an unexpected dilemma. She knew she must use her title as her last name, but should it be Kitty or Kathryn? Lady Cateril had given her a deep dislike of being Kathryn, but Kathryn Dauntry seemed more dignified.

She realized she was still troubled by Dauntry's reaction to the officers and Kit Kat. *To Hades with that!* Kitty she was, and Kitty she would always be. She signed Kitty Dauntry, then folded and sealed the letter. She put the letter in the foyer for Edward to take to the post office.

Next, she summoned her courage and invaded the servants' quarters. Henry had told her that the ruler of the kitchen was a Mr. Kingdom, who was surly and easily angered, though he'd melted for Sillikin. Kitty hoped that would count in her favor, but she must confront him. She was now mistress of this establishment.

The cook did seem surly, but he was also short, fat, and had a patch over one eye. "Yuz, milady?" he growled in a heavy accent, perhaps from Worcestershire. "Y'ave a complaint?"

Kitty resisted a desire to back out of the small room. "Not at all, Kingdom. Everything's been excellent. I merely wondered if you had all that you need."

"Yuz, milady." She could almost hear him thinking, *Except the space you're taking up.*

A pot simmered on a very compact stove. The wooden table was spread with vegetables. Did the servants eat in here? With the addition of Henry, it would be crowded. Perhaps the cook was surly because of that.

Kitty still wanted to retreat, but she held her ground. "The stove is quite small. I assume you buy baked meats."

"Yuz, milady."

"And bread and cakes."

"I sometimes make his lordship's favorites, milady."
Reluctantly, he added, "Is there aught you'd like, milady?
While you're here."

Kitty was very tempted to reprimand him for that,
but if Braydon kept such a servant, he must value him.

"Stewed oysters," she said. "Thank you. Carry on."
She left, blowing out a breath. *What an odd creature.* She
soon found Henry and asked about Kingdom.

"He was a ship's cook," Henry said, "so he'll be used
to a confined kitchen. I understand many of the sets of
rooms here don't have one at all—only a hob on a fire
where a pot can be boiled. He's more bark than bite. I
think he's nervous around women, and aware he's not
the prettiest sight."

"He might have feared I'd try to get him turned off?
Poor man. Though he did make it clear he expects me
to soon be gone."

"That might be my fault, dear. To keep the peace, I
told him we didn't expect to be here for long. I think he
was imagining us a fixture."

"Are families permitted here? I know in some sets of
gentlemen's rooms they aren't."

"Permitted but not encouraged. And even such elegant rooms aren't suitable, are they?"

"No." Kitty thought wistfully of the house, but there'd
be no reason to open that up for a week or less, and she
must soon return to her duties.

She hoped the Hartleys replied soon. Discovering
Diane Dauntry's whereabouts might be the only truly
useful thing she could do while in London. In the meantime, she must consider what to wear to this dinner—her
first social engagement as Viscountess Dauntry.

And after?
The night.

Her husband would have no excuse to be out till all hours tonight.

After an afternoon with little achieved, Braydon arrived home to find his wife secluded in the second bedroom, preparing for dinner. He washed and changed for the evening, troubled by that. Was she intending to sleep there tonight?

Because of their falling-out about her admirers?

When he entered the drawing room he found her ready, but with a challenging look in her eye. Devil take it, why had she chosen to wear the pagan red gown and the cashmere shawl? With the addition of a very fetching red and gold turban, she'd stop men dead in the street.

He made sure to smile. "You look magnificent, my dear."

"Too magnificent for a dinner?"

She'd caught his misgivings anyway. "Of course not."

She was his, and tonight he intended to wipe all thought of other men from her mind. As he put her cloak around her shoulders he murmured, "Tonight, you sleep in my bed."

Her look was startled but not resentful. Heat flickered behind her green and gold eyes, and her full lips softened, perhaps on the edge of a smile.

Damned witch.

Damned dinner. Braydon arrived at Beaumont's, house wishing the event already over.

They were warmly greeted by Beaumont's wife. She performed under her former name, Blanche Hardcastle, and was famous for her prematurely white hair and her habit of dressing only in white, on- and offstage. She was clearly keeping to that even in this time of mourning.

He'd been delighted by her on the stage, but it was

pleasant to find that she was as charming and beautiful from only a yard away. She wore the lightest powder and paint, which showed that her looks were all her own, and it seemed her nature was genuine as well.

Even as Braydon greeted her, an uncomfortable scrap of information popped into his head. She'd been known—might still be known—as the White Dove of Drury Lane. Again, a reference to her coloring, but with a slight implication of a disreputable past, as loose women were sometimes called spoiled doves. It wouldn't be entirely surprising, for actresses were not always pattern cards of virtue, and Beaumont was unlikely to be ignorant of her past.

Especially as—another inconvenient fact—she'd been the mistress of the Marquess of Arden for a number of years, and Arden and Beaumont were old friends. It wouldn't be the first time friends had shared or passed on a mistress, but for one to marry the lady was unusual. How fortunate that he was able to keep a smooth demeanor while digesting alarming facts.

There was nothing alarming about the Balls. Sir Stephen was certainly not a military type, having a more intellectual appearance. Dark-haired Lady Ball was an elegant charmer.

The other two guests were a fresh-faced young Canadian lawyer, Grantford Torlie, and Miss Feathers, a snub-nosed, bright-eyed actress from Drury Lane. Torlie was introduced as the son of a man Beaumont had known in Canada, and the young man was clearly very happy that Miss Feathers had been invited to balance the numbers.

Despite Braydon's wish that the event be soon over, he had to admit that the food was excellent and the conversation interesting and frequently amusing. Kitty played her part with ease.

Miss Feathers was young and lively, but she was no fool. When Torlie paid her a compliment that was a little too warm, she dropped into the conversation that she lived with her mother, who was, sadly, strict. "But," she added, "you would be most welcome to call and make her acquaintance, sir. She was once an actress herself."

"And an excellent one," Blanche Beaumont said. "Harriet could still be on the stage in older parts if an infection hadn't damaged her voice."

Beaumont said, "It's time we conquered infection," and discussion turned in that direction, touching on folk remedies, including maggots. Miss Feathers pulled a face, and Torlie declared he'd not have maggots eating his flesh.

"You'd be a fool not to have them eating an infection that would otherwise kill you," Beaumont said. He hadn't said "that could cost you a limb," because that would cause distress, but it had to have been what he'd thought. Battle-damaged limbs were frequently amputated to remove any danger of infection, but with time and care they might have been saved.

Laura Ball deftly turned the talk toward charities for wounded soldiers and the need for employment for them. That moved them all to the economy and the signs of improvement. It was more substantial talk than would be approved at most dinner tables, but skillfully avoided disagreements or jarring debate.

When the ladies left, none of the men raised difficult subjects, except when Braydon asked Torlie what brought him to London.

"To hone my legal training, sir. I wanted Boston, but my father insisted on London."

"Canada is ruled by British law," Ball said.

"But not forever, Sir Stephen. It's inevitable that we join the American states in time."

Braydon raised his brows with the others.

"That could be seen as treason," Ball pointed out.

Torlie colored, but he stood his ground. "Canada must at the least become self-governing, sir. We're thousands of miles from St. James and Westminster. If we then choose to become a republic and join with America, I hope no one will attempt to prevent it."

"I wouldn't stake my life on that," Braydon said, passing the port but considering a new twist. *Would Canadians who wished to join the Americans seek to create dynastic chaos in Britain?* Sufficient disorder, most especially a civil war, would make it easier for them to slip away. But, again, it would be a very long-term plan.

"Some are willing to die for freedom," Torlie declared, threatening the harmony of the evening.

Braydon said, "Your skill in British law could be more useful than your blood, Torlie. Know thy enemy. There was a time in Spain when one of the men knowing local custom turned the tide."

He told the story, and then Beaumont added another, and the moment passed. Soon after they all rose to join the ladies in the drawing room.

Beaumont took a moment with Braydon. "Apologies for young Torlie. I suspect his father shipped him over here to get him away from others of similar mind."

"We all tend to crackbrain ideas when young."

"It might not be entirely crackbrained."

Braydon raised a hand. "I have enough on my plate without a North American mess. Three princes and a peerage."

Beaumont chuckled. "How are you coping with becoming a viscount?"

"Much as one copes with a long march through enemy terrain in winter."

"As bad as that? Your wife must be a help. A strong and sensible woman, and she deserves an easier march."

"It was bad?" Braydon asked, wanting to know.

Beaumont grimaced. "Who knows the secrets of a marriage, and I visited there only a few times, years ago. But Marcus Cateril was fiery by nature, and that didn't change except in being confined. A man can't help resenting injuries at times."

Did he refer to himself and his missing arm? If so, he didn't dwell on it.

"His were severe," Beaumont went on. "Walking pained him and he was ungainly, which might have pained him even more. He'd once been a fit, athletic type. It had to have made him difficult at times, but he loved his Kitty. No doubt of that."

"And she him."

"Of course."

Unreasonable to let that sting. "Ball seems sound. I'll bring him in if he's willing. There are matters to discuss tomorrow. Perhaps here?"

"Of course."

Chapter 32

Kitty enjoyed the dinner. She'd expected awkwardness, but their hosts put them at ease and the company was pleasant, even the wet-behind-the-ears Canadian. His enthusiasms made her smile. She remembered many young officers like him. And that many were no longer alive. *Thank heavens for peace.*

She felt she played her part well, and she enjoyed the drawing room conversation with the other ladies. It surprised her a little that the very elegant Lady Ball was on such easy terms with one actress and accepting of another, but so it seemed.

The Balls would soon be traveling to the country for Christmas, but the Beaumonts would spend the season in Town. As Kitty would like to do. Beneath all the social pleasantries, however, rippled her awareness of the coming night.

Thank heavens the party broke up at a reasonable time, so it was not yet half past ten when Kitty entered the hackney carriage with her husband. She was to sleep in his bed. Did that mean "stay there all night"? It must, when the alternative would be to slip back into bed with Henry.

"That was very pleasant," she said, "Excellent company, though Torlie is a bit raw."

"But mostly minds his manners well enough."

"Do you think Canada should join with the Americans?"

"I refuse to even consider the question. How delightful that a turban is no impediment to kissing."

His lips brushed against hers playfully and she responded in kind, already warm with desire. They deepened it together until she broke the kiss, flushed and breathless. "I'm sorry. I can't be moderate. It's been so long."

"Since the night before last," he pointed out, tracing her sensitized lips with a gloved finger.

She shifted on the hard leather seat. "Before then, I mean. And I confess . . . I've always had an appetite."

"Which I appreciate. But unless we want to disgrace ourselves, we'd best wait."

He lowered his hand, and she wove her fingers with his. "How do people survive forever without?"

"Are you asking about my mistresses?"

"Of course not!" Her protest was instinctive and not entirely truthful. She slid a look at him. "I wouldn't mind knowing how many there have been."

His smile reached his eyes. "Very few, if we're being precise. Most have been more temporary partners—"

She put fingers over his lips. "Don't. It's none of my business. Though I would like to know. . . ."

He pushed her fingers aside. "Yes?"

She asked the burning question. "Do you have a mistress now?"

"No. Why think that?"

"Your longing for Town. Ruth and Andrew assumed . . ."

He laughed. "Life as a clergyman must incline one to suspect the worst. Not that such an arrangement is the worst. But no, I don't have a barque of frailty tucked away in a little house somewhere, awaiting my convenience."

"I'm glad. It would be complicated."

"I'm surprised you don't feel more strongly than that."

"I'd have no right, given our arrangement."

"Not a trace of jealousy?"

"I didn't speak of how I'd feel." Kitty saw where he'd led her, the tricksy man. *Sauce for the gander; sauce for the goose.* "I was more aware of possible complications. She might have been a fashionable widow whom I'd meet at some event. A more beautiful and elegant woman than I. Heavens! I must have drunk too much."

He kissed her. "I like it when your tongue is loosened into truth."

"I wish yours was."

So, suddenly, under the influence of wine, they were at a serious point.

"I'm a private person, Kitty. I'm not sure I can be otherwise, but I'll try not to keep important matters from you."

It might be the unimportant ones that matter.

"I don't want to be demanding."

"You can be as demanding as you like," he replied. "Now that we're home."

Heat blossomed. She might even be sweating beneath her cloak. He climbed out, helped her down, and paid the cab driver. Then he led her into the house. "Come, my wife, to bed."

Johns was waiting up, but Braydon dismissed him and led Kitty into his bedroom.

"Have you ever played a card game where the forfeits are clothes?" he asked.

"No. And I don't want to now."

"Nor do I, but I propose that we undress each other, layer by layer."

Kitty would rather rip off clothing in whatever was the most efficient way, but she could match him move for move. "A glove, then, sir." She drew a leather glove off his right hand. His beautiful right hand, which she wanted on her skin.

"A glove," he said in turn. Her gown had long sleeves, so her silk gloves were short and one was easily removed. Soon he could say, "Hands bared. All the better to remove other items. A shoe, madam."

She'd expected the cloak to go next, but she raised a foot. He untied the ribbons and took off her right shoe.

She almost demanded his shoe, but why follow the pattern he set? "Greatcoat, sir." She unbuttoned it and took it off, tossing the heavy garment over a chair.

"Stocking," he said in turn.

Ah. "Stocking" meant "garter," up around her thigh. She'd gone naked to bed with Marcus without a blush, but this . . . This was different.

"Raise your right foot onto the chair," he said.

She obeyed, putting a hand on the back of the chair. He pushed up her red skirt and white petticoat until her frilled drawers were revealed, with her embroidered garter beneath her knee. He slowly, very slowly, untied it.

"I could say the garter was your item, sir," she said, hearing her own huskiness. "But I'll permit."

He eased her stocking down slowly, the brush of his fingers on calf and ankle delicious torment. Her body clenched. Her breath shortened. He lifted her foot to take off the stocking, and then raised her foot higher to kiss the arch.

Despite her drawers, Kitty was aware of being open to him, and how very much she wished he'd take advantage of that. She'd joined with Marcus only when naked, but she knew from scurrilous cartoons that men need only unloose their member and her split drawers would present no serious obstacle. That was often the way with men and whores, but she wouldn't mind being taken like a whore. In fact . . .

When he let go of her foot, she used it to push him backward toward the bed. Eyes widening, he stepped back and sat. She put down her foot, shed her cloak, and then walked to him and unbuttoned his flap. She soon had his member free, firm and rising. She raised her skirts and straddled him, filling herself, hands on his shoulders, exhaling with slow satisfaction.

But he stood with her. "Legs around me," he commanded, thrusting her back against the wall.

And he took her like that, standing, thrusting her up again and again with a power she'd never experienced before. Squeezing her legs around him, head thrown back in passion, Kitty had to choke back cries as he drove her into hot, dark oblivion.

Chapter 33

She came to tangled on the bed, still mostly dressed, but in complete disorder.

"Not what I planned," he mumbled, kissing around her jaw and ear. To her mouth, for a kiss as devastating as the rest.

After the kiss, after recovering, she asked, "What did you plan?"

"I've forgotten."

"You?" she teased.

He half opened his eyes to meet hers. "You are a wicked woman."

"Do you mind?"

"Only an idiot would." Kisses later he asked, "Do we dare to undress any further?"

"Probably not," she said, running a hand through his tousled hair. *Not so beaulike now, my lord.* "But I'm sure we must."

It was many minutes before they found the strength to get off the bed.

"I can undress myself," he said, shrugging off his jacket, "but you'll need assistance."

"Another unfairness between the sexes."

"If that's your mind, I should introduce you to the Marchioness of Arden. She's an enthusiast for the rights of women."

"Does she wear corsets?"

"I doubt Arden would appreciate my knowing."

"It would be obvious from the look of her gowns."

"Then yes, she wears corsets."

"The rights of women go only so far." Kitty turned her back. "Release me, husband." As he undid buttons, she said, "Some of my everyday gowns unfasten at the front. Fine gowns could, too."

She undid the three buttons at her cuffs herself and took off the gown, letting it drop to the floor. He set to work on the knots and laces of her stays, saying, "These garments could be simpler."

"I have soft bodices that I can wear instead of boned ones. They fasten at the front. But a gown never looks the same."

"It's an ancient struggle—comfort over appearance."

"Women have had more rational dress at times," she said, taking off her stays and petticoat, but watching as he removed his neckcloth and then sat to take off his boots. "A medieval style, perhaps. Loose, with a girdle at the waist."

"Like a shift?"

She was down to her shift—and one stocking. She turned to the long mirror. The shapeless white garment hung down to her shins. "A gown would be longer, but . . ." She cinched the waist with her hands. "It looks like a sack tied in the middle. What fools we women be."

She turned back to see that he was down to his breeches with his flap unbuttoned, which in some way was more enticing than complete nakedness. "What aspects of men's clothing would you improve?" she asked.

"Neckcloths and collars. No starch."

She took off her stocking slowly. "They'd just flop."

He watched, slowly releasing the waistband of his

trousers. "Our fathers had soft collars or none, and soft muslin neckcloths to tie around their necks."

"Why do men need anything about their necks?" she asked, walking over to touch the base of his throat, but leaning her body into him lower down. "Why can't they go low necked, especially in summer?"

He trapped her hand. "I'm sure many men have asked the same. There are countries where men wear long, flowing garments and are not felt less manly for it."

"You supposedly set the fashion, Beau Braydon. Bring it into style."

He escaped her touch to take off his breeches and drawers.

"In Greece," she asked, closing her hand on his cock, "did men often go naked, as in statues?"

"Do we care?"

She eyed him, smiling at the heat in his eyes and at the growing heat in herself.

Better than with Marcus.

The thought felt wrong, wicked even, but it was true. With Marcus she'd always known what to expect, and always had to be careful. This was an adventure, and he could endure anything.

"Into bed," he commanded.

She shed her shift and climbed into bed to lie on her back in the middle, liking very much the way Braydon looked her over, head to toe, his cock rising higher.

She'd expected another fierce joining, but he lay down at her side and explored her with only one hand. His touch was delicious and wandered to places never touched in that way before, but she wanted to protest the delay.

Especially when he stopped and said, "Sit up."

Trying to anticipate the next surprise, she obeyed.

He began to take pins out of her hair. She raised her hands to help him, but he said, "No. I'll do it."

"Damn you," she muttered.

Though her back was to him, she could sense his smile.

All very well, sir, but your need is more urgent than mine, I'll go odds.

She sat as still as she could as her hair was loosed, but struggled under every touch. Could he know how arousing she found it?

He fingered through her hair, his mouth playing on her shoulders, then on her back. All the way down her spine, even to the cleft at the top of her buttocks. She wanted to command him to cease, to turn and take him. She was sure he was beyond protest. But there was mysterious pleasure in this slow, torturous play.

This is seduction, she realized. Seduction of her body. It had never happened before.

She broke and turned, lying back, legs wide, pulling him to her.

He resisted, hotly smiling.

"Damned torturer!"

He trapped her hands and tormented her breasts. At first he only licked and kissed, but then he drew a nipple deep in his mouth, and a cry escaped her. She clenched her jaw to prevent another, but wanted to plead.

He released her, but instead of entering her then, he slid fingers inside her. She couldn't help but thrust against his hand to drive to her release, and he caught her choked cries in a blinding kiss. No sooner had she crested and sunk down, gasping, sweaty, spent, than he entered her, thick and hard.

Her mouth was free and the noise she made might have been protest, but immediately she was caught up again, driven up again, with nothing to do but surrender to the pounding wave of passion even more intensely than before.

Eventually, surely much later—in fact the candles were almost spent—she opened her eyes to see he was as hot, sweaty, and disheveled as she.

"A box of fire," she said.

"What?" he mumbled without stirring an inch.

"Nothing."

Stroking him, she recognized that that had been a performance of sorts. It might simply be to outdo Marcus, but it probably rose from jealousy. *In that case,* she thought, *there is something to be said for jealousy.*

Relaxed in sleep, his handsomeness came close to beauty, and she wanted to stroke his lean cheek and straight nose and even the little indentations about his nostrils. She wanted to lick and kiss, but he deserved his sleep and, in truth, she felt worn out. She might be a little sore tomorrow, but she had no complaint.

None at all, for here was a man capable of many variations. Odd that she'd never imagined variety in marriage, even though she'd seen pictures. She'd separated one from the other, but there was no reason for that.

She couldn't help wondering about other marriages. Did all couples play games with undressing, join together standing up, or drive one another to the brink? She closed the door on that. Each to their own, but her own was full of promise.

She woke in the pitch-dark night to find his arm over her, holding her close. Thinking him asleep, she curled a hand around his forearm, but he said, "Are you all right?"

"Of course. Did I wake you?"

"No."

"Are *you* all right?" she asked.

"Of course."

She realized the simple questions were meaningful. They were nothing to do with the physical, except in it being intensely pleasurable. In that heat they'd forged an unexpected connection. She couldn't call it love, whatever that was, but it was like wrought iron, folded and beaten together until it became unbreakable. He might not have expected that. Would it change anything?

The inevitable problem had slid back into her mind. They wouldn't spend many nights together. Best not to mention it, but that wasn't her way.

"I'll miss you when we're apart."

"And I you." He kissed her shoulder.

She turned to face him. "You needn't spend so much time in London."

"Perhaps not, but what would I do with myself at the Abbey?"

Make love to me, she thought. But she said, "Sort papers."

He nipped at her ear, and she obliged with a squeak.

"Many men seem to enjoy country living," she argued. "In addition to running their estate, they hunt, shoot, and fish. Meet other country gentlemen . . ."

"To talk about hunting, shooting, and fishing. And crop yields and the diseases of cattle and sheep."

"Discussions on the improvements in agriculture. Exploration of mining and local industries."

"You can do that for me."

"I doubt a woman would be allowed."

"And it's not your interest, either, is it?"

A tricky subject. "I'll keep to our agreement."

He kissed her. "I want your happiness."

She kissed him back. "I want *our* happiness, but we can't leave the Abbey estate to the dowager. You'd never be happy if things went awry there."

"You give me too much credit."

"Do I?"

He sighed. "No." He rolled onto his back. "It should be easy for me to simply spend more time there with you, but there are serious matters in play, Kitty, all centered on London, and I can be useful."

"Can't others do those tasks as well?"

"Perhaps. Perhaps not. The truth is, it's my life."

"You did similar things in the war," she said.

"Yes. Looking at the larger picture, holding more in my mind than most and finding the patterns. And the keys. And strengthening small alliances. Remembering details helps there, too. Family histories and rivalries, small misdemeanors and desires, careless words . . ."

She moved over him. "Thus we are as we are. For now at least. Circumstances might change."

"You hope Britain will become more orderly, peaceful, and just? I don't expect it soon."

"I wasn't being so visionary. Perhaps once we have everything in order at the Abbey, I can spend more time in London."

"Optimistic visionary! But you'd like that, wouldn't you?"

"That's what we're discussing."

He brushed hair off her face. "I mean that it's not just me. London's in your blood."

She sighed. "Yes. Many people dislike the crowds, the noise, the smoke and smells, but it's *alive*. There's something exciting around every corner. The arts, the sciences, the fairs and shops. If I can move the dowager elsewhere . . ."

"Dreaming on a star?"

"There has to be a way. To make everything right, I mean."

"You'd think so, wouldn't you? Perhaps we can't achieve international peace, but we should be able to put one country estate into a healthy and stable condition." He brushed tangled hair off her face. "Don't fret about it for now, Kit Kat. We're here and have reason to stay a while. Take pleasure in the day. And the night."

She smiled and kissed him, then enjoyed the simple pleasure of falling asleep in her husband's arms.

He'd called her Kit Kat.

Chapter 34

As they breakfasted the next morning, Kitty wondered if the servants could recognize the momentous change. She felt that it radiated out of her and showed in every look and smile they shared. Perhaps this was love. They were behaving much as lovers do, with sudden smiles and lingering looks.

Though her husband had the same cool elegance on the outside, the marble box had melted away to reveal warmth and passion. He'd been tender in ways she'd never known and forceful in others. They'd talked in the intimate dark, but often lain in each other's arms in comfortable silence. They had been physically comfortable, but she felt sure that he, like she, had been aware of how few nights they would have together.

She'd resolved to enjoy what they had, however, even such simple pleasures as breakfast.

Then, with the door closed, he shared his secrets. He told her his reason for coming to Town and invited her comments. She'd have done her best to help him anyway, but now it was a gift.

"An attempt to blow up three middle-aged princes to prevent their marrying seems deranged," she said.

"There are all too many deranged people active at the moment, and some capable of doing damage. Only months ago, a woman attempted to blow up Westminster, hoping to trigger a revolution similar to the one in France."

"Madness! How?"

"Using a gasometer."

"At least that's a novel idea," Kitty said, buttering another slice of toast. "In contrast, this seems clumsy, and very old-fashioned. A barrel of gunpowder in the basement? All too like Guy Fawkes."

"The Gunpowder Plot could easily have worked," he pointed out. "If there'd been no warning back in 1605, Catesby and Fawkes could have blown up king and Parliament and changed the course of history."

Kitty nibbled her toast, as delighted by this discussion as she'd been by their lovemaking in the night. Almost. "If it was so easy to get the barrel of gunpowder into the house, why not deliver it later? Then they could have overwhelmed the footman, set it to explode, and escaped with the task completed."

"I hope you never put your mind to mayhem," he said drily. "But a daylight delivery would be normal, whereas an evening one wouldn't."

"True. And they'd be busier then, so might refuse the delivery." She sipped some chocolate. Again he was drinking ordinary coffee. He'd said that he kept the Turkish for special moments. She'd teased him about this not being special. . . .

"Interesting thoughts?" he asked.

"Not on the current matter." He reflected her smile, but she dragged her mind back to the problem. "Let's return to the beginning. You said that even if the plot had succeeded, there'd be no immediate benefit to anyone beyond alarm and distress. Could there be some unsuspected benefit to anyone?"

He leaned back in his seat. "It wasn't to do with the

succession at all? A direct plot against one of the princes, disguised by the presence of the others?"

"I'd not even imagined that. It would be vile—to kill three to get one. How many people could think like that? And what could drive them to it?"

"People kill over remarkably petty matters—a grudge, a slight, a few shillings of debt—and often they don't consider the effects on others, but I agree. It would be astonishing to feel that way about royalty, and be willing to make the attempt."

Kitty considered matters. "The most dramatic event in recent times was Princess Charlotte's death. Could the plot arise from that?"

"The succession," he said.

"Put that aside. There's sympathy for the Regent's loss, but anger about the treatment Charlotte received. Many think the queen should have been in attendance, and some hold her and the Regent responsible for the choice of doctors."

"But the plot was aimed at neither."

"Perhaps our crackbrain realized he couldn't strike at the main players and went after the Regent's brothers instead. You don't believe that?"

"I don't believe any of it, but there's one large problem. The meeting of the princes was a quickly arranged plan known to very few. How did our crackbrained would-be Guy Fawkes find out?"

Kitty pulled a face at him.

"And," he added, "the queen is not that strongly guarded in Bath. She'd have been an easy target."

"Perhaps the crackbrain didn't care to strike against an old, sick woman?"

"Illogical."

"Crackbrained," she shot back. "In any case, the death of three sons would be a great blow to her. Dead sons and grieving mothers," she said. "That seems to be a running thread for us. We're getting nowhere, aren't we?"

"We've indulged in flights of fancy, which is always amusing, but often the simplest solution is the true one. Most evildoers are not clever enough to be complex."

"How many are willing to wait decades for any benefit of their plan?"

"A point. Perhaps our plotter is a country man. There's a plantation of trees at the Abbey begun by the fourth viscount that will be felled for timber round about the time the last of the king's children might die."

Kitty rolled her eyes. "I'm sure there's some deep philosophical point in that, but if the plotter is of that mind, you have a difficult time ahead."

"Unless they intend to pick off the royal family one by one."

"Doesn't that make your situation more difficult rather than less?"

"If there are repeated attempts," he said, "the hand will eventually become clear."

"If there are repeated attempts, the country will be thrown into ferment. The purpose?"

"Possibly. Which is why we must put a stop to it now." He'd drunk the last of his coffee and came to kiss her lingeringly, a hand cradling her face. She knew his pull back to the bedroom was as powerful as hers, but he straightened. "What are your plans for the day?"

A honeymoon, she thought. But that wasn't possible.

"A dressmaker. She's also a friend, so that's a pleasure jaunt."

"Your comments have been useful, Kitty. Thank you."

He went to the door, but Kitty suddenly had another thought. "Speaking of mothers, what about the Princess of Wales? Caroline of Brunswick might be blaming the royal family for her daughter's death."

"Oh, dear God. And she is crackbrained enough for anything. I'm not sure whether to thank you or curse you for putting that notion on the list."

Kitty wasted a few moments smiling at the closed door, and then had to bite her lips on tears. Why was everything always bittersweet? She could try harder to persuade him of the delights of rural life, but how, when she didn't see them herself? With his work here being so important, it was hopeless.

She could probably arrange matters so she could spend more time in London, but that wasn't what she wanted. Greedily, she wanted to be with her husband every day and every night. She wanted the passion, but she also wanted his company and the sort of discussion they'd just enjoyed. She wanted to share her life with him.

"Oh, I'll fall into a fit of the blue devils this way," she said, startling Sillikin awake. "Time to visit Janet Saunders."

With some difficulty, she left Edward behind.

"I'm going to a very simple place, Edward. People will stare if I arrive with an entourage."

"The simpler the place, ma'am, the more I should be with you."

"For heaven's sake, I lived in Moor Street for eight years with never a scrap of trouble. I have friends there."

"All the same, ma'am, his lordship would wish me to accompany you."

"Then you must tell him I bullied you unmercifully, which I will do if you don't do as I say."

With a sigh and rolled eyes, he went to summon a hackney for her and allowed her to ride away with only Henry and Sillikin to defend her from the barbarian hordes.

Chapter 35

Janet Saunders was a sturdy Scots widow who'd set up as dressmaker in a house close to Kitty's former home. She did simple work at economical prices, and Kitty had used her services. In time they'd become friends, and also become more adventurous. After all, Kitty was an honorable, and she played hostess to many gentlemen of high birth.

Janet had taken to walking around Mayfair, observing the fine ladies. She'd then draw similar designs, but adapted for Kitty's slender purse. Soon her other clients, mostly wives of professional men and local tradesmen, wanted finer garments, and Janet could employ more workers.

She was clever at making do. She visited warehouses, haggling over the ends of bolts and slightly damaged cloth and trimming. She hunted through cast-off finery for trimmings that could be salvaged. Kitty had always paid Janet as much as she could afford, but she'd known she was worth more.

Janet beamed to see Kitty and Sillikin, and when told the news almost had palpitations. "A viscountess! Havers! You've come to make my fortune!"

She was teasing, but Kitty realized it could be true. "I have, Janet. My gowns are excellent, aren't they, Henry?"

Henry smiled and agreed, but with provisos. "In a middling sort of way. No offense to you, Mrs. Saunders, for you've had to make do, but now you'll be able to afford the finest materials and trimming. Your talents will shine, and when ladies beg for the name of Lady Dauntry's mantua maker, my mistress can reluctantly be persuaded to share the secret."

Janet's eyes were sparkling at the idea, but she said, "They'll never want to come here to Moor Street."

"You'll be surprised, Mrs. Saunders. Ladies who hear of a secret treasure will hunt it down like pigs hunt truffles."

They laughed at that, but then Kitty said, "I do want you to make me new gowns for spring, Janet, but today I'm hoping for an instant miracle. I've brought the sapphire blue gown you made for me two years ago. Can you make it more stylish before this evening? I'm to go to the theater."

She expected dismay, but Janet sparkled. "I love a challenge, as you know, Kitty. Is it all right if I still call you Kitty?"

"I'll be cross if you do otherwise."

"Come with me."

She led them to her inner fitting room. "Let's see the gown." Henry passed it over and helped unpeel the muslin.

"In good condition," Janet said, inspecting seams and hem. "Does it still fit?"

"Yes."

"I thought so. Chenille is quite out," Janet said, brushing dismissively over the decoration on the bodice, "and floss. Both will have to come off. Vandyke lace is all the thing and I have some to hand, dyed black. Always black, black, black, these days! I'll put black gauze over the skirt and bodice."

"Gauze?" Kitty asked.

"To darken it. I'm doing that for many of my clients, muting brighter clothing to provide somber wear without them purchasing new."

"I heard that mourning was affecting trade. Is it very bad?"

Janet shrugged. "People around here need new clothes in much the same way, for they wear things out, but there's few who are buying fancy stuff. Who wants more black and dull? I'll retrim this and have it to you by the evening."

"You're an angel. I wish you could magically provide a warm black cloak. My mantle will be too bright."

"I've nothing ready-made, and it would be heavy wear in any case. You might find something fancy in the West End." Janet smiled at the Russian mantle Kitty had put off in the warm room. "I remember making this. Such a bold idea, you had, but we made it cheap as could be. I have one myself and I've made a few others. Most think they'll look too grand. That never bothered you."

"I never saw why it should. Prepare some designs for me, Janet. In spring I intend to blossom, no matter what the world says. Now, can we beg a cup of tea so you can tell me all the local gossip?"

Janet must have sent word to some neighbors, for a number of women just happened to drop by and were thrilled to tears to hear that Kitty had done so well for herself. It turned into a lively tea party, and Kitty found herself promising to come back to Moor Street as often as she could. But then she had to say that she would mostly be living in the country.

"In a grand house," said Sally Sand dreamily. "With an estate all around, I'm sure."

"And deer," Kitty said, because they were enjoying this so much. "And a lake with a temple on it."

"A perfect heaven," Rachel Pollard declared. "And no one could deserve it more."

Even here, however, the women spoke of the succession, grumbling over the lack of royal grandchildren and the irresponsibility of the princes who hadn't married.

"Even the ones who marry can't get it right," Janet complained. "Look at the Duke of Cumberland. Married, fair enough, and to a German princess, but to one near forty! No wonder there are no children."

"Then it must have been for love," Kitty said.

"The royal family has no business being foolish over love," Janet said. "They have their duty."

Kitty remembered such discussions in the past. Some of the newspapers provided royal gossip, and broadsheets sold on the street spread even more, some of it scandalous, and people drank it up. In the past, such talk had seemed merely amusing, but now, with danger hovering, she was uncomfortable.

"The Duke of York married just as he ought," Amy Lassiter said. "It seems most unjust that he has no children from that after more than twenty years."

"Just as he ought, perhaps," said Janet, "but they soon found they didn't suit, and no one gets children when living apart. It's as if they go out of their way to make things difficult!"

"I've heard," said Sally in a low voice, "that the Hanoverian royals are *cursed*. For stealing the throne."

"Only think of Princess Charlotte!" Rachel exclaimed. "And the king's madness."

Kitty quickly intervened. "They were invited, I believe, so the nation should be cursed, not them. And we were victorious over Napoleon."

"And that's another thing," Sally said. "Now we could end up with a Bonaparte on the throne!"

"*What*?" Kitty wasn't the only one exclaiming.

"It was in the *Chronicle*—a list of the Protestant succession. One of Napoleon's brothers married a German princess with a right to the throne, and they had a son."

"I don't believe it," Kitty said.

"That's what it said!"

"Yes, yes, but sometimes they invent nonsense to alarm. And even if it were true," Kitty said, "the Bonaparte must be far down the family tree. One or more of the royal dukes will soon marry and we'll have a proper British heir."

Kitty took her leave soon after that. When they were on the street, she said, "Such nonsense. A Bonaparte on the British throne!"

"It could well be true," Henry said. "Napoleon liked to marry his brothers and sisters into royal families around Europe."

"All the more reason for the royal dukes who are free to marry to get on with it. At least one of them has to be able to sire a child." Kitty pointed right to one of the simple two-story terraced houses. "That was our house. How small it looks. We had only the ground-floor rooms, of course. But there were good times."

"People don't need much to be happy," Henry said.

"That's not what many think."

"And having plenty doesn't make people happy."

"Such as the dowager. In my experience, having plenty only makes life more complicated! Come along. We can get a hackney nearby." But then Sillikin pulled against the leash and Kitty saw why. "There's Captain Edison." Immediately Kitty wished she could avoid a meeting, but he'd seen them and was crossing the road to greet the dog and then her.

Kitty greeted him with a smile. "I'm surprised to find you here, Captain Edison."

"Why? It's familiar enough territory. You've been visiting your old home?"

"No, my old dressmaker. Or, rather, my current one. We must make haste. I have another commitment." Kitty walked on, annoyed with herself for feeling uncomfortable.

He kept pace with her. "I'll escort you."

Kitty saw Henry sending her a question. Either of them could get rid of him, but only with unpleasantness.

"No coach?" he asked.

"I'm not so fancy as that. I came by hackney. I'll get one on the Edgware Road."

"Your husband is neglectful."

"Nonsense."

Kitty quickened her pace, glad of Henry close behind. She wasn't afraid of Edison, but she didn't want any embarrassments.

"Why did you marry him?" he demanded.

"That is a most impertinent question."

"You must have known how I've always longed to make you mine."

"Then you should have acted sooner." Immediately, she knew it was the wrong thing to say. She stopped to retract it. "I—"

"So you *would* have married me! Damn fate that had me far away!"

"Away?"

"My regiment was posted to Corfu. I returned only three weeks ago, and then visited my family, but I intended to seek you out. If only I'd made haste."

Kitty always preferred honesty, but for his sake she must lie. "I'm sorry, Captain Edison, but we were already committed."

"He didn't act that way a short while ago, mentioning you in a club as if he hardly knew you."

Damnation. Braydon had told her that. "I shall have to take him to task for that," she said lightly, turning into the Edgware Road and seeing the line of hackney carriages not far away. "And no cattle clogging up the street. They bring them this way to the cow yard," she said to Henry behind, "and then on to the butchers. That's why this area is cheap when it's quite close to Mayfair."

"Kitty . . ." Edison said.

"Ah, here we are!" She gave her address to the driver of the first hackney.

Edison opened the door for her but said, "I can't give up hope."

"Of what?" she demanded. "My husband's death? Have an end to this, sir. I have only ever regarded you as a friend. We would not have suited."

"You're wrong."

"Good day to you."

She picked up Sillikin and climbed in. Henry followed and soon they were on their way.

"Devil take it," Kitty murmured. "Oh, I'm sorry."

"I don't mind, dear. You'd no idea he felt so strongly?"

"None."

"Would you have married him?"

Kitty thought about it. "If he'd presented himself at Cateril Manor a few months ago? Quite possibly, but it would have been out of desperation. Truly, he's had a lucky escape. He would have been jealous of other men, and I would have lost my temper with him."

Which had almost happened with Braydon.

"Oh, enough. That should be the end of it." Then she exclaimed, "Edgware!"

No wonder Henry looked bewildered, and perhaps worried that Kitty had lost her wits.

"The Edgware Road," Kitty said. "It must go from

here to there, and I don't think it's very far. I wonder how large a place Edgware is."

"Why?"

"The viscountcy seems to own a property there, but no one knows exactly what it is. I wouldn't mind looking into that."

"What a one you are for curiosities. Remember what curiosity did for the cat."

"And satisfaction brought it back. One thing's sure— there'll be no danger from anything to do with the fifth viscount."

Chapter 36

Braydon was at Beaumont's house with Sir Stephen Ball and a friend of Ball's, the Earl of Charrington. Charrington had arrived in Town on a brief visit and been roped in because of a familiarity with delicate matters in high circles. He was a dark-haired man with a notably Continental air, having been born and raised in diplomatic circles, mostly abroad. Braydon had met Charrington in Turkey back when the then Lord Haybridge had still been in the diplomatic service. He'd been born in Turkey to diplomatic parents, and traveled with them apart from the years he'd spent at an English school. He was an elegant sophisticate who spoke eight languages, and Braydon had enjoyed his company.

Not long after that, Charrington had been swept into the army as an aide to Wellington with particular duties to smooth away temperamental crises among the great. Braydon had no need of a sophisticated linguist, but a smoother of crises might well prove useful—especially if the chaotic Princess of Wales was, in fact, involved.

"Are you likely to be here long?" Braydon asked him.

"I planned on only a few days." There was a humorous, resigned tone to that, and Braydon smiled.

"I'll try not to delay you, but you might be the very person to interrogate the Duke of Sussex."

Charrington's brows rose at the word "interrogate."

"About whether he staged a plot to blow up his brothers? He could have slipped away at the crucial moment."

It was a joke, but Braydon considered it. "Any one of them could have planned to dispose of the other two, and it's not the most harmonious of families."

"Jockeying for positions in line for the throne?" Ball asked. "That should rule out Sussex. He's currently sixth in line."

"Are you seriously considering prosecuting one royal duke for the attempted murder of two others?" Charrington asked.

They looked at one another in silence. Nothing good could come out of that, for the nation or themselves.

"We simply find the truth," Braydon said. "Then we decide what to do with it. I'll toss in another alarm. My wife wondered if the Princess of Wales might be involved, striking at the royal family for neglect of her daughter."

"Jupiter!" Charrington exclaimed. "A grieving mother could be capable of that, especially an unstable one. But she's in Italy."

"Which could explain why she's not acted until now," Ball said. "I understand that the Regent didn't even write to inform her of her daughter's death. She heard of it by accident. Not surprising if she immediately dispatched someone to do harm."

"I am not," Charrington said, "traveling to Italy to interrogate the Princess of Wales on a matter of murder."

Ball said, "How fortunate, then, that her apartments at Kensington Palace are being prepared in anticipation of her arrival."

Braydon looked to see if he was joking, but clearly not. "I'll talk to Sidmouth," he said. "Not about our speculations, but because the government will have people keeping an eye on her, if only to find the evidence the Regent needs for divorce."

"And if she is the culprit?" Charrington asked. "And coming here with yet more vengeance on her mind?"

Beaumont broke the silence. "I don't believe it. There's a cunning to the plan, and if Caroline of Brunswick had been capable of cunning, she'd have fared much better in her marriage."

They all nodded.

Ball said, "We need to focus on the princes and find out what each has to say about the arrangement of the evening, and, if possible, about who might hold a personal grudge against any of them. Though Charrington has the social address, I have a reasonably good relationship with Sussex because of his interest in reform. I'll take him."

"A thousand thank-yous," Charrington said. "That frees me to approach Clarence. I have no relationship there, but Bath isn't far from Temple Knollis, so my speedy return there becomes a noble duty."

Until recently, Braydon would have thought such desire to return to family odd, but no longer. He was aware of being slightly distracted all morning by thoughts of Kitty. He might even forget some parts of this discussion. Charrington's willingness to return to live most of the year in the country was less easy to understand, especially in a man who'd lived in some of the greatest cities in the world.

"Which leaves a trip to Brussels," Beaumont said with resignation. "As Dauntry needs to play spider in the middle of this web, I assume I take on that mission."

"Thank you. Also, Kent might deal better with a military man and, if you'll excuse my mentioning it, a maimed one."

"Good that it serve some purpose."

"If you take a couple of pigeons, you could wing important news back. That's probably not necessary with Bath, Charrington, but take some if you wish." Braydon went over everything in his mind. "I believe we've completed our business for today. I thank you—"

"One moment," Charrington said. "I'm intrigued by your wife's question about immediate benefit. Could anyone have already gained by this?"

"No," Beaumont said, "because it failed."

"Not quite what I asked."

After a moment, Braydon said, "Benefitted by the *failed* attempt?"

"I merely pose the question."

"But hardly anyone knows," Beaumont objected. "So how could it serve someone's aim?"

"The three princes know," Braydon said, "and probably their immediate households. The Regent knows, and he was going to discuss it with the Privy Council. Possibly people in Sidmouth's office know. Mrs. Courtenay and her household do, plus anyone they gossiped to."

"The queen," Ball added. "Clarence might have told her when he returned to Bath. Was it directed at her as suggested?"

"A warning shot only?" Braydon asked. "Dashed odd. Let's return to the excellent question—what, if anything, has already been achieved?"

"Other than disturbing our lives?" Ball asked drily.

"Other than that."

They all considered it.

"The princes are now accepting increased protection," Beaumont said at last.

"Then perhaps," Charrington murmured, "Sidmouth or some other person in the government did the deed."

"Devil take it," Braydon said. "Do I now have the task of interrogating the Home Secretary about his role in the plot?"

"Unfair that you escape scot-free."

"This would be a simpler matter if the gunpowder

had exploded and taken them all to kingdom come! As it stands, it's beginning to resemble a farce." Braydon remembered something. "Perhaps it's appropriate that I'm attending the theater this evening. You would all be welcome to join us in our box at Covent Garden if you're free. And Lady Ball as well, of course. Mrs. Beaumont, too, if she's not engaged at Drury Lane."

"She's not," Beaumont said, "and will enjoy scrutinizing rivals."

Braydon thanked the other men for their assistance and Beaumont for his hospitality and set off home, hoping Kitty had returned from her dressmaker.

But then he took a detour, pleased at the thought of purchasing more gifts for his wife.

Chapter 37

When Braydon returned home, he shed his outerwear, put his boxed gift on his bed, and went in search of his wife.

He found her in the library, writing a letter, curls of her burnished hair escaping around her nape. She was as perfect a part of the room as his carefully chosen furniture. When she returned to the Abbey, these rooms would feel hollow, especially without the warm smile she turned on him.

Her dog came over, tail wagging, which was strangely pleasant.

"Have you had an enjoyable outing?" he asked, fondling Sillikin.

"I have," Kitty said. "I've begun the process of obtaining new gowns for the spring. Brightly colored gowns."

"You're weary of mourning, but you must wear sober colors this evening."

"I know, and Janet is bringing an old gown up to the mark."

In mere hours? he wondered, but he didn't say it. He wondered if the new gowns Kitty had ordered would be fine enough for the spring season in the beau monde, but that was a difficulty for another day.

"I have something to assist you," he said. "In the bedroom."

The look she gave him was decidedly saucy and possibly hopeful. God save him.

She saw the box and went quickly to open it, as eager as a child.

"A new gown?" she asked, untying the ribbons. "After all Janet's work . . ." She drew back the muslin. "Black velvet?" She stroked it, but he saw she was still reluctant.

"It's not a gown."

She glanced at him and pulled it out. "A cloak! Oh, it's beautiful." She swirled it on and hurried to the mirror. "So wonderful. The way it hangs. The figured design down the front. Janet suggested I might find a black cloak in the West End, but Henry and I visited three places and nothing. Even if we had, I'm sure I'd never have found anything as elegant as this." She pulled up the hood and turned to him, her face and hair glowing in the dark frame. "Thank you."

She stole his breath. Her strong features and coloring made a perfect whole that was simply Kitty. No wonder Kit Kat had enchanted so many men.

But she was his now. His, and coming to him to offer glowing thanks. He gathered her into his arms, the embodiment of passion wrapped in slithery silk velvet. . . .

But the door was open and it was the middle of the day. He'd not previously been aware of the limitations of his rooms, where little could be truly private.

"If you don't let me go," he said, "I won't be able to give you my other present."

"More?" she asked. He delighted in her frank acceptance of pleasures—of all kinds. *A night in black velvet . . .*

He picked up the jeweler's box and gave it to her. "You already have some jet, but I saw this and wanted it for you."

She opened it and smiled again. "Thank you. It's lovely. Forgive me, I must show Henry!"

Greedy of him to have wanted yet more enthusiastic thanks, and foolish, too, for his control wasn't absolute. In her absence, after a while, he was able to sit to make notes of the earlier meeting. He'd definitely need them.

There was always the night. As long as Kitty was in London, there would be wonderful nights.

Perhaps he could come to appreciate rural life.

Kitty went into the other bedroom, where Henry was doing mending. "See!"

"A perfect cloak for the theater."

Kitty turned to swirl it. "Isn't it? And he's given me this as well. Look. Every bead is carved into a rosebud, and the central pendant is a filigree heart. There are earrings to match."

Henry touched the heart. "Exquisite work. Why are you crying?"

Kitty sniffed. "Aren't women supposed to cry when they're happy?"

Kitty had heard that, but it had never been the case with her. She was crying because she'd instantly seen the jet as a sign of love, then instantly known he wouldn't have meant it that way. He was simply concerned with appearances.

Then she'd thought that perhaps in time he might love her, and then realized how foolish she was.

She'd soon be back at Beauchamp Abbey, and he wouldn't care a jot. It was their arrangement. She must do as she'd promised to do. But she couldn't help hoping he would mind their being apart at least half as much as she would.

She gave jet and cloak into Henry's care and returned to the library. She found Braydon had taken her place at the desk and was writing.

"Do I disturb you?" she asked. "I'm ready to eat lunch, if you'd care to join me."

He rose and smiled. "Of course. Hungry work, tussling with knotty problems."

"You're no further forward?"

"Not greatly."

"I heard something odd today. Is a Bonaparte truly in the line of succession?"

"Yes, but half the noble families of Europe would have to die out before he got a sniff of it."

"Still, it's extraordinary. I'm surprised the papers mention it at all."

"They're probing the succession as much as anyone, and his presence can't be denied. He's merely a three-year-old child."

"All the same, his lurking on the list of heirs should inspire the royal dukes to greater enthusiasm for marriage."

"So it should. What of your mysteries?"

As they settled at the table, she told him about the Hartleys.

"They may not reply," he said. "We don't know what drove Diane Dauntry to flee. If she was treated cruelly, she might have written to her parents about it."

"And they will shun anything Braydon? I find it hard to believe that her husband was cruel."

"Some weak men turn vicious when affronted. And then there's his mother."

"Yes, indeed. The dowager is capable of tyranny. She might even have thought it her duty to check a wild spirit."

Edward brought in the dishes and tea service, then left, closing the door.

"Is there any progress in your investigation?" Kitty asked as she made the tea.

"We've decided to find out what we can about the

three princes and the way the meeting was arranged, but other than that, no."

"What of the Princess of Wales?"

"A possibility, but in that case, we'd need to find her agent. Damnation! Your pardon."

Kitty smiled and waved away any concern about strong language. "What?"

"I should have realized that makes nonsense of it. Even if she sent someone from Italy to do what harm he could, the chance of that person happening to find out about the hastily arranged meeting defies belief. It has to arise out of the princes' households."

As they ate their soup, Kitty considered the situation. "What did the princes do when the alarm was raised?"

"Fled to the safety of Carlton House. Why?"

"Only that random questions might help. What, precisely, was the purpose of the meeting?"

"According to Sidmouth, to spur the Regent into taking up his duties. The plot did bring him racing up to London. Result achieved? Danger over? Your random questions are effective."

She smiled at the compliment and helped herself to stewed oysters. At least Kingdom was prompt to please. "Whom else do you have to discuss this with? Major Beaumont and Sir Stephen?"

"And another, the Earl of Charrington."

"Such high circles I'm brushing against!"

He gave her a look. "I'm sure some of the men who attended the Kit Kat Club were of high rank."

"Ah, so you heard that term. It wasn't at all political."

"I never imagined it was."

"It wasn't all frivolity, either. The talk was often of weighty matters, especially to do with the war. As for high rank, the noblemen were nearly all younger sons." She took some bread and buttered it. "Is the Earl of Charrington a friend?"

"An acquaintance only, but a friend of Beaumont and Ball. He came up to Town to deal with some business and probably wishes he hadn't. You'll meet him tonight. I invited him to join us at the theater, along with the others."

Kitty was pouring herself more tea, and paused. "And *wives*, I hope."

"You worry about being in only male company?"

"Not worry, precisely, but in public I'd rather present a more commonplace appearance."

"Impossible."

"Perfectly possible! I don't want . . ."

"To remind anyone of the Kit Kat Club? Did you mind your husband's hospitality? Being adored by a horde of young men?"

Kitty wanted to protest that word again, but he needed an answer. She took time to complete the pouring of her tea and topped up his cup. "I didn't mind the hospitality. Marcus would have hated lack of company. He didn't like reading or any handicraft, and so had no occupation when alone."

"He had you."

"And we enjoyed some pleasant times, but he needed the company of men."

"You might have enjoyed the company of women."

"Heavens, are you imagining me in confinement? I went around the area to the shops and such, and took Sillikin for walks, often meeting other women and enjoying some gossip. Janet Saunders, my seamstress, is a friend. I enjoyed my visit there today."

He stirred sugar into his tea. "And at the Abbey you have only Ruth Lulworth."

"Ruth is enough," Kitty said, though inside she knew it wasn't quite true. She was like Marcus in enjoying a merry group. How hard to please she was. "Let's return to your business. Have you considered that the dukes of Clarence, Kent, and Sussex might have gathered to concoct a deep, dark plot to usurp the throne?"

"I must confiscate your novels."

"I haven't had time to read one for ages. I know history, however, and brothers have united to remove an unjust or inadequate ruler."

"True, but you imply a plot against the Regent. Wallowing in grief is not so heinous a sin."

"I'm sure the queen would like to slap the Regent's fat bottom for it. I've heard she has a stern way with her children."

"Which is proof only that a stern way with children doesn't achieve desirable results."

Kitty sipped her tea, eyeing him. "Were your parents stern?"

"Not particularly. School was another matter. Yours?"

"Not at all, and not at school, either."

"Which probably explains everything."

She wrinkled her nose at him. He smiled, but a topic lurked, unacknowledged. "So, if we have children," she said, "we will be indulgent?"

"No. But not unkind, I hope."

"Never unkind. I'd insist on that. But it is unlikely," she reminded him.

"And as promised, you'll hear no recriminations from me."

But will you mind?

She was beginning to think she might. Being childless with Marcus hadn't bothered her. She'd never thought deeply about it, but must have known it would create an impossible situation. Now, with three homes and ample money . . . There was no benefit to dwelling on that, and truly it was a hazardous business for women.

"What will we see at the theater tonight?" she asked.

"*Guy Mannering.* It's the first time it's been staged, so an unknown quantity. And a farce. I forget what."

"Forget?" she teased.

"You've scrambled my wits."

She couldn't help but smile. "I'll enjoy my first trip to the theater no matter what's on stage." She considered a plate of damson tarts, but decided she'd eaten enough. Braydon was staring into space. "Penny for your thoughts?" she asked.

He blinked. "My apologies. Thoughts of theatricals. We've let our imaginations run wild because the affair of the three princes does feel like a farce, where no plot device is too wild."

"Which might be why I'm enjoying talking about it. I might be less gleeful about a true attempt at murder."

"As you should be. Someone intended something and took a great risk over it. The attempted murder of three princes would not be treated lightly by the courts, whether it was intended to work or not. The culprit could still hang."

"Then who took such a risk and why? What gain was worth the possible price?"

"Precisely. I'll visit Sidmouth this afternoon to see if anything new has come to light. What are your plans?"

"A walk in the park for Sillikin, and another visit to the house. I want to take a more serious look at what needs to be done if we're to use it in spring." She couldn't resist asking, "You're not tempted by such delights?"

"Extremely, but there is a serious matter beneath the farce, and I must attend to it."

That could be true, or it could be a polite excuse. She had no doubt he enjoyed her company in the night, but was less sure about during the daytime. Perhaps all Kit Kat's adoring men only enjoyed her company in a group.

Except for Edison. She hoped she'd seen the last of him.

Chapter 38

Complete with entourage, Kitty gave Sillikin exercise and then continued to the house on foot. She did intend a more thorough inspection, and would have some furniture unshrouded, but she had a purpose beyond that. If the house was as it had been when the fifth viscount died, it might tell her more about him.

Consequently, when she arrived at the house, she set Henry to chatting to the housekeeper and getting as much gossip as possible, and Edward to inspecting the mundane parts of the house and the yard behind. Keeping her cloak and gloves on, she went directly to the bedrooms. If anything personal remained, it would be there.

She entered Lady Dauntry's bedroom first. No matter what the sleeping arrangements had been when Diane had been a dutiful wife, once she'd gone, her husband would surely have used this rather than his dressing room.

Kitty opened the doors of the clothes press, but there were no clothes there. She took the cotton dust covers off the bed, night table, and washstand, revealing no secrets. But then, as she fully opened the small drawer in the night table, she found a slim brown book. The gold title on the spine said *Town Follies*. She opened it and found humorous and often salty poetry about society's foibles.

That fit with her assumption that the fifth viscount had not been a man for serious matters. But when she flipped through the pages, she found dried rose petals between tissue paper in one space. Did the petals belong to some other person, or had he been the romantic sort to treasure such mementoes?

Of Diane, once?

That verged on tragedy.

She put the book in her pocket and went to the dressing room. She found no personal items there, either. Some damnably efficient person had cleared out everything.

She went next to the library downstairs, where there were still books on the shelves. She unshrouded the desk, but all she found in the drawers were some stray ivory gaming counters and a few tradesmen's cards. She studied them but could see nothing of importance.

She walked along the shelves, wondering if there were any secrets to be found in the books. *More dried flowers, or even love notes?* A search would be exhausting, however, and she didn't have the time.

But then a slim, tall book caught her eye.

It almost filled the height of the shelf and had been put beside one of the wooden dividers so that the brown spine seemed part of it. *Placed there deliberately so as not to catch the eye?* When she eased it out, she found it was a ledger quite similar to the ones at the Abbey. This one was used for accounts.

Unlike Braydon's neat records, the handwriting was messy and often wandered off the lines. She recognized it as the fifth viscount's.

> *To repair of leading on the front window.*
>   *For new fire irons.*
>   *To repair thatch on the north side.*

Not this house, then. There was no thatch here, and it was rare in London these days.

She checked the flyleaf and found *L Cottage, Edgware.*
Edgware!

So the fifth viscount had taken an interest in a place
there, but it had somehow slipped out of the rest of the
viscountcy's records.

Or been hidden?

Braydon would shake his head at that, but the way
the book had been placed on the shelf was suggestive.

She flipped through a few more pages, hoping for
secrets, but all she found were entries for maintenance
of the property and furnishings. There was nothing to
do with food or drink, so he'd been maintaining it but
not living in it. She'd thought before that the Edgware
property could be something like the Beecham Dab
almshouses—a forgotten charity. But why would that be
secret? Had the dowager been so domineering that the
poor man had even hidden his benevolence?

When she looked at the last entry, she saw it had
been made only a few weeks before his death, perhaps
just before he'd returned to the Abbey for the last time.

For the new rosebush by the back door.

Would he care about such a thing for almshouses?

Kitty returned to the front. The first entry had been
in 1814, years after Diane had fled, but there could have
been previous books.

In a novel she'd find Diane at this house in Edgware,
run mad and being cared for under her husband's loving
supervision. That would explain why he'd never sought to
divorce her. Braydon would scoff at the very idea, but
there was a mystery here and it needed to be solved.
She'd find time to go to Edgware. It wasn't many miles
from Mayfair.

The book was too large for her pocket so she put it in

her muff. She didn't have time for a longer search of the library, so she joined Henry and Mrs. Grant in the house-keeper's parlor.

There Kitty carefully posed one question. "There must have been an inventory when the fifth viscount died, Mrs. Grant."

"Oh yes, milady. And very thorough. Down to the last spoon."

"Where would that be?"

"I think Mr. Palfrey has it, ma'am. His lordship's solicitor. I hope you don't think anything's gone missing, ma'am."

Kitty made haste to reassure her. "I'm simply curious. I'll obtain a copy and read it in due course. I disarranged some of the covers in order to get a better feel for the house. It's pleasant, isn't it?"

"I think so, ma'am. Nothing fancy and a bit faded, but well-done."

"I'll make arrangement for someone to come about the Rumford stove and the boiler. There will be some disorder as it's fitted, and I may require some repainting as well. If you wish to move out for a little while, you must do so."

"Oh, no, ma'am. I'll stay to make sure it's all done right."

Kitty took tea, hoping for some scrap of gossip, but all she achieved was confirmation that the fifth viscount had spent little time in this house.

Mrs. Grant turned sad. "When I think, milady, that he spent only two nights here before traveling to the Abbey, and was dead a week later. We never know, do we, when God will call us?"

"No," Kitty said. "We don't."

She was weary of thoughts of death and turned her mind to the spring, when this house would come to life and she and Braydon would be here for months. They would entertain, and perhaps she would be able to hold a weekly Kit Kat Club. Isabella would still be in mourning, but she could enjoy the quieter delights of Town.

It was beginning to grow dark when Kitty left the house, and she was glad of Edward. He got them a hackney, but as there was time, Kitty had it take them to a gaslit street where she could browse the brightly lit windows. She saw ideas for her rooms at the Abbey, and some for the town house, but her main target was Hatchard's Book Shop. She must fulfill Isabella's request.

Henry had never shopped after dark, and was as delighted as Kitty by the show. After buying a number of novels of the less-dramatic sort, they spent a pleasant hour wandering back past enticing shops and sometimes entering to make purchases. Kitty chose some items to be sent directly to the Abbey, but carried most of her purchases with her. Or, rather, with Edward, who was disappearing under a pile of packages. He got some relief when some of Kit Kat's admirers took their share, but they were becoming a group likely to block the way.

"Gentlemen! I must hurry home, for I'm to attend the theater tonight. Please, someone find me a hackney."

Major Porteous obliged, but by the time Kitty, Henry, Edward, and the packages were inside, they'd teased out of her what theater she was to attend. It had been impossible to refuse, but she hoped they wouldn't be tiresome.

Chapter 39

Kitty found that her refurbished gown had arrived and was delighted by Janet's work. The blue gown had been transformed by the gauze overlay and Vandyke lace. The black gauze should have made it dismal, but there was a silvery sheen to it that caught the candlelight. Janet had made a bandeau to match, and when Henry had arranged Kitty's hair in a confection of rolls and curls, she put it in place. With the jet, Kitty knew she looked in the height of style.

She was still keen to get Braydon's opinion, but she saw it instantly in his eyes. He kissed her hand. "In that frame, you glow like a candle."

She admired him, too, in his formal evening wear. "I've never seen you in all black before."

"You approve?"

"You shine like gold and ivory," she said, "and I've always appreciated a well-dressed gentleman. It's probably why I liked uniforms so much."

"London uniforms," he said, as they went to the dining room. "There's rarely anything elegant about them on campaign." He seated her and went to his own chair. "Tell me about your afternoon."

"I visited the house again. I'm not sure what makes one house pleasing and another of the same design not, but it's pleasing. I'll enjoy spending time there. I remembered that there would have been an inventory when the fifth viscount died. Was there anything interesting in that?"

"Three good beds, four good mattresses, five silver porringers. . . . I never read it."

"Tut-tut! You might have found explosives or bloody daggers."

"Novels," he said again as he served her with soup.

"Some are very sober and improving."

"Then I go odds you've never read them."

"Are you saying I'm unimproved, sir?" she asked, dipping her spoon into chicken soup.

"Unimprovable, perhaps," he said. A smile suggested a compliment, but it could be taken another way.

She ate some soup, then said, "Do you remember Edgware?"

She could almost see him rifle through mental records. "You found a letter from the fifth viscount—no, to him— about the lease of a house in Edgware."

"Do you remember the date?"

"September 1808. Perhaps the twenty-eighth."

"You could be making that up. Oh, very well, but it's uncanny."

"My burden to bear. What is significant about Edgware?"

They'd finished their soup, so Kitty rang for the next course. "I found a record book concerning a place in Edgware. In the fifth viscount's handwriting."

"Where?"

Edward came in to take away the soup. Kitty decided it wasn't a secret subject. "On a bookshelf, in a way that was partially concealed."

"I suppose you now want to search the town house from cellars to attics. Hoping for skeletons?"

Her speculations about a madwoman were definitely not for the servant's ears. She'd dismissed it at first, but had reconsidered over the past few hours. People did go mad, and family sometimes tried to conceal that fact.

"No," she said, "but I intend to make time to visit Edgware." Before he could object, she said, "The records are all of repairs and replacements—I'll show you later—so the repairs might have stopped, as with the almshouses in Beecham Dab."

"L Cottage sounds singular," he pointed out.

"Very well, not almshouses. Perhaps a place for an old servant. His nurse, even."

Edward had laid out sliced beef in a sauce and dishes of vegetables, and brought over some wine that had been waiting. He left and closed the door, and Braydon poured.

"Possibly, but you're being a curious cat again."

Kitty helped herself from the dishes. "I admit it, but it could be of some importance, and apart from buying things for the Abbey, I don't have much to do."

She told him about some of her purchases as they ate, but though he was polite, she could tell he thought them trivialities.

"Your visit to the Home Secretary?" she asked, sipping her wine.

"Probably best not discussed here. Later."

Later, in bed, after much more interesting matters? "I suppose," she said, "my priorities for later make me a shallow person."

"Impossible," he responded with a smile, "for then I'd be shallow, too."

"We don't squabble, do we?"

"We don't. Thus far we haven't fought, either, which is probably as well. I suspect you're a fiery warrior."

"I'm not meek. I doubt I could ever be."

"I have no complaint."

She rang for their final course. "Nor have I. I feel as if I won a lottery."

"We did both gamble," he agreed, "but not so blindly. I knew you were a dear friend of Ruth Lulworth's, and you must have known something of me from them."

Kitty waited until the sweet course was laid out, along with dried fruits and nuts.

"Let's see," she said, taking some pear tart. "You were not objectionable—"

"High praise!"

"But unlikely to abandon your London ways."

"True."

"But you had Andrew Lulworth's approval as a good man, and that was enough for me."

"We still could have been incompatible."

"Which was why I wanted to delay the wedding. I was expecting a week to learn about you, but you made haste back to Town."

"I was terrified of Isabella."

"Ha!"

"Truly. I couldn't discount the possibility of her sneaking into my bedroom one night, stripping naked, and then screaming for help. It seemed much wiser to be out of reach. I didn't think of it from your point of view."

"We must get Isabella away from the dowager."

"Perhaps the Hartleys will be kind, warmhearted people with whom she'd like to live."

"A mere baronet?" Kitty asked. "The worst of her might come from the dowager, but she has a fine opinion of herself. A visit, perhaps, but not a home. She needs a grand marriage, and unless we can free her from the dowager, as soon as possible."

"I'll not force her to it."

"Of course not. But if a duke proposes . . ."

"As long as it's not a royal one!"

Kitty chuckled, and they spent the rest of the meal harmoniously discussing future plans. But Kitty wondered if he, like her, was thinking of the time between— the winter, when she would be tussling with Beauchamp Abbey, and he would be mostly in Town, entangled in plots and mayhem.

A bit more Shakespeare. Something about a winter of discontent. The countryside in winter. Stark trees against frosted fields, and chilly journeys to even the closest places. Despite the Dutch stove, her breath would frost in the Abbey as she went from room to room, and if the weather turned really bad, she could be trapped there for days or even weeks by snow and ice. She thought wistfully of the neat town house, which would be easy to keep warm and where shops and amusements would be only streets away.

I have such pleasures for now, she reminded herself, *and I will enjoy every moment.*

Braydon had hired a livery carriage to take them to the theater, so they didn't have to take their chance on a hackney. It came provided with hot bricks, so that in her velvet cloak Kitty was comfortable all the way. Edward and Henry had gone ahead to ensure their box was ready for them, and they'd stay as personal attendants.

The outside of the theater was lit by brilliant gaslight, and the same greeted them inside. Kitty wrinkled her nose at the smell, but it wasn't too bad, and the brightness was magical. They had come for the play, but the pit and high gallery were already filled by people who'd come for the earlier parts of the program. Kitty wanted to put her hands over her ears. The intermission chatter approached cacophony.

Nearly everyone was in sober colors, but most particularly in the rows of boxes. Kitty was thankful for the black gauze and velvet, for her unmodified blue might have seemed too bright, and her blue cloak would have been disastrous.

Lady Ball was in a dark, steely gray, but Mrs. Beaumont was in white. It was a very simple design, however, and she wore a large and lovely black lace shawl over it and pearl and jet ornaments.

"White was the color of mourning, you know," she said as she took a seat in the box. "And people understand that the White Dove never wears colors, not even on the stage. You're fortunate, Lady Dauntry. Dark colors frame you. White would never suit."

"What's it like to be on the stage, looking out at so many people," Kitty asked, "all expecting wonders from you?"

The actress grinned. "I love it, especially when the play's a good one. The response flows back from the audience to the actors. It's a heady brew. Of course, if the play isn't good, we're more likely to get rotten fruit."

"Truly?"

"Never for me these days. I choose my parts carefully."

"And Blanche is much loved," Lady Ball said. "Are you enjoying your time in London, Lady Dauntry?"

The ladies had been given the front seats, and Kitty was to the right of the other two. "I am very much. But I lived here for eight years until my husband died."

"Ah yes," Lady Ball said. "He was a hero, sadly left crippled. I give thanks daily that the war is over."

"Amen," Kitty said.

The Earl of Charrington arrived then, and Kitty was struck by his effortless elegance. He rivaled Braydon in that, but in a subtly different manner. He kissed her hand in a way she found just a little flowery.

When he turned to speak to Braydon, Kitty leant close to Mrs. Beaumont. "Is he foreign?"

"Clever of you. No, but he was raised and mostly lived abroad until recently. His friends tease him about his Continental ways. Did you ever hear of Sebastian Rossiter?"

"The poet? He's not him, is he?" Kitty looked at the suave earl in astonishment.

Mrs. Ball almost choked on laughter. "Never. But he married Rossiter's widow, his 'Angel Bride,' if you're familiar with that poem. Judith's a lovely woman, but you wouldn't expect the match. She's very down to earth. We'd love to see more of her, but she prefers country life."

An unexpected match. Kitty's marriage could be seen as that, and if the Charringtons' had worked out well, she'd take it as a good omen.

"Do you pine for copse and pasture?" she asked.

"Only on stage," the actress said with a chuckle. The curtain rose, and she added, "There's a farce first. A rollicking bit of nonsense, or so they say."

The plot was quite ridiculous, but Kitty was instantly enthralled by the action on the stage. She was sucked into the events there as if she were watching real people through a window. She worried as Captain Tickall was chased by bailiffs and Captain Wingem by the law, even though she didn't approve of debt or dueling. She gasped in shock but couldn't help laughing when the rascals persuaded two honest wives to help them escape by telling the pursuers that they were their husbands.

The farce ended in an "all's well that ends well" manner, and the curtain came down for the first intermission. Kitty tried to pretend carelessness, but Braydon said, "I think you enjoyed that."

She plied her fan. "It was silly stuff, but very well done."

"And I can't help thinking," he said softly, "that it's no more ridiculous than my business."

She raised her eyebrows at him. "You think the princes weren't the princes at all?"

He groaned. "Don't toss that speculation into the stew!"

Edward was serving wine and cakes from his place at the back of the box. A German gentleman came in to greet the Earl of Charrington as a long-lost friend, and they left to stroll the corridor together. Then Sir Francis Burdett came and sat with Ball to talk politics. Kitty knew he was one of the fiercest reforming members of Parliament.

Lady Ball murmured, "Can we never escape politics?" but with a wry smile.

Braydon went to join them.

He had a seat in the House of Lords, whether he wanted it or not, but was he inclined toward reform? That could be dangerous, as it so often seemed to involve gatherings and riots, and then military action to keep the peace.

"Is something amiss?" Mrs. Beaumont asked.

"Politics," Kitty said with a wry smile.

"The curse of our age, but I support reform. Why shouldn't a woman of property be allowed the vote? Don't seek an answer," Mrs. Beaumont said. "There isn't one. But as long as men are allowed to imagine women inferior, everything will go to wrack and ruin."

"Blanche is a fierce adherent of women's rights," Lady Ball said.

"You don't think you're inferior to men," Mrs. Beaumont said to her.

"No, but different. We bear the children."

"Which doesn't deprive a woman of all wit and sense. And what of those of us who don't?"

It was perhaps as well the curtain rose on the main play of the night, but Kitty wondered if her barrenness explained her bold spirit and desire to control her fate.

Chapter 40

The play was an adaptation of the successful novel *Guy Mannering*, with the addition of songs. Kitty had read the novel and knew the plot, but that didn't affect her enjoyment. Indeed, she thrilled to see it come to life, with lost children, smugglers, and wild Meg Merrilies.

She had to stifle a protest when the curtain came down for the next intermission. Everyone left the box to stretch their legs and meet others. Kitty strolled with Braydon, talking about the performance when not being introduced again and again. She'd not expected this to be her first night amid the ton.

Again and again they were congratulated on their marriage, but twice a gentleman said, "Kitty!" before recollecting himself. At least no one called her Kit Kat, but Major Corcoran put his hand to his heart and enacted a tragedy over her being snatched before he had a chance.

"Don't be foolish, Major. You know we would not suit."

"Ah, but the not suiting would have been magnificent for a while. Your pardon, Dauntry, but a man can't help but envy you."

"And I can hardly object to such fulsome praise of my wife, sir." There was a steely edge to it, however. Corcoran waggled his gingery eyebrows at Kitty and went away, leaving her annoyed.

"Please don't bristle at such foolishness," Kitty said, "or you'll be bristling morning, noon, and night. I can handle such matters for myself."

Before he could respond, three officers were coming toward them, including Edison.

"You look splendid," he said to her, as if he had a particular right.

Kitty smiled at all three. "I'm delighting in the play. I've never attended one before. It's so *thoughtful* of Dauntry to arrange this treat so soon." She made sure to give him a besotted smile.

"I invited you to the theater once," Edison said.

Kitty wanted to hit him, and had to admit it might be useful for Braydon to freeze Edison away, but she'd claimed to be able to handle such matters herself. "What a shame it wasn't convenient, sir. Are you soon to be posted abroad again?"

At her tone, he colored. "I must go where I'm sent."

"And I wish you all success, Captain Edison." She turned to one of the other men. "What prospects for you, Hallward?"

He'd caught her interaction with Edison, but he answered amiably. "I'm kicking my heels, but if that keeps me in Town while you're here, Lady Dauntry, I don't feel too hard done to."

She appreciated his deliberate use of her title, which Edison had avoided, and settled to a light discussion of military prospects. She was glad when Edison stalked off. Surely that had been strong enough to stop his folly.

The next act was announced, and the other two men took their leave. Kitty prepared for something scathing from Braydon, but a thin, middle-aged gentleman approached.

Braydon greeted him with a bow. "Sidmouth. My dear, I present Lord Sidmouth, our Home Secretary."

Kitty dipped a curtsy, wondering if some new drama had unfolded, for Lord Sidmouth looked odd.

"A word with you, Dauntry."

Braydon escorted Kitty to their box door. "You'll excuse me for a moment."

"Of course."

She watched him return to the Home Secretary and observed the brief exchange of words. It looked to come close to an argument, but she couldn't hover there. She went in and took her seat just as the curtain rose. Even as the play captured her again, she was aware of Braydon entering behind her, and wished she could ask what had occurred. Later, unless his jealousy put him in a sour mood.

However, at the next intermission people came into their box and private discussion was impossible.

When the play came to an end, with all the villains dealt with and the virtuous rewarded, Kitty was keen to return home and learn what Sidmouth had said. However, she learned that they were to host a supper at the nearby Bedford Hotel.

As they walked there with their guests, she said, "You didn't mention this."

"Did I not? A theater party must be fed."

"It could be seen as a wife's duty."

"Then be pleased I spared you it."

His terseness could only be because he was still simmering over the scene with Edison. Surely he couldn't fault her for that?

Sir Francis Burdett and his wife were of their party, and the German gentleman Herr Grassmyer. They had been invited during the evening, and she wished she'd known and invited a few of her own acquaintances. In particular, her most ardent admirers!

The arrangements were perfect, however, largely

because the Bedford Hotel was expert at such events. Their private room was elegantly furnished and the supper delicious. There had been no difficulty over the extra guests, and it seemed the hotel expected that. Two extra tables stood against the wall, and one was easily added to the end, and covered and set in a moment.

Braydon had probably arranged such suppers a hundred times and she hadn't, but she couldn't rid herself of grievance. She made sure it didn't show, however, as she played hostess, and gradually her pique faded as she watched him play the charming host.

He was so comfortable in this setting and so well liked by this variety of people. At first impression she'd judged him aloof, but she should have remembered then that he'd quickly become friends with Ruth and Andrew.

It couldn't be easy for him to have men clustering around his wife, and Edison had been outrageous. And yet, once she'd objected, he hadn't interfered. Perhaps he wouldn't have criticized her if he'd had a chance. It was doubtless Sidmouth who'd put him on edge earlier.

She relaxed into good food, fine wine, and excellent company that was sufficiently varied to be interesting. They mostly even avoided politics. Sir Francis did once mention the Regent's visit to London, saying he wished he'd lingered to attend to business, but no more than that. His wife, a very gracious lady, complimented Kitty on her gown—and then asked the name of her mantua maker.

Kitty was delighted to be able to say, "A Mrs. Saunders of Moor Street, ma'am. A simple establishment, but Mrs. Saunders is very talented."

"So I see. I will visit her."

Kitty had to suppress a grin at the excitement likely to land on Moor Street in the near future, but she was delighted for Janet. And this would be only the beginning. No matter what happened about the Abbey, she'd return in spring for the season and wear wonderful gowns, and Janet's fortune would be made.

As they returned home in their carriage, Kitty told Braydon.

"More exciting than you realize. Lady Burdett is the daughter of Coutts, the banker, and not short of money to spend. Nor are her well-married sisters or her wide acquaintance."

"How lovely. But what of Lord Sidmouth? More drama?"

"In a manner of speaking." She thought perhaps he wouldn't tell her what had been discussed, but then he said, "He ordered me to cease investigations."

"About the attempted assassinations? Why? They've found the culprit?"

"He said it was the Regent's wish. That the Regent wished to avoid any alarm."

She read his tone. "That makes no sense. Those who know, know, and any enquiries won't make matters worse."

"So why?"

It was a serious question. Despite a glass of wine too many, Kitty applied her mind to it. "They don't have the culprit, or he would have said so. The Regent is the culprit? No, that's incredible." She looked at him. "The Regent is afraid of what you might discover?"

"Clever lady. Seems the most likely, doesn't it? Or Sidmouth is afraid of what I might discover. I have no proof it's the Regent's wish."

"Heavens! But if Sidmouth devised the plot, why bring you in to investigate? He could have kept it in the Home Office and muddled it away to nothing."

"An excellent point. You could be an investigator."

"If I weren't a woman," she said, remembering the conversation in the theater box, "with a feeble woman's brain."

"Have I ever accused you of that?"

"No."

"And I never will, unless justified."

"Am I allowed to challenge you for feeblemindedness?" She pulled a face at him. "I can't imagine it."

"I have many flaws, and I invite you to correct me as necessary. As for investigations, there are many situations where a woman can poke around better than a man, and some where she might have unique insights."

She studied him. "You're serious. But what of the Abbey?"

"Oh, damn the Abbey!" He took her hand. "Can we consign it and all it involves to the devil?"

He'd opened a door to an exciting possibility, but she had to say a regretful, "No."

"No," he agreed.

"Perhaps one day. But as matters stand, I should return soon. I dread to think what the dowager's been up to."

"Nothing significant. I get a daily report from Worseley."

She pulled her hand free. "And not a word to me, sir?"

"There's been nothing to say. I apologize! Again." He captured her hand and kissed it. "We have been joined in wedlock for only a very few days, my dear Kitty. Neither of us can transform in a moment."

"No." She studied him. "Am I? Your dear?"

"Begging for compliments?"

"More than a compliment."

"You are very dear to me," he said. "A part of my life I would miss if you were gone."

That was not quite love, but it was precious. "As, alas, I must be."

"But not yet. Nothing is awry at the Abbey. Linger. There are more plays to see and more shops to plunder."

"And always will be." But he wanted her to stay, and would miss her when she left. "You know I have to return, and that you must stay here until this matter is untangled. You can't allow Sidmouth or the Regent to turn you from the path."

"Is that a command?"

"Does it go against your inclinations?"

He kissed her hand again. "No."

She tightened her fingers on his. "I have to say this, Braydon, even though it can't change anything. I don't want to part, and I wish we could live most of the year in London. Together."

"It would be delightful."

"Even though I'll continue to attract my old acquaintances?"

He grimaced, but said, "Even so. As long as they hold the line."

She was glad to reach the point. "Edison. I think that shot will have warned him off."

"He's dangerously besotted."

"I never realized before. He has to see now that it's hopeless."

"He might wish for my early demise."

"He'd never try to *kill* you," she protested.

"He might try to kill you. No, don't dismiss it too easily. It's a madness that takes men at times—that if they can't possess a woman, no one should."

"I can't believe it. I won't believe it. But before you ask, I will continue to take my entourage when I go out."

"Thank you."

She leaned comfortably against him and indulged in dreams. "If I was able to live mostly in London, we'd need to use the house. Would you mind? I like it, and it's as if it's dozing, hoping someone will live happily in it."

"A sentient building? Do we dare speculate what the Abbey is thinking and feeling?"

"Miserable thoughts. Oh, dear—now I want to rescue it. How? Even if we evict the dowager, if we have our way, it will stand empty. I don't suppose we can lease it?"

"It would cause a lot of talk, but if we reach that point, it might be the only solution." She caught the smile in his voice as he added, "You want to rescue the world, don't you?"

"No, that's you. I restrict myself to my immediate sphere. I'll do what I can for the town house. New paint and paper. Some additional furniture. Piped hot water to your dressing room, so it could serve as a bathing room."

"A large bath," he said, "so we can bathe together."

"Why?" But then she envisioned it. "You're making me blush."

"I love to make you blush. I've read of projects to use steam to heat a whole house."

"That would be delightful. We'll be a winter haven for gatherings of whatever sorts of people we each like." She shifted so she could see him when she added, "Including a weekly Kit Kat Club."

She saw no reaction. "If there's not enough space," he said, "we could take one of the houses to either side."

"Have two houses?"

"Knock them together."

"I never imagined that."

"Expand your mind," he said, and they both smiled at memory of their first encounter.

"Anything is possible?" she said, but then she pulled a face. "Not everything. Or not for some time. And if I were to live mostly in London, I'd miss Ruth. Having only just moved close to her, I'd be far away again. So the Abbey isn't so terrible after all."

"Except that we won't be there together."

He'd put it into words. She responded as calmly as she could. "Sometimes perfection isn't possible, and we have more, much more, than we expected, my dear Braydon."

"We do," he said, as the carriage halted outside their rooms.

Chapter 41

Kitty woke early the next morning, and lay, in low spirits, close to her husband's warm body. She'd woken in the middle of the night, at that time when darker thoughts seem able to invade.

She must soon return to the Abbey, and putting it off wouldn't help. Rural Gloucestershire wasn't the Slough of Despond, but her dark-hours mind hadn't been able to escape that image. The chilly house with the even chillier people, and the wintry countryside where little was alive.

Unfair, unfair. It could be lovely in the summer.

Yet even those who enjoyed their rural estates in balmier seasons didn't live there in winter, if they could help it. They visited at Christmastide and then hurried back to Town.

Christmas at Beauchamp Abbey.

She'd have to attempt some celebrations, because not to do so would be to knuckle down to the dowager. But how could she arrange matters without starting a war? And whom should she invite? And would they attend?

She'd always enjoyed the Christmas season in London and resented leaving it for Cateril Manor. Now, in early December, the streets were already bright with gaslight and the shops full of delicacies and delights. The theaters would be at their best at Christmastime, even with the lingering mourning. There'd be pantomimes, which she'd heard were great fun. Now there was no reason she couldn't go to one, except for the damned Abbey.

She put aside the dismals and did her best to raise her spirits before Braydon awoke. She managed well enough to be able to put on a smile for him at breakfast.

"What are your plans for the day?" she asked.

"To continue with my investigations. I've had some thoughts on the matter."

"Yes?"

"Sidmouth seemed as annoyed by the situation as I am, so it's probable that he told the truth and the Regent gave the command. The most likely reasons for that are that the Regent was himself responsible, or he knows who was and doesn't want it known."

"The Princess of Wales?" Kitty suggested.

"Definitely not. The Regent would want to blast that news everywhere."

"One of the three princes, then."

"That seems most likely."

Kitty sipped her chocolate. Braydon was drinking ordinary coffee and, as usual, eating a sandwich. "If that's so," she said, "it's over, isn't it? The culprit will never dare try again."

"That does depend on the why. For example, if Kent has his eye on the throne, getting rid of Clarence would move him one step closer."

"But why wait for a gathering of three?"

"Because he needed to coax Kent back to England from Brussels."

Kitty considered that. "But assuming he slipped away before the explosion, his brother Sussex would die."

"A sacrifice in the cause."

"Is he truly so callous?"

"I've met Kent only twice and can't claim to know him at all, but in the army he had the reputation as a strict disciplinarian. When he was in Nova Scotia, a group of soldiers tried to seize and murder him."

"Good heavens. Last night you suggested the whole thing might be a farce. This isn't farcical."

"It isn't, is it? If it was a pretend plot, we're back to the puzzle of whose purpose that serves."

"And who might have already gained by it. I'm glad you're not going to cease investigations."

"Sidmouth can't think he can call off the hawks so easily, and it's best if the Regent doesn't, either. Beaumont will be leaving for Brussels today, as planned."

"On a Sunday?"

"The matter is urgent enough. Charrington returns to Somerset tomorrow."

"Which church should we attend?"

"Saint George's."

"But I assume you won't have a day of rest?"

She expected agreement, but he said, "Why not? There's little useful to do, and the weather looks fair. We could drive out somewhere. To Richmond, perhaps."

"If we're going so far, we could drive to Edgware."

"Edgware?" But then he remembered. "Curious cat."

"More interesting than an idle drive. We should see what house the fifth viscount was maintaining there, and make sure that the care is continuing."

"Very reasonable," he said, "but it's curiosity, pure and simple."

"And what's wrong with that, sir?"

Perhaps he remembered something from the night, for he smiled as he said, "Nothing. Nothing at all, my dear."

After attending the Sunday service, Braydon hired a carriage from the nearby livery, and instructed that it be warmed by hot bricks. In her mantle and muff, Kitty was perfectly comfortable as they left London along the

Edgware Road. She'd decided to leave Sillikin behind. The dog wasn't fond of carriage rides and had the servants enslaved.

When they passed close to Moor Street, she pointed that out and shared memories of some of the familiar places nearby. The road was unusually straight, but that was because it followed an old Roman road called Watling Street.

"I've always liked the Roman way," she said. "Go directly to the target without dithering around for valleys and hills."

The Edgware Road ran along the west edge of London, with streets to their right but few buildings to their left. Once they passed through the tollbooth at Paddington village, they had countryside to their right as well. There wasn't a great deal of traffic, it being a Sunday and Edgware not being a popular pleasure jaunt, especially in winter.

When they arrived at their destination, Kitty was somewhat surprised. Because it had a road named for it, she'd expected a town, but it was merely a straggling collection of houses along the street, with a few more significant ones nearby.

They climbed out of the carriage at the White Hart, which had no pretensions of grandeur. On such a significant road she'd expected a large coaching inn, but perhaps Edgware was too close to London to be a popular place to change horses or seek refreshment. Hostlers took charge of the two horses, and Braydon gave the postilion his freedom for an hour or so. The innkeeper, thin and keen, asked what other service he could offer.

"L Cottage, sir? All I can think of is Laurel Cottage, just off this street. If you walk five houses down, you'll see the lane, sir. Fox Lane."

As they followed the directions, Kitty said, "What do

we expect to find? My money's on the fifth viscount's nurse. Where do you place your bet?"

"You've stolen the most likely explanation. It's a little out of the way for a mistress, so I'll plump for an old friend, down on his luck, housed out of charity. After all, it would seem he kept these expenditures secret. Why would he do that for his old nurse?"

"A good point. I know—the dowager took against Nurse and dismissed her. He was afraid to let his mother know that he was taking care of her."

"Overly dramatic, but in this case all too likely. What a milksop he was."

They turned the corner and were soon assessing Laurel Cottage.

"Rather a grand cottage," Kitty said, for the building was two full stories beneath its thatch. "Large for Nurse. You're probably correct about the friend, especially if the friend has a family."

"Or he was supporting more than one unfairly dismissed servant. There's only one way to find out."

As they walked up a short path to the door, Kitty heard children shouting in play from behind the house. "I fear you'll win. An old friend with a family. Perhaps a wounded soldier."

Braydon knocked at the door.

It was opened by a woman who certainly wasn't an old nurse but didn't look like a servant, either, despite the apron over her brown gown, and a mobcap over mousy brown hair. *Wife of a wounded officer?*

"Yes?" she asked, clearly surprised—and why not?— to find unexpected visitors on the doorstep on a Sunday afternoon? "May I help you?"

Braydon said, "We hope so. My name is Dauntry, and my wife and I are taking the opportunity to satisfy mere curiosity. An imposition, I know, but may we come in?"

Kitty saw no flicker of reaction to the name Dauntry. How to explain that?

After a brief hesitation, the woman stepped back. "Of course, sir."

They entered a narrow corridor, but were taken into a fair-sized parlor to the left, which was warmed by a large fire. No sign of penny-pinching. The woman invited them to sit. All the furniture was of good quality, but nowhere near new. No sign of extravagance, either.

Kitty and Braydon sat on a slightly battered sofa, and the woman sat on a straight chair. She wasn't offering her name, which perhaps wasn't surprising with such unexpected guests, but Kitty wondered if there was wariness in her expression. *A mistress, after all?* She didn't seem the type, being so soberly dressed and with a face that was more sturdy than beguiling.

Braydon had brought the account book. "This is our curiosity, ma'am. It records expenses for the maintenance of a property. On the flyleaf you'll see it says, L Cottage, Edgware."

He passed it to the woman, open at the flyleaf. She took it without any sign of recognizing the book, but when she looked at the words, she frowned. She turned some pages and then looked up, alert and perhaps alarmed. "How did you come by this, sir?"

"On a shelf," Braydon said. "You recognize it?"

"I recognize the writing. It's my husband's." Then she asked, quite desperately, "Do you know where he is?"

Chapter 42

Kitty saw it in a moment. Not a mistress, or, at least, not in this woman's mind. She thought herself married, and she'd not heard from her husband in months.

Lord above, what to do now?

"Your husband's name, ma'am?" Braydon asked. Kitty wondered how he could sound so calm.

"Braydon, of course. You didn't know that? I'm Mrs. Braydon. Dorothy Braydon. Please tell me where my husband is, or at least where you found this book!"

Kitty wanted to rush to her and hug her, but it would only alarm the woman more.

"My name is Dauntry, as I said, ma'am—it's Lord Dauntry. The book was found in my London house. I have reason to believe your husband left it there, but in order to be sure, do you have a picture of Mr. Braydon?"

Oh. Kitty saw his reasoning. It was just possible that the fifth viscount had been taking care of some indigent relative and his family, and it was the indigent relative who'd disappeared.

"A picture? Yes, of course." The woman hurried out of the room and returned in moments with a small oval portrait, no more than a foot high. The artist wasn't as skilled as the one who'd executed the portrait that hung at the Abbey, but it was clearly the fifth viscount. He still looked slightly anxious, but in a generally more optimistic way.

He'd been happy here, despite a bigamous marriage, but he'd left this woman in a terrible situation. Especially if . . .

"You have children, ma'am?" Kitty asked.

"What? Yes. Two. Please, where is my husband?"

Kitty went to her then, taking her hand. "I'm very sorry, ma'am. We have sad news for you."

The woman looked into Kitty's eyes and clutched her hand. "He's dead."

"Yes."

The woman sat down. Kitty knelt beside, because the woman kept her grip on her.

"I've feared as much. He's frequently been away on business and sometimes for a month or more, but never so long." She looked at Braydon. "Why has no one told me? And how? Where?"

Braydon replied in that cool tone that Kitty had encountered at first meeting. It was his defense, she saw, against high emotions.

"He died of a fever, ma'am. In Gloucestershire, at a place called Beauchamp Abbey. He never mentioned it?"

"No. Why was he there? Were they buying pewter?"

"Pewter?"

"That was his business. Trading in pewter. I never understood it, but it brought in enough money for us to live well. Did he die alone?"

"No," Kitty said quickly. "He wasn't alone, and he had the best possible medical care, but it couldn't help him. A number of people died of the illness at the same time."

"I don't understand why nobody told me!"

"Nobody knew, ma'am. About you, I mean."

"But he must have had things on him. His business cards. Letters. Something."

Kitty looked to Braydon, not knowing what best to say. She saw it in his eyes. Only the truth would do.

But at that moment, four young children burst into the room—two boys, two girls. "Mama! Look what. . . ."

They all went silent, and then one, a dark-haired lad, said, "I'm sorry, Mama. We didn't know you had guests."

"Yes. Best you go away for now, dears."

The children backed out, perhaps just abashed by their intrusion, but Kitty suspected they'd picked up the atmosphere of disaster.

This was disaster. Not only was this woman not a legal wife, but her children were bastards.

There was no doubt, however, who the boy's father was. The resemblance to the picture of the fifth viscount as a child was potent. One of the girls had a similar appearance, but the other two children were sandy and round-faced.

"Fine children, ma'am," Kitty said.

"Heavens, they're not all mine! Johnie is—the one who had the grace to apologize—and the girl in blue. Alice. The other two are their friends. They'll have found something horrible. . . ."

She suddenly put her hands to her face and started to rock.

Kitty moved another chair close and took her into her arms, simply holding her, but she sent Braydon a desperate look. What were they to do next? Could this poor woman take the additional blow that she was not a widow? That she'd never been a wife?

Braydon rose and left. Had he decided this was woman's work and abandoned her?

"Please, ma'am, try not to worry about your future," Kitty said. "I assure you we will take care of you and your children."

The woman looked up at that. Her eyes were only slightly damp, but hollow with shock and grief. "Why would you do that?'

"Because our name is Braydon, too. Your Mr. Braydon was a distant relative of my husband's."

"A lord? Alfred never mentioned that."

"What did he say about his family?"

"Very little. His parents were dead, and he was an only child."

Kitty knew that the bereaved generally needed to talk about their lost one.

"Where did you meet?"

"In Cirencester. One of those silly moments. I was returning from market with an overloaded basket, and a cabbage rolled out. He picked it up for me. He had such kind eyes." She blinked and swallowed. "The cabbage wouldn't stay in the basket, so he offered to carry it for me. I normally wouldn't have encouraged such a thing, but he had such kind eyes. And he seemed anxious, as if he expected me to refuse."

"That was kind of you, then."

"It was for my own benefit as much as his. Not just the cabbage. I was so lonely at that time, with rarely anyone sensible to talk to. I was nursing my father, you see. My mother had died three years earlier, and I'd had to leave my job as a governess to look after my father. He'd slowly been losing touch with reality, but was still in good health, if you know what I mean."

"Like the king," Kitty said.

"Perhaps, though Father never raved. I do feel sympathy for the queen, except that she doesn't have the daily care of His Majesty. I understand she visits him only once a month. My father took all my time. When I had to leave him, he'd do odd things, sometimes dangerous things, so I had to pay a neighbor to sit with him. Sometimes he'd wander off."

"That must have been very difficult."

"It was. I didn't want Alfred to come in, but he insisted

on bringing the cabbage into the kitchen. Father was in one of his better days, insofar as he thought he was younger and that Alfred had come to visit him. Invited him to sit and take tea. So he did. Father spoke of his younger years, when he'd been in the militia. I remember Alfred mentioned the victory at Talavera—the news had just arrived—and Father didn't notice that it didn't fit with the wars of his youth. I sat sipping tea, feeling as if I'd fallen into a pleasant dream."

"And Alfred returned," Kitty guessed. "He wooed you."

"He did. I tried to send him away. What use was I to anyone, burdened as I was? But he continued to visit, even though Father rarely remembered him and sometimes treated him as an intruder or enemy. Within two weeks, he asked me to marry him!"

"You protested again."

"Of course, but he made the practicalities so appealing, and I was at the end of my tether." She looked directly into Kitty's eyes. "I didn't love him. I feel I must say that. I was very fond of Alfred, and deeply grateful, but I never held a poetic passion for him. I felt bad about that, but such feelings can't be commanded, can they? And I gave him all possible kindness and tenderness. He was happy here with us. He often said so, and I know it was the truth."

"I'm sure he was. May I call you Dorothy? I'm Kitty."

"You're being very kind."

Braydon returned then with a wide-eyed young maid bearing a tea tray. So that's where he'd gone. The tea was already made in the pot, so Kitty poured it and stirred in two lumps of sugar. She passed over the cup and saucer. "Drink this. It will help."

The woman sipped. "Thank you."

Kitty poured tea for herself and Braydon. "I told Dorothy that we'd take care of her and her family. I explained that you were distantly related to her husband."

He took the tea and sat on the sofa. "Of course. Are you in need at the moment, ma'am?"

Dorothy's face was still marked by the news, but she seemed composed. She was a strong woman. She'd need to be.

"In need? No. Alfred arranged an annuity when we married. I didn't see the need, for his income was ample, but he insisted. It provides a monthly income, and I was told that will continue until I die. It's provided the necessities for us in his absence. There was also some arrangement to provide for the children's future. He was a good man." She looked between them. "You are quite sure he's dead?"

"Quite sure," Braydon said.

Dorothy sighed. "Where's his grave? I'll want to visit it."

"In the grounds of Beauchamp Abbey."

"Why there? Is it a ruin?"

"No, it's a house. My house, in fact. Ma'am, I'm sorry to say that we have some more bad news for you."

"More? What could be worse than my husband's death?"

Kitty wished desperately she could fend off the coming blow.

"That your husband wasn't your husband, ma'am. He wasn't free to marry you."

The cup and saucer tilted. Kitty caught them in time.

"I don't believe you! Alfred would never have done such a thing! We were married in Cirencester, in good order."

"All the same, he was already married to a woman called Diane. She left him for another man, but he never divorced her. He was not free to marry."

"I don't believe it," the poor woman repeated, but she did. She'd aged in the minutes since hearing the news. "Oh, my poor, poor children! How am I to tell them this?"

"I suggest you don't, ma'am," Braydon said. "There's no need to make this public in any way."

Dorothy stared at him. "Not . . . I'm to live a *lie*?"

"For your children's sake and your own. There's no reason anyone should find out."

He was being cool and logical—the marble box again—but Kitty wasn't surprised when Dorothy shot to her feet.

"You speak as if this is a matter of mere practicalities, my lord! My husband is *dead*, and now you tell me I'm a bigamous wife and my children are bastards, but I should put it all out of mind?"

Braydon had risen. "It's the only sensible thing to do."

Kitty stood, too, shooting him an angry look. "It's all a terrible shock, Dorothy, but Dauntry's right. Of course you can't put it out of mind, but do nothing hastily. What purpose will be served by your telling the world? You and your children will suffer."

Dorothy's hands gripped her apron. "But what if someone finds out? Can I be jailed for this?"

"No, I'm sure not. She can't, can she?"

Braydon said, "You're an innocent party, ma'am. If the truth does come out, we'll deal with that together. However, there is more."

"More." Dorothy wavered, and Kitty eased her back into her chair. "Perhaps we shouldn't . . ."

But Braydon continued, "Your husband was Alfred Braydon—"

"Well, thank God for that!"

"But he was also Viscount Dauntry. His travels were not on business, but to keep up his role as Lord Dauntry in Parliament and at his estate. I'm sure he didn't enjoy that part of his life and that you and your children were his joy, but he couldn't neglect his duties entirely."

"Viscount Dauntry." Kitty wondered if Dorothy would faint, but instead she gave a kind of laugh. "Poor Alfred. He must have hated that. Did he speak in Parliament?"

"I don't know," Braydon said. "I never thought to check."

"Probably not. He had a stutter, you see. It wasn't too bad at home, but it sometimes afflicted him when we were with others. It always seemed worse when he returned from his trips."

"I'm not at all surprised," Braydon said. "I must tell you that he also had two children by his wife. The boy, Alfred, died of the same fever, which is how I came to inherit the title, but the girl, Isabella, was spared. She's nearly seventeen."

Kitty thought all this information might tip poor Dorothy's wits, but it seemed to help.

"Seventeen, and he never mentioned her."

"How could he? I'm sure he felt a fatherly affection for her. One of his last acts was to make sure she was well provided for."

"Will I be able to visit his grave?"

"I recommend that you don't. It would be bound to raise questions. I suggest that you commission a memorial for the church here. It will serve the purpose as well."

Kitty wondered about that, but Dorothy said, "I suppose so. I've never felt attachment to my parents' mortal remains. He had my father moved here when we married. He wanted to be close to London for business purposes — or so he said." She shook her head, still coming to terms with the reality. "So he bought this house for us. He moved my father here and hired an attendant so I needed only to supervise his care and was free to come and go. Like the queen, though at that time we didn't know the worst about the king, only that he was unwell . . ." Perhaps she realized she was wandering, for she composed herself. "He was a good, kind man."

"He loved you," Kitty said. "And you made him happy."

"I do hope that's true. It's so very odd to think he'll never return here. That we made no special farewells." Dorothy straightened and looked at Braydon. "What should I do now?"

"Inform your children and your friends and neighbors of the death, as you would do if matters were regular. You can say that he died of a virulent fever and it was thought best to bury the body quickly. It's true. Then continue on that road. Can you do that?"

"I can do whatever I must for my children's sake."

"You are a splendid woman. Do you know if he made a will?"

Kitty looked sharply at him. There'd been a will. What happened if there were two?

"I don't think so," Dorothy said. "I did ask him about it once, thinking he should, but he assured me he'd made all proper arrangements for us with the annuities. I didn't like to pursue it."

"As you say, he made other arrangements. However, I suspect that legally this house now belongs to the viscountcy. I'll sign it over to you as soon as possible."

"Thank you. This is all hard to take in."

"Time will solve that, at least. If you have need of anything, cousin Dorothy, don't hesitate to contact me."

"Cousin." That comfortable word that acknowledged a family connection without necessarily implying a close one.

He took out a card and wrote something on the back. "Any of those addresses will find me."

"And we'll visit," Kitty said. "To make sure you're all right. After all, Johnie and Alice are relatives of ours, no matter the legalities." She hated to leave. "Are you sure you're all right? We could stay longer."

"No, thank you. You've been as kind as possible. I have friends here."

And we are not friends, Kitty understood, *but strangers bearing bad news.* Cousin Dorothy could be a difficult woman, but she was a strong one.

Braydon said, "If I may offer one more piece of advice, cousin, keep that portrait out of sight. The chance of someone visiting here who would recognize it is remote, but why take the risk?"

Dorothy was sensible enough to recognize good advice. "I'll keep it in my bedroom."

Tears were beginning, and she blotted them with a handkerchief, but Kitty guessed she'd rather they leave. She had friends, she'd said, and why not? She'd lived here for something like seven years.

They took their leave, saving their comments until they were well away from the house.

"How extraordinary," Kitty said, "but I find myself pleased that the fifth viscount had happiness in his life. A stutter. Poor man."

"Yes, but if he'd divorced his wife, he'd not have left that woman in such a situation. Milksops create more problems than bullies."

"This is all the bullying dowager's fault. That's probably why he didn't divorce Diane."

"How do you reason that?"

"At first it would have been too much attention and drama for him, but when he met Dorothy, he might have realized that getting the divorce and marrying her legally—"

"Would have taken a long time? Worth waiting for."

"Don't put words in my mouth. Marrying her legally would have made her Viscountess Dauntry and dragged her into the dowager's orbit. After what happened to Diane, he'd want to protect her from that."

"Leaving her in this situation? Illogical. But I think the dowager is innocent of one crime. I've been holding her responsible for the missing money in the viscountcy's accounts, thinking that she'd secretly squandered it on yet more ornamentation of the Abbey and on bribing gifts to the servants. Instead, it was almost certainly Alfred sneaking out funds to support his Edgware love nest. Shall we see if the White Hart can provide some decent food?"

"I think it best that we leave Edgware without drawing any more attention to ourselves. There will be other inns on the way back to Town."

"Wise lady."

Chapter 43

They stopped at an inn in Brent Bridge, which served them a meal in a hastily warmed private parlor. Kitty kept her cloak on. As they ate their soup, she said, "I thought I'd heard that if a spouse disappears for seven years or more, a person could marry."

"I believe so. Some people's deaths aren't clear, for example in foreign parts."

"Eaten by a tiger in India. Swallowed by a whirlpool in the South Pacific."

"Perhaps you should take to writing novels."

She smiled at that. "My point is, if Alfred could have had Diane declared dead, he could have made an honest woman of Dorothy a few years ago, without the scandal of a divorce. He wouldn't have had to announce her to be Lady Dauntry. To marry, he'd only have to use his name, Alfred Braydon, wouldn't he?"

"Yes, but consider this—he'd have had to confess to Dorothy that their original marriage had been bigamous, and the new marriage wouldn't have legitimized Johnie and Alice."

"Ah. Poor innocents. But any future children would have been legitimate."

He pushed his soup plate away. "Which could have made matters worse with a title in the mix. A son born after the legal marriage would have inherited the title over Johnie."

Kitty also abandoned the soup. It was very dull. "I see. That would be a very difficult situation."

"Something similar is currently haunting the Cavendish family. As things stand, if Dorothy's nerve holds, her children will be none the worse for all this. The fifth viscount did his best for her and his children."

The next dish was rather tough roast beef.

Kitty sawed at it. "I've just realized that the dowager has more vessels of the Godyson blood than she knows."

He looked up from his plate. "You're intending to inform her?"

"Heavens, no! Though perhaps she might welcome them?"

"Only if they can inherit the title and preserve the glory that is Beauchamp Abbey." He put his fork down. "Shall we abandon this sorry excuse for food?"

Kitty was hungry, but she agreed.

Once they were on the road again, she considered the Braydon family. "So many odd mothers and unsatisfactory marriages. Ours feels blessed by comparison."

One of his rare smiles lit his eyes. "It's blessed by any standard."

"Then we should burn incense to the goddess of chance."

"And a comment like that confirms it." He tugged at the bow in her bonnet ribbons to loosen it and remove the obstruction to a gently satisfying kiss.

The light was fading on the short winter day, and they paused so the carriage lamps could be lit. That made the countryside beyond their glow seem darker, and Kitty was relieved when they entered the outskirts of London, and especially when they reached the lamp-lit streets.

Soon after that, they were home, and Sillikin was giving Kitty an ecstatically wriggly greeting.

"Yes, yes," Kitty said, fondling her. "I'm sure you've had wonderful adventures and not missed me at all."

Braydon said, "I hope a decent dinner's preparing, Edward, and can be served soon. We dined poorly on the road."

"Yes, sir. There's a message, sir."

Kitty glanced over. *A message on Sunday?*

She had to straighten so Henry could take her cloak. "Perhaps your jaunt was pleasant otherwise, ma'am?" Henry asked.

"It was certainly interesting." Kitty would have liked to say more, but the fifth viscount's adventures were definitely better kept to as few people as possible. As, probably, were the contents of the message Braydon was reading. *Sidmouth again?*

"From Sir Stephen Ball," Braydon said. They went into the library and closed the door. Sillikin came with them, but she could keep secrets.

"*'Took an opportunity at church to speak to Sussex,'*" Braydon read out. "*'He wishes to speak to you.'* So I don't escape that duty, after all, but it can wait until tomorrow."

"Will he, too, urge you to cease investigations?"

"If so, it'll be an interesting indication."

"That Sussex was behind the plot?" she asked. "He's sixth in line."

"The explosion could have disposed of two of his older brothers, and the Regent is unwell. That would leave only York and Cumberland in his way, both of them in marriages that are unlikely to provide offspring."

"If that's the situation, would Sidmouth and the Regent want the matter forgotten?"

"What purpose would be solved by making a public scandal of it?"

And what steps might be taken to avoid that? Kitty wondered.

"Perhaps you shouldn't obey the summons," she said.

"Why not?" He must have guessed her concern. "No, Kitty, that would be too Gothic."

"We're talking about a royal duke. In the past he would have been able to throw you into the Tower."

"But no longer. He can't even vent spite on me. I can't be deprived of employment or evicted from my title, unfortunately. I need no royal favors in the future, and I certainly don't pine for an approving word. That's one reason Hawkinville involves a number of gentlemen of independent means."

He seemed certain, so Kitty let her fears subside. "And perhaps ladies?" she said.

"I shouldn't have put that idea into your head."

"But you did." She put a hand on his chest. She needed to touch him, even through layers of clothing. "I enjoyed unraveling the mysteries of the fifth viscount's affairs, and I did well, didn't I?"

"It mostly unraveled itself," he pointed out, but he'd covered her hand with his.

"Once we visited Edgware." She crept her hand upward. "Which was my idea."

"You do have a nose for the important detail."

She touched his nose. "So?"

But there was a knock at the door. By the time Edward came in and announced dinner, they were decently apart. As they went to the dining room, she remembered the reality of their situation. It would be a long time, if ever, before she could investigate any mystery, unless the crime took place at Beauchamp Abbey.

There'd be no benefit from going over that, so as they

began their meal, she said, "Do you realize that we've not spent a Sunday at the Abbey? How does it go?"

"The chaplain conducts a service in the dowager's boudoir. The senior servants attend. After one such service, I chose Beecham Dab instead."

"I'd forgotten the chaplain. Where does he live?"

"In a house in Stuckle, close by the ancient chapel. He conducts a service there for the Stuckle people and is well regarded."

"So even he avoids the Abbey. Things will have to change." Kitty rang for the next course. "There's some hope for Isabella. She's not immune to the enticements of the world, and she asked me to buy her some new novels."

"Will they improve her temperament?"

"I chose them carefully. Not all are Gothic horrors."

They went silent as Edward brought in portions of roast duck in sauce and side dishes. When he'd left she said, "It's not yet a full week since we married. Isn't that extraordinary?"

"Do you regret our lost honeymoon?"

"Not at all." She ate some of the tender duck, comparing it to the inedible beef. "So delicious. What is a honeymoon, after all? If it's for enjoyment, I've enjoyed the past days more for being here. If it's for increased ease with each other, I suspect that's also better for being away from the Abbey."

"Despite the plots and connivances?"

"Because of them, most likely. I don't think I'm made for a tranquil life."

"Nor am I, but there are times for tranquillity."

The look in his eyes told her he was thinking of the night. She smiled to show she echoed it.

In due course, at a proper time, they retired for the night, and if their explorations were not entirely tranquil, they were slow and gentle in parts. Braydon surprised Kitty with some soft laughter at one point, so that she woke in the middle of the night with tears dampening her pillow. It had come upon her, not as an explosion but as a powerful wave, that she loved him. She'd known she admired him, delighted in him, desired him, and enjoyed him. But enhancing everything now was that insane magic the poets tried to capture, and that had eluded Dorothy, despite her best intentions. Romantic love, which brought passions, addictions, and even tragedy, but, if blessed, was the most delicious delight.

Yet soon they must part.

Many loving couples spend time apart, she reminded herself, *especially if the husband is a soldier, sailor, or merchant.* Dorothy hadn't found it odd that her husband had to spend stretches of time away from home.

Men came to Town for Parliament and didn't always bring their wives and families. Many wives preferred to spend spring in the countryside, especially if their children were young. Perhaps a honeymoon was designed to wear out the first mania so that married lovers could resume a normal life.

Very well. She would not be manic. She must return to the Abbey soon, so on the next day, she must attend to Abbey business more seriously.

She breakfasted with Braydon, but when he went out to visit Sussex, she sat to make lists of what she needed to buy or order. She took the list to Henry for advice, and she suggested a few additions.

But then Henry said, "I was thinking this would be a good opportunity for you to interview some lady's maids, dear. You might not be back in Town until the spring."

Kitty wanted to protest, but Henry had only been on loan to her.

"Miss Ecclestall must be missing you," she said.

"She is, but I miss her and Lady Sophonisbe, and my family thereabouts. I'd like to be home for Christmas."

"You have family? You've never mentioned them."

"Two brothers and a sister, and many nieces and nephews."

"Then of course you must go home," Kitty said, hoping her good cheer was convincing. "How do we go about hiring a new maid?"

"There are agencies. You could write to ask them to arrange interviews in the next day or two."

"Very well. But you must assist me to make the right choice."

"Of course, dear. I won't leave until I'm sure you have the right person."

That tempted Kitty to be dissatisfied with all of them, but she wouldn't. Henry deserved to be happily in her right place.

She sent the letter to the agency and then, with her entourage, she toured shops and warehouses to select everything she needed to make her suite of rooms at the Abbey tolerable. She regretted not having Ruth to advise her, but she'd do her best. She also stayed alert for Christmas trimmings—the brighter, the better—and anything that might be a suitable gift.

She'd never clung to a dark mood, and this day was no different, especially when she could make choices without a care for the cost. She couldn't help but enjoy the way she was treated as a titled lady with two servants. Frequently the owner of an establishment would hurry out to give her special attention, offering refreshments and an abundance of samples to take away.

At one point Kitty murmured to Henry, "I could have refurbished my rooms in Moor Street with all these so-called samples."

"Then you'll be able to pass them on when you no longer need them, dear."

Benevolence. Something else she'd rarely been able to indulge in. When she thought of Beecham Dab and the Abbey, she didn't see much need, especially with Ruth and Andrew doing their duty so responsibly.

There's an abundance of need in London, which is why there are so many charities, many needing noble patrons and patronesses.... That way lay the dismals, so she plunged into the investigation of some small rotating bookcases. As she turned one, testing how smoothly it moved, she wondered how Braydon was faring with the Duke of Sussex.

This was 1817, not the middle ages, or even Tudor times, but she worried that a royal duke could retaliate if threatened. Braydon had been too dismissive of that.

She shook her head. They described love as a madness, and it must be if it led to her thinking Braydon couldn't cope without her at his side.

Chapter 44

Braydon had previously seen the Duke of Sussex only at a distance. He knew Sussex suffered from asthma, but there was no sign of the ailment as the prince greeted him. His frailty as a youth had prevented him from taking up a military career, which might have left him free to develop reformist and even egalitarian ideas. It was said the king had favored the military for his sons to remove them from idleness and indulgence.

That hadn't been a great success.

Sussex had the family tendency to run to fat, but he seemed in reasonably good health. Of course, he was only in his forties, whereas the Regent was approaching sixty.

Braydon gave Sussex credit for being true to his principles, for he was invited to sit down, gentleman to gentleman. Such a shame those principles had led to his making an illegal marriage, so that his children were technically bastards. He'd married in Italy in a wild passion, or so it was said. The relationship hadn't survived the subsequent storms. Did he now regret it, thinking that he might have married with approval and produced legitimate heirs? Or had that ecstasy of love been worth it?

Ecstasy of love . . .

"Dauntry?"

Braydon grappled together his distracted thoughts.

There'd been no hint of guilt or fear in the prince's manner, so what was the purpose here?

He was in a chair placed across a table that held a chessboard. He hoped he wasn't going to be obliged to play. He didn't care for the game, and he certainly didn't care for the delicate diplomacy of playing with princes. Sussex was reputedly cleverer than his brothers, so it might not be too hard to lose.

"I understand that you are enquiring into the recent event at Mrs. Courtenay's house," Sussex said.

"I am, sir. At the request of the Home Secretary. As you were there, sir, perhaps you can shed some light on the matter."

"I know no more than anyone else of the event."

"Someone knows a great deal." Braydon watched Sussex as he added, "The person who planned the explosion, sir, and the person or persons who attempted to put it into action."

Sussex put a finger on a chess piece, as if contemplating a move. "You think them two different parties?"

"It's no light matter to plan the assassination of three princes. The person capable of that is unlikely to choose to trundle beer through a backyard and into a cellar."

Sussex chuckled. "True, true."

Interesting. That was knowing humor. Either Sussex was amused at the thought of delivering the barrel himself, or because it was equally ridiculous about a known other. The tone implied the latter.

Who?

Braydon also realized there was something indulgent in the prince's manner. Sussex didn't believe the plan had ever been murderous.

"We have considered," he said, "that the plan went forward exactly as intended, sir. That there was never any intention of an explosion."

"Ah." Sussex attempted surprise, but however clever he might be, he was a poor actor. "What would be the point of that?" he asked, brows high, eyes wide.

"To alarm one of the supposed victims."

"To what end?"

"That, sir, would be the key to the puzzle."

Sussex leaned forward and considered the chess-board, and then he moved a white knight. He gave no indication that he expected Braydon to take part.

"Have you considered," the prince asked, "what you might do when you detect the culprit? It is the Regent's wish that the incident be kept as quiet as possible. He fears the mob, you know, especially after his carriage was attacked earlier in the year. In his darker moments, he fears the guillotine. He worries that the mere idea of murdering princes might be infectious."

"Not entirely without reason, sir."

When the Red Band plotters had been destroyed in the summer, parts of a guillotine had been found in a ware-house near the docks. Quite likely the Regent had been told, which might not have been wise. The revolutionaries would never have succeeded, but they'd been serious in their intent, and there were others of similar mind.

"Not entirely without reason," Sussex agreed, looking up from the board. "It's a delicate business, reform, Dauntry. As you know, I work for it. We will have it—we must have it—but every step opens cracks that can be exploited by those of evil mind. Evil must be stopped, but freedom must be preserved. I do not like Sidmouth, but I'm not opposed to the work that Hawkinville does."

"I was given to understand that you assisted in the establishment of his unit, sir."

"Sometimes my position gives me useful authority. Mostly, you know, I find it a damned bore."

He meant it, but Braydon suspected that if the prince

was suddenly made a commoner, he'd be miserable. That contrasted whimsically with himself. He'd thank God if he could be restored to that state.

Sussex moved a white castle. If he'd been playing both sides of a chess game, it should have been black's turn. Braydon focused on the board. Both kings were safe, but the black queen was now in a very difficult situation, boxed in by the castle and surrounded by three knights: two white, one black.

Mothers and sons; sons and mothers.

Sussex straightened. "As one of the interested parties, I would be pleased if the matter were quietly put to rest. Kent and Clarence feel the same. No purpose will be served by pursuing it, and we're sure you and Hawkinville have more important matters to attend to. The unpleasant elements are skulking at the moment, but they will creep out in time."

Braydon considered the board again and then looked up. "Yes, sir. You're undoubtedly correct."

"Good, good." Sussex rose. "I thank you for coming. May I hope you'll take a stance for reform in Parliament, Dauntry? It's the only way."

Braydon rose. "I agree, sir. But orderly reform."

Sussex surprised him by disagreeing. "Radical change can't help but disrupt order. Many see reform as infringing on their ancient rights and privileges, and they're right. The Crown had to shed powers under Magna Carta, and then in the Civil War and Restoration. In the coming years, many entrenched powers must be undermined. There will be howls and some will fight, but I have faith change will be achieved without bloodshed. With your help?"

"I will do my best, sir."

Sussex put out his hand, and Braydon shook it. "I know you'll do the right thing, Dauntry, and I thank you."

He wasn't talking about reform.

*   *   *

Braydon left Kensington Palace, considering what to do next. Nothing, of course, other than call off the hawks. It was over.

As for the other matter . . .

He spent the walk home exploring his new, not entirely pleasant, state of mind. *No, not mind, heart.* Weren't lovers supposed to dance and sing and scatter flowers toward the sun? The sun lurked behind clouds and he felt naked, even raw.

Vulnerable.

There were no flower sellers at this time of year, but then he passed a girl hawking posies of silk violets. He bought one, and then felt damned stupid carrying it through the streets. With a wry smile, he wondered if an aspiring dandy would see Beau Braydon with a posy and decide it was the latest fashion.

He entered his rooms, hoping Kitty was home. She was in the drawing room with a great many parcels piled on chairs and floor. Her dog was snuffling about them, stub tail wagging.

"I had the larger items sent directly to the Abbey," she said, delightfully unapologetic. "But I had the smaller ones sent here, and we brought some with us as well. I seem to have acquired rather more than I thought. Oh, what a pretty posy."

Is she, too, wondering if it is the latest manly fashion?

"For you," he said. When had he ever offered a gift so gauchely?

She didn't seem to notice, but smiled brilliantly. "Thank you!"

She raised the bouquet to her nose, so he said, "They're silk. Not real."

"But with some perfume. Smell." She came to him and raised the flowers. A hint of violet did rise from them.

"Clever," he said, wanting to kiss her, but oddly uncertain. As if something might break.

She turned to look at her purchases. "How will I transport them?"

"Wagon. Or if you need more speed, an extra carriage."

"For my purchases?"

"Why not?" He needed to get her into a private room. "Would you like coffee?"

Her eyes lit, but, then, they had lit at sight of him. He thought. He hoped.

As soon as they were in the library, door shut, alone except for her dog, he took her into his arms. At last. He wanted to declare his love, but the words stuck. From fear that she did not love him? He wouldn't wish to embarrass her with unwanted devotion.

"You've enjoyed your morning," he said.

She kissed him lightly—too lightly—before answering. "I have. I found a delightful needlework table with a musical box included."

"Are you a needlewoman? I've not seen you stitching as yet."

She chuckled. "It might encourage me to be one. I can mend quite well, but I've never had the patience for ornamental work." She turned serious. "How did it go with Sussex?"

Sussex, princes, and plots all seemed irrelevant, but he said, "Amazingly."

"In a delightful way, it seems,"

He realized he was smiling. How could he not? *This is the heart of love,* he realized. *The essential element. To be with the beloved. Always.* "The delight is from other matters. Let's sit and I'll tell you all."

They sat, but he kept hold of her hand—how could he

not?—as he related the interview in detail. Of course she understood.

"The *queen*?" she said at last. "But why?"

"*Pour l'encouragement des autres*, as Voltaire wrote about Admiral Byng."

"Why?"

"Byng was shot for not doing his utmost to relieve a British garrison on Menorca during the War of Spanish Succession. He didn't have the ships for the task, but his execution warned the other admirals to not be so sensible."

"What has that to do with blowing up three princes?"

"*Not* blowing them up, remember? The queen's not so strict a mother as that." He raised her hand and kissed it. How could he not? "Dr. Johnson is reported to have said that knowing he is to hang focuses a man's mind wonderfully. I assume she thought awareness of mortality would focus her sons' minds more urgently on the important task."

"Marriage and children. It might well. Whatever sort of mother she is, she's a strong queen."

"She's rarely intervened in significant matters—as best we know. However, she might feel that procreation is a family matter."

"So, there's no danger to you. Unless you pursue the investigation."

"I see no reason to."

Smiling, she squeezed his hand, and then, perhaps hesitantly, kissed it in turn.

He was about to draw her onto his lap when a knock on the door brought Edward. The footman put down the tray and left. It would be a shame to waste the coffee, and he'd enjoy her uninhibited enjoyment of it.

He poured for them both and then toasted Kitty with

his cup. "To our completed investigation. You were the one who first raised the possibility of it being a sham."

"But with no notion of who and why." She sipped and smiled, lids lowering slightly with sensuous pleasure.

His heart thumped, but he thought he managed to speak normally. "That's often the way. We gather bits and pieces with little idea of how they matter, and then one day they come together, especially with a meeting of minds."

"And with someone remembering all the bits. You did this sort of work in the army, didn't you?"

He realized he hadn't drunk any of the coffee and took a sip. It was delicious as always, but seemed bland compared to the woman looking at him with warm interest in her eyes. Only interest? Was there anything more on her side?

"At times," he said. "It sometimes helps that I retain details that seem unimportant at the time, though that's played no particular part here." He picked up a plate of small cakes and offered it. "Try one."

"What are they this time?"

"Revani. Honey and almonds."

She chose a piece. "Sticky again." Her smile invited licking and more, but, oddly, his new awareness made the merely physical irrelevant at the moment. Love, he realized, was so much more.

"Delicious," she said, and the way she licked her fingers could change his mind.

He realized she was beautiful. Unconventionally so, but with noble features and a glorious vitality. If only fashion allowed for her to walk the world with her hair down and in vividly colored gowns that hugged all her curves. Men would tremble and fall to their knees.

Men already tumble into love with her. . . .

"What are you thinking?" she asked, head cocked. "You see difficulties after all?"

"About the princes? No."

"Then is there any reason you can't return to the Abbey with me?"

The reminder of reality was like a shower of icy water. "Damn the Abbey. Stay here."

No wonder she frowned. "It can't be abandoned, by me or you."

"In a just world, a man would be allowed to refuse a title. It's enslavement." She chuckled, but he said, "I'm serious. In what other respect does an Englishman have no choice about his destiny?"

"Most would welcome the burden. You, sir, are too fortunate for your own good."

"True. I have you."

Her sudden blush entranced him, as did the way she looked down, perhaps bashfully. *Kit Kat, all aflutter?* She looked up again, as serious as he'd ever seen her. "And I have you. But are you saying you love me?"

"Yes, I love you!" He stood and pulled her into his arms, regardless of her piece of cake, which went flying. "I love you. I love you. I think I have for days, but I didn't recognize it." He kissed her, and it was perfection, making it hard to end. "You've shaken my world, Kitty, but I assume it will steady in time."

The light in her eyes turned wicked. "Are you sure?"

"No, damn you. And I thank God for it. I'll spend all possible time at the Abbey only because you'll be there. That need was a symptom I recognized."

She laughed against his shoulder. "A disease, am I?"

"I'm feverish, but I want no cure."

"Nor I." She looked up, still aglow with laughter. "What does the Abbey matter when we have this? The dowager will be conquered, the place will be made warm, and the servants will share our joy."

"Optimist."

Her dog sneezed.

They both looked and saw Sillikin pawing at her nose, the piece of cake nearby. Kitty went to her to clean honey syrup off her nose with her handkerchief. "I told you you wouldn't like it."

Kneeling there, haloed by firelight, she smiled up at him. "Even if we can't solve all the problems in a moment, we'll have my rooms and yours. We'll talk and play, and drink coffee and eat sticky cakes with our fingers."

And enjoy many other pleasures, she implied. It was a glimpse of heaven, but he couldn't entirely dismiss reality.

Reality be damned. He would make everything perfect for his brave and wonderful wife. Somehow.

Chapter 45

Kitty couldn't believe how the sweetness of love filled her life. She couldn't stop smiling, especially as they spent the rest of the day together as if tied with strings. A persistent gray drizzle couldn't dampen their spirits at all.

They went to the town house, without entourage except for Sillikin, to go over it and make plans for the spring. Then she took him to Moor Street to meet Janet. To Kitty's amusement, her friend and her husband were soon engaged in an intense discussion of her future wardrobe. She tended to forget that the world saw him as a beau.

"And if I don't want Nile green with bronze sequins?" Kitty asked at one point.

"You'd be wrong," Janet said.

Determined to assert some control, Kitty said, "You will *not* reline my mantle with more expensive fur."

"Then I'll buy you a new one," Braydon said, "and insist that you wear it at times."

"How?"

"I'm your husband. I can beat you."

"La, la!" Janet exclaimed laughing, and Kitty knew why. The way he'd said it had turned her hot, the wicked man.

For pride's sake, she had to say, "Sauce for the goose, sauce for the gander, sir."

But he responded, "I won't object to wearing furs for you, my lady."

Janet was so lost in giggles, she couldn't speak, but Kitty was sweating at the vision he'd summoned. Even Beauchamp Abbey wouldn't be able to chill these fires.

They went next to Westminster Hall, where duty and honor would oblige him to attend Parliament and push for steady reform.

"Standing here," he said, "I realize that the title is a privilege as well as a burden. It will strengthen my hand for reform. The next years will be crucial," he added apologetically, "and those in favor of reform will be beleaguered. I can't shirk the fight, which will take place here."

"I understand, and I believe everything will work out for the best." *Somehow,* she silently added.

As they returned home, she told him about Henry's leaving.

"She was only ever a temporary measure," he said.

"And excellently thought of, but I'll miss her. I hope I can find someone as skilled, wise, and kind."

"And willing to live mostly in the country. Johns hovers on flight at all times, especially now we're in Town, with other men tempting him."

"Is he truly so important to you?" she asked.

"There's a great deal of tedious labor in fashion."

"You make it look easy to be just so."

He smiled. "And therein lies most of the work, which Johns does."

"I can't believe you truly care."

"But I do. A weakness, but deeply rooted. Would you rather I be scruffy?"

"I love you as you are."

That required a kiss, even in a hackney carriage, and they arrived home probably appearing idiotic. Kitty found she had a letter from Ruth, and sat in the drawing room to read the latest news from Beecham Dab. Yet again the lines were crossed. What new delights did Ruth have for her?

Soon expectation turned to dismay.

I'm fighting tears as I write this, Kitty, for our short time together was such a joy to me, but Andrew and I can't deny the call. We are too comfortable in Beecham Dab, with too few demands upon us, and we know we could make a true difference somewhere else.

Andrew will urge Dauntry to support some older clergyman to the living, perhaps one who's done noble service for most of his life and deserves a tranquil resting place. We have accepted a parish in the East End of London, so as you settle here, we will soon be there! If Marcus were still alive, we might have managed some fairly frequent meeting. There I am, crying again, but this is the right thing to do.

What of the children? Kitty wanted to protest. The East End was mostly strung along the river and inhabited by those who served the shipping trade and sailors from all around the world. Many parts were rough and crime infested.

However, she recognized the cause of the unease she'd sensed in Ruth. Not trouble in her marriage, but questions about her life's purpose brought on in part by the death of Princess Charlotte. Kitty couldn't bear to read the rest for now.

"Why does my life always turn awry?" she asked Sillikin, then remembered she was trying to break herself of that habit. It wasn't hard now she had someone to

talk to. A friend. She had not only love, but also friendship in marriage, which was a blessing. But they would
often be apart, and now Ruth would be lost to her, too.
Was it something she brought upon herself?

Her marriage to Marcus had probably been rash, but
she'd seen his need and responded to it. She'd had no
choice other than to move to Cateril Manor, and she'd
definitely needed to escape it. Impulsively, she'd found
escape, and thus freedom and purpose with the delight
of Ruth nearby. Now she'd be alone much of the time in
a new prison.

Why couldn't Ruth and Andrew have moved somewhere else entirely? Birmingham, Liverpool, Africa! It
would feel less cruel than their moving to London,
where Kitty wanted to be but must leave. *The spring,*
she told herself. She would be in London in the spring.
That would be better than nothing.

"Bad news?" Braydon had come in.

It must be written on her face. "Ruth and Andrew
have decided their path is too comfortable. They're
leaving Beecham Dab for Shadwell, the better to minis-
ter to rascals and sinners."

"Ah. Andrew had mentioned such a thing a time or
two, but I didn't think he'd do it. Too saintly for his own
good, or his family's."

"I know. The children. But I can understand feeling
underused, unfulfilled."

"The Abbey won't make the most of your talents," he
agreed.

"At least I won't be short of work," she said as cheerfully as she could. "Will you be able to return with me and
stay over Christmastide? We'll make it merry and say a
grand farewell to Andrew and Ruth. We still have a ball
to arrange for the Abbey servants and tenants. After that,
we'll hold a Christmas one for the whole parish."

"Of course I'll return with you. How could I not? And Christmas brings mistletoe."

That required a kiss, a lingering kiss, but it had to end. One benefit of the Abbey would be that her boudoir would be far from other rooms, and if they wanted to progress from kisses to sheets in the middle of the afternoon, no one would know.

Her thoughts turned to Christmas. "I wonder if there are any handsome young officers with nowhere to go for Christmas."

"Kit Kat will pine for her entourage?" It was a tease, not an accusation.

"For Isabella! That would shake her out of vile servitude."

"Perhaps too far. After being in seclusion, she'll fall in love with one or more on the spot."

"More than one wouldn't be so bad."

"Remember, she's a considerable heiress. Make sure they're decent fellows and would make tolerable husbands. I don't want to have to shoot anyone."

"Would you?"

He seemed surprised. "Probably, but I'd try to be more subtle in dissuading and disposing."

"Sometimes I forget," she said.

"What?"

"That you were a soldier. One day I would like to hear about your military career."

She felt the beginning of resistance, of the marble box, but then he said, "One day. A house party is a good plan. It could even be a kind of exorcism. Would you like to go to the theater again? Blanche is performing at Drury Lane, and our box is available."

He'd slid away from her request, but there was time. A lifetime. Kitty beamed at him. "I can't wait!"

And barring any new emergency, he would return

with her. They'd have a month or so before a new separation. Anything could happen in a month.

Kitty knew they must return to Beauchamp Abbey, and so she set Thursday as the day.

Wednesday morning was taken up with interviewing six potential lady's maids. Kitty could be overwhelmed, not least by the need for employment she saw in some. The poor economy meant that even some fashionable people had had to cut expenses or go abroad, as the Duke of Kent had, to find cheaper places to live.

She had to be practical, however, and choose one who would suit. She knew she didn't want a maid who was younger than herself, even though one was lively and charming. She certainly didn't want a sour one, which crossed another off the list.

In the end she chose Miss Sarah Land, a woman of forty-two who seemed to have a calm, competent way about her. She'd been employed for fourteen years by a Mrs. Compton-Huffington, until that lady's sad death from an infected cut. Mr. Compton-Huffington gave her an excellent reference, and Kitty noted the fact that Miss Land had been allowed to live on in the family home until she found a new position. That spoke well of her and the family.

Henry asked some challenging questions about procedures and skills but was satisfied with the answers. Terms were agreed, and Sarah Land was to travel with Kitty back to Beauchamp Abbey, whereupon Henry would go north, back home.

Kitty could turn tearful over that, but she'd allow no such nonsense, and plunged into a last-minute flurry of shopping for perishable delicacies such as fruits and cheeses. She also purchased a large amount of candied fruits, in hopes of sweetening the dowager.

As she paused outside a greengrocer's, Edward was suddenly relieved of some of his teetering pile of packages by an officer.

Edison.

Kitty suffered a flutter of panic, but she was on a busy street in daylight.

"Thank you, Captain. I'm in a mania of shopping, for we leave for Beauchamp tomorrow."

"Dauntry goes with you?"

"Of course." She couldn't dismiss him when he held some of her purchases hostage. She could only pray he wouldn't enact a scene on Oxford Street.

"I, too, leave Town," he said.

"To spend Christmas with your family?" With relief, she saw their hired carriage ahead.

"Yes, but then to go abroad."

Kitty tried not to look too delighted. "A new posting. Congratulations."

"There isn't great competition to go to Van Diemen's Land."

They'd arrived at the carriage, and Edward was putting packages into the boot. The footman had to extract the ones Edison was carrying, as he seemed fixated on Kitty, as if expecting something.

"Where is that?" she asked.

"South of Australia. It's a penal colony."

Kitty could see it now. She was supposed to protest at such an exile, which he would take as a sign of love. "I'm sure that's very important work," she said, "and it is greatly to your credit that you're willing to undertake it."

"You don't care."

"About what?"

"That I'll be on the far side of the world."

She hoped she was a picture of blank incomprehension. "You'll be serving your country, Edison, and I expect you'll find it a grand adventure. Australia is an astonishing place, I understand. Perhaps you'll see kangaroos."

"Perhaps I will." His tense jaw had relaxed a little, and now he simply looked miserable. She longed to comfort him, but knew any hint of fondness would undo all her work.

"I wish you a very happy Christmas with your family, Edison, and a smooth journey to the antipodes. You must tell your mother how well Sillikin goes. And now I must plunge back into the shops, for I've completely neglected to buy a Christmas gift for my husband!"

With a cheerful wave she did just that, but muttered to Henry, "Is he following?"

"No. Gazing soulfully, and now walking away. You did well."

"I hope so, but I hate to cause anyone pain. He's sending himself into exile, and he'll be no more than a prison guard there."

"Don't be silly. You were right to call it an adventure, and he'll be an officer with many opportunities. I hear some people are doing well for themselves in Australia, and even that some are going out there freely, not as transportees. If there's anything to him at all, he'll make the most of it."

Kitty smiled at Henry. "Thank you. I'm going to miss you."

Edward had caught them up. "Where to now, milady?"

"I'll wander the shops a bit more."

Mentioning finding a present for Braydon had made her realize the lack. But what sort of present could she find for such a man? She lacked the skill to make him a worthy gift, but worried that anything she purchased would not be up to his standards. She knew he wouldn't mind, but she wanted whatever she chose to be perfect.

She considered paintings in one shop, then items of

jewelry in another, but he had plenty of both, and they were exactly the sort of items she could get wrong. Then, in an odd shop full of old stuff, she saw a small ivory box, yellowed with age. All four sides and the lid were intricately carved, but the detail was blurred by time and handling, so they were mysterious. It should really be cool marble, but she much preferred the warm ivory.

She bought it, and from another shop a white silk handkerchief to line it. Though it was getting late, she hunted for the next essential item, and at last found a red-jeweled heart. She'd rather ruby than garnet, but garnet would do.

Bubbling with satisfaction, she returned home and assembled her gift. Once it was ready, she couldn't wait for Christmas to give it to him. Then she saw an excuse to give it to him now. She put it in her right-hand pocket and went in search. She found him in the library, working on some papers, and kissed the top of his head.

He turned to kiss her properly, then said, "A letter came for you."

Kitty took it. "It's not from Ruth."

"One of your many admirers?"

There was no suspicion in it at all, but it seemed a good moment to tell him about Edison. Again, she said, "I don't like the feeling of sending him into exile."

"Which is probably exactly what he intended. He hoped for tears and pleas not to go."

"Yes. Yes, he did, the wretch! All the same, I wish him well."

"As do I—at the antipodes."

She smiled and wanted to give him the gift then, but she had the letter in her hand. She snapped the seal and unfolded two sheets of paper. "Whoever it is hasn't tried to save us money. Oh! It's from the Hartleys. Now we

might unravel the last mystery and learn what happened
to Diane. I'd like to have something to tell Isabella."

"As long as it's suitable," he warned.

"She has to know it's scandalous," Kitty said, and
read the letter aloud.

My dear ma'am,

*I have delayed in responding to your enquiry, for
I couldn't decide what best to do. The Braydon
family treated my daughter shamefully, and I hold
no kindness for them.*

She looked to the bottom of the letter. "It's from her
mother, Lady Hartley. Is Sir Allenby dead?"

"Read on and we may find out."

*The fifth Viscount Dauntry seemed a kindly
man and truly fond of our dear child, who was
only nineteen at the time of their marriage. My
husband and I gave our consent, having no suspicion of the place to which he would take her, nor
that he would fail so miserably in protecting her
from one intent on crushing her bright spirit.*

"I sympathize with a grieving mother," Braydon said,
"but I suspect that Diane was a spoiled chit."

"Sympathy with the dowager?"

"She's selfish and domineering, but I don't think
she's evil or mad. She must have had some reason for
attempting control. Continue."

*We were horrified by our daughter's abandon-
ing her husband and children and confess that if
she'd come to us, we would have had to send her*

back, though we would have attempted to improve matters. Perhaps that is why she fled abroad, and died in foreign parts.'

"Ah, poor Diane," Kitty said. "I hope she flew free in happiness for a while." She turned to the second sheet.

We chose not to inform her husband that he was free to marry again. My husband had already informed Lord Dauntry that if he sought to divorce Diane, we would present her letters in court as evidence of her ill treatment. It would not have blocked a divorce, but it would have exposed him and his mother to the eyes of the world. In retaliation, he refused us all contact with Diane's children.

"The dowager's work," Kitty said.
"Read on."

If the viscount had known of my daughter's death, he would have married again and we wished to prevent that. An unchristian attitude, I admit, but he deserved to suffer.

"He did," Braydon said. "For allowing his mother's actions."
"She's a hard woman to oppose."
"One only needs a spine."

However, your letter alerted us to the fact that there is a new Viscount Dauntry of only the remotest connection to Diane's persecutors, who perhaps should know the facts. Sir Allenby still wished to ignore your request for information, but I felt it

*right that the truth be recorded now that it can do
no harm. My poor daughter lived less than a year
after leaving her husband. She died on board a
ship to America on the eighth of August, 1808.*

Lady Allenby had simply signed her name at the end.

"How sad," Kitty said, refolding the letter. "I'd hoped for better."

"So much unhappiness sprung from one woman."

"But the dowager might not have been so ruinous if her husband and children had lived."

"Wounds do not excuse viciousness."

"At least now we know, and the events are all in the past. Can we hope for a simpler future?"

"I think we can."

His tone alerted her. "What?"

"Heaven has smiled on me after all, and on you, I hope. Will you weep tears if you are not Viscountess Dauntry?"

"Of course not, but how?"

"If Diane truly did die in 1808, my predecessor's marriage to Dorothy could be legal."

Kitty stared at him. "Not bigamy at all?"

"As long as he married in proper form, using his real name, and it seems he did. It will depend upon the date. Dorothy mentioned the king being unwell at the time but not known to be mad, so before the Regency in 1811, and probably before 1810."

"Your memory again. But I can add something. She mentioned Alfred talking to her father about the Battle of Talavera. When they first met."

"Did she, by gad! My brilliant darling. That nails it. Talavera was July 1809, after Diane's death."

"We're free?"

"As good as." He was actually grinning. "It will have

to go before the courts and the College of Heralds, but I see no reason that little Johnie shouldn't be accepted in due course as the sixth Viscount Dauntry, replacing me."

"Oh, but should we inflict that on him?"

He chuckled. "Such horror over a title. In fact, we have no choice. If the truth ever comes out—and why shouldn't it?—the situation would be more complicated than it is now. I judge Dorothy to be strong enough to withstand the shock, especially with our help, and the lad is promising. I'll stand patron to John, Lord Dauntry, and arrange for his schooling."

"Away from the Abbey."

"Precisely."

"We should evict the dowager before they arrive," Kitty said. "No?"

"That decision will be Dorothy's once she's in full possession of the facts. It's lamentably weak of me, but I feel Alfred's mother should have her chance at repentance and reform. She will have a new vessel for the Godyson blood, which might gentle her. Consider the fact that Isabella doesn't hate or even dislike her grandmother. She must have good memories of her."

"Definitely not a cold marble box," Kitty said, smiling. "I have a gift for you." She took the box out of her pocket and offered it.

He rubbed his thumb over the old ivory. "It's lovely, but why?"

"You've given me gifts. And this is the one-week anniversary of our wedding."

"Is it only a week, Mrs. Braydon?"

"Mrs. Braydon?"

"It's only prudent to cease using the title when my right is so uncertain. Do you mind?"

"Not in the slightest! I thought once that it suited you—Dauntry and daunting—but no longer. And I'll be much more comfortable without pomp, precedence, and protocol."

"You would have looked magnificent in scarlet robes and coronet."

"But as compensation, we're no longer tied to the Abbey. We can live in Town all year round."

"How your eyes shine. We'll have to take care of the place during the transition and to assist Dorothy."

"But it won't be a life sentence. And Ruth and I will be close again. What's the Shakespeare play? *All's Well That Ends Well.* How clever he was."

"I could add *Much Ado about Nothing*, for the princes' affair."

"And even *The Comedy of Errors*," Kitty said. "But not *The Taming of the Shrew.*"

He traced her cheek. "Shrewd, but not shrewish. Insightful and perceptive. Perhaps it comes from all those years observing and being kind to young men."

She had to ask. "No jealousy?"

"I'm determined to transmute it into pride. Don't answer if you don't want to, but did Cateril ever hit you?"

Instinctively, Kitty wanted not to answer, even to deny it, but she said, "A few times. When his pain was bad and his spirits low."

"That's no excuse."

"He never claimed it was. He was always repentant. Once I cracked a jug over his head, so I wasn't above violence, either."

"No meek Desdemona. I love my bold, strong wife, but I could wish you'd had a gentler life."

"I'm not sure about that. Too much peace and quiet and I'd probably seek out mayhem. So I do hope you'll find a way to involve me in your work." But then she said, "Open the box."

He did so. "A heart. Yours?"

"You have my heart, but that is yours. When we first met I thought you a cold marble box, but I sensed fire inside. There is fire, but above that, there's a warm heart, and there's nothing of cold marble about you, my love."

He drew her onto his knee for a kiss that, as always, turned passionate, but they both controlled it. In this she could be patient, as could he. Especially as a kiss could last as long as a feast, with a banquet to follow in the night.

Epilogue

Christmas Day at Beauchamp Abbey

The five children chased Sillikin and Pirate around the brightly decorated hall, the dogs sometimes skidding on the marble floor. Pirate was Johnie's dog and was a black-patched mongrel, but she had a friendly disposition, and she and Sillikin played together well.

The children were Johnie and Alice Braydon, their Edgware friends Harry and Bella Pickering, and little Arthur Lulworth. Arthur had been hesitant, but Johnie had befriended him, and Sillikin had added encouragement.

Three mothers and two military officers kept an eye on the noisy chaos. Isabella was watching from the gallery above, looking as if she wished she wasn't too old to join in, especially given the involvement of the officers.

Kitty and Braydon had delayed their departure from Town to take the news to Edgware, and then set in train the legal processes to do with Johnie's claim to the title. They'd ceased using the title and sent notices to the papers to that effect, and then worked hard to convince the world that they were at peace with the situation. Sir Stephen Ball had called to learn more details, promising to help in any legal matters, and to write to friends around the country about the matter.

Dorothy's first reaction had been dismay and, Kitty suspected, fear, but her son's situation ruled. He was a viscount and must have his due. Wisely, she made no attempt to have either Johnie or herself referred to by a title until all was formally settled, but she did agree to move to Beauchamp Abbey. The children were less positive, for the prospect of wealth and a title meant nothing to them, whereas leaving their friends and familiar area did.

Again wisely, Dorothy invited her friend Mary Pickering to come with them, along with Harry and Bella, her children and the best friends of Johnie and Alice. Then it all became a huge adventure, especially when Braydon mentioned the probability of ponies. Mary was also a widow, but less well provided for than Dorothy. She was now Dorothy's official companion and treated like one of the family. She was blossoming day by day.

Kitty had been impressed by the ease with which Braydon had arranged the transportation of two families and much of their worldly goods to Gloucestershire, undaunted by a blast of wintry weather that had put inches of snow on the ground.

At first the Abbey had daunted the new residents, and the Abbey servants had been thrown into confusion. They'd wanted to call Braydon "my lord," and if not he, who? Braydon had made the situation as clear as it could be, and Kitty had worked with Dorothy to hand over the management of the house.

Braydon and Kitty had taken on the task of informing the dowager of the situation.

"My son married without a word to me? Nonsense."

"I have the documents with me," Braydon said, "if you care to see them."

"I do not. I don't believe a word of it. It's part of your plot to evict me from my home."

"You have two new grandchildren," Kitty said. "One a son."

"You are trying to foist guttersnipes on me for your amusement."

Kitty recognized that she'd become so accustomed to being aggrieved and difficult that she was chained by it. She left to get Dorothy and the children.

As soon as the dowager saw Johnie, she'd melted, tears welling in her eyes. "My boy. It's as if my boy is returned to me! Come to me!"

Not surprising if the child held back from the mound of black on the thronelike chair, but Dorothy gently steered him forward. "Make your bow to your grandmother, dear."

At which, miraculously, he'd smiled. "Grandmother?" He'd bowed and said, "I've always wanted a grandparent."

And the dowager had smiled. If her eyes hadn't been so pouched, a twinkle might have shown. She didn't insist on an embrace, but said, "I will try to be the best grandmother possible, dearest boy."

The sweet mood hadn't held, and once the children and their mother had left, the dowager had settled, perhaps with relief, into bitter complaint about her son hiding his marriage and her grandson, the hope of her line, from her. They'd decided not to tell her he hadn't known he was free. The fewer who knew about that, the better.

Over the next weeks she had mellowed, and she'd certainly become careful not to create too much trouble. She'd been indulgent, perhaps overindulgent, to Johnie, but he—perhaps instructed by his mother—had refused any treat that didn't include the other children.

As Kitty had said to Ruth on her first visit to the parsonage, "I thought the old beldame would turn vicious at that, but she's not stupid, and she has Dorothy's measure.

There'll be no visits from the children except on Dorothy's terms, and if the dowager's not careful, she'll end up in the Dower House or worse."

"She deserves to be evicted. Are you sure it's wise to allow her to continue at the Abbey?"

"Where's the quality of mercy and all that?" Kitty asked. "She is thawing, especially as Dorothy has agreed that they'll be Godyson-Braydons."

"That odd obsession."

"Bloodlines mean a great deal to some people. It helps that the dowager was instantly besotted with Johnie. He does quite resemble her son, but he has the bright spark the fifth viscount always lacked."

"She was disappointed in him?" Ruth said. "Poor man."

"Mothers and sons," Kitty said, tempted to tell Ruth about the queen, but she overcame that. "As Dorothy says, the addition of a name is a small adjustment in order to win peace. There couldn't be a better woman for this situation, Ruth. She's so steady and calm. Exactly, in fact, the sort of woman Braydon wanted for a wife."

Ruth looked alarmed for a moment, but then she smiled. "No longer, I assume."

"No longer. We get along very well."

"More than well, I suspect."

Kitty just smiled. For some reason, confessing to a madness of love seemed impossible, but she was sure Ruth understood.

"The children have certainly shattered the ice palace," she said. "They are no longer awed by Abbey, parkland or anything, and are running their servants ragged. Yesterday Harry Pickering tried to ride one of the deer."

"Was he injured?"

"No, thank heavens. His mother spanked him, and Braydon arranged riding lessons on the quiet horses until the ponies arrive, which should be soon. The horses are far too big for them, of course, but they're content for now to sit on their backs and be led around the paddock."

"And you drove over here," Ruth said.

"With a groom, of course. I won't have much need to drive myself when living in Town, but I think I'll improve my skill. I enjoy it."

"Will you be one of those dashing, fashionable ladies with her own curricle and pair?"

Kitty laughed. "I doubt that. But I might enjoy being fashionable in other ways."

"You won't miss being mistress of Beauchamp Abbey?"

"Not a bit! Like Braydon, I've had a very lucky escape."

"How is Isabella behaving?"

Kitty pulled a face. "Cautiously. She's become accustomed to following her grandmother's lead, but now she doesn't know what to do. I think she feels that Johnie is supplanting her brother, but yesterday she helped Alice and Bella to make love knots out of scarlet ribbon to decorate the hall."

"A promising development."

"I'm hoping military reinforcements will carry the day."

Ruth raised her brows in a question.

"I've invited two young officers to spend Christmas at the Abbey. Cully Debenham, who for some reason wants to avoid his own family Christmas, and Captain Fallerton, who comes from Northumberland and can't take the time for such a journey in chancy weather. I'm hoping they'll crack her shell."

"I hope that's not a euphemism!"

Kitty chuckled. "For a maidenhead? Certainly not. They're good fellows. Handpicked for the job. You'll meet them on Christmas Day."

And here they all were, in a merry throng. They'd all gone to Beecham Dab for the service and were now waiting for Christmas dinner to be served, which would happen when the dowager came down. Or without her, if she delayed any longer. But here she came, carried down the stairs by two sturdy footmen, whereupon Quiller announced the meal.

Everyone was present except baby Maria. Johnie, pink with excitement and perhaps embarrassment, was seated at the head of the table, with his mother at his side. The dowager had the next-most-important place at the foot. Her mourning was a little less dense today, and she was wearing a short string of very large pearls.

Kitty suspected they belonged to the viscountcy, not her, but that was no longer her concern. She had regretted, just a little, the jewels she'd been shown, but it was already clear that Braydon would amply replace them. Today she was wearing rubies with her red dress and cashmere shawl.

Isabella was wearing a tiny black cap and a set of delicate pearl and silver jewelry that had also been a gift from Braydon. She was seated, glowing, between the two officers.

There were additional guests. The Misses Purslow, Mr. and Mrs. Whitehall, and Dr. Lowell. Worseley was spending Christmas with his family, but he had agreed to stay on at the Abbey to serve Dorothy and Johnie. He was young enough to perhaps be a good influence on the lad, but soon there'd be a tutor and a governess in residence to attend to the children's education.

Every now and then, the dowager would slip into a sour face, but whenever she looked at Johnie, her expression softened. He often smiled down the table at her without any reserve. John, Lord Dauntry could well prove too clever and charming for everyone's good, but Braydon would steer him right, and for now he was perfect.

After dinner they all played games, including a very complicated game of Speculation, in which the adults connived for the children to win most of the points. After the children had been reluctantly persuaded to go to bed, Arthur going with them for now, Kitty suggested some dancing. Though she made it seem impromptu, it was planned. She'd made sure Dorothy had no objection, and one of the servants was ready to play tunes on his fiddle. She could only hope the dowager wouldn't rage.

She didn't, only saying she was weary and would retire. It could even be true.

Dr. Lowell asked Miss Mary Purslow to dance, and gallant Cully asked Miss Martha, which caused her great but pleasurable confusion. The Whitehalls danced together, as did Ruth and Andrew, and Braydon led out Mary Pickering. Dorothy had said that she wouldn't dance.

Captain Fallerton asked Dorothy if it would be proper for Isabella to dance. This, too, was prearranged, and Dorothy said, "I can't imagine why anyone would object." She turned to Isabella. "Would you like to dance, dear? This is a private affair, and I'm sure your father and brother would only want your happiness."

Isabella seemed torn between an attachment to mourning and a strong desire to dance. Of course, dancing with a handsome young officer won and she went forward, cheeks flushed and eyes bright.

Kitty sat with Dorothy, Sillikin over her toes, watching the merry couples. "Do you feel blessed or cursed?" she asked.

"Blessed to high heaven," Dorothy said. "You and your husband truly didn't want any of this?"

"Truly. We all have different ideas of heaven, don't we? For my first husband, clouds and harps would have been torture. I have to hope he's found the Norse heaven, where the men fight battles every day and rise from the dead to fight again."

"Why on earth would anyone want that?"

"As I said, different blessings and curses. Thank you for agreeing to sell the town house to us. I don't know what it is about it, but I believe we can be happy there."

"I gather it's not part of the entailment, and I can see no use to us for many years, especially as you've agreed to introduce Isabella to the world in due course. It's odd to think she's my stepdaughter when she generally terrifies me with her haughty ways."

Kitty chuckled. "You hide it well. She'll improve in time, I think, and be off your hands entirely in a few years. You know that you and the children will be welcome at the town house at any time."

"That will be rarely. Country life suits us very well."

"All's well that ends well, indeed."

The first dance ended, and Kitty captured her husband as partner for the next.

First he steered her beneath the mistletoe.

Kitty put on a frown. "I believe, sir, that a couple's supposed to kiss only once beneath the mistletoe, and this would be our third."

"Fourth. I never forget a kiss, and I know which rules to ignore. Happy Christmas, Mrs. Braydon."

Their kiss was light, but special, as always. Then Sillikin gave a little yip.

"You object?" Braydon said, looking down.

"Simply agreement, yes?" Kitty said to her dog.

"Yip!"

Braydon chuckled. He, too, had fallen into the habit of talking to the spaniel, though perhaps he didn't understand the responses as well. Yet.

Author's Note

I've written most of my Regency historicals along a timeline that began in 1814, so I've known that eventually one would have to include the death of Princess Charlotte, and it worried me, because I knew I couldn't treat the subject lightly.

The death of the Regent's daughter and the only legitimate grandchild of the king was as dramatic and traumatic as shown in this book, equally as much as the death of Diana, Princess of Wales. The death of any young woman in childbirth is always a tragedy, but it wasn't as uncommon as it is today. The death of a princess, however, hit hard enough to throw the whole nation into sincere mourning, and the implications for succession were serious.

So the event would intersect with my fictional story line, but I didn't want to dwell on the details of the event itself and couldn't imagine how it could fit well into a love story. In the magical way that sometimes happens in writing, it slotted into Braydon and Kitty's story as if it had always been planned that way.

The Viscount Needs a Wife is about mourning, and the crucial death and widespread mourning fit into Kitty's life. At the same time, the tragedy had implications for Braydon, because it did have the effect of dampening unrest and deterring the extreme antimonarchists. The calm wouldn't last long, but over the winter, there was relative order and quiet.

The plot against the three princes is completely my invention, and to begin with, I didn't know who was responsible or how it would turn out. I was as surprised as Braydon and Kitty were when all was revealed. However, again in the magical way these things sometimes happen, the Prince Regent did indeed make a flying visit to London at just the right time.

How do I know?

When writing a book I read the newspapers of the day online. *The Morning Chronicle* is good for society comings and goings and lesser matters, such as the demand for mourning clothes of all sorts. I learned some things about the time that I couldn't fit into the book, such as there being a "black ball."

As time passed after the princess's death, people's emotions naturally moderated, but the social pressure to keep to mourning black persisted, especially in the ton. Thus one lady had the idea of a ball where everyone would wear black. It seems it was a great success, and a good time was had by all.

I am putting some of them into the next book, which follows the same timeline, though the characters don't know one another. There's an All Black horse race, and a soberly colored ball, among other fashionable events in December 1817.

It was also from the papers that I learned that a Bonaparte was in line for the British crown. Three-year-old Jérôme Bonaparte was the son of Jérôme Bonaparte, one of Napoleon Bonaparte's brothers. The child's claim came through his mother, Catherine of Württemberg, a great-granddaughter of King George II. As said in the book, many people would have had to have died to put the boy on the throne, but the mere notion alarmed many, and the discovery amused me.

My characters are generally happy to spend most of their time in the country, so it was interesting to have two people who aren't. Again, I wasn't sure when I began how I was going to give them their truly happy ending, but then the plot laid the way.

This novel stands alone, with new principal characters, but as it follows my timeline, it takes place within what I call the Rogues' World.

I have written a series of historical romances about a group of men called the Company of Rogues, who came together at Harrow school to create a protective band that has lasted into their adulthood. The first one, *An Arranged Marriage*, was published in 1991 and the last, *To Rescue a Rogue*, in 2006. There are nine books and an overarching story line, so they are best read in order.

You can find that order on my Web site, jobev.com/rogues.html.

I have written other romances that are spinoffs, using characters who appeared in the Rogues' World books, but from now on I will be writing about new characters, and there may not be any clear connections from book to book.

However, in my creative mind there exists a Regency England that has been formed over nearly thirty years where my characters exist. Therefore some old characters are likely to pop up—hosting a ball, attending a meeting, or giving a helping hand, especially in London, where the nobility gathered for the season and meetings of Parliament. Readers unfamiliar with previous books won't notice, but those who are will meet old friends. In this book, Hal Beaumont, Stephen Ball, and Lord Charrington are Rogues, and Sir George Hawkinville, who is off in Paris, is a spinoff character.

If you're new to the Company of Rogues and wish to know more, all the books are available in print and e-book form. Again, you can find a list on my Web site.

I also have a Georgian series about the Malloren family, and the details of those books are also on my Web site. There are four medieval romances, six traditional Regency romances, and a number of novellas. *The Viscount Needs a Wife* is my fortieth novel. Enjoy!

I have an author page on Facebook at www.facebook .com/Jo.Beverley, and sometimes I tweet. You can sign up for my occasional newsletter on most pages of my Web site.

As always, I appreciate it when readers leave a review online, as reviews help other people find the sort of books they will enjoy.

All best wishes,
Jo

Read on for an excerpt from Jo Beverley's next romance, coming soon from Signet Select.

Lady Barbara Boxtall has been alarmed by the death of Princess Charlotte. It has made it all too clear that life is unpredictable, and if her younger brother, the Earl of Langton, were to die, the title and all that went with it would fall into the hands of their wastrel, gamester uncle. As he's a neck-or-nothing sportsman, she's determined that Norris must marry, and soon.

She herself is resigned to spinsterhood. Her six-foot height has deterred most local gentlemen, and a disastrous season in London has turned her off social events outside her Hampshire neighborhood. Norris, however, is a splendid figure of a man and, being an earl, can marry as soon as he wishes to. He has no right to be quibbling about his youth and love.

"What's the matter now?" asked her lady's maid, Ethel, putting aside the stocking she'd been mending by the fire.

"Norris," Babs said.

"Ah."

Ethel was more of a companion than a maid, and dressed accordingly. Her black gown was made of a fine wool-and-linen blend, and she wore no apron, nor a cap on her wiry black hair. She played the servant well enough when she and Babs were in company, but they'd been together now for twelve years, and in private they were equals and friends.

"You and your brother always seem to be butting heads," Ethel said. "It'll pass." She'd remained sitting, as she always did if not needed for some task, but her composed attitude, hands in lap, suddenly stirred exasperation. Even Ethel didn't seem to realize how dire their situation was.

"It won't pass," Babs said, "because I can't let it. It's the matter of the future of the earldom and his marriage."

"You addressed that subject with him?"

"Of course I did!"

"As soon as he arrived?"

"Why wait?" Babs asked, but she grimaced. "Very well. Perhaps that was a mistake."

"More haste, less speed." Ethel was irritatingly full of sayings.

"How long was I supposed to wait? And then he had the gall to throw it back at me!"

"How did he do that, then?"

Babs paced the small room, reluctant to put the absurd suggestion into words, but she couldn't keep secrets from Ethel.

"He said that if I marry by the end of the year, he'll marry by the end of January."

Ethel's brows rose. "I didn't think he had the wits for that."

"He's not stupid."

"No, but you can't expect an old head on young shoulders. He is young to be marrying."

"At twenty-five, I'm considered past hope."

"Young for a *man*," Ethel said.

"He's not just a man—he's an *earl*. He has a duty to start his nursery, and no right to turn the tables on me. My marriage won't help."

"True enough."

Babs continued to pace, wishing that Ethel would share her outrage, but it wouldn't happen. Ethel was the personification of placid calm.

"He'll have to come to his senses," Babs said.

"A leopard can't change its spots."

"Stop spouting proverbs at me! Especially when they do no good. Oh, I'm sorry. But really . . ."

"You need a ride," Ethel said.

Babs almost argued against that, but Ethel was right. Brisk exercise would burn off her agitation and let her think more clearly. There had to be a way to get Norris to the altar soon, and she'd find it.

Ethel went with her into the dressing room and helped

her into her habit. It was dark blue, and a relief from constant black. Babs left the house hoping for an encounter with her brother so she could relaunch her arguments, even though she knew it would be wiser to give him time. She felt as if every minute, every second, mattered.

An hour later Babs returned calmer. Ethel had been correct about more haste, less speed. There was no extreme urgency. True, Norris could kill himself at any moment in some sporting wildness, but it was unlikely. She could allow him a month or two, but he must turn his mind to finding a bride.

As Babs dressed in black silk for dinner, she said, "It's not surprising that Norris isn't thinking of marriage at the moment, with the world in mourning for such a dreadful reason."

"A wife dying to give birth to a man's child."

"Trust you to put it bluntly."

"Why not? Any man with a heart has to be considering the matter."

Babs doubted her brother was shying away from the altar for that reason, but perhaps it was possible. "Life must go on," she said.

"True." Ethel finished fastening the back of the gown. "What ornaments?"

"Something with a little brightness. My amber beads and bracelet."

Ethel fastened the triple row of beads that sat neatly at the base of Babs's throat, just above the high neck of the gown. She added the matching bracelet at her right wrist, overlapping the long dark sleeve, and added short black net gloves.

She liked to wear amber because it matched the color of her hair, which was easy to manage since she'd had it cut to shoulder length. The shorter hair at the front and sides meant that curls framed her face without the slightest need of curling irons. Since she disliked fussing with her appearance, it was a blessing.

Unasked, Ethel had brought just the right shawl—a long Norwich one, woven in a design of black and gold.

"Thank you. Any advice?"

"More flies are caught with honey than with vinegar," Ethel said.

"That's true."

"And it is your mother's birthday."

"Which I'd forgotten! Very well. Honeyed sweetness all evening. But I must catch my fly."

The meal progressed well enough, for Babs didn't stir discord and Norris gave a firsthand account of the events around the princess's death. Babs and her mother had received letters, but they valued his view of how London had reacted.

"I understand the princess's doctors are being blamed," Babs said as the soup was removed and the first course laid out.

"And the queen," Norris said, eying the various dishes with approval. He had a mighty appetite. "She wasn't there, you know."

"She isn't well, poor lady," their mother said, "and seventy-three years old. Her granddaughter's death and all the traveling and ceremonies will have taxed her."

"You fear there could soon be another funeral?" Babs said. "We'll all be in mourning forever."

"Hope not," Norris said. "Town died on the same day. The theaters closed, and most of the shops as well."

"It is touching to see such general respect for the poor princess," their mother said.

"Aye, though it's made Town remarkably dull."

Babs restrained herself from commenting.

"At least the theaters have opened again," he said. "The shops opened within days, of course, but no one's putting off mourning or throwing grand entertainments."

"People are truly sad," Babs said.

"It's thrown up a few oddities," he said, helping himself to more ragout of mutton. "Last week a foreign ambassador's wife turned up to a reception in white."

"No!" Babs exclaimed.

"Why?" asked their mother.

"I'm told white's a mourning color in some countries. That'd make our spring assemblies pretty sad affairs, wouldn't it, with all the hopeful misses in their pale silks and muslins?"

Babs almost said something about hopeful misses but managed to repress it. She did say, "I doubt you've been inside Almack's in years."

"Gads, no. Dull stuff there. Cribb's Parlor's more my style."

"Pugilism?" his mother exclaimed.

"All the thing, Mama. Keeps a fellow in trim. A man'll hear it from Cribbs if he's bellows to mend."

"Don't sink to cant, dear."

"Apologies, Mama."

"And I don't like to think of you under attack."

"It's all in good fun." Norris flashed a look at Babs. "No danger at all."

At that taunt she could hardly hold herself back, but speared a chunk of meat instead. "What do you find to do with yourself in Town amid all the gloom?"

"There are still private parties to enjoy, and I took part in a splendid steeplechase near Chiswick. The Great All-Black."

"All black?"

"In keeping with mourning. Men to be dressed in

black and riding completely black horses. The price of an all-black horse rocketed the week before, but of course I had Torrent."

Lady Langton smiled at him. "Then of course you won, darling."

Norris was a brilliant rider and could afford the best horses. And Torrent was his best.

"Neck and neck with Arden on Viking and Templemore on Beelzebub, but then Torrent put a foot in a rabbit hole and down we went. Damned shame."

"Is Torrent much injured?" Babs asked.

"Dead," Norris said, lips wobbling. "Broken leg."

"How very sad," his mother said, "but thank heavens you were unscathed."

"Pretty well. Knocked out by a damnably placed rock. I came round to find I'd nothing but a headache and bruises, but Torrent was a goner. He was a fine beast." He pulled out a handkerchief and dabbed his eyes. "A fine beast."

"He was," Babs said. "But. . . ." She cut another piece of meat, though she wondered whether she could swallow it.

Norris had almost *died*.

The idiot made light of it, but a slightly harder blow could have killed him. Or he could have broken his neck or been mortally injured in some other way. Not long ago young Lord Scorton had broken his back in a similar accident. He'd lingered a day or so but died. At least he'd had a son.

Babs struggled through the meal, making general remarks to conceal her inner turmoil while trying to come up with a conquering argument. She knew her brother, however, and knew now that he'd dug in his heels, nothing would move him.

There was only one thing for it.

She waited until they were in the parlor and the servant who brought the coffee had left. Once they all had their cups, she gathered her courage and made her announcement. "Very well, Norris. I accept your challenge."

He sipped. "What challenge?"

"If you will marry after I do, I will marry by the turn of the year."

"No, you won't, Babs. You're a confirmed spinster."

"I've had offers!"

"First I've heard of it, and clearly you've accepted none of them."

"Now I will." Despite the sick churning inside, she took satisfaction in his alarm.

"You'll accept a man you've rejected simply to force me to the altar? I don't believe it."

"To force you to start filling the nursery, I will."

He surged to his feet. "You damnable woman!"

"Norris!" his mother exclaimed.

He froze. "I'm sorry, Mama, but it's more than a man can bear to be bullied so by a sister."

"An elder sister," Babs said. "Elder and wiser."

"A foolish woman."

"Now you're insulting our mother."

He clutched his curls. "No, I'm not! *She's* not supporting this mad plan. Are you, Mama?"

"Whether I support it or not, Norris, you did propose this arrangement. I don't see how you can back out now."

"It's a petticoat conspiracy, is it? Very well. I'm a man of my word. But I feel safe in the certainty that Babs will never take herself to the altar. A harpy like her will never promise to obey any man."

With that he slammed out of the room.

Babs bit her lip at his very real anger. "I'm sorry, Mama. I've ruined your birthday."

Her mother sipped her coffee. "That's all right, dear.

It's time you married, and I'll be happy to have grandchildren. But please be sure to marry as agreeable a gentleman as you can find."